Laurels and Liquor

Pack Saint Clair Book 3

Thora Woods

Contents

Dedication VII

Content Warning VIII

Prologue IX

1. Alexandra 1

2. Lucas 8

3. Lydia 14

4. Mateo 23

5. Lydia 29

6. Lydia 44

7. Lucas 53

8. Alexandra 59

9. Lydia 67

10. Rhett 79

11. Alexandra 89

12. Mateo 99

13. Lydia 108

14.	Lydia	116
15.	Lucas	128
16.	Lydia	142
17.	Lucas	151
18.	Mateo	157
19.	Rhett	165
20.	Alexandra	174
21.	Mateo	188
22.	Lydia	200
23.	Lucas	207
24.	Lydia	215
25.	Lydia	225
26.	Lydia	233
27.	Alexandra	246
28.	Rhett	253
29.	Lydia	259
30.	Lucas	269
31.	Alexandra	276
32.	Rhett	283
33.	Lydia	294
34.	Lucas	301
35.	Mateo	311
36.	Rhett	319
37.	Alexandra	327
38.	Lydia	333

39. Lydia   341

40. Lydia   352

41. Alexandra   362

42. Mateo   370

43. Rhett   380

44. Lydia   392

45. Lydia   401

46. Lydia   411

47. Rhett   418

48. Alexandra   430

49. Lydia   437

50. Mateo   443

51. Lydia   451

52. Rhett   459

53. Lydia   465

54. Alexandra   471

55. Lydia   478

56. Ma-   486
    teo

57. Lydia   493

58. Lucas   502

59. Lydia   510

60. Alexandra   518

Epilogue   523
Rhett

Acknowledgments   531

Want more?   534

Join the Conversation!   536

About the Author   537

To you, dear reader, for coming with me on this journey. No matter where or when you joined, I'm so incredibly grateful to have you with me.

Thank you for everything.

Content Warning

The book contains material that is not suitable for all audiences. This is an adult romance, with graphic descriptions of sex, including same sex encounters (MM and FF) and polyamory, as well as fetish activities, including BDSM, D/s relationships, degradation, blood play, DD/lg, and more.

This story also contains graphic descriptions that may be triggering to some readers, and will touch on topics that are sensitive in nature. These descriptions and topics include, but are not limited to, the following: physical, emotional, mental, and sexual abuse; religious trauma, with quoted scripture; homophobic language and behavior; mental health crises, including dissociation, depression, anxiety and panic disorders; gun and knife violence and injuries.

Reader discretion is advised.

Prologue

LYDIA

MY LIMBS TREMBLE AS I listen to Rhett Cooper's limping foot-steps, his drying blood still covering my hands. Each thump down the stairs grows fainter until he's gone, leaving only shouting voices. Too many conflicting commands, words garbled with the echoes bouncing off the roof and walls.

Freeze. On your knees. Hands in the air. Don't move.

I barely manage to catch the charges as someone reads Rhett his rights. Assault. Attempted murder. Fleeing the scene. I want to scream, to tell the police they're wrong, but I can't move. My knees ache from when they hit the floor of the private jet, all strength gone from my legs. I look down again, the red-brown stains on my hands stark against the deep, inky purple of my skirt. Sounds fade as I stare at the blood. Rhett's blood.

This is my fault. He's gone, and it's all my fault.

"They're leaving. Prepare for takeoff."

My head snaps up at the sound of Caleb Novak's soft-ly Eastern European accented order. My bodyguard isn't looking at me, but at the flight crew, who've been huddled in the galley since the police arrived. The pilot nods and disappears, and the flight attendants look relieved to have some sort of direction, something safe and routine to do. They start the pre-flight checks, speaking quietly to each other.

I envy them.

My world is shattered, my life completely upended in a few short minutes, and I have no one to blame but myself. Everyone tried to tell me not to do this, not to attend my eldest brother's wedding. They told me this trip could only end badly, and they were right. Silence settles over us as the police cars file out of the hangar, and my ears ring. I try to settle my stomach with deep breaths, but the smell of whiskey and leather and chocolate invades my nose, and my throat closes up in response.

Rhett lost so much blood. Would the police keep their word and take him to a hospital? Or would he bleed out in the back of a squad car? Or in a holding cell? What if they tear the hasty stitches Caleb put in?

"Lydia."

I jump at the whisper and gentle touch on my bare shoulder. Looking up, I meet the steel-blue gaze of Lucas Klausen. My beta. Rhett's beta. Our lover. I don't fight him as he helps me to my feet, but I lean heavily against his chest as we stumble back through the sitting area and into the bedroom.

We made love here, my thoughts unhelpfully remind me.

The sheets aren't rumpled anymore, but I can still smell Rhett in the room. Still see how Lucas, Rhett, and I tangled together not two days ago, when we still believed we had a plan that would work. How naive of us. How stupid of me to drag the people I love into my problems.

"Just sit here, and I'll get some towels. That's it, sweetheart," Lucas says, voice soft and calm like he's speaking to a frightened animal.

He guides me to sit on the edge of the mattress, and the vibrations of the engines come to life beneath us, even if their sound is almost entirely muffled. I'm only able to blink, dazed, my attention locked onto my blood-stained fingers. Lucas is back, a warm washcloth massaging my hands with tenderness. Pink drops fall onto my dress, soaking through the tulle and silk until they're seeping onto the skin of my thighs. I want to tell Lucas to stop, that it's no use.

"We're going to be okay, Lydi-bug. It's going to be okay," Lucas keeps whispering, a chant repeated over and over until the words lose meaning.

What's "okay" even mean?

"I don't know, but we'll figure it out once we get back home. Lex'll know what to do," Lucas replies.

I didn't realize I'd spoken the question out loud.

The plane begins moving, and I blink again. Now my hands are free of blood, and Lucas has me on my feet. Judging by the tilt of the floor and the pressure in my ears, we're off the ground. Lucas's hands are hot against my skin, helping me out of my ruined dress and into a simple t-shirt and yoga pants. I nearly sob as Rhett's scent surrounds me fully. It's one of his.

I grip the neck of the cotton shirt tight, wanting to rip it off and clutch it close in equal measure. Rhett should be here, holding me, holding us both. But thanks to my arrogance, he's gone, and each second takes us farther away.

"We're going to be okay. He's going to be okay," Lucas whispers, stepping close and wrapping his arms around me after I'm dressed.

I don't know how long I stand there, letting him prop up my limp body, but each moment breaks something in my heart. His shoulders shake, and I finally find the strength to move my hands. I wrap them tight around his ribs, burying my face in his chest as hot tears splash against my skin.

"I'm... I'm sorry," I rasp, voice trembling as much as my hands.

Lucas doesn't answer right away, and the silence is like a blow to the gut. This is all my fault, and he knows that just as much as I do.

I hope one day he'll forgive me for taking his alpha away. Lord knows I'm never going to forgive myself.

CHAPTER ONE

Alexandra

THE FOOT I HAVE crossed over my other leg bounces rapidly, hitting my shin every now and then, but I can't get it to stop. I scroll through my email, refreshing again and again, but no new messages come through. At the sound of an engine, I nearly sag with relief at the sight of my pack's private jet as it taxis past the lounge. I've been sitting here for the last three hours, ever since Caleb texted me that they'd taken off. As I watch the plane finally approach the hangar, I rush out, ignoring the desk attendant's cries for me to wait until it's parked. Fuck him. I've waited long enough.

The engines are just powering down as I descend the stairs and push through the doors. By the time I reach the plane, its stairs are already lowering, and I take them two at a time. I scan the sitting room once, and I find Lydia and Lucas curled up together on the sofa. His eyes are closed, but hers are open wide, staring at nothing in mute horror.

"Ms. St. Clair, I'm so sorry—"

I turn a stern frown on Caleb, the bodyguard I'd hired to protect Lydia. He's more disheveled than I've ever seen him, his normally pristine white shirt stained with dried blood, no tie, suit jacket missing, shoulder holster on full display. His words stick in his throat, his gray eyes saying more than he could ever put into words. But they're things I've been thinking to myself all night. We'd prepared for everything, and we still failed to get everyone home safe. The guilt is written in every line of his tired expression. My heart softens, but I don't let it show.

"Go home, Caleb. We can... we can debrief later, once we've all slept," I say, trying to keep my tone neutral.

My voice breaks, and I have to clear my throat. I don't know what Caleb reads in my face, but he sighs and nods, moving off to gather his things. Turning back to Lucas and Lydia, I find both of them are looking at me with mixed expressions of concern and exhaustion. I motion silently for them to follow me, but it takes a moment to get Lydia moving. It doesn't escape my notice that Lucas is half carrying her as they follow me out of the plane, out of the hangar, and into the parking lot.

"Is she hurt?" I ask quietly, holding the door for Lucas.

"I don't think so. Her face is a little swollen, but she—we've been—"

I nod, sparing him the need to finish that sentence. My heart twists as the smell of dried lilacs fills my nose, which is almost worse than her burnt-sugar fear. I've seen Lydia upset before, but this silence is more disquieting than her tears. This wordless anger, the rage burning like emerald fire in her eyes, takes me aback, and my instinct is to soothe and comfort. But as I move to touch her, she flinches, looking down and away. I walk them both out to my car, knowing the luggage will make its way back to the pack house eventually. I have more important things to worry about right now.

Lucas and Lydia slide into the backseat as a unit, and I close the door behind them before rushing around to the driver's seat. As we exit the airport, Lydia still isn't looking at me, or doing anything really. She's so pale, the rising sun catching on the tear stains running down her face. Her makeup is smudged, hair askew, but she's still beautiful enough to take my breath away. I keep glancing at her through my rearview mirror, waiting. After several long, silent minutes of driving, I can't take it anymore.

"What happened? The last I heard, you were leaving the wedding—"

"Rhett got arrested, Lex. Something about felony assault and attempted murder. I don't know. Everything happened so fast," Lucas rasps, shaking his head slightly in disbelief.

"What happened? Caleb wasn't able to provide a ton of details, just that he saw Rhett punch Darren," I press, trying to be gentle, but not sure I succeed.

Operating with limited information doesn't sit well with me on a good day. But being left in the dark about my pack is setting off every anxiety response I have. Sweaty palms, a tremble in my stomach that won't stop. The tick-tick-tick of my childhood piano teacher's metronome in the back of my mind. The itch in my fingers to do something other than grip the steering wheel like I can strangle the information I need out of it.

"I don't know. I... Lydia said there was a knife?" Lucas stumbles, voice lifting in a question as he looks down at the omega in his arms.

We wait, hoping she'll answer and fill in the gaps. Caleb told me about the confrontation with Lydia's family, about the threats her parents made against her, and how Darren tried to get in one last verbal blow but ended up with Rhett's fist in his face. Only, even he didn't know what happened inside. How Rhett came out of the venue with a stab wound to his thigh, or how Lydia's dress had been damaged, her face coming to bear the distinct shape of a handprint.

"Dar—*he* cornered me in the bathroom. There was a knife and Rhett—" Lydia's words are faint, barely audible over the sound of the engine and the tires, and she tucks her chin to her chest with a frustrated growl as she tries to hide her silent, angry tears.

"So Darren stabbed Rhett?" I ask, not sure I want to know the answer anymore.

She nods, pressing her hands to her mouth. "I'm sorry. This is all my fucking fault," she grits out.

Lucas holds her tight, and we lock eyes through the mirror. He's saying the soothing words, but there's a dark cloud in his eyes I don't like. He's furious, but not at her. No, never at her. At himself, maybe?

"No, it's not, sweetness. None of this is your fault. Either of you. We all decided to do this. Everyone, Rhett included, knew the risks," I say firmly, gripping the wheel hard enough for my hands to hurt.

"He said something about Seth being arrested?" Lucas asks, rocking Lydia and rubbing her back.

I don't blame him for trying to shift the conversation, but this topic is nearly as painful, if not worse. Seth Douglas, the curse I brought upon my chosen family, the demon who refuses to die, has vanished.

"No, not yet. They went to serve the warrant, and he was gone," I admit in a monotone, my gut twisting painfully.

Lucas lets out a string of particularly colorful and creative curse words, and I grunt in agreement. The engine revs as I rush through a yellow light, my heart beating hard in my chest. Mateo is home alone, and our nightmare is on the loose. I need my pack together... or as together as we can be right now. Once we're safe at home, I can get to work on returning Rhett to our arms.

The rest of the ride back to Bristol Point—the housing development we built to surround our pack house as another level of protection—is silent. Lydia's tears stop, and she's tucked into Lucas's arms, nearly curled into a ball, and I can't see her face. I want to say something, anything, to reassure her, but everything I think of just feels like false platitudes. We don't know if he's going to be okay. We don't know if he'll be home soon. There are so many unknowns, too many. So, I'll work on the things I can control. I can get my pack home safe, and then I can get to work.

The car isn't even fully parked in the garage before Mateo is there, pulling open the rear passenger door and extracting Lydia. His scent of burning grass fills the space as I step outside, and I try my best to smother a cough as his fear chokes me momentarily. Before I even get the chance to stop him, he has her scooped up in his arms and is marching away into the house. I turn to look at Lucas, sighing heavily. A moment later, arms wrap around my shoulders, pulling me into a warm embrace, one that smells like freshly cleaned sheets. I let myself be held, be vulnerable, but only because we're alone. I squeeze my eyes tight against the tears burning in the backs of them, gritting my teeth. I try to step back, but Lucas only holds tighter.

"Don't... don't pull away, Lex. Not this time. Please," he whispers into my hair.

"I have a duty to—"

"I don't need my prime alpha right now. I need my Lex. And we need to do this together," he insists, voice shaking slightly in his passion.

Breathing out a long sigh, I lift my arms to return the embrace. He's right. For too long, this pack hasn't operated as a unit, and it's cost us dearly. Not that I can blame anyone but myself for that. I let us drift apart when I focused on keeping my secret more than I focused on my pack mates. But we can't let that happen anymore. I tried to solve this problem by myself, and I failed. I need them as much as they need me.

"I love you, Luc. I'm so—"

"Rhett knew what he was doing. He wouldn't apologize, and we shouldn't either," Lucas interjects darkly.

I scoff a half-hearted laugh. He's right again. Rhett would never apologize for his actions when it comes to our safety. There are more than a few people in my life I know to be capable of committing murder, but he might be the only one who would be proud of it. I'd let Ted know to watch out for Rhett's prison phone call, and hopefully I'll get more details of what happened last night. But for now, I just need to be present for my pack.

I look up at Lucas with a grateful smile. His eyes are still sad, and there's a smear of something dark under his fringe that looks suspiciously like blood, but he's still looking at me with the familiar warm smile I know and love. We meet in the middle in a tender kiss, and I let myself forget the world for just a moment and enjoy this. But as soon as we pull apart and start walking toward the house, reality comes crashing down with the ringing of my cell phone. As soon as I see the number on the screen, my heart drops. Lucas gives me a confused look, but I give him a little shake of my head and motion for him to go. My ringer cycles for the third time, but Lucas relents and goes inside. Once the door latch clicks behind him, I swipe to answer.

"Hello, Father."

Chapter Two

Lucas

Pausing on the other side of the door, my jaw clenches as she answers to Leopold St. Clair. There's a heartbeat when I consider going back out, grabbing her phone and hucking it into a lake, but I manage to resist. Instead, I stalk through the mudroom and into the kitchen. I know there's a bottle of something brown in here, and I fucking need it.

When Lex texted—God, was it only eight hours ago?—and told me Rhett and Lydia were making a hasty exit from the wedding, I don't think anything could have prepared me for what I saw in the backseat of Caleb's SUV. Rhett, gray and nearly unconscious, his knuckles and face swollen, and Lydia, dress half torn away, and arms covered up to the elbows in his blood. And the worst of it is not knowing how or why. I knew Lydia's dickwad ex, Darren McLaughlin, must have been the culprit, but how did things escalate to stabbing?

The questions nagged at me the entire flight home, but I couldn't bring myself to ask. It was all I could do to keep it together for Lydia as she sat motionless for long stretches, then would jump randomly like a ghost had tapped her on the shoulder when I tried to comfort her, to only then break down into tears in my arms. She never spoke, and while she'd let me hold her and soothe her, I doubted it really did any good. I didn't know what to say or do. All my experience with my sisters and mother never prepared me for this level of panic.

I step through the open doorway to the kitchen and reach out toward one of the upper cabinets to look for that bottle, but I stop short. There's a black leather folio on the island counter, a red bow on the cover.

"What the actual fuck..." I whisper, frozen with confusion.

"We closed on the Magnolia Garden."

Mateo's forlorn words pull my attention, and I turn to find him coming up the stairs from the basement, running a hand through his hair. He makes his way to the fridge, opening the doors and staring at the contents but not seeing them, eyes distant.

"What are..." I start, but then stop.

The Magnolia Garden Theater. The project. *Rhett's* project.

"Lex and I signed the papers on Friday. We'd planned on driving by after we'd picked y'all up from the airport and telling Lydia. And then we'd come back here and celebrate," he goes on, words wavering with anger, or something else, I can't tell.

"We have got to fucking stop trying to surprise Lydia," I spit under my breath, redoubling my efforts to find that bottle.

"What's that supposed to mean?" Mateo snaps.

I shrug. I hadn't meant for him to hear me, but too late. I find the bottle of rum behind my collection of exotic spices, right where I'd hidden it. Not even bothering with a glass, I flick off the cap, watching it ping off the floor before rolling under a piece of furniture. Fuck it. The bastard can stay there. I'm sure as hell not going to need it again.

"Think about it. We tried to throw her a surprise party for her birthday, and she nearly died in a car accident. We tried to throw her a surprise party to celebrate her joining the pack, and someone broke into her apartment. Now we try to surprise her with this and—"

I gesture vaguely as I take a long pull from the bottle, but my meaning is clear enough. I gasp as I pull away, licking my lips and enjoying the spicy burn as it slides down my throat.

"If this pattern continues to escalate, the next time we try to surprise her, someone's going to end up fucking dead," I finish.

Mateo thinks for a moment before he huffs an ironic chuckle and shakes his head. I glance around the room, a little lighter now that the alcohol is mixing with lack of sleep. Offering him the bottle, he takes a long drink.

"Lydia's downstairs, in her nest. Had to carry her, though. She got to the dining room and just… froze." Mateo sighs, passing me the bottle.

I breathe deep, sighing on my exhale. But I realize right away why Lydia shut down. After living here for so long, I've sort of gone nose blind to my pack's scent unless I really concentrate. They're part of the intangible aura of "home" this building has. But now, I can smell Rhett everywhere. It's like the absence of him amplifies his scent, and my heart aches. With the state she's been in, it's no wonder she reacted like she did.

"Yeah, I figured as much," Mateo replies heavily after I explain my theory. "My first instinct was to take her up to Rhett's room, but..."

He trails off, but I can finish the thought easily enough. If the hint of Rhett's scent that lingers in the common spaces was enough to make her go catatonic, then plunging into a sea of it would definitely do more harm than good.

I look between his face and the basement door, my heart squeezing. I'm so lost, so out of my depth. Rhett would know what to do, how to soothe her. Mateo is doing his best, but there's something special about the bond Lydia and Rhett have. He runs his hand through sandy brown hair before gesturing for the bottle again. We share another long pull each, and I might as well be floating. Too much liquor without food, but I can't make myself move to address that. Mateo gives me a searching look, and the words forming in his soft brown eyes make me growl in warning.

"If you have the fucking nerve to even *think* the words 'I told you so' right now, Mateo Hutchenson, I will shove this bottle so far up your ass—"

"Now *there's* something I wouldn't mind seeing," Lex comments as she enters.

Mateo and I both whip around to face her as she crosses toward us. She snatches the bottle out from my grip and takes a swig, grimacing at first, but then she goes in for a second, longer pull.

"What'd Leo want?" I ask.

She rolls her eyes and hands me the bottle. Mateo lets out a surprised choking cough, his eyes wide as he looks at Lex.

"Your dad called? When?" he splutters, retreating a step back unconsciously.

Lex shakes her head and sighs. "Just now. But I'm handling it," she says simply.

I give her a sharp look, and her cheeks flush pink. The liquor makes my head fuzzy, and my patience that much thinner.

"And you're going to tell us how," I prompt, not bothering to keep the patronizing tone out of my voice.

"Yeah, I will. Just... not today, not right now. He's tomorrow's problem," she returns heavily.

"And what's today's problem?" Mateo drones.

Lex looks around before her eyes come to rest on the basement door, eyes softening and mouth pulling down in a little frown. "Lydia," she whispers, the single word full to the brim with emotion.

We all exchange a look before setting into motion. Without needing to speak, we gather bottled water and other easy provisions and move as a unit downstairs. The door to Lydia's room is cracked, and the air is quiet, which is a bit of a relief. We set down our supplies on her vanity before shedding excess layers and hesitantly crawling onto the oversized mattress that is Lydia's bed and nest. The only clue to our omega's location is the slow rising and falling of one particular lump of blankets, and she doesn't move as we settle in around her. Mateo slides his arms under and lifts her into his lap, holding her close. Lex leans against a pile of pillows nearby, and I squeeze into the space between them. One of my hands finds Lydia's back, my thumb rubbing idly against the soft emerald green material she burrowed into while my other hand wraps around Lex's ankle. We don't speak, and Mateo's eyes drift closed, his face buried in the space where I assume Lydia's neck would be. Lex stares off into the middle distance, in her own head again. I want to do something to bring her back, but I'm loathe to disturb the silence. So I close my eyes and let the exhaustion sweep over me.

But as I do, my heart aches. Even with four people, there's still too much space without Rhett here. He'd run his hands through my hair and purr for me, and I'd know everything was going to be okay. Rhett always steadies me, and without him, my soul is like a toy boat adrift in a hurricane. But I need to find the strength to go on, because Lex needs me. And Lydia needs me. I can't let this family down.

Chapter Three

Lydia

CLAY AND TOBACCO FILL the air, invading every corner of my mind. Muddy brown eyes staring at me through the mirror, his hand on my neck, holding me down.

"What the fuck is this?"

I can't speak, can't move to fight him off. He cuts my dress, not stopping at the lace but slicing everything away until I'm naked and shivering.

"These sorts of marks only go skin deep. But don't worry. I can fix that."

Ripping, shredding pain, like the night he tried to force the bond on me. But this time, he's carving away my pack tattoo, the symbol of my new family, my new beginning. But I should have known better, should have known I could never escape him.

"Omega whore."

The words ring in my ears as I fall forward, no longer supported by the sink. My knees hit the ground, and I'm looking down at Rhett, his golden blond hair stained with blood, ice-blue eyes open but not seeing.

A blast of heat, and the world erupts into flames. Omega whore. Letters outlined against the blaze, the accusation, the truth. I look back at Rhett's cold, pale face, the knife, Darren's knife in my hand.

"You did this."

I look down as the hissing whisper bounces around me, stinging and biting like so many blood-thirsty insects. My hands drip with blood, Rhett's blood. I try to move my arm, to throw the blade away, but I can't let go.

"You did this."

It's Alexandra's voice. I failed her, broke my promise. I told her I'd bring us all home, and I failed.

I open my mouth to scream, but no matter how hard I try, no sound I make can drown out the voices.

"Omega whore."

"You did this."

"Ungrateful bitch."

"Omega whore."

Hands shake me hard around the shoulders, dragging me out from under the fog of sleep. Someone's screaming, a blood-curdling sound that fills the air. I fight and struggle, but my hands get caught in something. My heart kicks in my chest, the screaming getting louder—

"Omega, stop."

My body locks up at the command, and it's only when the screaming stops that I realize I was the one doing it. Alpha barks usually feel like ice water crashing down on me, and while there's a moment of frigid shock, glowing, soothing warmth takes its place almost instantly. I open my eyes, and I realize I'm on my back, Mateo kneeling over me with panic written on every line of his face.

The compulsion of his bark slides away, and he shakes his head, like he's trying to rid himself of the sensation as well. My throat is raw and my deep inhales ache. I try to move, but I've managed to twist myself up in a blanket, and I don't know where to begin extracting my limbs. Swallowing hard, I frantically pull and twist as the panic sets in, but Mateo is there, steady hands helping me escape. I try to move away, but a gentle hold on my wrist stops me before I can get far. I look up to see Mateo's fawn-colored eyes soft with an emotion I don't dare name. Glancing away, unable to stand it, I find Lucas and Lex nearby, concern pulling at their features.

"You were having a nightmare," Mateo says simply.

Not looking at him, I instead focus on the emerald green blanket pooled around me, but regret it instantly. This was Rhett's first gift to me. I try to pull my arm free of Mateo's grip, but he just holds a little tighter. How can he stand to touch me right now, especially after what I did to his best friend?

"Talk to us, baby," Mateo pleads.

"Don't shut us out, sweetheart. Please," Lucas whispers, shifting closer.

I wince at the vulnerability of his plea, my heart squeezing in my chest. How do I even begin to describe the depths of my failure?

"If we know what happened, we can help you. There's nothing you can say that will upset us, sweetness," Lex implores, crawling around Lucas to kneel on my other side.

I contain the hollow laugh that tries to come up, glancing up at her for a moment before I have to look away, face hot with anger and shame. I don't deserve her comfort, and the kindness in her eyes burns through to the core of me. The words come before I can stop them, pouring out of me like a cathartic tidal wave.

"It all went wrong from the start, like they knew what we were going to do and did everything they could to ruin it. Caleb was stopped at the door, and I couldn't avoid my parents because of that goddamn receiving line. It looked for a minute like we'd get out okay, but then I fucked up and went to the bathroom by myself. That's where Darren cornered me. Tried to charm me, gaslight me, the old song and dance. But when I pushed back, he..."

I trail off as my left cheek pulses with phantom pain, and I stop myself from reaching up to check my skin for marks. Lex leans in and tucks a stray piece of my hair behind my ear, and I shiver at the trail of her finger against the sensitive shell. I want to move away, but my pack has me surrounded, no place to run. Yet my primal mind doesn't panic like before, and even seems to settle a little more. Their scents are everywhere, the calming pheromones I've come to recognize as home and safety.

"Then he saw my pack mark, and he pulled out the knife and... he cut my dress—"

I choke back a frustrated shriek behind closed lips and gritted teeth, my eyes burning with tears. Now that the shock has passed, I'm deep into the anger stage. I want to scream and cry and make something or someone hurt like I'm hurting. But I'm pinned here, unable to escape the understanding looks on my pack mates' faces. Out of the corner of my eye,

I see Lex leaning in. I want to move, but I don't react fast enough, and she grabs my hand and holds it tight between both of hers and refuses to let go. And despite myself, her touch and scent of mulled wine and orange peels helps to quiet a little bit of the furious static in my mind.

"Why did he cut your dress, baby?" Mateo asks, words quavering as he struggles to keep calm. I appreciate the effort, but I almost wish he wouldn't.

"He saw my pack tattoo, and he was going to..." I trail off, throat closing.

These types of marks are only skin deep.

Lucas curses under his breath, and I catch him subconsciously rubbing the place on his left side ribcage where he has his own pack tattoo. Part of joining Pack St. Clair was agreeing to have their motto tattooed on me, and I chose to have mine on my back to cover the scar from Darren's attempt to force a mating bond. I'd done it to reclaim that part of myself, to turn something ugly into something beautiful. But now the flower and Latin script I'd put there seem like a stupid, reckless move. How could an alpha not take offense to someone trying to cover their mark, even if the bond never formed? I should have known better.

"Is that when Rhett came in?" Lex asks, pulling me from yet another guilt spiral.

I nod tersely. "He and Darren went back and forth. Darren used to be all bark and no bite, so I wasn't—things escalated so fast. One minute, they were talking, and then... then the next..."

I blink, and I can see the moment again behind my eyelids. A flash of silver as Darren's arm cranks back and darts forward. Rhett's barely contained scream of pain. Both alphas locked in hand-to-hand combat, tumbling backward into the stall.

"So that's how Rhett got stabbed," Mateo sighs.

"He told me to run, to get to Caleb," I reply with a nod. "I thought he'd be right behind me, but then I went outside, and I ran into my brothers, and then my mother showed up and—Oh, my God. I'm so fucking stupid. What was I thinking, leaving him there by himself. I should have tried to get Darren off him, or called for help, or—"

My words get faster and faster, as my mind whirls out of control. This is all my fault. Why didn't I pull Darren back? Or hit him with a trashcan? Or do something, *anything* other than just running like the coward I am?

"Rhett is a better trained fighter than all of us combined, baby," Mateo says, cutting across me. "If he told you to run, then that was the best thing you could have done to help him."

"But if I'd—if I'd done something, maybe we could have—"

"Lydia, listen to me," Lex starts, letting go of my hand to cup my face and turn my head so I can't look anywhere other than her hazel eyes. I try to flinch away, to pull back, but she refuses to give in, even as I whimper pathetically. "Rhett did what he had to do to protect you. If he were here, I have not a single doubt in my mind that he would tell you that you did the right thing."

"But he's not! He's not here, and it's because of me!" I cry, tears breaking free at last.

It's my fault. All of it. If I hadn't talked back to Darren, I could have prevented the situation from escalating. If I hadn't drunk so much at the wedding reception, I wouldn't have needed to go to the bathroom, and never would have given Darren the chance to catch me alone. If I'd agreed to leave when Caleb wasn't allowed inside with Rhett and me, then we wouldn't have had to face Darren at all. If I hadn't insisted on going to the wedding, we wouldn't have had any of this. If I hadn't been such a stupid, pathetic, worthless—

"No, it's not. It's not your fault, sweetness. We made this decision together. And we're going to figure out how to fix it together," Lex pushes, stroking my cheeks with her thumbs.

I try to shake my head, but she doesn't let me deny it. Mateo moves in closer, sliding in behind me and wrapping his arms tight around my waist. Lucas fills the gap until I can't see anything beyond them. Their scents mix, lemonade and fresh towels and spices forcing out everything else, and I slump, exhausted. Didn't they understand? Why aren't they shouting their fury at me?

"You don't believe us now, and that's fine. I'll tell you every day if I have to," Lex says gently.

I close my eyes and try to block her out. I take another deep breath, and my heart aches. Even surrounded by the scents I've grown to love, there's still a missing piece. Whiskey and leather.

Mateo's purr rumbles against my back, and despite myself, I melt into his embrace. Lex whispers comforting words over and over, and Lucas is there, brushing away my tears. No one is yelling, accusing me of the things my mind is telling me they should. The steady calm persists, reinforced by my alphas' purrs, and my beta's peaceful pheromones. They care for me and hold me until I'm settled again. Closing my eyes, I lean my head against Mateo's chest, threading my fingers through Lex's, and resting my hand on Lucas's knee.

"We're going to be okay, sweetheart. We'll get through this together," Lucas says softly, and I find myself able to believe him.

"Nothing that happened at that wedding was your fault, Lydia. Rhett did what he had to do to protect you, and I have no doubt in my mind he would have done much worse without batting an eyelash. He loves you; we all do," Mateo says into my ear, kissing and nuzzling my neck.

I sigh and give the slightest nod. He squeezes tighter for a moment and then a hand on my cheek brings my attention to Lex. She's nearly nose to nose with me, her hazel eyes bright with affection. I lean into her touch, captivated.

"I know standing up to Darren couldn't have been easy for you, but you did it, and I'm so proud of you. You did everything you could have done, and that's all I could ever ask of you. I know Rhett well enough to confidently say that, if he could do it all over again, he wouldn't change a thing. So no more tears, okay, sweetness? I hate seeing you cry," Lex says, voice lifting a little as she smiles.

I can't help but giggle and nod, and her answering grin makes my heart skip a beat. She leans in and slants her lips over mine in a brief but breath-stealing kiss. But as she pulls away, her words sink in and my heart throbs painfully in my chest. I keep my face blank, hiding my spiraling descent into despair as a realization crashes down on me, slamming me against the rocky cliff of truth.

There was something I could have done different. Not on the night of the wedding, but before we ever stepped foot on the plane. It would have nullified any need to bluff or lie. Hell, we could have avoided going to Louisiana altogether.

But most importantly, it would have given Rhett a legal shield to justify what he did to Darren.

If I'd bonded with Pack Saint Clair, then it would have solved everything.

CHAPTER FOUR

Mateo

LYDIA SHIFTS FROM MY arms to Lucas's lap, though to my surprise, the beta doesn't go far. Instead, he leans against me heavily, closing his eyes. My heart throbs for him; he's been carrying the emotional burden for the last thirty-six hours, and he must be exhausted. I find a blanket and tuck it around him and Lydia, running my fingers through his soft but unruly hair. His lips twitch up in a little sleepy little smile, but then he drifts off along with Lydia. When I look around, I find Lex still with us, which genuinely surprises me. She crosses her legs under her as she relaxes into the pillows, her fingers idly playing an imaginary keyboard on her thighs even as her eyes show that her mind is a thousand miles away. In the distance, the grandfather clock in the formal living room chimes nine, and I let the last *ding* echo and fade.

Lex has always been the strong, sure leader of our pack. She makes decisions with ease, and never shows a shred of doubt once she starts down a path. But we're poised at a crossroads now, with too many competing directions at our feet. We need to figure out what's going on with Rhett, take care of Lucas and Lydia, and there's still the looming threat of Seth Douglas in the background. And the longer the silence stretches, the harder my heart hammers in my chest. The morning sun filters through the frosted windows, making Lex's smooth skin glow with an almost angelic golden aura. It's easy to forget that she's only a few years older than me, but in this moment, she looks as young and lost as I've ever seen. So I straighten my spine and set my shoulders.

"We should have heard from Ted by now," I start, trying my best to emulate the confidence Lex so often exudes.

"Yeah, I suppose so," Lex breathes, noncommittally.

"When does his office open?" I prompt.

Lex blinks as the question hits her, and a little clarity comes back to her expression. "It's Monday?"

"Sunday," I correct.

"Right," she sighs, nodding. "He won't be in the office, but with a situation like this..."

I nod. "Would Rhett know the number to call off hand?"

Lex hums, tilting her head. "Probably not. If the police took his phone, then he wouldn't be able to find it. That might explain why we haven't heard anything," she mutters, sounding more and more focused with each word.

My shoulders relax slightly. I glance at Lucas, whose eyes are open now, not even bothering to feign sleep. When I give him a stern little look, he just rolls his eyes.

"You can sleep, Luc," I chastise lightly.

"You're not my supervisor," Lucas teases, sticking out his tongue.

I give him a little growl, but it lacks any real heat. My heart twinges, a little guilt creeping in. This is hardly the time for teasing and joking, not with so much to do and so little time to do it. But Lucas always brings out the petulance in people, even when he isn't trying.

"Are you going to tell us what your dad wanted?" Lucas asks, turning his attention to Lex.

I catch the way her shoulders tense for a moment before she relaxes again, but she doesn't speak for a while. And then she sighs and rubs her face with both hands.

"I have no fucking clue how, but he found out Seth's been charged, and that he's on the run," Lex groans.

My body locks tight at the mere mention of *his* name. Seth Douglas. The omega who's ruined my life several times over. He wormed his way into my bed, and through me, my pack. He's a manipulative narcissist who trapped me and Lex in mating bonds we never wanted. For years we tried to get rid of him, but he blackmailed Lex into giving him a monthly stipend, and God knows however many other concessions. When Lydia came into our lives, he took umbrage at our relationship with her, and turned his evil, twisted focus onto her. There seemed to be no limit to what he was willing to do to get her away from us: hiring someone to stalk her, convincing his followers to harass her any chance they got, even grooming a vulnerable fan into going kamikaze, causing an accident bad enough to kill him—one that nearly killed Lydia too. But finally, we had a breakthrough. It took months of searching and digging, but we finally managed to get enough evidence to prove Seth's guilt and get him sent to prison.

But just when we thought we'd won, he had to fuck things up. Again.

When the police went to serve the arrest warrant, they found Seth gone without a trace. It's only been twenty-four hours since then, so they haven't had a chance to even start chasing leads. The fact that Leopold St. Clair knows about Seth's warrant when even the nosiest gossip rag, The Everton Review, doesn't, strikes a nerve.

"So what did he have to say about it?" I ask quietly.

"Oh, you know. After he got done telling me how right he was about Seth, and that I should have known better than to associate myself with 'his kind,' whatever the fuck that means, he wanted to know what I was going to do to keep this out of the papers and away from the St. Clair name," she says, words getting faster and more clipped in her anger as she speaks.

"'His kind?' Does he mean, clout chasers?" Lucas asks harshly.

"If I had to hazard a guess, he probably meant omegas, but who knows. His disdain for everyone who isn't kissing his ass knows no bounds," Lex returns, just as venomously.

"I hope you told him to take his nose out of our business and shove it up his ass," I grumble.

"As much as I would have loved to, I didn't. I told him I was working on it and if it became something he needs to know about, I'll tell him." Lex sighs, a defeated sound that tugs at my heart.

"So what is the plan?" Lucas asks with a resigned exhale.

"When I have one, I'll let you know. But my priority right now is getting Rhett out of jail and back home," Lex drones, letting her head drop against the headboard and closing her eyes.

Hearing her admit it is something else, even if I'd already come to the same conclusion. And the look in Lucas's eyes, the flash of worry and exhaustion mixed with sorrow, steels my resolve.

"One thing at a time. We'll get in touch with Ted, and get him down to New Orleans to spring Rhett from the slammer. We can let the police deal with Seth for now. That's sort of their job," I say, ending with a humorless chuckle.

Lex's shoulders relax once more as she latches onto my steady words, nodding to herself. She still doesn't move, and I don't blame her. This little bubble of safety we've created is ready to shatter at any moment, and when it does, reality will come flooding back in. But I resolve to stay positive, because someone in this pack has to keep us from slipping into a sea of depression. Even though there's a massive, Rhett-shaped hole in our pack, the rest of us are together and that sort of feels like a minor miracle.

"Maybe we'll get lucky and Seth'll overdose on steroids or something and cease to be our problem," Lucas snarks.

Lex's head snaps up, eyes wide as she gasps. But then her face morphs into a serious frown with a furrowed brow, eyes darting back and forth in thought. Lucas and I stare at her, waiting for her to say something, to elaborate on whatever epiphany she just had, but she continues to converse with herself in her head.

"For the record, that was a joke. You know that, right?" Lucas questions, leaning forward with a concerned expression.

"Yeah, yeah. For sure," Lex replies faintly, not looking at him.

And before either of us can say anything further, she's clambering out of the nest, and out of the door. Lucas and I stare at each other, exchanging silent concern. Lydia whimpers in her sleep, shifting a little in his arms, and Lucas's expression darkens, his shoulders slumping. The impulse to shield him from whatever burden he's carrying hits me hard, but I push it aside. He's never reached out to me like that, and now's not the time to test the waters.

"Do you think she'd actually do it? Kill Seth?" Lucas asks, turning to me.

The concern in his steel-blue eyes has become true worry. I want to tell him that Lex wouldn't do something so extreme, but I hesitate. I've known Lex for a long time, over a decade, and I've never seen her like this. So, I settle on the only thing I can say honestly.

"I don't think there's anything she wouldn't do at this point."

CHAPTER FIVE

Lydia

THE WARM WATER SPRAYING down on my face brings me out of the waking dream I've been living in for God knows how long. These days, time slips through my fingers like sand, and I slide from one moment to the next, often not really aware of how I got there. It can't have been too long, as I still feel the soreness in my knees from when my father forced me to them at the wedding. I look around, realizing I'm in my bathroom, and that I'm not alone.

The humidity makes Mateo's lemon and ozone linger against my skin, and I lean into his touch, happy to let him support my weight for a moment.

"Is that warm enough, baby girl?" he asks into my ear, nuzzling it gently with the tip of his nose.

I nod, too tired to speak. Mateo turns me so my head sits under the spray, and I catch the last trace of his frown before he wipes it away. Guilt tugs at my heart, and I look down at our feet. Water swirls down the central drain, and as I watch the vortex, I can feel the beckoning event horizon of the black void that's appeared in my chest. I do my best to keep from falling into it, but when I'm left alone with my thoughts, it's almost too easy to let go and drown in the pain and longing. Even now, with only the sound of the water to fill the air, the ache builds higher and higher, and tears form in my eyes.

Mateo's fingers in my hair, massaging my scalp, catch me off guard, and I gasp before leaning back into his touch. He works the shampoo thoroughly into the strands, and for a moment, I almost feel relief. I reach out and run my hands up and down his chest, the muscles jumping under my fingers. The vibration of his purr against my palms makes me shiver. Even when he walks me back into the spray, rinsing my hair clean of the suds, I keep exploring with my touch. I follow the trail of soft hair down the middle of his stomach, then lower, but he catches my wrist just as the back of my hand brushes his half-hard length. My eyes snap open and I look up to see him staring at me with heat and concern dancing in his eyes.

"You don't have to—"

"I'm sorry."

We speak at the same time, and I duck my chin, looking away as my cheeks heat. He adjusts his grip and brings my hand up to his face so he can kiss my palm.

"Don't apologize. You've got nothing to be sorry about," he mutters, pressing my hand to his cheek, his much larger one covering mine.

I look up at him, confused. "If you need—"

Mateo shakes his head. "I don't need anything like that right now. I can't help but get hard when I'm near you, Lydia. You make me feel like a teenager again, popping boners left, right, and center."

We both chuckle at his joke, and my chest warms a little. I look down at his cock, still impressive even though it's not fully at attention, and sigh. I would do anything for him, even if my heart is too heavy for it. He can't be comfortable like this. Maybe...

"No, you're in your head again, baby girl. Look at me," Mateo says, suddenly very firm.

I snap my wide-eyed look of surprise up to his face, swallowing hard. Mateo is an alpha, but it's sometimes easy to forget that with his easy smiles and carefree attitude. Stern and dominant aren't usually words I'd use to describe him, but those are the only ones that come to mind as he looks down his nose at me. This is a new development for him, and based on the way my pussy flutters, I'd be lying if I said I don't like it.

"If you want to do something for me, then you can let me finish cleaning you up. Then you're going to let me get you into some comfy clothes, and we're going to go upstairs and see if we can get Lucas to decide on something to make for dinner. Can you do that for me, baby?" Mateo says, a hint of his softness sneaking back in.

The urge to address him with an honorific hits me hard, but I shove it away. Even if he is acting like such a dad right now, he made it clear he doesn't want to play, so I nod. And his answering smile lights up the steamy little cubicle, pushing down the darkness for the moment.

Once Mateo is satisfied that I've been properly scrubbed, buffed, and lotioned, he puts me in one of his stolen t-shirts and a pair of my own sleep shorts, holding my hand as we make our way up to the main living floor. Letting him care for me like that wasn't something I'd normally allow, but it was so obvious how happy it made him that I couldn't fight him on it. Not to mention that letting go of control and following his gentle commands worked wonders on my mood. I'm almost feeling like myself when we reach the kitchen, but then my heart plummets as I see Lucas at the kitchen island.

He looks rough, to put it mildly. Normally, he keeps himself tidy out of habit, since there are health codes and safety concerns while working in a kitchen. But now, he looks downright homeless, with a deep shadow of stubble on his cheeks and jaw, and wild, even slightly matted hair sticking up in every direction from his head. I realize with a pang that Lucas is wearing one of Rhett's shirts, even if it hangs loose on him, giving him an almost starved appearance. The dark circles under his steel-blue eyes are near purple, and he's swaying slightly on the spot.

He doesn't look up at us, still studying the marble like he's trying to decode the location of a buried treasure. Mateo sighs, running a hand through his hair. My heart thuds in my throat. I want to help, but I don't know what to do. Lucas has always been the steady constant, the unshakable one. To see him like this breaks my heart all over again, the guilt I'd managed to shove aside, coming back with full force.

"Why don't you get cozy on the couch, baby girl? Lex'll be home soon, I think," Mateo suggests, but the calm confidence he'd had before is gone.

I can only nod, shuffling away meekly and wrapping myself in a cashmere blanket on the sectional. Mateo watches me until I'm settled, but then strides over to Lucas, wrapping an arm around his back and pulling the beta into a sideways embrace. Not that Lucas notices. He's still looking without seeing. He reminds me of people I've seen on the news, the ones who witnessed the worst atrocities and were being forced to recount them. Shells, existing on momentum alone. How much longer can Lucas last before his runs out?

The front door banging open makes me jump, and I muffle my yelp in the blanket, ducking and covering my head. But a scent drifts toward me, not mulled wine and oranges, but something entirely unexpected. Apples. Caramel.

Gabby.

"All right, you mopey bitches, listen up. Pity party's over and we're getting this shit cleaned up," she declares, striding into the room like a general taking charge.

Lucas and Mateo look up at her, too bewildered to speak. My best friend stops in the middle of the open-plan space, looking around with an assessing eye. She flicks her long, cherry red braids over her shoulder before she plants her hands on her perfectly shaped hips, setting her back straight. Her dark brown eyes scan over once, the slight softening there making me flush hot. But then she turns to examine the boys and her expression falls.

"Lukey-poo, my boy, you look like a hot pile of shit," she says, her disappointment somehow making the insult more of a joke.

Lucas jumps at being addressed directly, and awareness seems to come back into his eyes. "Don't call me Lukey-poo," he snaps, but there's not much force behind it.

"Okay, Lukey-poo," Gabby says with her signature tact and grace. "If you're not too busy feeling sorry for yourself, would you mind going upstairs and taking a shower? You're in my way."

I blink at the almost unnecessary level of dismissal in her words. Can't she see how badly he's hurting? But her expression stays calm, even when Lucas starts sputtering with indignation.

"Feeling sorry for myself? Who gave you the right to come in here and—"

"I did."

Lex's stern voice comes from the doorway to the foyer, and we all turn to find her standing imperiously, arms crossed over her chest and expression unreadable. Her hazel eyes are fixed on Lucas, who's gone beet-red, mouth agape.

"Lex told me what happened, and I can't begin to tell you the things I've imagined doing to that fuck weasel ex of yours, babe, but you're just circling the drain right now. All of you. I can't fix the legal drama, but I'm going to help y'all get your shit together," Gabby says, speaking to me and then to the room at large.

I can't respond, because she's absolutely right. Mateo and Lucas are likewise silent. Lex's heels crack like whips as she crosses the room, coming to rest next to the boys.

"Let's get you upstairs, my love," she says, gentle but with absolutely no room for refusal.

Lucas lets Lex lead him out of the room and up the stairs, and Gabby gets to work right away. Chasing Mateo from the kitchen, she starts pulling ingredients from the cabinets and fridge, a one-woman cooking tornado. And like a cyclone, I can't help but get sucked closer, moving from the sectional to a stool at the breakfast bar to watch her. I've seen Gabby cook plenty; some of my best memories from the last five years are from the days she and I spent making hundreds of Christmas cookies in the tiny apartment kitchen where she lives with her grandmother, Wila. They were days spent laughing and pushing away bad memories to replace them with good ones. Me, forgetting about how I left home on Christmas Eve after Darren raped me, and her forgetting about how she lost her parents in a car crash as they were coming home from a Christmas party. Refusing to dwell is such a fundamental part of Gabby's personality, and she is bringing it down like a sledgehammer onto me and my pack.

"You know, I owe Caleb twenty bucks, but I'm hoping if I avoid him for long enough, he'll forget," she starts, mixing and pouring, following some sort of mental recipe.

"I doubt it. But what bet did you lose this time?" I reply with a smirk.

"That Rhett would kill Darren on sight. Fuck, I know I would, and that was before he went all—" She mimes shanking someone with her spoon, pulling a bark of surprised laughter from my chest.

"Rhett's not a murderer," Mateo counters, sitting beside me.

He leans back and rests his arm across the back of my stool, his thumb tracing nonsense patterns on my lower back. I shiver a little at the touch, smiling to myself. I catch the twinkle in Gabby's eyes, but thankfully, she doesn't comment on the casual affection. Instead, she gives Mateo a look that tells him exactly how much she believes him.

"He's not!" Mateo insists, but the laughter undermines his efforts.

"I mean, yeah, he's probably not going to start going all Jeffrey Dahmer or anything, but like... you can't tell me you wouldn't have been surprised to hear that Darren ran into Rhett's knife ten times that night," Gabby says, slamming a stock pot onto the cooktop.

I suck in a sharp breath, flashes of the fight in the bathroom making me wince back. Rhett's grunt of pain as Darren's arm flies forward. The blood.

Run, Lydia! Find Caleb!

I whimper and rub my chest, my heartache manifesting as physical pain. But then Mateo is there, an arm around my shoulder and his purr in my ear. His lemon and cut grass scent surrounds me, even blocking out the spices Gabby's working with. It takes another few moments, but when I finally get a hold of myself, I look to see Gabby giving me a genuinely apologetic frown.

"I'm sorry, babe. I know... it's hard to lose someone, even temporarily. But he'll be okay. And I'm sure he's chomping at the bit to get on that collect call to you," she says gently.

I nod, wiping away the tears that threaten to fall. Mateo's heavy sigh pulls my attention, and I look up at him curiously.

"Do you remember our talk yesterday?" he asks, picking his words carefully.

I try to think, but the only thing I remember before coming to in the shower is falling asleep in my nest with Lucas, both of us crying without speaking. If I spoke to anyone, then it must have been when I was lost in the black hole.

When I don't answer, Mateo sighs again, pushing my hair back from my forehead and kissing my hairline. "Ted finally got in touch late Sunday night. We've been advised that it would be wise for us to not contact Rhett while he's still in the parish jail. Due to the nature of the crime, he's worried that our conversations could be recorded and..."

Mateo trails off, but I can imagine the rest. It's not a stretch to think that Rhett has exactly zero regrets about what he did, but if the New Orleans DA gets him admitting that on the record, then it'll be all too easy to convict.

"Speaking of phone calls, did you drop your phone in a lake, or are you purposefully ignoring your brother?" Gabby asks, skillfully redirecting before I can sink into the void again.

I blink and look around, as if I'm going to spot my cell phone just laying around. But now that I'm thinking about it, I honestly don't remember the last time I had it in my hand, or even saw it. Was it at the wedding? On the plane? But before I can answer, Gabby scoffs and rolls her eyes.

"If your head wasn't attached, you'd lose that, too," she grumbles, but her smile softens the jab.

"I've been..."

"A mess, I know," Gabby finishes when I trail off. "But it's not like the rest of these chuckleheads suddenly lost their phones. A simple text, that's all I'm saying. But now I have to invoice you for the salon trip I needed to cover up these gray hairs y'all gave me."

Mateo growls a little, but she just sticks her tongue out at him. He relaxes at the sound of my giggle, nuzzling my neck with his nose. In his distraction, he misses the wink my best friend throws my way.

"I would love to hear the story from your side, babe. That wedding sounded like a total Hot Mess Express," she goes on, stirring the pot again.

I flush and swallow as my mouth goes dry. "Maybe another time, Gabs. It's still a little… raw," I reply, words fading to a whisper.

"Oh, no. Totally get it. When you're ready. You know how much I love a juicy family drama," she counters, and we share a laugh.

"I'm sure you got plenty of gossip from my brother," I comment.

"Oh, yeah," Gabby says, drawing out the vowels for effect. "Jace called me that night, trying to find out if y'all made it out. After I recovered from the freaking heart attack he gave me, and reminded him you have a pack he can call, I got him to spill. Speaking of which."

She cuts herself off, reaching into her back pocket and sliding her phone to me across the slick marble surface.

"He's not going to stop blowing me up until you talk to him. So fucking call him before he has an aneurysm, woman," she says, moving to cut up some chicken.

I hold back my sarcastic retort, simply pulling up her contacts. I'm momentarily taken aback by the number of messages between them, as well as the frequency and length of their call history. She's got some explaining to do, but that can wait for another day. After pressing the dial button, the line only rings once before Jason picks up.

"Gabs, what's up? Is everything okay?" he asks urgently.

"Hey, Jace," I say sheepishly.

There's several moments of coughing and spluttering, and I even catch a few colorful curses in the mix, and I can't help but giggle.

"Lydi, holy shit. I thought—are you okay? You made it home?" he asks, voice barely above a whisper.

"Yeah. Are you okay? Why are you whispering?" I ask back, confused.

"I'm at the office. Listen, I can't talk for long, but it's good to hear your voice. The radio silence thing was killing me," he goes on, more relieved now.

"Sorry, Jace. I've been... yeah," I say, finishing lamely.

"No kidding," he mutters with a humorless chuckle.

Biting my lower lip, I hesitate before speaking. "Were you okay after we left? Things were..."

"Yeah, they sure were," Jason says emphatically, picking up where I trail off. "Mom and Dad have had some long meetings with Mr. Greg."

I swallow. Greg Thibodeaux has been the family lawyer for as long as I can remember, and if he's been called in, it can't be for anything good.

"They're playing things uncharacteristically close to the chest, but if I hear anything, I'll make sure Lex knows. I'd tell you, too, but I don't trust Mom as far as I can throw her, and I don't want to put you at risk," Jason goes on when I don't respond.

"Thanks, Jason. How are you doing, like, personally?" I ask softly, playing with the hem of my shirt.

There's a long, heavy pause, but I don't try to fill it, giving Jason the space to answer. When he exhales, I can almost see the crease between his eyebrows, the stressed frown tugging at his mouth.

"Let's just say that the things I've been finding out in the last few days have been... eye-opening, to say the least. Lots to think about," he says at last, the dark, cryptic undertone of his voice making me shiver.

I frown, trying to figure out how to respond. I'm partially responsible for the sudden series of revelations he's had to have, because I hid my mother's manipulations from him when I shouldn't have. She threatened to disavow him and have him thrown out of the pack if I didn't go to the wedding, and I fell for it hook, line, and sinker.

"It's not your fault, Lydi. This shit's been a long time coming," Jason says, interrupting my thoughts.

People keep telling me that, but it's hard to believe. Even if I'm not wholly responsible, my actions still contributed to the clusterfuck of a situation my friends and lovers have found themselves in.

"You only did what you thought was best, what you thought you had to do to protect me. I'm not going to blame you for that instinct, ever. Even all the shit that went down outside, none of that is on you. Dad should have stepped in and got his mate under control. Darren didn't have a right to put his hands on you, and Adam sure as fuck didn't have the right to speak to you like he did. They're to blame for everything."

Jason's words fade into a growl, a deep, furious rumble that makes my eyes go wide. He didn't mince his words, but what he's left unsaid speaks just as loud. A spark of something flares to life in my chest, a bitterness that I'd long abandoned. I had to let go of my anger toward my parents in order to move on from what happened to me five years ago. Pointing fingers wouldn't fix anything, and I had to focus on my future, not the past. But that advice rings hollower than ever.

I've tried to move on, to forget them and live my life. But they won't let me go, and are clearly willing to go to any lengths to drag me back.

Maybe I did make bad choices, but we were set up to fail from the start. There was no way we could have avoided confrontation that night, and looking back on it, we're lucky things only escalated as far as they did.

I'm about to ask more questions, but Jason sucks in a breath, swearing to himself.

"Listen, I have to go. I can't text or talk all the time, so I'll let you know the next time I'm able to call. I'm working on something, but don't worry about me. Just take care of yourself, okay?" Jason says, words flying out now, like he can't finish fast enough.

I stumble over my response, but only manage a brief farewell before the line goes dead. Pulling the phone away from my ear, I look at it until the screen goes black, trying to wrap my head around what just happened. I thought speaking to my brother would help, but I'm left with more questions than answers. And asking me not to worry about my baby brother is sort of like asking the sun not to rise.

"What the fuck have you done to my kitchen?!"

I whip around to see Lucas and Lex in the open doorway to the foyer, though it looks like Lucas has frozen in place in horror, judging by his expression.

"I'm cooking," Gabby replies, nonplussed.

Lucas sputters and then charges around the room, moving to put away the bottles and jars and bowls that Gabby pulled out and left on every available flat surface, making her cry out in defiance and go behind him, pulling the stuff out again. The two go back and forth, but their bickering is good natured. And it's nice to see Lucas with some life in his eyes. He's shaved and dressed in his own clothes, looking far more like himself than he did a few minutes ago. Lex slides onto the stool on my other side, smiling to herself.

"Why do you look like the cat who got the canary?" Mateo asks conspiratorially.

She just chuckles to herself and nods at Gabby and Lucas, who are playing tug of war over a bulk bottle of garlic powder, until Gabby lets go suddenly and sends Lucas staggering back into the cabinets while she cackles. Thankfully, she doesn't fight him for much longer as she works on the gumbo she's got going. The smell drifting out of the pot makes my heart squeeze with nostalgia, and I catch the knowing look in her chocolate brown eyes as she tastes it. Only for her smile to dissolve into an affronted gasp as Lucas dips his whole pinky into the pot and tastes it.

"Not enough Tony's," he grumbles, moving off to dig in the back of the cabinet.

I look to Lex as Gabby and Lucas work together to add the finishing touches to the gumbo, giving her a grateful smile.

"How'd you know?" I ask softly.

"Know what, sweetness?" she asks back, giving me a curious look.

"Know to do this? To bring Gabby over?" I clarify, nodding to the pair of betas.

Lex's smile widens, and she leans in to kiss my temple. I smile at her easy affection, leaning into her warmth. Her mulled wine scent is mixed with pine smoke and marshmallows, Lucas's scent, and her hair is slightly damp. She's changed into leggings and an oversized sweatshirt, and she's removed her makeup, but she's still radiant.

"She called me and told me she was coming over, and I could either let her in, or she'd climb the fence," Lex admits.

As I look back to my best friend, my heart grows full to bursting. I'll never understand how or why it happened, but I'll never cease to be grateful for the force of nature that is Gabby Fitzgerald.

Chapter Six

Lydia

THE RELIEF OF HAVING Gabby in the pack house only lasts for a few hours, but after she leaves to go back to Wickland House for the night, the creeping ennui moves in fast, swallowing me whole. And even if I'm more aware of my surroundings, I still find myself slipping away for hours at a time, the phantom ache in my chest throbbing like an open wound. I try to keep up appearances, to hide the worst of my longing from my pack, with limited success. It takes some convincing, but Mateo agrees to go back to work after a few days, because there are still clients to handle, and with Rhett gone, a lot of his work has fallen onto Mateo's plate. Lucas is still taking a leave of absence, staying home with me as we wait for any news about Rhett.

I think about him nearly constantly, even when I'm actively trying to distract myself. Everything reminds me of my alpha in some way or another. The books I try to read are too like his scent. The sky is too close to the color of his eyes. Even the rumble of traffic sounds too much like his purr. And every reminder sends me back to the edge of the black hole, and it's always so easy to let myself fall into the flat dissociative episodes.

As I blink myself back to awareness after one such episode, panic fills my chest. I don't recognize my surroundings right away, but the scents of cedar and snickerdoodles calm my heart moments later. I'm in the Novak's living room, though I can't recall for the life of me how I got here. Looking around again, I catch a glimpse of Lucas in the kitchen, humming to himself as he works. A rustle of paper on my left draws my attention, and I find my stern bodyguard reading the newspaper. He's dressed in jeans and a band t-shirt for a group I've never heard of, and the casual image is startling enough to bring me fully back into my body.

"I was wondering when you'd come back," Caleb says softly, not looking up from the newspaper he's reading.

"I'm sorry," I mutter, toying with the edge of the blanket draped across my lap.

"I'll admit that I wasn't expecting to have you and your pack mate show up on my door this morning, but I can't say I'm not glad you did," Caleb goes on, still casual.

I flush hot, looking away, even though he's not looking at me. Lucas is making an abnormally loud racket, his slightly off-key singing making me smile to myself.

"I'm worried about you, *voyin*, and so is he. We think we might know a way to help, if you're up for it," he says, paper rustling again.

I don't answer, not sure what to say. But when I look back toward him, the piercing gray stare cuts through the half-baked denial I'd been about to form. In truth, I'm a bit worried about me, too. My soul feels unmoored, and I'm adrift with no shore in sight. I know Rhett is safe, and it's a matter of time before I'll be able to speak to him again, but that gaping void inside of me sucks away my hope and reason, and I'm helpless to fight it. So, I nod, willing to try anything at this point.

"Sylvie is going to be home in a few minutes, and she'd like to talk to you. Is that okay?" Caleb asks, voice warm and downright paternal.

"What about?" I rasp, my throat dry.

Caleb sighs, turning in his chair slightly to look at me. "Lucas suggested that you may need to talk to an omega about what you're going through. And based on what he told me, Sylvie and I agree."

I frown, guilt creeping in again. If Lucas and all his experience with omegas is at a loss for what to do with me, I must not be hiding my emotions as well as I thought. And they've got enough to worry about with me adding to the pile.

"It's not like that, sweetheart," Lucas says gently, appearing in the doorway.

I jump and look up at him, flushing. His eyes are kind, his smile understanding, but the way he's drying his hands on a kitchen towel is positively sexual. I swallow the sudden moisture in my mouth and give him a questioning look.

"It's been years since I was around my family, and none of them ever had to go through what we have," he says, looking away slightly as memories darken his countenance.

I press my lips together in thought. I'm about to respond when the sound of tires on gravel outside draws all our attention. Caleb jumps to his feet and makes it to the front door right as it flies open, catching it before it can slam into the wall. Sylvie waddles in, her pregnant belly slightly rounder than I remember, but not quite to ready-to-pop levels. She shoves a few strands of her bubble-gum pink hair out of her face after she shucks her coat. Her smile is kind as she looks at me.

Watching him fuss over her twists my heart in a peculiar way. He helps her put her feet up and takes off her shoes, treating her with the utmost gentleness. And even though she throws me a look of amused exasperation, she doesn't stop him. They seem to communicate without words, holding eye contact for a long moment before Caleb leans down and kisses the top of her belly, and then her cheek.

"Hello, Lucas. Glad you decided to come over," she says with a grin.

"Thank you for letting us loiter for a few hours," he replies with his usual disarming charm.

"As long as you make good on your promise to cook us that incredible pasta thing Caleb won't shut up about, then I think I can forgive the intrusion," she jokes, one of her hands rubbing idly on her belly.

"I'll do one better. I'll teach him how to make it himself," Lucas says, throwing a smirk in the alpha's direction.

Sylvie and I chuckle, and Lucas starts back toward the kitchen, but Caleb sticks around for a few more seconds, tucking the blanket around his mate's legs, fluffing her pillow. Finally, she lets out a huff and shoos him away for his cooking lesson.

"You'd think this was his first with the way he worries." She sighs, relaxing back and turning her attention to me.

I chuckle slightly, glancing at the pictures on the mantle. Sylvie isn't the first person Caleb has had a child with, but his previous partner Beth has primary custody of their son, Leo. There are a few pictures of Caleb, Sylvie, and the little boy together, placed centrally among the collection of snapshots and professional portraits, as well as handmade art pieces.

"I heard about what happened to your mate, and I can't—"

"We're not mated," I say, cutting across her sharply, but my frustration is with me alone.

Every day without Rhett, my mind replays the same guilt-ridden thought, the one I haven't spoken to my pack about. When I'd decided a while ago that Pack Saint Clair is it for me, I couldn't bring myself to let them force my heat so we could bond. But I should have faced the memories and fear and done what I had to, to protect Rhett and the pack.

I have no one to blame but myself that we aren't mated.

"Oh, I'm sorry. I thought based on how you've been—hmmm."

Sylvie starts sincerely, but then breaks off with a hum of thought, pressing her lips together as she furrows her brow.

"What?" I ask, a little more harshly than I'd intended.

"Are you the first omega in your family?" she asks suddenly, turning to me with bright but serious eyes.

I shake my head. "My mother is an omega. I have a few cousins, and cousins-in-law who are omegas, too. But I don't know—why does that matter?"

She sighs and almost absently twirls a piece of her hair between her fingers with one hand as she rubs her belly with the other.

"I have a strong maternal line of omegas, so I knew what to expect when I found my person. I don't want to assume, but it seems like no one really explained what being an omega means," she says, picking her words carefully.

I let out a sharp breath. "No, not really. I learned more about mating and knotting in my public school's sex ed class than I did at home. The only thing my parents made sure I understood was my place in the hierarchy, which was firmly at the bottom," I grumble.

Sylvie chuckles, but her smile is understanding. "That's okay. I just... I know it might seem like overstepping, but Caleb has been telling me about how you've been over the last week, and I thought maybe I could help."

So it's been a week. That answers that question, but it certainly doesn't make me feel better. If anything, knowing only makes it hurt worse. I've let all that time slip away, and for what? Why can't I pull myself together? The rest of my pack has. The brief moments of clarity I do have aren't enough, and they never last. Frustration at myself and this situation build under my skin, warring with the ever-present longing that fills every cell of my body every minute of every day.

"It feels like you're ripped in half, doesn't it? Your body is here, but the rest of you is somewhere else?" she prompts gently.

I look up at her, eyes wide. She put it into words exactly what I couldn't.

"Caleb was called overseas very suddenly a few days after we bonded, and it was non-negotiable. He was only gone for six weeks, but I will never forget the soul-crushing loneliness of those first few days. We hadn't figured out how to feel each other yet, let alone do it over distances. It felt like someone had dug my soul from my chest with their bare hands and left me to bleed. Caleb knew something was wrong, and he was going through his own struggle, but couldn't figure out how to help me. I went to the emergency room, but no one could find anything physically wrong with me. My mother was the only one who could help, the only one who understood that I was going through agony because my bond mate was taken from me," she explains.

I blink at her, trying to get my mind to comprehend her words. Everything she said makes sense, and she's describing my struggle perfectly, but Rhett and I aren't bond mates. When I went through my heat a few months ago, Rhett and I had been on one date and barely knew each other. He very specifically wouldn't let me touch him despite my wanting to, and even after my heat broke, none of my alphas have bitten me hard enough to break the skin. It's been one of my limits since the beginning. They can nip and suck, but they can't draw blood. After taking these precautions, there's no way this could be true. And yet...

"When my mother and grandmother explained bonding to me, they told me that the sex and the bites are only part of the equation. A true mating bond, one that lasts, has to be formed on a foundation of love and trust. They said that an omega can form a sort of pseudo-bond with an alpha without ever going into heat if the connection between them is strong enough," Sylvie goes on.

I gape at her for another long moment, letting the words rush over me. Could I already have this pseudo-bond with Rhett? I've never heard of it, but then again, there are plenty of things about omegas and mating I'd never heard of until after I left my family. I didn't even know heat suppressants were a thing until I went through my first heat cycle. It wouldn't be entirely out of character for my mother to hide this sort of thing from me, if she even knew it existed. Though with how hard she pushed for Darren and me to be together, I'm sure she would have jumped on any chance to claim I belonged to him. It almost seems crazy, to bond with someone without ever knowing it.

But considering how I've felt this past week, and everything I've been through with Rhett, I can't dismiss the thought out of hand. While I don't think of my relationship with him as being any different from the ones I have with Mateo, Lex, or even Lucas, I can't deny that Rhett has always had a certain potent effect on me. His touch could calm me from my worst panic attacks, and the sound of his voice is enough to turn me into a puddle. Even thinking about him now, and acknowledging the possibility of a pseudo-bond, seems to soothe the raw edges of the wound in my heart.

"Is there anything I can do to make it better?" I whisper, rubbing my chest absently.

"Short of him coming home, I doubt anything is going to make this go away entirely. But I can tell you that curling up in a ball and waiting for it to blow over won't help," she replies with a chuckle.

I smile a little despite myself. I can't deny that I've been wallowing in self-pity. And that's not fair, not to my pack and not to myself. The only person who's continued to blame me for this mess has been me, and it's high time I stop doing that. I've got to take my own advice and stop acting like the world stopped turning. And there are things I can do to make sure that, when Rhett does finally get to come home, I'll be ready for him.

Sylvie leans over and takes my hands, holding them tight. The touch makes my skin jump, and I return the hold as best as I can, squeezing gently.

"I'm always here to talk about things, if you need it. I think you may have missed a few lessons at Omega School," she says softly, her smile serene and knowing.

I nod and go quiet for a minute, just enjoying her soothing cookie scent. Anxiousness still twists my gut, but I don't think that'll go away until Rhett is back where he belongs. Until then, I owe it to him to not dwell on or make myself sick over this. And as I consider my next steps, of what I need to do while I wait, a plan begins to form.

"Actually, there is something I want to ask."

CHAPTER SEVEN

Lucas

WE STAY AT THE Novak's through supper, and the change that comes over Lydia is like night and day. She's spent the last week drifting in and out, sleeping most of the time, but even when she was awake, there were times when her body was there, but the rest of her was miles away. I'd tried every trick I could think of, but I'd run out of options. I'm not afraid to call in an expert, and Sylvie Novak did the trick.

Once we're back at the pack house, Lydia and I find Lex and Mateo sitting on the sectional, the TV on, but neither of them watching it. Lex is on her tablet, which is not unusual, but then so is Mateo, which very much is. They both turn to look at us as we enter, relief sliding over their faces.

"Did y'all have a good time?" Mateo asks, getting to his feet and vaulting over the couch to gather Lydia in his arms.

She smiles at his affection, and my heart skips a beat. An easy smile, almost a normal smile. I don't want to get my hopes up, but maybe we're turning a corner at last. My relief is palpable; I don't think I could have watched Lydia be miserable for another minute.

"It was good. Caleb and Lucas made the house special carbonara from Alice's," Lydia says brightly, following Mateo as he leads her back over to the sectional.

I shove my hands into my pockets as I trail after them, catching Mateo's questioning look, asking the question with his eyes rather than his words. *Did it work?* I give a tentative nod and a hopeful smile, and the returning grin makes my heart flutter a little. It truly isn't fair how handsome that man is.

"Giving away trade secrets, I see," Lex teases, locking and setting her device to the side as I flop down next to her.

"You're just mad because he won't tell you any of his recipes," Mateo tosses out.

"We could get them patented and protected—"

"Joke, Lex. It was a joke," Mateo says with an exasperated sigh, making Lydia and I laugh.

She's tucked up under his arm, a soft blanket over her shoulders, leaving only her adorable face poking out. Her green eyes sparkle with life and awareness, and I get lost in them for a moment. I missed that look, the innocent curiosity she wears when she doesn't think we're watching her. Like she's still trying to figure out if we're real.

"Can I ask something?" she says into a lull in the conversation.

"You just did," I retort before I can stop myself.

She sticks her tongue out at me, and I grin.

"What was that folio on the counter? The day we came home?" she asks hesitantly.

I look at Lex and Mateo, assessing. Lex tenses and swallows hard while Mateo's smile falls flat. It's only for a moment, but it's still long enough to make Lydia go pale and start apologizing. I flap my hands at her to stop before she can build up a full head of steam.

"That's the next Foundation project, right, Lex?" I prompt pointedly, turning to give her a hard stare.

She nods and clears her throat, sitting up a little as she composes herself. "Right. The Magnolia Garden Theater," she says firmly.

Lydia nods. "I know that place. It's just off Church Street?" she says, words lifting in a question.

Mateo nods, jumping on her change in mood. "Yep. We've been trying to get it for a while, but we had to wait for the contract to end and then the auction took forever to close and—"

"Long story short," Lex says loudly, cutting off Mateo's eager ramblings, "we closed the deal on the Friday you all left for Louisiana."

Lydia hums thoughtfully, and I can almost see the wheels turning in her head. I want to see if she'll work it out on her own, but the longer the silence stretches out, the more doubt creeps in.

"What do you think you're going to do with it? Restore it and sell it?" she asks conversationally.

Mateo, Lex, and I share a look, and I sit forward a little, twisting my fingers together between my knees as I rest my elbows on my thighs. Lydia's eyes go wide, surprised but not fearful.

"That's actually the thing, Lydi-bug. We want you to decide what we do with it," I say as gently as I can.

She pauses for a minute, and I see the exact moment the realization dawns on her. Each of us in the pack has had something of a pet project. Lex had Bright Hills, and

Mateo drooled over The Valencia for the longest time before they finally acquired it. For all of Lex's illegal chicanery in the bidding process, Rhett took point on the Wickland House restoration, and designed every miniscule detail of the house around us. For me, it was my restaurants. With Lydia a member of this family in all the ways that count, even if we're still waiting for the formalities to be completed, it's only right for Lydia to have something like this.

"Y'all, that's—I mean, insane doesn't even begin to cover it," she says, exhaling in disbelief.

"Well, since you won't let us buy you a new car..." Mateo says, trailing off.

Lydia elbows him in the ribs, but we all laugh at the half-joke. We've been trying to tell Lydia that we want to do things for her, spoil her completely rotten, and make sure she never wants for anything for the rest of her life. Hopefully now that we've bought her a whole-ass building, she'll bend a little on the less extravagant things.

There's another long moment of silence as Lydia processes, and we give her the space. Though Lex continues to fidget, her fingers of her left hand dancing across my back as she subconsciously plays the bass line of whatever classical song is filling her mind. I put a hand on her knee, squeezing slightly in silent reassurance. Lydia's face isn't exactly unreadable, but the emotions that flicker across it move too fast for me to fully process. Shock, awe, joy, sadness, longing, back to shock, more joy, and then finally settling on determined resolve. She looks up at Mateo with her brow and lips set in a serious expression, and then she looks to me before finally coming to rest on Lex.

"I want to get my implant removed," she declares.

A pin hitting the floor would have sounded like an explosion in the silence that follows her words. Her implant. She wants it removed. Does that mean...

"I'd need to start supplements as well, and I'd obviously want to talk to a doctor to see if it's even possible, but I think we could make it happen," Lydia goes on.

"Make... make what happen, baby?" Mateo stutters, still in the complete disbelief phase.

"My heat. I've only got a few weeks before I'm supposed to go into heat again, but if y'all are serious enough to buy a theater for me, then—"

"No, Lydia, that's not why—" Lex cuts herself off after nearly shouting over Lydia, clearing her throat. "You don't have to do that—get your implant removed, I mean—just because we bought The Garden."

Lydia shakes her head. "It's not about the theater. Today at Caleb and Sylvie's, I talked to her about it, and she gave me some advice. I wasn't going to bring it up like this, but..."

She trails off, and everyone waits for her to continue. I'm hardly breathing in anticipation of what she might say next. This can't be real. She fiddles with the edge of the blanket, not looking at us, and my skin prickles with electric excitement. And when Lydia looks up at us, her emerald eyes are firm, resolve pulling her mouth into a line.

"In my head, and in my heart, I know that you—this pack—are it for me. I've known it for a long time. I want to be your pack mate, and... more. I want the bonds. I want everything. What I was going to say was that if y'all're out here, buying buildings to show me how serious you are about your feelings for me, then the best way I can show you how serious I am about joining this pack is to get my implant out, get on supplements, and do whatever I can to be ready by the time I go into heat again. And then we can bond, all of us."

Lydia's voice cracks from the passion and emotion she pushes through her words, and my heart aches from it. Mateo is there, wiping away her tears and kissing her hair, but I'm frozen. The implications of her words are hitting me in waves, and that last bit nearly stops my heart. I look at her, and she nods, reading my expression, and I'm glad for it. I don't know if I could ever ask it of her, but my Lydi-bug knows me well enough that I don't have to.

After three years, I'd genuinely lost hope of ever bonding with Rhett or Lex. The shit Seth put us through left deep wounds, ones we only managed to heal with Lydia's help. I could never imagine a life without my alphas, but to ask an omega to share her bond mates with a beta like me would go against her very nature. But my Lydia, my perfect omega, will do this for me.

"As long as this is what you truly want, then that's what we'll do. Make your appointments, and we'll do our parts to make sure we're ready and available, too," Lex says, drawing our attention.

The darkness in her eyes falls like an ice cube into my gut. Right. We all have work to do over the next few weeks. But if the smoldering ember I see in the depths of her hazel eyes is anything to go by, I don't think anything is going to stop Alexandra St. Clair anymore.

CHAPTER EIGHT

Alexandra

I STARE OUT OVER the Everton skyline as I wait, my fingers tapping on my thighs in patterns I recognize as Chopin after a moment of consideration. It's almost sunset, but there's one last thing I have to do before I can go home for the night. I've already sent Erica home, and the building is growing quieter with each employee who exits and drives away.

My day has been a series of phone calls from hell. I'd spoken with Officer Lee Nyueng of the Everton Police Department and the ADA about Seth's case. They've got alerts out on all his accounts and credit cards, but Seth has hidden himself remarkably well. My only explanation for this level of stealth is preparation. He must have known we were coming and may have even run long before the warrant was issued.

The sole reason I know he's not dead is the fact that money is still being withdrawn from the account I pay his stipend from. He never goes to a physical location to make the withdrawals, using apps instead to keep the currency digital, which makes using the money trail to pinpoint his location impossible. I'd considered every angle, and finally settled on a plan, one crazy enough that it just might work.

So I'd had to make my second hellish phone call to the one demon I'd promised myself I'd never make a deal with again: my father. I'm still recovering from the pounding headache that came on during that two-hour nightmare conversation. But at least it wasn't for nothing. Leopold had agreed to lend his assistance, if I was willing to pay his price. I shouldn't have been surprised. Leopold can't do anything out of the kindness of his heart on account of not having one.

A month ago, I would have gone ahead and agreed. I would have handled this and been done with it, and already moved on to solve the next problem. But not anymore. I have to do better for my pack, and it starts with including them when the situation calls for it. So when my office door opens and Mateo strides inside, I brace myself for a hard talk.

"For being a new build, this place is fucking creepy after hours," he starts with a chuckle.

I hum a small laugh, turning my chair to face him. The room is bathed in reds and oranges, the fading sunlight throwing harsh shadows across the marble floor. Mateo's dressed for business, which soothes me a little. I'd been worried he'd shut down after he took a few days off to take care of Lydia, but he's at least trying to keep up appearances while Rhett's gone. He tosses his jacket over the back of one of my armchairs, rolling up his sleeves to the elbows as he strides over to the bar cart. The muscles under his tattoos flex while he pours himself several fingers of his favorite bourbon into a glass before taking a swig. I tilt my head to the side, curiously studying him as his throat works. Grimacing at the burn, he turns to face me with a hand in his pocket.

"So. I'm here, as requested. What's so important that you couldn't talk to me at the pack house?" he asks dully, slowly pacing toward me.

I bite the inside of my lip to stop myself from firing back. A little crease appears between Mateo's brow when I don't respond to his goading, but I ignore it. Taking a deep breath, I set my shoulders and look up at him. "Seth," I state simply.

The scowl that crosses his face strikes a nerve in my chest. Mateo is too good to have been caught by someone like Seth, but that may have been why he'd been targeted in the first place. I remember the affable, boisterous alpha I'd met at the conference in Las Vegas all those years ago, the one so passionate about making a difference that I couldn't help but like him. But he's been hardened by years of Seth's abuse, and I can hardly stand it. And with Lydia ready to take things to the next level, we no longer have time to spare. Which is why we have to deal with him once and for all.

"Has anyone spotted him?" Mateo asks, words stilted.

As I shake my head, Mateo curses under his breath. I stay quiet as he moves toward the window behind me, stopping when he's just past my chair. Turning and standing, I cross my arms as I settle next to him. I breathe in the smell of the bourbon as it mixes with the citrus notes of his aura on his next sip. As Mateo shifts his weight, his arm brushes mine, and I shiver, moving away from the ceiling vent I must have accidentally stood under. We don't look at each other for a long time, the air charged with four years of accumulated unspoken feelings. We'd stopped playing the blame game a while ago, at least out loud. But there were times he's looked at me, and I can read the bitterness in his eyes. If it weren't for

Rhett, I'm sure he would have disappeared into the sunset a long time ago. Mateo takes another drink and I sigh.

"I've got a plan to flush him out, and hopefully deal with him," I murmur, keeping my voice down despite us being functionally alone in the building.

"Is this you asking for permission or forgiveness?" he shoots back with a scoff.

"Permission. Because this is as much your decision as it's mine, Mat. Trust me; I'd love to give you plausible deniability here, but it's not possible."

Out of the corner of my eye, I see Mateo throw back what's left of his drink and turn to me. He leans sideways against the glass, running his free hand through his sandy brown hair. I don't know how, but his hair always settles into a frustratingly handsome coif, regardless of how much he messes with it. Wet, dry, tangled, or combed, his hair is always perfectly ruffled and soft enough to run your fingers through. Not that I've ever done that intentionally or anything. He puffs his cheeks, and then lets out a slow breath.

"All right, lay it on me," he says at last.

As I explain, I specifically don't look at him, because if I see one shred of doubt or anger in his eyes, I'll abandon this entire endeavor without a second thought. It's risky, with too many places for things to go wrong, but the safe road has failed us. This plan is the only way I can see to get us free. When I finish, there's a long, heavy silence. It stretches on and on, until I can't take it anymore. I turn and find Mateo looking off into the middle distance behind me, brow furrowed in thought.

"So... what do you think?" I ask hesitantly.

"You know, of all the batshit things I thought you'd suggest, I have to admit that this didn't even make the list," he says slowly, turning to look me in the eye.

His soft brown gaze shines in the last rays of sunlight, full of too many emotions for me to sort through. He's not dismissing me out of hand, which is encouraging. And I swear I see a spark of hope in the depths of his pupils.

"My father's already agreed, but you know how he is," I reply softly, but not weakly.

"What's the going rate for Leopold St. Clair's assistance these days?" Mateo snorts with a small shake of his head.

"He wants The Valencia. Outright," I reply shortly.

"Ah. So just our firstborn. I was afraid he'd ask for a favor," Mateo retorts with a sigh.

I can't help but huff a little chuckle. Mateo's lips twitch up at the corners at the sound of my laugh, his little grin bringing a strange heat to my cheeks. But the expression drops as he looks away, thoughtful again. I don't blame him for wanting to really think through any deal that involves my father. Even though it's the scene of the crime, so to speak, we've always held The Valencia in a special place of honor. It was the first project we picked as a pack, the first restoration under the combined banners of the St. Clair Foundation and C&H Design. Giving up our firstborn, as Mateo so eloquently put it, will be tough, but it's better than pretty much every alternative offer he brought to the table, worst of all a flat IOU. I'd rather sell my soul to the literal Devil than owe my father an unspecified favor. The Devil, at least, would wait until after I've died to torture me for eternity.

"And it'd be clean? No way for it to get traced back to us?" Mateo asks into the silence.

I nod once. "I want to keep Rhett, Luc, and Lydia out of this. If we limit the people involved, it'll reduce the risk of leaks."

He sucks his teeth skeptically and tilts his head, making me sigh.

"I know, but it'll be safer this way. Plausible deniability," I reply flatly.

"Were those your first words?" Mateo shoots back.

"No, my first words were 'I'll do it myself,'" I reply, completely deadpan.

"Wait, really?" Mateo splutters, turning to look at me.

I roll my eyes with a smile. "No, of course not. It was Nana."

Mateo throws his head back and laughs, clutching his stomach. I can't help but join him; his laugh has always been more infectious than the common cold. The silence that follows the last of our humor is more comfortable, and we both look out over the skyline and the setting sun.

"After what Seth did, you'd really trust me with this? To have this secret hanging over your head?" he asks seriously.

I close my eyes, my lips pressing into a thin line. He's not wrong. I'd promised myself I'd never let anyone have leverage over me again after Seth. I foolishly told him about how I'd lied on a government grant form to secure the necessary funding for the Wickland House project. He's been holding the threat of alerting the authorities to my fraud ever since, preventing me from enforcing consequences for his repeat violations of court orders. Trusting Mateo to keep this secret and take it to his grave isn't easy, but it's what has to be done.

"To be fair, I'll have the same leverage over you," I snark in return.

Mateo chuckles and shakes his head, putting his hands on his hips, going quiet again. The sun slips below the line of buildings, setting them in a sharp silhouette against the oranges and pinks of the cloudless sky, and as I look out over the city, my heart swells with affection. Everton is more than a city to me. It's the first place that's felt like home since I moved out of the family compound after college. There's so much life and vibrance, a pulse of excitement I'd felt the moment I entered the city limits for the first time. It's been nearly a decade since then, and my love for this place and its people hasn't dimmed. I'll never stop trying to help this city, but I can't do that with the albatross that is Seth Douglas around my neck.

This won't be the first time I've gotten my hands dirty to do what needs to be done, and I doubt it'll be the last. It's just a matter of whether Mateo is willing to do the same.

"You do realize what'll happen if we get caught, right?" Mateo starts.

"Bare minimum, possession of a controlled substance for the bond breakers, more than a few Omega Protection Act violations, and I'm sure there's something illegal about selling property for the purposes of funding criminal activity," I drone, swallowing hard.

"I'm glad you've thought about the legal stuff, but I meant to our pack mates. They'll never trust us again, especially after we promised not to keep any more secrets," he goes on, mussing up his hair again.

I nod, heart plummeting and eyes burning. I don't want to do this, but we've run out of options. Taking the high road has landed us here. The law won't help us anymore, so we have to take matters into our own, extralegal hands.

"They're going to be questioned, and I won't make them lie for us. Rhett's alibi is airtight, but ignorance is going to be the best shield Lydia and Lucas can have. Maybe one day we'll tell them, and hope they forgive us, but..."

Trailing off, my voice cracks as I consider the alternative. I can try to lie to myself and say that I'm okay with accepting the consequences of this plan, but I still remember the way Lydia looked at me after that massive fight a few weeks ago. I'm not sure if my heart can go through that again, but I don't want to live like this anymore. More than anything, I want to give myself fully to her and Lucas, and I can't do that while Seth is still in the picture.

"I know, Lex. So, let's agree that if this goes tits up, we're going to throw your father directly under the bus," Mateo drones, not looking at me.

I whip my gaze to him, face draining of heat. It takes me a few seconds to comprehend his meaning, but once I do, I can't help but laugh outright. Mateo looks down at me and returns my chuckles. When we're quiet, our eyes stay locked together, and there's a flicker of something in the fawn-colored depths. But I brush it off as a trick of the light.

Mateo turns on his heel and goes back to the bar cart, refilling his glass and pouring a portion into a second glass. When he comes back, he passes me the bourbon and holds his up.

"To freedom, by any means necessary," he declares.

I roll my eyes but clink my glass to his and repeat his toast.

CHAPTER NINE

Lydia

I STARE AT THE orange bottle in my hand, the heat suppressants inside rattling slightly as I turn it back and forth. There's still half a bottle left, but it doesn't matter. Ripping the cap off, I turn to my toilet, emptying the pills into the bowl, and pressing the flush soundly. I wait until I'm sure the pills are down the drain before tossing the now empty bottle in the tiny wastebasket under the vanity. As I look at the new bottle of pills on the edge of the sink, my heart flips slightly in my chest. But before I can dwell, my arm throbs dully and I wince, looking down at the band of neon pink self-adhering gauze tape wrapped around my bicep.

I've just gotten home from my appointment at the omega clinic, where I'd made the decision to get my implant removed. I'd expected Dr. Miller to make a big fuss of it, maybe even try to talk me out of it, but she'd been weirdly excited for me when I'd declared that I was ready for a bond.

It's been a few days since Sylvie's intervention, and I've been at her house every day since. I've learned more about what it means to be an omega in three afternoons with her than I did in nearly twenty years at home. Pseudo-bonds were only the tip of the iceberg. She helped me to finally master my omega purr, a sound I can make to soothe anxious or distressed alphas. I'd gotten so good at it that I'd nearly put Caleb to sleep where he was standing, three rooms away from where Sylvie and I were practicing. She'd even told me exactly how to initiate the bonding process, and what I'd have to do to help an alpha bond with a beta—ya know, just in case I might need that in the near future.

But what had become increasingly clear was the need for my body to be in a true heat. Nothing short of that would do if I wanted the bonds to stick. And they had to. There were too many dangerous pieces on the board for anything less. Beyond my own personal desires, the practical solution to almost all my problems is this bond.

So I'd made sure that the clinic knew about that when my implant was removed. And they've prescribed a round of hormone enhancers. I'm to take one a day every day until I go into heat. Combine that with plenty of "attention," the doctor's exact words, from my pack, and I should be ready for my alphas.

Well, I'll be ready. I just have to hope Rhett will make it home. And Lex and Mateo can get free from Seth.

Popping one of the tan tablets into my mouth, I swallow it down with little effort. I leave my bathroom and flop into my nest, listening to the quiet of the pack house. I'm alone for the first time in a long time, with the pack at work and Caleb busy with Sylvie at a birthing class. Mateo will be the first home tonight, what with Lucas covering a closing shift and Lex's meetings running late, but it's almost nice to have time to myself for the first time in months. And unlike before my lessons with my omega mentor, the silence doesn't send me spiraling with my thoughts and longing. She's shared some of the coping mechanisms she used when she has to be apart from her mate, and they've worked.

As I drift in my longing for a while, the sunlight fades outside of the frosted windows above my bed. I must fall asleep at some point, because when I surface again, I'm curled around a pillow that smells faintly of Rhett. Whiskey and leather and dark chocolate just barely cling to fabric and my heart twists. This is normal, I remind myself. My primal instincts are seeking out the comfort of his scent, even if it hurts. I've yet to muster enough courage to go into Rhett's room, convincing myself that it would be wrong to disturb the space. But now that I'm alone, maybe it's time to stop lying to myself.

I drag my feet up the stairs from the basement to the main floor of the pack house. The silence of the house is oddly comfortable as I make my way up the stairs to the second floor. The hum of electricity in the walls, the central air kicking on, just the general ambience, is oddly soothing. There's no one to stop me from entering Rhett's room, no one to judge me for the tears that burn the backs of my eyes as traces of his scent leak out through the gaps around the door. When my shaking hand turns the knob and the door swings open on silent hinges, I stagger into the frame as the strength goes out from my legs.

Nothing has changed, no one having gone in here since we've been back. So, seeing the slightly mussed sheets, the clothes in the hamper, even the haphazard pile of folders and boxes next to his desk, it's almost like I've stepped back in time. Like any moment, he's going to come in behind me and close the door before gathering me up in his arms.

I rush for the bed, launching myself into the center and burying my face in the pillow. My heart throbs and twists in my chest as I inhale the whiskey, leather, dark chocolate, and old book smell that's so much stronger here. I can scent traces of Lucas's pine smoke and s'mores, but the overwhelming concentration of Rhett's essence in the fabric breaks the fragile control I've managed to keep on myself.

I roll onto my side and hug one of his pillows to my chest, curling around it as much as I can. Fishing my phone out of my hoodie pocket, I open my photo app, flicking to my favorite picture of him. He sent it to me early in our relationship, when he left to visit his family to celebrate the birth of his nephew, Mason. The picture is a candid, clearly taken without Rhett's knowledge, because his attention is so utterly focused on the tiny bundle in his arms. He's holding the baby for the first time in the hospital, his excitement and joy palpable even through the screen.

He's going to be a good dad.

The thought wanders idly across my mind, and I'm surprised by the happy little flip in my stomach at the thought of Rhett being a father, specifically the father of my children. I shake my head a little, flipping to another picture in my camera roll. This one is a snapshot he took when we were spending a lazy day in my old apartment. He's behind me, one arm banded tight around my chest as he looms over me. His ice-blue eyes sparkle in the light falling over our faces, his smile infectious even now. He's framed the selfie just so, hiding the fact that we're both naked, but it hardly matters. I can't take my eyes off his face, the warmth shining through the pixels filling the lonely hole in my chest just a bit.

The longer I look at the image, the warmer my body gets. I shed my jacket and pants, leaving me in a tank top sans bra and my underwear, and I shiver slightly as I settle back on my side and flip through the pictures of the two of us together. It's not that I haven't been given attention by the others, but they've been going at my pace, and this is the first time I've truly been in the mood for more than snuggles. Now, surrounded by Rhett's scent, feelings that have been lying low are surging, and it's easier to pretend the blanket I've wound around my stomach is his arm, the pillow his chest, and I close my eyes to sink deeper into the fantasy.

I turn over, adjusting until I'm positioned similarly to that photo, and I can pretend I'm back there, in my shitty studio apartment in the nest I'd built through years of tweaking until it was perfect. The mental image is sort of ruined by the distinct lack of lumps in the mattress below me, but I push that aside with another inhale of Rhett's scent.

He'd nuzzle my neck with his nose, taking deep inhales of my scent as he buries his face in my hair. I let my fingers trail down my stomach, over the material of my shirt, trying to pretend it's Rhett teasing me. But my fingers are too small, too thin. So the daydream changes, and I can hear his voice in my ear, rough with desire and full of that lilting Irish accent.

Show me how wet you are for me, sweet girl.

I dip a finger below the waistband of my panties, shifting one of my legs to allow me better access to my core. As I slide a finger between my folds, I gasp and arch, more sensitive than I'd realized. I lose myself in my own touch, trying to keep it light and teasing as I circle my opening, resisting the urge to touch my swollen, throbbing clit.

Taste yourself, see how sweet you truly are.

I nod mindlessly, my body obeying the imagined command even as I fight the impulse to keep touching. But even this version of Rhett that lives in my mind holds my will in an iron grip. Carefully, I extract my hand and bring my finger to my lips, my tongue darting out to taste the wetness clinging to the digit. A moan escapes my throat before I can stop it, and my lips close around my finger. As I clean my finger, the sweetness of the fluid catches me off guard, honey and vanilla and something refreshingly earthy filling my mouth.

Good girl. More.

The command is more of a rumbling purr, but I rush to obey. Using two fingers now, my touch is much bolder, the tips of my fingers dipping shallowly into my entrance. My hips roll on their own, and I gasp and whine, the sounds muffled as I bring my fingers back to my mouth and suck them clean.

I'm about to repeat the motion, when suddenly, the bed sinks. I sit up, whipping around to find Mateo climbing in behind me. My face flushes hot with embarrassment. How long had he been here without my noticing? He's only in his boxers, but I'm too distracted by the absolutely predatory look on his face. He prowls closer, soft brown curls falling into his smoldering tawny eyes. I try to move backward, but he's too fast. He grabs my wrist and pulls me down, replacing the pillow at my back with his body.

"How'd your appointment go?" he mutters into my skin, hands roaming over my clothes.

I swallow, catching my breath and trying to regain some of my composure. But the warm trail of his fingertips is more than distracting. I whimper and arch back, feeling his hardening cock pressing against my ass. He chuckles, grinding just a bit but pulling back to tease.

"Were you touching yourself and thinking about Rhett, baby girl?" he asks lowly as he drags me back down into the fantasy, looping an ankle around my leg to hold me securely.

I swallow again, breath shaking. I don't know how to best answer, so I settle on silence.

"I don't blame you. I miss him, too," he goes on, nuzzling my neck as his fingers splay out over my stomach.

Settling back into the embrace, my arousal banks slightly as a wave of compassion replaces it. Mateo has been so strong for us, a pillar for the pack to lean on as we've navigated this uncharted territory. Until now, I haven't really considered what sort of toll this might be having on him. Lucas and I may have lost a lover, but Mateo lost his best friend.

"I'm sorry I haven't been...as attentive to you lately," I trail off, shrugging slightly.

Mateo kisses my neck. "You have nothing to apologize for, Lydia. You needed time, and I am more than happy to give you the space you need. I'm not going to die if I don't get my dick wet, I promise."

We share a laugh, but I still feel a little residual guilt. I know it's my trauma that's making it hard to believe him, but it doesn't change what I'm experiencing.

"If it comes down to it, you could always ask Lex for a hand," I comment, deciding to push my guilt into a little box to be unpacked another day.

Mateo scoffs, and I can practically hear him rolling his eyes. "Yeah, okay. That'll happen the day we can have a snowball fight in hell."

I smirk to myself, glad for the distraction. Teasing Mateo and Lex about their undeniable sexual tension has been one of Lucas's favorite past times, and he's recently introduced me to how much fun it can be to get them worked up.

"Well, then maybe Lucas. You two have been hanging out more lately. I'm sure he'd—"

Mateo sputters over me, but he's not conspicuously denying. Once he's gathered his wits, he nips at my ear, squeezing me a little tighter.

"I said I'm fine, and I mean it," he grumbles in my ear.

I giggle. "I know. But I'm just saying. If you and Lucas wanted to blow off some steam, and you let me watch, that'd be kinda hot," I admit, flushing a little.

Mateo's laugh is more of a sultry purr, and I shiver as his lips ghost over the skin of my throat. His hands, which had gone still for a moment, start up again, and I bite my lower lip to stop myself from groaning.

"Would you be the director, telling us what to do to please you? Or just the audience, touching your pretty little pussy while you enjoy the show?" Mateo asks, tone dripping with desire.

I gasp as he trails a hand over my stomach, fingers slipping below the hem and traveling back up to my breasts. His touch is firm, massaging me with just the right pressure to make me whimper his name. I lift my head as he moves his other arm, letting my head fall back into his chest as he surrounds me more completely. Ozone mixes with whiskey, and my nipples harden as I let myself drift in the sensations.

"What dirty little fantasies do you dream about? Rhett and me fucking Lucas from both ends? Or are you with us, Rhett fucking his beta's cock into your ass while I'm balls deep in your cunt? Don't leave me guessing, baby girl. Tell me what you were thinking about before I came in," Mateo asks, breath hot against my neck.

I swallow roughly, my tongue suddenly too big for me to form words. But as I hesitate, Mateo's fingers stop, touching my nipple but not moving or squeezing like I want. An unspoken challenge.

"I was...thinking about Rhett behind me, like you are. He was telling me..." I trail off with a gasp as he pinches both of my nipples hard, adding that edge of pleasure-pain that makes my pussy clench.

"Keep going. Don't stop," Mateo breathes, words ragged.

"I could hear him telling me to touch myself, to taste how sweet I am," I continue, grateful he can't see how flushed my face is.

Mateo purrs low in his chest, a rumble I can feel against my back. He rolls his hips, the evidence of his enjoyment pressing hard against my ass. One of my hands drifts back to cling to his hip, nails digging as I try to drag him closer.

"Do it for me. Show me," he commands, and the tone is so alpha that my whole body shudders.

I wriggle my other hand free, slipping it between my legs and pushing my panties aside so I can access my dripping slit. Whimpering at the contact, I circle my clit with teasing brushes before moving to my entrance. I push the tip of one finger into my channel, and it's so wet, there's no resistance. I don't want to stop, but Mateo twists my nipples again, grinding his cock against me, and I remember myself.

Withdrawing my finger, I hold it up so he can see my sticky arousal shining in the afternoon sun. Snatching my wrist, he pulls my finger into his waiting mouth. I moan at the feeling of his talented tongue wrapping itself around the digit, and I push back against his throbbing cock.

"I need you, Lydia. Please, let me—I want—"

"Please, Mat, please. I need you, too," I whimper, speaking over him even as I'm dragging his boxers down.

We're a tangle of limbs as we shed the few layers of clothes we have left, and then he's on me. He pulls my top leg back and over his hips, opening me up to him fully. We work together to line his cock up with my entrance, and then he thrusts forward in one smooth motion, my body so keyed up that there's almost no resistance. There's still the delicious stretch as my body accommodates his size, but it feels too good. His mouth finds mine as we move together, faster and faster, as we seek mutual release.

"I love you so much, so fucking much," Mateo pants when we pull away, and he rests his forehead against mine.

"Love you, t—Oh, God," I start, breaking off in a moan as he shifts his hips and hits that perfect patch of nerves and makes me see stars.

"I know, baby girl. You feel so perfect, squeezing me so tight."

He shifts again, pressing me face down into the mattress so he can thrust even deeper. I try to meet his powerful strokes, but I can only do so much. He has me pinned just the way I like: held enough to feel secure but not enough to feel trapped. I can drift in pleasure, my pleas for more growing higher and louder as he pushes me toward my peak.

"Gonna fill this perfect cunt, give you so much cum it'll stain the bed and Rhett'll smell us for months. Then we'll take turns breeding this perfect pussy," Mateo snarls, speaking so low and fast that I'm not sure he even realizes what he's saying.

Something about that thought, about being fucked so hard and often that I can't help but end up carrying a child, makes my pussy clench just right, and I shatter. I scream into the sheets, my orgasm flooding from me and filling every corner of my body with tingling warmth. Mateo curses loudly and drives deep, and the feeling of him pulsing, his cum filling me just like he promised, sets off another smaller wave of heat that makes me moan long and low.

We stay like that for a moment, Mateo holding his weight above me until he can't take it anymore. He hisses as he pulls out, and I flush as the rush of our mixed release trickles over my thighs. It's obscene and I can't help my little dazed smile as I roll onto my side again, squeezing my legs closed to hold it in for just a little longer. Mateo cuddles up behind me, kissing my shoulder lightly. The house is still quiet, the only sounds our breathing and our heartbeats slowing back to normal.

"I needed that," I sigh, speaking the thought as it occurs to me.

"Happy to be of service." Mateo chuckles, still a little out of breath.

I smile to myself, letting my mind wander. In the silence, my thoughts creep back to the idea of Mateo and Lucas together, or Mateo and Lex, for that matter. And it's more than a little shocking to realize that there's not a shred of jealousy in my heart. A year ago, I may have gone into a spiral of self-hatred if I thought about a partner being with someone other than me. But now it's just... natural. Like the last piece of a puzzle falling into place.

"Lucas might need you, too," I whisper.

Mateo sits up and looks at me, concern in his eyes. "Lydia, that's not—"

But I cut him off with a kiss, and just give him a reassuring smile when we pull away. "Only if you want to, and he wants to. But I don't want you to think you have to be monogamous with me," I state simply.

Mateo considers me for another long moment before shaking his head with a smile. "I appreciate that. I don't know if it'll happen, but I'm glad you're comfortable enough to tell me that."

He kisses me again, and we let it linger, not escalating, but just enjoying the feeling of closeness. When we pull away, Mateo settles behind me again, holding me close as he curls his larger frame around mine. My mind goes blank as his warmth fills me to the brim. But the warm afterglow is cut short as my phone's ringer cuts through the silence. It takes us a minute to find it in the mess of sheets and blankets, but when I do finally extract it, my heart leaps into my throat. I swipe to answer, hardly getting it to my ear before I'm shouting.

"Rhett?! Oh, my God!"

CHAPTER TEN

Rhett

IF I'VE LEARNED ANYTHING from the last two weeks in jail, it's how to hurry up and wait. Hurry up and get to mess for lunch, but then wait your turn to be served. Hurry up and get to your bunk but wait for the guards to take their sweet time doing inspections. Today has been especially torturous, because it's been hurry up and wait for my release. But after hours of bureaucratic nonsense, I'm finally on my way out.

I'm dressed in a thin white tank top that barely covers my stomach and a pair of jeans three sizes too big that I have to hold up to keep from tripping. They threw out my blood-soaked clothes at the hospital, and I'd given my phone to Ted for safe-keeping, but my wallet, watch, and a few other odds and ends I'd had on me at the time are in a comically large clear plastic bag, bouncing against my good leg. The deputy at my side sighs pointedly, stopping to let me catch up and then taking exaggeratedly slow steps to match me. I can't help but smirk. My limping isn't entirely fake, but after the bullshit of the last several days, I deserve this petty revenge. He can be the one to hurry up and wait this time.

Thankfully, my ride is waiting for me, as he promised he would be. As the deputy and I are buzzed through the last security door between the cell block and the waiting room, I spot Jason Anderson sitting in one of the plastic folding chairs, scrolling through his phone. When he hears my approaching shuffle, he looks up and grins before getting to his feet. Seeing his face makes my heart squeeze painfully in my chest. I'd noticed how similar their eyes were before, but seeing that shade of emerald green, the same as my omega's, cuts deep. I need to get my phone back as soon as possible.

Jason's smile is wide as he closes the last few yards in a two strides, slapping my hand with his and pulling me in for the universal one-armed "bro" hug. The non-hostile contact makes my eyes burn. Touch starved doesn't begin to describe me right now, but I don't want to make it weird for my omega's brother.

"Sign here, if ya could. Just an acknowledgment that you're taking custody of the inmate and transporting him directly to the prearranged housing location," the deputy says in a bored monotone, holding out the clipboard he'd been carrying.

"Can't even take him through a Popeyes drive thru?" Jason chuckles, taking the clipboard and scanning the documents.

"No, sir. Any deviation from the shortest route will be a violation of the inmate's release agreement," the deputy says, either not getting the joke or intentionally ignoring it.

"You can call me Rhett Cooper, Deputy," I snark, holding out one of my hands for a shake.

The officer looks at it, narrowing his eyes before looking at my face. I roll my eyes and shake my head before dropping my hand. The pen scratches on the paper for a moment before Jason hands the paperwork back and takes the plastic bag from me. The deputy doesn't even look back as he turns on his heel and high-tails it back through the secure door, probably heading for the air-conditioned officer lounge. I stop myself from flipping him off, because even if he can't see, the dozens of cameras watching this area definitely can, and I don't want to get sent back before I've even fully left.

Jason doesn't comment on my condition, just keeps pace with me as we make our way out of the building. The first steps outside of the Orleans Parish Prison are the most wonderful I've ever taken, despite the pain still shooting up from my thigh. The sun has dropped behind the skyscrapers, but it's still bright and hot enough to make me wince as I limp out from the shadow of the entrance and out into the parking lot. His Jeep is parked relatively close, but I'm still sore by the time we reach it.

"You've got a care package waiting for you at home," Jason says, heading to the driver's side.

I hum curiously, moving to the passenger door. It takes all the strength I have not to scream as I climb up into the cab, and I nearly face-plant as my ankle monitor catches on the running board. The grim reminder of the conditions of my release makes my jaw clench. Despite Ted's best efforts, I'm not out of the woods yet. But I'll take Lex's luxury apartment to the hellhole in Jason's rearview mirror any day of the week. We leave without speaking, and I only really relax once the complex is well and truly out of sight. I don't regret what I did for a single heartbeat, but if I had to go back and change anything, it would be not getting out before I was caught.

"I spoke to Lex on my way here," Jason starts.

"How is she? How is…" I trail off, throat closing up as I try to say her name, but fail. Clearing my throat, I look away, watching the traffic around us on the highway.

"She's good. They all are. It was a bit touch and go there, not that any of your pack mates would say as much. Had to find out from Gabby how much of a mess things were in the beginning, but they've gotten their shit together," Jason says, words twisting with a little touch of annoyance for a moment.

I nod and swallow hard, trying to pull myself together. The longer we drive, the more it's hitting me that I'm going to be able to talk to my pack again. I haven't gone this long without speaking to them since I met them. Even in the worst of mine and Mateo's love-hate freshman year fighting, we'd still talk, if you counted shouting obscenities at each other as talking. And since meeting Lydia, I don't know if I've gone a day without at least texting her. God, I miss her so much it hurts.

"How are you holding up?" I ask, directing my thoughts away from my pack for the moment.

Jason blows out a sharp exhale and shakes his head. "Just peachy, my guy. Everything is sunshine and rainbows in my world," he replies, knuckles going white as he grips the steering wheel.

"That bad, then. What's been going on?" I press, straightening a little in my seat.

"Sam and Ally moved back into the pack house a few days ago, which has sent the whole place into chaos. I guess they had a house lined up to move into, but the deal mysteriously fell through at the eleventh hour, and they lost the down payment, and yeah. It's just a mess from top to bottom. So, now they're living with us until they can figure out what happened and get their money back and find a new place. And Mom has been in one hell of a mood," Jason explains, words turning bitter and biting as he speaks about his mother.

The mere mention of Diane Anderson sets my teeth to grinding. If there's an ounce of justice left in this unforgiving world, the trash heap who gave birth to one of the loves of my life will suffer and die alone after years of torment and misery. I'd had plenty of time to contemplate all manner of endings for that miserable, festering, pus-filled waste of oxygen. Not that I would act out any of them. At least not without just cause.

"Did something else crawl up her ass and die?" I snark cruelly.

Jason snorts. "Well, she found out Lydi's trust account was emptied the other day. She can throw a tantrum with the best of them, but we're still patching the walls she busted, throwing shit all over the place. Now she's pushing to have my dad officially challenge y'all's claim on Lydia."

I swear under my breath, clenching my fists in my lap. If they find out it was all a bluff, I have no doubt in my mind Diane will stop at nothing to get her daughter, and the several-million-dollar inheritance she claimed, back. And if that happens...

No. I won't even think those sorts of thoughts. It'll bring bad luck, and we've had enough of that for a lifetime. Though, I resolve to make sure I tell Lex about this development, if she hasn't already been informed.

A short time later, Jason pulls up to the curb outside of the high-rise apartment building where I'll be trapped until this mess can get resolved. Jason doesn't stay, even when I offer, so I enter the spacious apartment alone, flicking on the lights. As promised, several legal-sized boxes are piled on the dining room table, along with my laptop bag, a suitcase presumably full of clothes, and another smaller bag of toiletries. And as I approach, I sag in relief. My phone is sitting on the table, fully charged.

Not even hesitating for a moment, I pick it up and navigate to my contacts, dialing her number with shaking hands. My heart kicks like a rodeo horse in my chest, faster and faster with each ring. *Please pick up. I need you to pick up. Please. Just let me hear your—*

"Rhett?! Oh, my God!"

I manage to catch myself on one of the dining room chairs as the strength gives out from my legs at last. It's only been two weeks, but even thinking about her every day and running through all the memories we've made, hearing the sound of her sweet, girlish voice again is more than I can take.

"Lydia—" I gasp, words cutting out as emotion constricts my throat, making it hard to breathe.

"Lex said you'd be released soon, but I didn't know it was going to be today," she goes on shakily.

"I didn't either, love," I admit with a chuckle. "I only found out this morning, and with the hearing and the ankle monitor—"

"Ankle monitor? What's going on? Aren't you on your way home?" Lydia asks abruptly.

I sigh, shoulders slumping as I sink down into the chair I'd been leaning on. "Unfortunately, I'm not. I'm on house arrest until this gets dealt with. The DA was able to convince the judge that I'm a flight risk."

"Lydia, is that him?"

A faint voice in the background makes my breath catch. Mateo. There's a moment when I can't hear anything except muffled, unclear words, but then there's a faint click and then they're both there.

"Rhett, holy shit. I can't—are you okay? How's your leg?" Mateo starts, disbelief dripping from his words.

I rub at the sore spot almost subconsciously. I can still feel the bump of scar tissue left behind, even though the stitches were removed the other day. I was lucky I didn't tear them as I went about the inmate's routine, not to mention trying to not look weak enough for someone to try to press an advantage.

"Healing. He didn't get any major arteries or tendons, so it's just a matter of time and rest," I tell them as reassuringly as I can.

"I miss you so much," Lydia says, and the pain in her voice cuts through me like a knife.

I purr on instinct, and she sighs. But that quickly turns into a sniffle, and my heart cracks a bit more.

"I miss you, too, sweet girl. And you, too, Mateo. So much it hurts," I admit, rubbing my chest again.

"Like physically? It hurts physically?" Lydia asks, suddenly curious.

I pause, trying to puzzle that out. "Yes. Sometimes it feels like—"

"Someone ripped your soul in two," Lydia finishes for me, and I can only sit in stunned silence.

"I've been talking with Caleb's mate, Sylvie, and she thinks we may have created some sort of pseudo-bond, and that's why it's been... hard to be apart," Lydia explains, voice catching for a moment before she finishes.

"Lucas asked his sisters about it, and I guess it's something that can happen if an alpha and an omega are particularly close. Most people don't realize it happens because they end up bonding before any of the adverse effects become noticeable," Mateo adds, tone light and inquisitive.

I frown a little deeper, trying not to let any of my worry seep through the phone line. I'd told Ted that I want to go through the grand jury process, because we think we have a good shot at avoiding indictment all together. But if being apart from Lydia is hurting her, I may have to ask if there's any form of plea deal I could take that would allow me to go back home to serve the sentence.

"I'm okay now, Rhett. It wasn't fun for the first few days, but Sylvie is helping a lot. She and Caleb went through something similar, and they made it just fine. If anything, I can come to you if things get too bad."

"No!"

Mateo and I shout the word at the same time, both with equal measures of panic coating our voices. I clear my throat and take a deep, calming breath. Lex and Mateo and Lucas can protect Lydia better if she's in Everton. As much as I want to hold her, to see that she's safe with my own eyes, I can't risk her parents ambushing us and taking her away from me.

"We're going to be fine, Lydia. Even just talking to you has made me feel that much better. It's better for you to stay where you are," I reply calmly.

"But what about my heat?" she protests, making my heart skip a beat.

"We've got time, love. The DA is on the clock to get charges to stick and—"

"I need you here for my heat, Rhett. I don't care what it takes," she interrupts petulantly.

I give her a little warning growl without thinking. She whimpers and I can almost picture the way her eyes would go wide, and she'd tuck her chin to her chest in silent apology. I sigh and run a hand through my hair.

"I'll do what I can, but you have Lucas, and Mateo, and Lex. They'll see you through your heat if I can't be there," I say, forcing the words out even if they hurt.

The idea of missing my omega's heat, of not being there to care for her when she needs me the most, drags on my soul like a rusty blade, but I have to remain realistic. My word is my bond, and I'm not going to make a promise I can't keep.

"Rhett... it's not just wanting—I got my implant out," she returns, barely above a whisper.

I nearly drop my phone as her words slam into me. If she got her implant removed, and she goes into heat, it could mean... it means we could bond. And not only Lydia and her alphas. It would mean Lucas and I...

"Are you sure about this, Lydia? With everything going on—"

"That's exactly why I'm sure. We've nearly lost each other too many times, and I don't want it to happen again. I love you, Rhett Cooper. I love you, Mateo Hutchenson. I love Pack Saint Clair, and I'm ready to be yours, completely yours," Lydia says emphatically, and I can hear the tears at the edges of her words. But she holds them back, and my heart swells with affection. My strong, beautiful, kind omega.

I don't know what I did to deserve someone like her, but I'll never cease to be grateful.

So I swallow and nod, even if she can't see me. If she's ready, then I have to find a way to be ready, too. There has to be a solution out there, and I have nothing but time to try to find it.

I will be home for her, no matter what it takes.

Chapter Eleven

Alexandra

To the Prime Alpha of Pack Saint Clair:

We have previously requested you provide any documentation to support your claim to the unbonded omega, Lydia Anderson. We have given you ample opportunity to prove your claim, but to date, we have received no response. In accordance with the relevant laws and statutes, this letter is our third and final attempt to reach you to clarify the claims you and your pack have made.

If you are unable to present proper documentation by end of business on the date stated above, I will be advising my client, Samuel Anderson Sr., Prime Alpha of the Chauvert Anderson Pack, to proceed with legal action to reclaim the unbonded omega. Once this process has begun, any attempts to interfere will be treated as an infringement on my client's Prime Alpha rights, and will be dealt with accordingly.

It's been a few days since Rhett was released on bail, and I'm staring at the latest intimidation attempt sent to my office by Samuel Anderson Sr. This is the second one to show up at my office this week and, while I know he's only sending these letters because he's legally obligated to do so, I can't say I'm not grateful for the time it's given us to try to work something out. He has to show a "good faith" attempt to confirm our claim before he can move forward with what is essentially legal kidnapping. It doesn't escape my notice that his lawyer only used Lydia's name once, otherwise referring to her like she's some sort of livestock we're haggling over.

Nothing could be further from the truth.

I slide the letter to the side, hiding it away for the moment. If everything goes according to plan, we'll be fine. I've had to put a lot on Ted Calhoun these last few months, and he's doing the best he can. But I made the call to pivot focus. We have to find a judge that'll squeeze us in for a pack status hearing. Based on my past experience, the whole process shouldn't take more than twenty minutes. There were some standard questions to establish that the petitioner, in this case Lydia, isn't being coerced into joining the pack, and then there's a basic loyalty oath that I, as the prime alpha, have Lydia swear. For our original hearing, I'd prepared something emotional and meaningful, but at this juncture, when time would be of the essence, I'd have to settle for the bare minimum. A few signatures later, and I'd have a new pack member. But as with all things involving the legal system, it's not official if there isn't a small army present to witness, which has been the holdup. We need a bailiff, an Omega Rights Advocate, a court stenographer, and a few other stars to align, and we'd burned a lot of favors to make it happen the first time only to blow everyone off. But I'd entrusted Ted with several stacks of extra persuasion power, and I wouldn't take no for an answer. Not when there's so much on the line.

Right on time, the intercom on my desk buzzes.

"Ms. St. Clair, your two o'clock is here," Erica chirps, tone light enough that a stranger might mistake it for friendliness. But there's a hint of cool Southern ice there that I picked up on after knowing her for so long.

"Thank you. Send him in," I reply, keeping my voice free of inflections.

Moments later, I look up at the sound of my office door opening, and only years of practice keep any sign of open contempt from my expression as I watch Leopold St. Clair stride into my office. He's a man who's paid to age gracefully, and it shows. His skin is tight across his face, complexion too even to be natural. His hazel eyes, the exact color and shape as my own, scan the room, searching for something out of place, I'm sure. As he gets closer, I can see the slight sheen of sweat across his brow, but he refuses to remove or even unbutton his expensive wool-blend suit jacket. October in Baltimore is cool, if not outright chilly, but Georgia is still clinging to its pleasantly balmy late summer temperatures. The petty part of me wants to crow and needle him about making such a mistake, for not doing the proper preparation and showing weakness, but I swallow my pride. Though I'm sure if the roles were reversed, he wouldn't hesitate.

"Swanky digs ya got here, Lexi," a new, but uncomfortably familiar, voice snarks from near the doorway, drawing my attention away.

An angry flush rises to my cheeks as I see who's entered my office in my father's wake. I haven't seen Delano Argentieri, Hunter Navarro, and my cousin, Gideon St. Clair, since I graduated from Brown. They'd been personally offended by the lack of "fun" at the luncheon and called in a bunch of their friends to crash. My father, of course, blamed me, and even after I'd begged them to own up, the Trio of Trouble just laughed. Now, they've wandered into my office like they own it, letting the door close with a harsh slam before they disperse.

"What are they doing here?" I snap at Leo, not even bothering with a greeting.

"Manners, Alexandra," Leopold retorts, deep voice icy cold.

"This is my office, and you said this was to be a private meeting," I say firmly, not backing down.

I get to my feet, but don't round the desk. My eyes flicker between Gideon, who's making himself at home in my bar cart, Hunter, who is running a finger along the spines of the books on my shelves, and Delano, who has thrown himself onto my white leather sofa, shoes and all. My jaw hurts from clenching it already, and we haven't even been in the same room for three minutes.

Gideon hasn't changed very much in his appearance, and as always, it's like looking into some sort of gender-bending mirror. He's taller than me, but our hair and eyes are the exact same color. We'd always been confused as siblings growing up, and I can't say that I'm upset that we've lost touch over the years. From what I've been told, he's positioned himself to be next in line to run St. Clair Holdings once my father passes, and I formally renounce whatever title he's going to inevitably try to pass down to me. Though if half the rumors I've heard about the things he and his pseudo-pack get up to, I'm surprised Leopold still acknowledges him at all.

He crosses to Delano on the couch, extending a glass of bourbon, but Delano takes the decanter Gideon has in his other hand and drinks from it directly. He tosses a few strands of his blood-red hair out of his face—a change from the highlighter yellow I'd seen in a recent mugshot—as he turns to look at me. I'd thought his light gray, almost silver eyes were contacts the first time I met him, considering how much of his appearance is for show. But no, it's the color he's had since the day he crawled out from Hades to curse my life.

"Glad to see your taste in booze is as good as it ever was," Delano says with a smirk, even going as far as to wink at me.

Mateo is going to lose his shit when I tell him someone is drinking his bourbon.

I don't deign to respond to the teasing, and turn my attention back to my father, giving him a pointed look as I stay silent and wait for an explanation.

"They are assisting me with your request," he says simply, sauntering toward me, hands in his pockets.

One step ahead of him, I sit back down in my executive chair. Like hell would I surrender the seat of power in my own fucking office. And least of all to my father. His lips thin ever so slightly and he stops, turning instead to look out over the Everton skyline, like that was his destination all along.

"How could they possibly—"

"You need a cadaver, an accident, and hard to come by pharmaceuticals, and they can get them," Leo says, almost sounding bored.

My stomach drops at his casual mention of the details of the plan, eyes flying to gauge the reaction from the others. But there's not a single batted eyelash or raised brow, like committing several felonies is par for the course for them. It has been several years since I last saw them, and while I do keep general tabs on my father and his business dealings, I certainly don't have dossiers for everyone on his payroll. I can't imagine how the tattooed band of miscreants loitering in my office could possibly help me.

"I run a funeral home, and am a board-certified medical examiner," Hunter comments softly, arms crossed over his chest as he leans against the bookcase he'd been examining.

Of the three alphas, Hunter Navarro has always been the enigma. His dark eyes and black hair, along with his tan skin, speak to his Colombian roots, but the jovial light I remember in him is gone. He's dressed in all black, mourning attire, except for the glitter of a gold chain at his neck. But I don't have time to ponder what could have happened to turn the human personification of "life of the party" from a decade ago into a somber undertaker.

"And here I thought you were still learning to read," I snipe, rolling my eyes and leaning back in my chair, crossing one leg over the other.

Hunter doesn't take the bait, but instead gives me a smile that doesn't quite reach his obsidian eyes. I turn my attention to Gideon and Delano, both now lounging on my furniture, and raise a brow in question.

"I happen to have a contact who is willing to misplace a box or two and not ask why I need bond-breakers," Gideon comments, holding his glass up to the light.

"How fortunate. And what's your excuse?" I drone, glaring at Delano as he takes another long pull from my bottle.

"I'm just here for the destruction, dollface. What is this, by the way?" he replies, swirling the liquor before sniffing it appreciatively.

"Smells like Omega, if you ask me. Something... floral?" Hunter says, and I realize he's moved on silent feet across the room and is now standing a few paces away from my desk on the opposite side as my father.

I blink once in surprise, the only reaction I'll allow, before I shut down my emotions completely, slamming the door with practiced ease. They're fishing for a weakness, and I won't let them find it. Especially not in front of my father.

"Or maybe it's the bouquet I have on my desk," I say with a bored sigh, motioning to the fresh arrangement Lydia made for me.

"No, it's sweet. Honey and... roses? Hmm, not quite—" Hunter breaks off as he breathes deep, closing his eyes. When he opens them, his stare pierces deep, and it's a struggle not to move or blink or react. "Lilacs," he finishes.

"Thought you would have had your fill of omegas, Lexi," Delano says, casual and almost sing-song.

The pause as I stare down Hunter is heavy. I can feel multiple pairs of eyes on my face, but I can't look away from the challenge in the large alpha's expression. But the longer I look, the more sadness I see. There's heartache in the way his forehead creases, and the downward pull on the corners of his mouth. Even his scent is melancholy, the amber and patchouli notes dull with dry, bitter ash. There's a story here, but I don't have the luxury of trying to find out what it is.

"We're meeting with Mr. Douglas today to advise him of his options. I want this over before the weekend," I say, turning back to addressing my father.

"It will be. Make sure you see to it that there aren't any distractions or complications," Leopold replies, still looking out the window.

His posture is imperious, hands clasped behind his back, chin raised so he looks down his nose all the time. A carefully sculpted image of a powerful man, carved from ice. Too bad the artist forgot to include a heart in his creation. But his mention of distractions makes my eyes flick to the letter, a corner of it barely poking out from the folder I'd placed it in. My phone screen lights up, Ted's number flashing as he calls. I reach for it, but my father clears his throat. When I look back, Leopold has turned to look at me over his shoulder.

"Once this is concluded, I expect your behavior to improve."

"My behavior stopped being your concern when I left," I snap before I can stop myself.

"So long as you carry the St. Clair name—"

"I would drop the St. Clair name like a bad habit if I could. But as it stands, you'll just have to put up with your legacy being associated with my philanthropic causes and charitable giving. What a shame," I retort, letting my temper get the better of me.

Delano lets out a cackle from the couch, but I don't look away. Leopold's eyes narrow slightly, and it doesn't take much to imagine what sort of diatribe he'd be spitting at me if we were truly alone. But I lift my chin, daring him to try to hurt me. I've come to terms with my own self-worth, and it isn't based on his opinions anymore.

"We're done here," he says at last, turning on his heel and marching out of the door without another word.

The Trio of Trouble doesn't immediately follow, much to my annoyance. Instead, Gideon gets up and strolls over to my desk. He sets his now empty glass down before reaching into his jacket and pulling out a matte, charcoal gray business card. As he extends his hand, a little wave of his scent hits me, pushing out the florals I prefer. It's like someone set a grove of orange trees on fire, using brandy as the fuel.

"My number. Your assistant gave me your card while we were waiting. I'll text you when the meds are in," he says softly.

I nod once, jaw clenched. I take it, barely letting my skin touch the paper, and dropping it on my desk as soon as I can. His eyes stare into me, and I don't like how he's trying to use his not insignificant height to tower over me. So, I sit back in my chair and cross one leg over the other, chin high. He'll have to try much harder than that to intimidate me.

"If what I read was right, you're going to want to find somewhere to hole up in while the drugs do their thing," Hunter says, walking a little closer, but stopping short of crowding me.

"And you're going to want a box of condoms," Delano says with an ironic laugh.

I'd done my own research into the side effects of bond breaking drugs, and all of them have some sort of variation of "increased sexual appetite" listed. Something about the drugs messes with hormone production, and anecdotally at least, it makes some people go insane with lust. We'll be fine.

Mateo's made it clear that he's not looking for that sort of thing with me. So why does my mind suddenly replay the times I've caught him looking at me with heat in his eyes, and Lucas's snarky comments about us just needing to "fuck until we don't hate each other?" I push that little, irrational voice away.

"That won't be necessary. Mateo and I don't have that sort of relationship," I answer coolly.

Delano snorts, setting down the decanter. "Raw doggin' it, nice. I like your style," he says, still laughing.

My stomach flips at his words, and not in an unpleasant way. My face heats, heart kicking like a wild stallion in my chest. I want to brush it off as a joke, but my primal mind latches onto the mental image of Mateo driving into me, filling me to bursting—

"Get the fuck out of my office before I make you," I growl, pushing a little of my alpha bark through my words as I force the blush from my cheeks by sheer force of will.

"Nice to see you, too, Lexi," he calls, and I've never heard a sound as sweet as his shoes on the floor as he exits.

Thankfully, Hunter and Gideon don't linger, following him and finally leaving me in peace. And just in time, as Ted's name lights up my phone again. I swipe to answer, but I don't even get out a greeting before he's shouting.

"Get your omega and haul ass downtown this instant! It's go time!"

CHAPTER TWELVE

Mateo

THE AFTERNOON SUN STREAMS through the windows to my right as I lounge at a table in Carter's, the bar and restaurant off the lobby of The Valencia. Lex might have thought it was a bit dramatic to have this confrontation here, but it seems more than fitting.

It's been a week and a half since we set Lex's bat shit crazy plan into motion, and it's been so far, so good. We've officially filed for Leopold to buy The Valencia for a price most newspapers are calling "suspiciously low." There's been speculation about the reason, but no one is even close to guessing the truth.

I sip on my neat bourbon as a smirk pulls at the corner of my lips. I shouldn't be surprised that it took so little for Seth to climb out of whatever hidey-hole he'd disappeared into, but it was almost laughably easy. Less than twelve hours after Lex drained his stipend account, the angry messages from a blocked number began pouring in. I'd been of a mind to let the bastard stew, but putting him on the defensive wouldn't help us in the long run. Instead, we'd sent him a single reply: a time, a date, and a location.

And right on schedule, the Devil appears.

As I look up as a nearby church bell chimes 3:00 p.m., an impossible to miss silhouette slides through the open entry arch, pausing only for a moment as he scans the room. His shoulders tense and his hands ball into fists at his sides the moment he sees me. And like the smug little shit he thinks I am, I tilt my glass ever so slightly in acknowledgement.

I use the time it takes Seth Douglas to cross the nearly deserted restaurant to look him over. I've intentionally avoided direct contact with him for the last eighteen months, just for my mental health. The last time I saw him, when we signed the court documents that sealed the conditions of our breakup, he'd been muscular, but proportionally so. Now, his arms bulge in unnatural places, his shoulder muscles nearly swallowing his thick neck as they strain against his gray hoodie. Massive, mirrored sunglasses, a baseball cap, and his hood cover most of his face, but I can still see his overly filled lips and the sneer he's twisted them into. When he's close enough, I barely manage to hold back a cough as a cloud of synthetic scent washes over me, something woody and spicy that only reminds me of the aftershave my father used. Even with the cologne, my alpha instincts still pick up on traces of grenadine and limes, his omega scent.

"What the fuck, Mateo," Seth snarls by way of greeting, stepping close to loom over me.

I look up at him in mock boredom, sipping my drink again. "Have a seat, Omega. We need to talk," I start smoothly.

"Don't fucking call me that," he snaps, roughly pulling out the chair on the opposite side of the table from me.

"Why not?" I ask with a look of feigned innocence.

"Where's Alex?" he asks, looking over his shoulder surreptitiously.

I shrug and pull out my phone, navigating to my messages. "I'm not her keeper," I deflect.

Me: He's here.
Lex: Good. We're almost there. Keep him busy.
Me: The things I do for love.

"She said—"

"Yeah, I know what she said. But things come up, Omega," I interrupt with a sigh dripping with a disappointment I don't really feel.

His little growl is almost adorable, but I swallow my chuckles. Laughing outright in his face wouldn't help me here. Still can't stop myself from smirking, though.

"Listen, if this is some sort of game, I'm fucking done playing. Where is she?" Seth spits, leaning toward me aggressively.

"But the fun is just getting started," I say, unable to keep my glee contained, and I revel in the second pathetic attempt at a growl.

"You think this is funny? Will your little bitch think it's funny—"

My smile drops, and I silence him with a true alpha growl. Being this close, I can feel that tug in my chest, the one I usually smother with medication. But I stopped taking them in preparation for the next phase of the plan, and I have no shame in using that connection to my advantage. I push my disdain and fury through the invisible line connecting us, and my smug smile isn't fake now as he winces at the sensation, almost like I'd smacked him.

"You're going to mind your manners, Omega, or I'll make you," I state, barely holding back the compulsion of my alpha bark.

Thoroughly chastised, Seth sits back, teeth gritted and bared at me. I wish he would test me. I could use an excuse to put this bottom-feeder in his place. Unfortunately, he's smarter than he looks, and chooses to stay silent.

"Lex has better things to do than meet with you, but she sent me to offer you a deal," I start, settling back in my chair and crossing one leg over the other.

He rips off his sunglasses and glares at me, half surprised, half furious, judging from what I can feel at the other end of our bond. Before he can speak, I shift in my seat, recrossing my legs as I talk, opening my shoulders and tilting my head slightly to one side. Purposefully approachable body language, designed to disarm a mark, is one of the many tricks I'd learned in my years in sales.

"We both know that your options are limited right now. You can probably run for a few more months, but eventually, the shit you've pulled is going to catch up to you. With the charges you've got hanging over you, you'll be lucky to get less than a decade, and the authorities don't even know about the blackmail scheme you've been running for the last few years."

"You don't know what you're—"

"Lex told us everything, Omega. There's really no point in denying it."

I cut across him with a roll of my eyes and a sigh. And his silence and lack of additional rebuttals is as good as an admission of guilt, if not in a court, then at least in my book. I wait for another heartbeat, drawing out the tension, making him subconsciously eager to know what I'm going to say next. I haven't hooked him yet, so I soften my face, even smile a little. When he doesn't speak, I continue.

"You're going to spend the prime of your life behind bars, and a sweet piece of omega meat like you is going to get chewed up and spit out in prison," I continue, letting myself indulge in the look of true fear that flickers in his eyes for a moment. I've got his attention now. Time to hook him. "But I'm here to put another option on the table, one that doesn't involve you becoming someone's bitch."

I'd spent some time with Lex, preparing my pitch. When Alexandra St. Clair steps up to the table, she comes fully armed, and she's set her sights on Seth Douglas. I've seen the evidence she's collected, and it paints an absolutely watertight picture of his guilt. Every text message, voicemail, email, court transcript shows the hell he's put her through, and us by extension, for the last four years, and the stuff she managed to track down to link Seth to the stalking and harassment Lydia had to endure is just as solid.

Seth snarls, but hesitates. The beautifully ironic thing is that he knows I'm right, even if he hates to admit it. I let him sit with that for a while, watching him try to figure a way out of this. But the little rat is trapped.

"You gonna tell me what it is, or what?" Seth snaps after several long moments of silence.

"In a few days, you're going to go for a drive after you've had too much to drink, and you're going to go off the road, where you'll pass out and tragically perish after your car bursts into flames."

The look of horror on his face as I speak makes nearly everything he's put me and my pack through worth it. He reels back, shoving away from the table with a harsh screech of chair legs on tile. I can't help but throw my head back and laugh, which stops him from bolting.

"That's not fucking funny," he growls, looking around again, not that anyone is paying us any mind.

"Maybe not, but I thought it was à propos, considering you burned down my friend's home and business," I say, still chuckling darkly.

"First, *I* didn't do that. Second—"

"One of your flying monkeys did, then bragged about it on camera. So yeah, technically, but you're still an accessory to arson," I interrupt, waving a flippant hand.

"Second, if you think I'm going to commit suicide willingly to avoid prison, you're crazy," he goes on, and it doesn't escape my notice that he doesn't try another denial.

"Trust me, as much as I would love for you to be the one in the car, Lex understands that's not a very enticing offer," I retort, finishing the last of my drink.

Seth blinks as I set the glass back down, brow pulled low in confusion. I'd tried to suggest that we actually go through with that version of the plan, but cold-blooded murder was just a bridge too far, apparently.

"We will ensure that the charred husk of a body that's found in your car will be convincing enough. Meanwhile, you'll be halfway to somewhere warm and sunny, a king's ransom in your pocket, along with a new identity," I finish, looking him dead in the face.

"How much, exactly?" Seth asks, a little too quickly.

I roll my eyes and relay the amount Lex deemed appropriate, enough to tempt him, but not enough to put us in danger of insolvency. I still think it's at least seven digits too high, but she was adamant that her figure would be enough. And judging by how round Seth's eyes go, she was right. He's still thinking as my phone vibrates on the table, and I snatch it up before he can see the screen.

Lex: Going in now. How's it going?
Me: Just laid the bait. Waiting for the bite.
Lex: He'll take it.
Me: He'd be stupid not to.
Lex: Despite all evidence to the contrary, Seth is a smart man.

"What's the catch?" Seth asks, drawing my attention back to him.

I shove my phone in my inner jacket pocket and sigh. "Once you're declared dead, legally, the bond between us will be severed. But you'll still have to go take the injections to fully break it. And we'll be doing the same. Seth Douglas is going to disappear. You won't bother us, and we won't bother you."

"I'm not—"

"It's part of the deal. A neutral third party will administer your dose and be present while they work to confirm efficacy. Then they'll drive you to the airport, where a private plane will take you to your new home," I say firmly.

"And how can I trust you to keep your end? How do I know you won't just send the police after me once the bond's broken?" Seth shoots back, raising an accusatory finger in my direction.

I give him a bland look, a mixture of exasperation and disappointment that makes him pull back.

"I don't know how this could have been misunderstood, but let me be perfectly clear," I start, uncrossing my legs and leaning forward until my elbows rest on the tabletop. "The day you entered my life was, unequivocally, the worst thing that's ever happened to me, and I'll remind you that my parents disowned me. I've spent every waking hour for the last year, seven months, sixteen days trying to forget you exist. You have violated me physically, emotionally, psychologically over and over again, and I will never forgive you for that. I may have loved you once, and I hated you for a long time, but I don't even spend my emotional energy doing that anymore. To say I couldn't care any less about whether you live or die would be a gross understatement. So believe me when I say that I cannot wait to be rid of you once and for all. I am counting the minutes until those vials arrive, and I will be taking them at the first possible opportunity."

Seth's mouth drops open in pure awe as I speak, years of venom unleashed at last upon the scum who ruined my life. I've dreamed of saying these things to his face, and finally being able to do it almost feels better than sex. Well, not sex with Lydia. Nothing is better than sex with the love of my life.

"What about Alex?" Seth rasps.

I snort a chuckle, and almost on cue, my phone buzzes in my pocket. I pull it out and open the picture Lex just sent. My smile is genuine for the first time since I sat down as I look at the image of pure joy on my screen. Lex and Lydia are kissing, holding the signed and sealed pack designation form to the camera.

"She's moved on, Omega. It's time you do the same," I say, turning my phone to show him.

Seth stares for a long time, and I'm not sure if he's even breathing. His face falls, eyes shining with moisture for a moment before he blinks the tears away. When he looks back at me, he's pale, truly at a loss for words. If I thought him capable of such an emotion, he almost looks heartbroken.

"When are we doing this, then?" he asks dully.

I pull a sealed envelope out of my jacket and slide it across the table. "All the details are inside. And I feel like it should go without saying, but if you tip anyone off to what's going to happen, the body in that car won't need to be fake, understand?"

Seth nods, and seeing him humbled like this touches a cruel, petty part of my heart. It's nice to finally be able to make his life miserable after all this time.

"Pleasure doing business with you, Omega," I say, buttoning my jacket. I clap a hand on his shoulder as I pass.

As long as everything goes according to plan, this is the last time I'm going to see Seth Douglas. And as I walk away, I don't even bother to look back.

Chapter Thirteen

Lydia

I'VE BEEN CLUTCHING THE papers since we'd left the court-house, too afraid they'll disappear if I let go. The car is silent, Lex driving as smooth as ever through the streets of Everton. But I hardly feel connected to anything around me. I read the lines of the form over and over, studying the witness signature, the judge's seal, the notary's stamp. It's real. It's done. I'm part of Pack Saint Clair.

I knew Lex was trying to get our court date moved up, but after so long, I hadn't expected anything to change, leaving us to have to wait until November. It would have been after my heat, making the proceedings if not a moot point, then just an annoying technicality. Bond mates aren't automati-cally members of their alphas' packs, but there would have been less pressure to get it done before my family could interfere.

What I never expected was for Lex to pull up on State Street, parking haphazardly in front of the burnt-out ruins of Grandmother Wila's, shouting at me to get in the car. For us to race to the courthouse, dashing through the doors right before the security guard went to close up for the night. And I never expected to take a pack vow in a hallway outside of a judge's office, surrounded by at least ten people, all crowding in so they could properly witness the event. The judge signed the documents against the wall, his pen running out of ink twice before everything was finalized, and then dashed out the door, grumbling about being late for his tee time.

"I will need to ask for those back eventually, sweetness. Ted needs to make copies and send them to the appropriate entities," Lex comments, turning off the road and into the Wickland House parking lot.

I look up at her as she comes to a controlled stop in one of the reserved spaces in front of the building. She's smiling softly, her shoulders relaxed. She's still in her work clothes, a wine red dress that makes my mouth water, and I once again feel supremely underdressed. I'd had no time to find a change of clothes, so I'm still in the sweat-soaked and soot-stained leggings and a tank top I'd thrown on this morning.

Lex looks at me, stopping my train of thought dead. Her hazel eyes are a glowing gold in this light, and I'm completely transfixed as she leans in and cups my jaw with one hand before brushing her lips with mine. I close my eyes and whimper, kissing her back once I manage to regain control of my motor functions. She tastes like citrus and something spicy, like cloves or bay leaves.

"I'm keeping you here tonight, sweetness. I need to give you a proper welcome," she mutters against my lips as we break apart for a moment.

My entire body flushes hot and then cold, goosebumps breaking out at the absolutely possessive edge to her words.

There's no room for argument, not that I want to. I'd dreamt of what it would mean to truly belong to Alexandra St. Clair, and it appears that my dreams are about to become reality.

I expect to go straight up to the suite, but we make a stop at the front desk where I'm issued my very own access card to the pack suite. My body is still on high alert from the kiss in the car, and I'm aware of every breath and movement she makes as we ride the private elevator. It's not that I expected her to be all over me in the lobby, as it was still packed with people checking in, but now that we're alone and she's still distant, my stomach twists nervously.

Once the doors open and we step into the suite, I hesitate just inside the familiar space. Lex kicks off her shoes and heads to the fridge, where she pulls out a bottle of wine. After uncorking it, she takes a swig and does a double take when she sees me standing awkwardly in the middle of the open space.

"What's the matter, sweetness?" she asks gently, moving back to me.

I try to put my thoughts into words, but I'm still stuck on how stunning she looks, and the way her scent makes me jittery with excitement and fear. She's too perfect, too good to want me like this. I don't know what I'm doing, and the fear of disappointing her is like a lead weight in my belly.

"I... I've never done this before," I admit, not looking at her.

Lex gives me a small, sympathetic smile that doesn't really do anything to help with my nerves before crossing back to stand in front of me. She looks me up and down, and I wrap my arms around my middle, slumping my shoulders forward to make myself smaller under her assessing stare.

After what feels like an hour, she reaches down and takes one of my hands in hers.

"There're no expectations of what happens tonight, Lydia. We can drink this wine and watch television and go to sleep, and that'll be just as satisfying as anything we could do in the bedroom. The only thing that matters is that we're together," she says emphatically.

As I look up slightly into her face, I'm struck again by how beautiful she is. The angle of her jaw, the perfect Cupid's bow of her red-tinted lips, the creamy perfection of her skin. Everything about her is perfect. And she's looking at me like I'm something extraordinary, when it's her who is too good to be true. I bring a hand up to brush along her cheekbone, and she leans into my touch with a gentle purr, closing her eyes. Her responsiveness emboldens me, and I lean in to give her a gentle kiss before moving down her neck, trailing soft kisses as I go.

"I want to, want *you*, so bad. I just... I don't know what I'm doing," I whisper, flushing slightly with embarrassment.

Her purr turns into a sultry growl, and her grip on my waist tightens. She turns us and I stumble a little as she leans forward, forcing me back until we hit the kitchen island. She sets down the bottle before seizing a fistful of my hair and cranking my head back. I gasp and shiver as I give in to her touch, staying in place even as she lets go.

"Such a good, obedient omega, you are. I'd love to just take you to my playroom and have my wicked way with you, but I think we need to have a conversation first, hmm?" she says lightly, leaving me plenty of room to respond how I want.

I blink for a moment, not quite understanding before it occurs to me. Before Rhett and I played for the first time, we talked about our rules and limits. Lex and I have talked a little, but nothing was ever set in stone. I tilt my head back up and grab the wine, taking a long pull before setting it back down with a nod. Lex leans in and kisses me again, leaving me panting after she pushes off and heads to the living room.

Following behind, I sit on one end of the couch with my legs tucked under me as Lex perches herself in one of the armchairs, sitting sideways so her crossed legs dangle over one of the arms. With the setting sun behind her, she looks like a goddess of light and sex, waiting to be worshipped as she rightly deserves.

"I've talked with Rhett, and I know a little about your limits. No spitting, face slapping, or name calling. Is it okay if I call you by your designation?" Lex starts, jumping right into the deep end.

I nod, flushing. "It doesn't sound like an insult when you do it. Not like…"

I trail off, trying not to lose myself in the memories that are threatening to bubble to the surface. Thankfully, Lex is plenty distracting, her spicy scent filling the air between us.

"My limits are very… niche, and at this stage, I think telling you about them would do more harm than good. But if you ever want to try something, don't hesitate to ask. I don't expect this to be the last conversation we have about limits," she goes on, looking at me in the face even as my eyes wander to the hint of cleavage this position offers.

I swallow, nodding again. My mouth is coated with citrus and bay leaves, fruit and liquor, and it's becoming harder to focus. I clench my fists hard enough for my nails to dig into my palms, the bite of pain helping me concentrate.

"Rhett and I use a traffic light system for safe words. I'd like to keep using that," I say, spine straightening.

Lex smiles and tilts her chin in acknowledgement. "I won't lie to you, Lydia. Playing with me won't be like playing with Rhett, or Mateo, even if he won't admit that's what he's doing. There's something inside of me that only comes out in that playroom, and while I'd never violate your trust, I need you to understand that I won't hold your hand. When I ask you to do something, it's because I know you're capable of it, and you will respect that. If I give you a command, I expect it to be obeyed without question or hesitation. And there will be consequences for not doing so, or for breaking my rules," she says seriously, her smile turning a bit feral.

My stomach jumps, the hairs on the back of my neck lifting slightly. The primal part of my mind sits up and takes notice of her, like a rabbit scenting a fox on a passing breeze. The threat of danger makes my heart race, but the promise of reward makes my pussy ache.

"What are the rules, then?" I ask, throat dry.

Lex gives me another assessing look, and I don't dare to move a muscle. Her eyes burn through me, all my worries crumbling to ash and leaving me raw, exposed, but in the best way. I don't know if I could feel more vulnerable if I were dancing naked in the middle of Times Square.

"I want your obedience, my lovely. Your complete submission. When you enter my domain, you are my toy, my little plaything. I don't want you to think, just feel and react. As long as you do that, then you have nothing to fear and everything to gain."

Her words drip like honey in the air, each one a decadent treat that I savor. It's almost as if she's casting a spell over me, pulling the deepest, more intrinsic parts of my nature to the surface. Letting go, being free to just experience sounds like heaven. And as the thought occurs to me, I fall from the couch and onto my knees, ready to worship the goddess before me.

"Please, ma'am. I want that, want to be that for you. Teach me," I gasp, closing my eyes and letting my head fall forward in supplication.

There's a long stretch of silence, and then I hear her move, shifting in her chair and getting to her feet. I don't look up, keeping my hands loose at my sides like Rhett taught me. Her warmth radiates from her body as she stops in front of me, but I don't look up.

"I'd had plans, but I can't say no to a pretty little omega, begging so nicely on her knees for me. I'll teach you a lesson in pleasing me, and if you pass, I will give you a reward. Does that sound like fun, my lovely?"

I can't nod fast or hard enough, eager for the chance to show her how much I want to please her. She laughs, and I let out an involuntary moan as she grips my chin hard and pulls my head up to look into her face. From this angle, I can't quite see up her skirt, but I can smell the fruit and spice of her arousal, and I don't miss the way her thighs rub together ever so slightly as she looks down at me.

"Words," she corrects sternly.

"Yes, ma'am. Please. I want to learn," I whimper, no hesitation at all.

"Good girl."

My whole body shudders under praise and after she pulls me to my feet, I practically float on air as she leads me down the hall that would normally lead to Rhett's room in the suite. But instead, we stop at the door I've only ever dared peek into once: the playroom. I expect to go right in, but Lex pauses and turns back to me with serious eyes.

"Once we step in here, you will address me as your Domina. You will be at my mercy, and only your safe words will stop what's to come. Do you understand?" she asks, looking me directly in the eye.

I nod. "Yes, Domina. I'm ready."

She smiles and gives me a sweet kiss, and then she turns and opens the door.

Chapter Fourteen

Lydia

THE FIRST TIME I'D looked into Lex's playroom, I hadn't stuck around long enough to truly appreciate the décor. But as I enter and Lex closes the door behind me, I get my first good look. The floor below my feet is a dark wood laminate, smooth but warm under my bare soles. The sliding glass door that leads to the balcony is covered in some sort of film that tints the glass while still allowing light to pass through, and a heavy set of curtains hangs to one side, thick enough to block the view completely if desired. There are several large implements arranged neatly along the wall farthest from the door: a St. Andrew's Cross, a chair with padded arms but no seat, a long bench, and a few others I don't recognize but can only imagine what purpose they serve.

I only get a glimpse of a pegboard with various bundles of rope, paddles, and Lord knows what else, but then Lex is there, hand around my chin, forcing my attention to her face.

"You'll get to know the board soon enough, my lovely. Eyes on me now," she says, a gentle chastising tut to her voice.

"Yes, Domina," I whisper, mouth suddenly very dry.

"Good girl. Clothes off and on your knees."

I'm surprised I don't rip anything as I strip down, throwing my clothes into the corner until I'm naked and kneeling on the floor in my wait pose, sitting on my heels with my knees spread, hands resting with my palms up on my thighs, and my back straight. The floor is very subtly padded, which I'm sure I'll appreciate if I'm going to spend an extended time down here. My chin is up but my eyes are lowered, but even then, I can see as Lex saunters away toward the bed, hips swaying hypnotically. My pussy pulses as she reaches behind her back and draws the zipper of her dress down, letting it drop in a pool on the floor, leaving her in only a lacey bra, a garter belt, stockings, and panties so transparent as to hardly matter.

She turns and perches on the edge of the black-velvet bench at the foot of the bed, crossing one leg over the other. She beckons with a single finger, tossing her hair over her shoulder. I keep my eyes down as I crawl toward her, aware of the way my heavy breasts swing below me, and I try to suck in my belly to stop it from doing the same. When I settle on my knees again in front of her, I keep my breathing shallow, trying to keep my pooch from sticking out too far.

"No need to stand on pretense here, my lovely. Your body is exactly as it needs to be, ripe and plump, and *perfect*."

Her voice has that strange subaudible hum that goes straight to the primal part of my mind and turns it to goo. Her foot traces a path across my collarbone, down between the valley of my breasts, before settling on my diaphragm. When I least expect it, she presses hard, and I gasp, coughing slightly as I let my breath out. I flush and close my eyes, or at least I try to. But Lex lunges with a growl, taking me by the chin again, nails digging as she forces my gaze back to her.

"Does my lovely little omega not understand me? Or is she trying to tell me I'm wrong?" she snarls, low and fierce.

"No, Domina. I'm not—"

"When I give you a compliment, you will say, "Thank you, Domina." Understood?"

"Yes, Domina," I whimper.

She smiles and sits back, releasing my face. As she does, she spreads her legs, revealing her soaked panties right at my eye level. She trails a hand down her stomach, humming her pleasure as she rubs the dripping fabric with perfectly manicured fingers.

"Look at this mess I've made. You have had me wet since we left the courthouse, knowing you're mine at last."

I stare as her fingers shift the material to the side, allowing me a full view of her dripping pussy. I can smell the citrus and cloves and my mind melts, everything except those glistening pink folds and her slim fingers fading away. Licking my lips, I try to keep myself from openly panting.

"You want to taste this, don't you, lovely? This alpha pussy that's so hot and wet, just waiting for a good girl to lick up?"

Her voice is high and breathy as she circles her swollen clit ever so slowly, and I can't help but follow the motion with my eyes, a pathetic little whine spilling from me as my pussy clenches on nothing, my slick dripping obscenely onto the floor below me. She sighs and tuts, and I have to fight the disappointed noises begging to escape my throat. She flicks her eyes down between my legs and then back up to my face.

"Clean up your mess, Omega."

The order sends a jolt of fire through my body, and I launch into motion, all instinct as I drop to my belly, ass in the air as I lick the floor. Her little hum and purr of approval only pushes me further into this strange, primitive place, where my only thoughts are of my Domina and her pleasure.

"Good girl. Now clean up mine."

I look up and my eyes go wide as I realize she's removed her panties while I was working, leaving her bare and waiting for me. She's leaning back on her elbows, back arched and legs spread wide. I chirp an excited little noise before scrambling forward on my hands and knees until my mouth is only inches from her core. But then I hesitate, insecurities creeping forward to pull me out of the moment again.

"You can't do this wrong. I'll tell you what I want more of," Lex soothes, hand petting my hair back in a gentle, reassuring motion.

Swallowing again, I take a deep breath of her intoxicating scent before leaning in. I run the tip of my nose along the joint of her hip, remembering how Rhett likes to tease me. My reward is a shuddering exhale, fingers tightening in my hair and pulling me back to her center. She's neatly trimmed, and I kiss feather-light along her outer lips before letting my tongue slip into her honeyed center.

Her flavor explodes on my tongue, fruit and spice mixing like the nectar of the gods. I moan as I dive deeper, all thoughts of technique fleeing at the first taste. I want to drink as much of her into my soul as I can, to truly get drunk on her until I can't tell up from down. As I swirl my tongue to gather more of her cream, her walls pulse, and she moans. I repeat the motion, my heart leaping as she reacts just as fiercely. I pull away for a breath before going back, looking up through my lashes at her—chest flushed pink and mouth open on a gasp from the pleasure I'm giving her.

The thought sends a rush of confidence and joy through my heart, and I redouble my efforts. Licking her opening from bottom to top, I search for her clit. I know I've found it by the way her legs twitch closed for a moment and her eyes pop open. I try little kitten licks, fast and light, that make her moans grow higher and louder. The hand that's not in my hair moves to her bra, pushing it down just enough to expose one of her breasts. She twists a nipple hard, head falling back and hips rolling against my mouth.

"More, more," she moans, her grip on my head almost painful.

I whimper, closing my eyes and letting her guide me to where she wants me, sucking and licking with everything I have in me. Her legs shake and I moan into her slit, dipping my tongue as deep as I can go. As I drag it back out, her walls close hard, harder than ever before, and I whimper.

"I'm so close, so close. Right there," she pants, legs coming to lock around my head.

I circle my tongue around the spasming muscle, and I'm rewarded with a shouted curse in her beautiful, elegant voice. I keep going, determined to do my best to please my Domina, to do exactly as she says. Her shouts echo off the walls, so loud I'm sure people three floors away can hear what I'm doing to her, and then all at once, she shatters. A fresh wave of her juices coats my chin and mouth, but I drink down as much as I can. With her legs locking me in, I keep going, as she clearly doesn't want me to stop. Her whole body shakes when I suck on her clit again, and she arches up hard, her heels digging into my back before she goes limp. I slow my pace to languid passes over her entrance, cleaning her up as she'd instructed. Her muscles pulse with her climax, and I have to hold in my satisfied little smile.

"Were you lying to me before, sweetness?" Lex pants, swallowing hard.

I look up in question, wiping my chin with the back of my hand. My heart kicks a little at the implications, fear making me tense. She looks at me for a long time, and then she sits up and leans close.

"You really haven't done that before?" she asks, tone genuine.

I shake my head, eyes watering as my mind whirs into a panic. "No, Domina, I'm sorry. Did I do something wrong?"

She caresses my cheek and I lean forward, mouth open in preparation to apologize again, but the warmth in her eyes stops me short. She leans closer and kisses my hairline tenderly.

"No, lovely girl. You were amazing. And you've more than earned your reward," she says, purring deep.

My eyes light up and I grin up at her, her praise making my heart soar and stomach dance. Before I can think better, I reach up and wrap my arms around her waist in an embrace, burrowing my face into her chest and inhaling deeply.

"Thank you, Domina," I whisper into her skin.

"Kneel on the bed for me, facing the headboard," she instructs.

I rush to obey, only stopping to kiss her cheek as I stand, and I move into her requested position.

"Are you going to want my knot today, lovely?" she asks mildly from behind me.

I hesitate, biting my lip. Ever since the day in the living room where I watched Lex have her wicked way with Lucas, and Rhett described the toy she uses to turn her lock, the tightening of muscles in her pussy that keeps a male omega cock inside, into a knot, I can't say I haven't been curious. Even now, just the mention of being knotted makes my primal instincts roar with desperate desire.

"I do, Domina, but... please don't bite me. Even if I ask," I answer at last.

"That's not a problem at all. Hands above your head for me, please."

I jump as I realize she's climbed on the bed behind me without my notice, but I do as I'm told. She slides leather cuffs onto my wrists, her touch gentle as she makes sure they're secure before guiding me to reach up toward the lattice of metal that spans the space above the mattress. There's a soft metallic click, and my wrists are secured to a hook I hadn't seen before. My breath catches as she nudges my knees apart, and I look down to see her strapping some sort of harness to my thigh.

"You have my permission to come as often as you want today. But you have to thank me every time. Do you under-stand?"

I barely hear her words as I stare, transfixed by the vibrator wand she's sliding into place in the harness. It's perfectly po-sitioned over my clit, and with a few tugs, it's strapped down tight, and I know without needing to ask that no amount of thrashing is going to shift it now.

"Yes, Domina," I gasp, remembering she asked me a ques-tion after a moment.

My only warning is her low chuckle, and then she flicks a switch and my body lurches from the sudden, intense pleasure flooding my system. I'm so turned on by everything that's happened so far that it doesn't take more than a few moments before I'm at the edge, whining and gasping for air. My instinct is to hold on, to not give in until I've asked for permission, and it takes me a moment to remember that I've already gotten it.

"Thank you, Domina. Thank you, oh God, thank you," I moan, long and loud as my climax crashes down on me like a tidal wave.

She purrs in my ear, still kneeling behind me, so close I can feel her body heat, and occasionally her breasts brushing against my back. Her hands come up to my breasts as my orgasm stretches on and on, with no sign of slowing as the vibrator continues to hum. I want to pull away, to ease off the pleasure for a moment so I can recover, but even as I twitch and buck, the wand moves with me. It's not long before another orgasm tears through my body, and my thanks only comes out in a thin whisper.

Lex's touch barely distracts me for a moment before even that is drowned in a sea of pleasure that's rapidly turning to pain as my over-sensitive body peaks again and again. I stop fighting against the wand after a fifth orgasm, hanging limply with my head thrown back. Staring up at the ceiling, my mind floats as I almost go numb. I only twitch and mouth my thanks as a sixth and then a rapid seventh climax pulses through me.

"You are so beautiful like this, my lovely little omega. Absolute putty in my hands."

Lex's voice seems to come from somewhere far away, and I can only manage a dull whimper, my pussy pulsing as yet another orgasm breaks free. But then I feel a touch on my swollen, dripping entrance and I jerk back, arching from the new sensation. But the hand moves with me, a slim finger slipping inside of my pulsing core with no resistance. And as it strokes and thrusts, the wet squelching sounds of flesh on flesh make my heart twist with feral joy.

I'm pure need, solely desire, and it's easy to slide away from my body and let the part of me that wants to submit and obey take over. I can't form words, only pathetic whimpers and whines as the alpha beside me plays my body with ease. She wrings me out completely of every drop of pleasure I'm capable of producing.

"Alpha," I moan, peaking again.

"What does my omega need?" she whispers, so close her spice-scented breath coasts over my face.

"Knot me. Fuck me, Alpha, please. Need—need you," I moan, finding the strength to thrust down onto the fingers deep in my pussy.

"You have me, Omega. You're mine," she declares, trailing off into a growl.

I gasp as her fingers withdraw, but I'm not left wanting for long. With surprising strength, she drags me backward by my hips, then suddenly releasing the clip on my wrist cuffs so I fall forward onto the soft bed. Instinctually, I arch back, sticking my ass in the air to present myself to the alpha, showing her how ready I am for her cock.

"Good girl. Such a good omega," she praises, a hand trailing along the curve of my ass.

The broad cockhead brushes against my folds, and it takes everything in me to not immediately start rutting back onto her thick, hard length. Instead, I wait, letting her set the pace, fucking and withdrawing until she finally bottoms out. Then, I can only hold on for dear life as she pounds mercilessly into me. Her nails scrape my back, marking me, but I need more.

"Alpha, please, claim me," I pant, thrusting back as best as I can.

She growls hard enough to rattle my bones, and I whimper, ducking my head from her wordless chastisement. But then she takes me by the hair and pulls me back until her chest is flush with my sweat-slick back. I'd gotten so used to the vibrator that when she reaches down and turns it up, I can only scream, shaking with renewed jolts of pleasure.

"You are mine, Omega. This cunt, this body, your pleasure, all of it is mine."

The alpha's snarl in my ear makes me moan, causing something powerful to surge inside of my chest. More than an orgasm, something unshaking that I can only barely hold back.

"You're going to come as I knot your needy cunt, Omega. And you're going to tell me who you belong to."

Her breathing is shallow, and I can feel her shaking now, too. I nod as much as her grip will let me. She releases my hair, both hands on my hips to help fuck me onto her unyielding length. My head lolls to one side, opening my throat to her.

"Say it. Fuck—tell me—"

"I'm yours, Alexandra St. Clair. You're mine and I'm yours," I whimper, body convulsing as one last powerful orgasm fills me with warmth.

Lex screams as she thrusts home, her knot locking into place behind my pubic bone. Somehow, she has the where-withal to shut off the vibrator right away, but it leaves the room silent except for the sound of our heavy breathing. I don't move, basking in the warmth of her body, the pulsing of her knot inside of me.

"Let me get that off you before we lay down, sweetness," she whispers breathlessly.

I just nod and let her work, still feeling like I'm detached from my body. She quickly releases the harness and my cuffs before we maneuver down to lie on our sides. Her arms encircle my chest and arms, holding me tight as she nuzzles her nose against my hair, kissing me softly every now and then.

"Was that okay?" she asks after a moment.

I don't have to think before I nod, smiling to myself. "Yes, Domina," I mutter sleepily.

Her little giggle makes my heart flutter. I don't know how I have the strength left in me, but as she shifts to massage my wrists, another slow climax crests and spreads to every corner of my body. I let her work, taking care of me as I drift closer and closer to the edge of consciousness. When she's satisfied that I'm not hurt, she settles, playing with the ends of my hair silently.

As her knot deflates, we still don't move. It's strange to still have the hardness of the toy inside of me, but I don't mind it. If anything, it makes me feel more connected to her. But my mind drifts in the quiet, only the sound of distant traffic below breaking the pure tranquility of the moment. And it occurs to me that I haven't been alone with Lex like this in a long time, since before I went to New Orleans. The memory of our last intense encounter plays out in my mind until I catch onto something she said that I never addressed.

"You told me you loved me once. Did you mean it?" I ask, my hazy mental state making me bold.

Her swallow is loud in the silence, and I can almost sense her bracing for impact. "Yes, sweetness. I meant it then, and I still mean it now. But don't feel like you have to—"

I turn over and kiss her before she can finish whatever qualifier she was about to spout off. She lets me control the movement of our lips for a moment, likely too stunned by the suddenness of the action to object. But when I pull away, I let my forehead rest against hers, closing my eyes with a smile.

"Good. 'Cause I love you, too, Lex."

CHAPTER FIFTEEN

Lucas

THE PACK HOUSE IS eerily quiet tonight, and I realize this is the first time I've been completely alone in a long time. Before Lydia, it wasn't uncommon for me to have the entire house to myself for hours at a time, usually during the day when the others were at work and I was working the closing shifts. Rhett always made a point to avoid it, but there were times when I'd go days without seeing Mateo, and even Lex, if her schedule was packed. I'm glad for the change, though. Our pack is more like a family than ever, and with Lydia's status finally being confirmed by the courts, it really feels like we're turning a corner.

I'm flat on my back in Rhett's bed, staring up at the ceiling and lost in thought, when my phone rings. Fishing it out of my pocket, I smile as I see the incoming video chat from Rhett. I turn over onto my side and swipe to answer, grinning.

"Hey," I chirp excitedly as his face appears on the screen.

"Hey, Luc," Rhett sighs, running his free hand through his hair.

Rhett's in bed, judging by the color of the pillowcase I can see under his cheek. His hair is damp, and with this angle, I can tell that he's not wearing a shirt.

"Lex texted me the news," Rhett starts, grinning to himself.

I let out a relieved sigh. "I don't know how Ted managed to pull it off," I admit with a chuckle.

"I'm not going to question it. Lydia's part of the pack now, and she's safe. That's all that matters," Rhett replies, eyes growing distant.

I nod my agreement, relaxing into the pillow below me. Rhett's scent is fading every day, and it's getting harder and harder to not be near him. I haven't brought up the idea of visiting, because it would be wildly unfair to Lydia if I could go to our alpha and she couldn't. But maybe now that she's officially part of the pack...

"I can see the plot in your eyes, Luc," Rhett says, voice low with warning.

"What? I was just thinking it might be possible for me and Lydia to come to you now," I reply defensively.

Rhett sighs, and his frown tugs at my heart. His ice-blue eyes scream that he wants to agree, but the set of his brow is worried.

"I'd love to see you, but I don't think it would be a good idea. If something should happen, and Lydia goes into heat early, I'd rather her be with you and the others," Rhett says heavily, rubbing his face.

I frown, not buying his excuse for a second. "What's really going on? I would've thought you'd jump at the idea of seeing us again," I ask, not leaving room for argument.

Rhett gives me a searching look, but I don't back down. After a long moment, he relents with a huff.

"Jason says things aren't exactly peaceful at the Anderson compound. Joe McLaughlin is raising holy hell, I guess, because Sam Sr. isn't forcing any of his boys to testify in front of the grand jury," Rhett explains tersely.

"Probably because Sam Sr. knows that anything they say will only work in your favor, or will be outright lies," I snort derisively.

Rhett grunts in agreement. "But if Lydia comes here, I wouldn't put it past that con artist to throw his weight around and have the DA subpoena her," Rhett finishes, rubbing his face again.

I hadn't considered that. I have no doubt that she'd handle herself just fine, but from what she's told us about the fight in the bathroom, everything Rhett did was in self-defense. But a good lawyer can spin any story to serve their own purpose. As the only witness, Lydia's testimony could condemn Rhett as much as it could redeem him.

"He could do that while she's in Georgia, too," I point out hesitantly.

Rhett shakes his head. "They'd have to have an address, and because Lydia never listed a forwarding address when she moved out of her old apartment, they don't know where she is to have her served. Diane has been hounding Jason about our properties for a few days, so I think they want to, but he's not going to budge."

A little bubble of gratitude and affection forms in my chest for Lydia's younger brother. Based on the few interactions we've had, I find that I like the man, and his protectiveness over Lydia only makes me like him more.

"Trust me, Lucas. It's not that I don't want you here with me, but it wouldn't be fair," Rhett says, genuine regret in his voice.

My heart falls a little as I snuggle closer to Rhett's pillow. Patience has never been one of my strong suits, and this situation is pushing me to the end of my rope.

"Are you in my bed?" Rhett asks randomly.

I nod, tilting the camera so he can see the room, which makes him purr. As I bring the camera back to my face, I notice the shift in his expression. A little flame of hunger is dancing in the depths of his eyes, and he licks his lips.

"Have you been sleeping there? In my bed?" Rhett pushes playfully.

"Once or twice. But I try not to disturb it too often. Don't want your scent to fade," I say, blushing with honesty.

Rhett hums with understanding, turning onto his back and sitting up a little against the headboard.

"What do you do when you're in my bed?" he asks in that casual, nonchalant manner of his that makes the hairs on my neck stand up. My body knows what that voice means.

"Crossword puzzles, mostly. Maybe the occasional fuck, but I like to come here to think," I say, hoping he'll miss the "slip up" and focus on my sass. But he's too smart for that.

"Do you fuck yourself, or do you have a friend?" Rhett demands, an edge to his words now.

"Lydia and I were here the other day, and I made sure to fill her with so much cum that it leaked out of her cunt and stained the bed. And judging by the scents here, I think Mateo did the same," I answer, the distance between us making me stupid.

"Good. She deserves to be fucked, thoroughly and often. And if my sheets smell like all of you when I get home, so much the better. But tell me, pet, are you alone now?" Rhett says, and I can see the flex of his bicep as his hand moves off screen.

"Just me, sir. All alone with no one to stop me from playing with your toy collection," I say, rolling over and sliding to the edge of the bed.

"Your Domina won't be happy if she knows you're playing with yourself," Rhett warns.

"Domina is busy celebrating with her other toy. And you know what they say happens when the cat's away," I say with a dismissive wave, getting to my feet.

I slide my jeans down, along with my boxers, and toss away my shirt, leaving me bare and hard as I make my way across the room to the chest of drawers Rhett uses as his toy box. Each drawer is meticulously organized, with plugs and vibrators, ropes and whips, gags and canes all arranged neatly. Rhett growls as I open the drawer with the dildos, running my finger over the multi-colored array. So many options, different sizes and textures and shapes, but I eventually settle on one that makes Rhett groan. It's black, large and thick, a perfect replica of my alpha's cock.

"Put your phone on the dresser next to the bed," Rhett commands, and I shiver.

"Maybe I will…" I sigh, trailing off as I head back to the bed and flop down backwards onto it. "Or maybe I'll lie here and fuck this rubber cock into me, and you'll just get to see my face as I come."

Rhett's answering growl makes my heart kick. I know I'm playing with fire, but the rush under my skin feels too good for me to stop. Maybe I'll pay for this later, but seeing Rhett visibly struggle to keep from shouting and barking is a sight to behold. I shimmy up the bed and find the bottle of lube on the bedside table, flipping open the cap. I let out exaggerated moans as I thoroughly coat the dildo, my progress a little sloppy as I'm only working with one hand.

"I want to see you take that in your ass, pet. Show me," Rhett orders, not a bark but close.

His arm flexes faster, and I can hear a rhythmic squelching, and I smirk. Instead of obeying, I position myself so I can press the tip of the slicked-up rubber cock against my hole. Not breeching, but just applying pressure. I don't move the camera from my face, letting Rhett see as my eyes roll back and I sigh.

"Feels so good against my ass, sir. Just barely entering me, stretching me out. Oh, God, you're so big," I groan, fucking myself a little bit deeper.

I'm almost always worked up enough to take Lex's strap on these days, but the stretch of my hole trying to take the stand-in dick is something I didn't realize I missed. So once the head slips past the ring of muscle, I push deep, crying out at the delicious burn that's just on this side of pleasurable.

"It's so deep inside me, filling me up," I pant, working the flared base out an inch or two before pushing in again, deeper still.

"My naughty little pet likes to get fucked, doesn't he? Can't get enough alpha cock?" Rhett replies, more of a statement than a question.

I nod, working in long strokes now, pulling the dildo almost all the way out before driving it back in again, making myself grunt and my hard cock bounce against my stomach.

Precum coats my lower abs, and I try to shift to hit my prostate, but it's hard holding the phone at the same time. But I move faster, letting my head fall back as the head of the dildo occasionally makes me see stars.

"I'm so fucking hard for you, Luc. I can't wait to fuck your slutty little hole, to mark up that perky ass of yours with my cane," Rhett growls, his hand moving faster.

I try to match his pace, feeling the sweat dripping off my forehead as I work. I'm close, so close—

"Hey, Lucas. What's for..."

My head snaps up as Mateo's voice comes from the hall. I'd left the door open, and he's got a perfect view of my leg hitched up, phone in one hand, fucking myself with a big, black cock with the other. I freeze, not sure what to do as he keeps staring. And then he starts advancing, soft brown eyes growing dark and predatory.

"What's going on, Lucas? Are you okay?" Rhett asks, genuinely worried.

"Hey, Coop. Just got home in time for the show, it seems," Mateo answers, speaking before I can get my brain to unfreeze and form sentences.

I swallow as Mateo peels off his shirt, approaching the end of the bed like a lion stalking a gazelle on the savannah. I start to move, but Mateo's growl makes me go still again.

"Looks like you're having some trouble, Luc. Want a hand?" Mateo asks, voice husky enough to make me shiver and clench on the dildo still deep inside of me.

"Sir..." I trail off, words sticking in my throat as I look back to Rhett.

Instead of possessive heat, there's a feral grin splitting my alpha's face, and I still hear him stroking himself, albeit slower now. He jerks his chin, silently letting me know that this is my call. I look back to Mateo, who's openly stroking himself through the material of his jeans, and swallow. I've seen his cock before, and the idle curiosity of how it would feel has lived in the back of my mind for years.

"I can watch, maybe take the phone so Rhett can have a better view. Or..." Mateo trails off, the implication clear.

I take a breath and nod eagerly, starting to pull the dildo free, but Mateo lunges forward and grabs my wrist. The movement shoves the dildo even farther into me, and I whine, arching. He guides my hand to fuck myself again, and only lets go long enough to shed the last of his clothes.

"Lucas has been a little brat for me, Mateo," Rhett comments, that dangerously casual tone back.

Mateo chuckles and crawls up the bed toward me, his cock nearly purple and leaking already. He takes the phone from me, and I try to sit up, only to have Mateo shove my chest hard, forcing me onto my back. My legs fall to either side as he settles onto his heels between them. His thumb presses a button, and he holds the camera up, and I swallow, knowing he's flipped to the rear camera for Rhett to see me better.

"Have you been misbehaving for your alpha, Lucas? Are you supposed to have this cock in your ass?" Mateo asks, almost laughing to himself.

I go to answer, but Mateo's other hand rips my hand away from the dildo, grabbing it and fucking me fast and hard, knocking the wind from me. Now that I'm not contorting myself, the head brushes against my prostate relentlessly, making my toes curl with white-hot pleasure. My hands fist into the sheets and I try to match Mateo's pace, but then he stops. I look up at him, indignant. But he's smirking, and something about the expression makes my stomach drop with another rush of need.

"Look at your slut, Rhett. He was about to come without anyone touching his cock," Mateo sneers, making me flush.

"So greedy, always wanting to come when he hasn't earned it," Rhett chides darkly.

Mateo spits on my cock, stroking it harshly with no warning. I clench on the dildo, trying to twist and thrust up into Mateo's fist, but he stops after only a few pumps. He laughs, and my cock throbs, so hard it almost hurts.

"So fucking needy, aren't you?" Mateo snaps, moving his knee to press against the base of the dildo as his hand returns to my cock.

I roll my hips, finally able to get leverage to fuck the dildo properly without having to touch it. But then Mateo grabs my balls and twists, making me scream. Pain streaks up my spine, and the wires cross in my brain, and to my horror, my cock throbs, cum shooting up my chest and stomach.

"Pathetic. Couldn't even hold it until you got a real cock," Mateo spits, releasing me.

I'm panting, skin on fire. My pulse thumps in my scalp, and I can't stop fucking the dildo, lost in the chase for pleasure. Mateo's hand grazes my stomach, fingers scooping up my cum, making me shiver. I open my mouth and stick out my tongue, ready to accept it, but he just laughs. Any retort I might have been able to come up with dies in a shout as Mateo uses my cum as lube, stroking my over-sensitive cock back to full hardness.

"Little slut wants something in his mouth. What do you think, Coop?" Mateo asks, condescending and arousing all at once.

"Give him something good to suck on," Rhett gasps, but it's almost distant as the never-ending wave of pleasure crashes over and over.

But then suddenly, the dildo is ripped from my ass, leaving me gaping and clenching on nothing. I'm about to protest when Mateo presses the broad head into my open mouth, nearly making me gag as he pushes it deep. I moan as he sets a steady pace, fucking my throat with the replica alpha cock.

"That's it, take it. Take that dick like the good little slut you are," Mateo snarls, pushing the limits of my gag reflex.

I take a shaky breath through my nose, trying to ride it out, but then his weight settles on me, and his cock presses against my ass. There's no time to prepare myself before he's fucking me, the speed of his hips matching the speed of his hand as he fucks me from both ends. I can only hang on, my cock still hard and sensitive as it brushes against Mateo's belly. It's not long before I'm right there at the edge again, whimpering around the cock in my mouth.

"Do you feel that, slut? That cock in your ass? Aren't you grateful to have an alpha fucking you, even though you don't deserve it?" Mateo snaps, losing his steady rhythm for a moment as I clench around him.

I nod, but Mateo growls, pounding harder, almost painfully.

"Answer, pet. Thank him for fucking your unworthy ass," Rhett snarls.

I attempt to speak, but it comes out a garbled mess. Thankfully, Mateo pulls the dildo free, tossing it aside before putting his hand around my throat and forcing my eyes up to meet his. He's got the camera poised over my face, and I look between him and it when I whimper, pleasure and pain mixing together as Mateo batters my sweet spot over and over.

"Th-thank you, sir. Thank you, Mateo, for fucking me," I stammer, tongue feeling almost too big for my mouth.

"Beg me for my cum, slut," Mateo orders, a wildness to him that I've never seen before.

His fingers squeeze and blackness closes in on the edges of my vision. I try to get the words out, but I only manage to mouth the word "please." He laughs cruelly, the sound echoing in my head.

"You don't get to breathe until I come. Make me come, slut. Squeeze that ass—oh, fuck, just like that. He's so good, Rhett. So tight," Mateo babbles.

I can only hang on, the world fading. I reach up and drag my short nails down Mateo's chest, not trying to escape, but for something to hang onto. With a shout, Mateo drives forward, until his knot presses against me and his cum spills deep. He releases his grip, and my body convulses, pleasure screaming through me as I come again, painting both of our chests this time.

There's a long stretch where we don't speak, and I look up at Mateo with wide, disbelieving eyes. I had no idea he had a side like that in him, but fuck if I don't want to bring it out again. When he withdraws, I'm left with that thoroughly fucked ache, and the feeling of his cum sliding out of my ass and onto the bed.

"Whoops. Sorry, Coop. Made a bit of a mess on your duvet." Mateo laughs, sitting back on his heels.

"Leave it," Rhett pants, making me laugh.

"Your sheets are going to look like a gym sock if you're gone for too long," I tease, stretching out slightly.

Mateo throws his head back and holds his stomach as he laughs, Rhett chuckling as well. When the laughter dies, Mateo looks down at me with a small smile.

"You okay, Luc? Do you need anything? Towel? Shower?" he prompts, genuine concern sparking in his eyes.

I shake my head. "I'm good. Thanks, uh... for the assist," I say, finishing lamely.

Moving before my brain catches up, I hold up a fist for Mateo to bump. I blush hard, about to put it down, when he returns the gesture. And then I hear Rhett, absolutely dying of laughter on the other end of the line. Mateo and I can't help but join him, albeit less raucously, and more bashful.

"You two get yourselves situated. We can talk more tomorrow," Rhett says once he's recovered.

Mateo and I say our goodbyes and as he sets my phone off to the side, I sit up, moving to get up from the bed. But Mateo catches my wrist, pulling my attention back to him. He's looking at me with an odd expression, not quite embarrassment, but close. I cock my head to one side in silent question.

"Are you really okay, Lucas? With what just happened? I know we've never... done that before, so I'm sorry if I overstepped—"

I cut him off with a laugh. His nervous rambles are almost adorable, but the worried frown on his face makes me pause.

"Yeah, it's fine. I can't say I've never thought about how you'd be in bed," I reply, still teasing but softer.

Mateo grins bashfully, face going pink. "Same, though I figured you had your hands full. But then Lydia mentioned wanting to watch us, and I couldn't get the idea out of my head, and—"

"Wait, *Lydia* said she wanted to watch *us*?" I ask skeptically, cutting across more of his rambles.

Mateo nods and laughs. I grin to myself, not sure why I'm surprised by this development, but not mad about it. I've known for a long time that I'd do just about anything that woman asks of me, but putting on a show for her wouldn't exactly be a hardship. And then maybe Lex would be there, too, topping Lydia while Mateo dominates me again. Or maybe once Rhett gets home...

I clear my throat, shaking my head from those thoughts before I get riled up all over again. Mateo is still looking at me with worry and hesitation in his eyes. My stomach clenches, and I reach out to pull his face to mine, claiming his lips for a brief but intense kiss.

"We're going to put a pin in that for the moment, but you bet your ass I'm going to ask about these little daydreams of hers when she gets home tomorrow. For now, I'm okay with what just happened, and the idea of it happening again if you are," I soothe, squeezing the back of his neck slightly for emphasis.

Mateo truly relaxes then and nods, kissing me again before sitting back. He looks me over, and the way his eyes linger on my cock for a half second longer than the rest of me makes my skin prickle. But then he blinks, remembering himself. "Let's go get cleaned up. It's almost time for kickoff. With the girls at Wickland House, we can watch the game in the living room tonight," he says, getting to his feet.

He leaves his clothes on the floor, but I can forgive him. The view as he struts away is worth it. After another moment's hesitation, I get up and follow him back to his shower. It'd be rude to leave the score unsettled, after all.

CHAPTER SIXTEEN

Lydia

"I'M STILL MAD AT you for not telling me you have a pool sooner," Gabby says for the fourth time this afternoon.

I roll my eyes and sip my cocktail, not answering. Wila still hasn't found a building to run the flower shop out of yet, so Gabby has been going out of her mind with boredom. There's nothing left for us to do on State Street anymore, and, in her own words, she can only stare at the same four walls for so long without wanting to climb them. So I'd offered to let her hang out at the pack house with me. She didn't get the full tour the last time she was here, so when she got here the first day and realized all the fun we could have been having between the pool table, the swimming pool, and the massive televisions with gaming systems, she's been here every day for the last week. She's declined my offer to sleep over more than once, claiming to not want to step on any of my pack mate's toes.

Not having her spend the night is, in all honesty, probably for the best. Mateo and Lucas have been keeping me busy, together and separately. Lucas, in particular, has been relentless in learning about all my deepest fantasies now that he's learned about the ones I've had about him and Mateo hooking up. At first, I thought he was so keen because he wanted to make sure I was respecting the polyamorous boundaries of our pack. Nope. Turns out he wants to know so he can make my sexual dreams come true. Sometimes I think Rhett has the right idea, keeping him on a short leash. It took mine and Lex's combined efforts to get him to go back to work and let my body have some time off.

Which is why Gabby and I are spending a third day in a row by the pool, sunbathing and enjoying the last of the nice weather before winter hits. Caleb is giving us a respectful amount of space, sitting on the deck above us, watching out. I tried to get him to come down and sit with us, but he'd insisted on having a better vantage point.

"When do you think you'll finally be able to ditch your muscle?" Gabby asks as she sees me looking up.

I shrug and look away with a sigh. "When they catch Seth, probably. Darren's going to be in the hospital for a while, I guess, and even after he gets out, I'm not sure he'll come near me after what Rhett did to him."

Thinking about that night brings all manner of confused feelings to my chest. I've stopped trying to blame myself for what happened, because I can recognize that we were set up to fail. The only part I regret is not getting out in time to avoid getting caught, and having Rhett taken away from me. Outcome aside, I can't deny that Rhett certainly taught Darren a lesson he won't forget any time soon. "I can't believe he's still a fucking ghost. Going three weeks without posting a gym mirror selfie must be torture for a guy like him," Gabby says with a snort.

"How do you know he hasn't posted?" I ask quickly.

"I followed him on socials after he ambushed you at the store. Figured it'd be worth it to keep an eye on the bastard," Gabby explains flippantly.

"You didn't have to do that. I'm sure it's not interesting or fun to look at," I mutter, brushing a stray hair out of my face to avoid looking at her.

"You can say that again. It's just hundreds of pictures of this face."

I turn and bark out a startled laughter as she twists her features into what someone might generously call a smolder, but it looks like she's sucked on a really sour lemon. She drops the expression and shudders comically, making me laugh harder, which then sets off her giggles. We're still laughing when my phone rings on the low table between us. As I look down, I gasp at seeing Jason's name on my screen, and I scramble to answer.

"Jace!" I exclaim as I bring the phone up to my ear.

"Hey, Lydi. It's good to hear your voice. How are you?" he starts, sounding more relieved than anything.

Jason and I have had limited contact over the last few weeks, due in large part to our mother watching him like a hawk. She's waiting for him to slip up and reveal any sliver of information she could possibly use against me. But he's been gray-rocking like a champion, even if that means not calling as often as I'd like.

"Better. How are you holding up?" I answer, sitting up slightly and tucking my legs in to sit crisscross.

Jason lets out a long, heavy exhale. "Um... not great, if I'm being honest. Are you alone?"

I furrow my brow with confusion. "Gabby's here, and Caleb, but he's not really in earshot right now. Why? What's the matter?"

Jason pauses, and I bite my lower lip. My excitement has melted into worry, not sure what to make of this tone from my little brother.

"I've talked to your alpha, and told her about it, and I don't know how much she's told you, but Mom's..."

"Angry?" I supply when he trails off.

He scoffs a laugh. "Angry doesn't even begin to cover it, Lydi. She's off the deep end. I don't know what on God's green Earth her plan was, but my God, did it not work. Pastor Joe's been here at the house almost every day since the wedding, bringing down all manner of righteous indignation on Dad for allowing him and his son to be embarrassed like this. Miss. Andrea has been weeping like a widow, wearing her funeral best as she sits in the ICU, and when she's not there, she's been at church, talking to all the other wives. You'd think Mom had the Black Plague with the way she's been dropped from every committee, council, and volunteer group. She's even been asked to step down from teaching Sunday school."

My jaw drops, and I am too stunned to speak as the weight of this news hits me. My mother has been a part of the Chauvert Assembly of God leadership as far back as I could remember. She spent more of her time planning church potlucks and ice cream socials than she ever did planning any family gathering, and half the time, the decorations she used for the family events were borrowed from their storage anyway. And to have that position of power stripped from her...

"Has she found out about my trust?" I ask as the thought occurs to me.

"Eh... yep," he replies, drawing out the words for emphasis. "Got the call from the bank, letting me know she tried to make an inquiry the Monday after the wedding. Of course, she turned around and tried to blame me for taking the money, and got up a real head of steam before I walked away, but—"

"I'm sorry, Jace. I didn't think she'd... I didn't want her to take this out on you," I interrupt, voice fading to a whisper as guilt creeps in.

"She's lashing out at everyone, not just me. I'm a traitor and a liar with no sense of loyalty or respect for my pack. Sammy's weak minded for letting his wife manipulate him—"

"Wait, what?" I blurt, blinking rapidly.

"Oh, yeah. I told you that Ally and Sammy moved back into the house?" Jason starts.

I hum an affirmative response, on the edge of my seat. I'm not particularly interested in gossip, but drama like this is like witnessing a train wreck.

"Poor Ally is Mom's latest punching bag, all for the crime of mentioning that what Darren did at the wedding was wrong and he got what was coming to him. Sammy's been questioning things for a while, and we've talked a lot since you left. He's not quite ready to fully ditch Mom and Dad, but he's calling them on their bullshit way more now, not letting them get away with outright lying when he's around. But Ally's the mastermind for trying to steal her baby or something," Jason explains.

I cringe back. "That's... just wow. He's a grown ass man with a functioning brain."

"That's what I said, but what do I know. Ally's a trooper, though. If she can handle kindergarteners, she can handle Mom."

We share a laugh, but the elephant in the room stares at me.

"And... Adam?" I prompt when Jason doesn't continue.

"I think he's trying to kiss so much ass that we'll all conveniently forget he was dishonorably discharged not that long ago. Mom has, of course, forgiven him, but Dad sure as hell won't. After the shit he said at the wedding, he can suck an entire bag of dicks and choke as far as I'm concerned," Jason says, ending on a snarl.

I can't help but smile. Of all the things that happened that night, Adam's victim blaming was hardly the worst of it, but something in his tone catches my attention.

"Did he say something after I left?" I ask hesitantly.

"Oh, yeah. I'd never repeat his exact words in polite company or otherwise, but he's lucky he's not in a bed next to Darren with his jaw wired shut, too," Jason spits.

I sigh, considering forcing the issue, but I can only imagine what horrors my brother could have come out with. Instead, I change the subject.

"You're still using the burner Caleb gave you," I start, picking at a chip in the paint on my toenail.

Jason grunts, a gruff, annoyed sound. "Mom's still trying to deny spying on me. I even asked a buddy of mine who's good with tech and he proved that she had my SIM card cloned, but she's still trying to act like it wasn't her. So I walked out and threw my phone into the bayou."

I can't help but chuckle. "She thinks you don't have a phone now?"

"Yep. Sammy and I communicate through Ally's phone, and I call Rhett every now and then, just to keep the poor bastard from going crazy, but otherwise, no one can get ahold of me. I should have done this years ago."

We share a laugh at his joke, then go quiet, the question bubbling up on his side of the line. We've texted some, but this is the longest conversation we've had in a while. It feels good to get everything out in the open. But I know he's got questions, and I owe him answers.

"Lydia, you said..."

"Yeah, Mom blackmailed me into going to the wedding. She said that she'd cut you off and have you disavowed from the pack if I didn't show up," I finish when he trails off.

I've been waiting for this. I'd known going to the wedding would be dangerous, and I'd even decided not to go at one point. But when my mother threatened to have Jason kicked out and disowned, there was no way I would let that happen. Jason has a place in the family, and I couldn't let myself be the one to take that away from him. I'd thought about everything leading up to that day, and I'd do a lot of things differently if I had the chance, but I wouldn't change this part. I would protect my little brother every time, period.

"Lydia, that's—why didn't you tell me? We could have talked about it, made plans—"

"You would tell me not to go, and I'm not going to make you an outcast to protect myself. That's not—"

"You're not hearing me. If I'd known in advance that Mom was threatening to kick me out, then I could have—"

"No, Jason!" I'm nearly shouting, my vision blurry as I clutch my phone hard. "I would never, could never, ask you to do that for me. You aren't like me. I was already gone mentally before I ran. You still want to be there, and I'm not—"

"Will you please stop and listen to me for a minute?" Jason shouts over me.

I blink in surprise, too stunned by the sudden heat in his voice to speak. He presses his advantage in my silence, words falling out in a tumble like he can't get them out fast enough.

"I've been planning to leave for months, since before you even knew about the wedding. I don't want to talk too much about it over the phone, but I found some stuff and I can't—I won't let myself be a pawn in this family's bullshit anymore. If you'd told me that Mom was planning to kick me out, we could have worked it out, staged everything to make it look like she won. I could have..."

He trails off again, but this time, I have no idea how that sentence could possibly end. What does Jason know that's so bad he's willing to give up his pack standing to get away from it? Why can't he tell me over the phone? More questions swirl in my head, and I can't get any of them to slow down long enough to be vocalized.

"Listen, I'm still getting things together, but it won't be long. I'll give you as much warning as I can, but expect the retaliation to come through fast. Dad's already sent three letters, and I think he's got the police on speed dial for the moment that clock runs out."

"That's been solved, Jace. I have the proper paperwork. He can't touch me now."

"Oh, thank God. That was my biggest worry, that they'd use you to make me come back once I leave." Jason exhales, relief dripping from every word.

"Jason, why can't you tell me what's going on?" I push, worry creeping forward.

"I will as soon as I can. But listen, I've been gone for too long and someone's going to get suspicious. I have to go. We'll talk again soon, okay?" Jason says, words rushing out.

"Wait, no. Jason, please, talk to me—"

"I'll explain everything as soon as I can. But for now, please, just stay safe and don't worry about me," he replies emphatically.

"It's a bit too late for that," I throw back with sarcasm.

Jason chuckles warmly. "I know. But I really do have to go. Love you so much, Lydi."

I sigh, defeated. I know when I've been shut down, and it's not worth it to pick this fight now. I'll try again another time. "Love you too, Jace. Stay safe."

We say our goodbyes and I lower my phone to my lap. I know he thinks he can handle himself, but I'm his older sister. I'm always going to worry about my baby brother. I have to stop my mind from running away from me, imagining the worst of the worst-case scenarios.

I turn back to Gabby, opening my mouth to ask her what she thinks, or if he's said anything to her, but stop short. She's sitting straight up, eyes wide and mouth agape, as she stares at her phone in horror. I move closer, heart already pounding. I don't think I could handle any more bad news right now. But the headline on her screen launches me into an entirely new tangle of confused feelings.

SETH DOUGLAS MEETS HIS DRUNKEN DEMISE

CHAPTER SEVENTEEN

Lucas

I REREAD THE WORDS over and over again, still in shock. Seth is dead. He got drunk and crashed his car into a tree. And now he's dead. I look away from my phone and rub my mouth in shock. When Rhett sent me the link a few minutes ago, I didn't know what to expect, but it certainly wasn't this.

I'm sitting in my office in Alice's Kitchen, the restaurant Rhett owns and I manage. It's still early in the day, a few hours away from the Friday night dinner rush. Not that I'd had plans to stick around for it. Lex and Mateo are in Savannah for the weekend, looking at a potential expansion opportunity, leaving me alone with Lydia, which will be nice. Three days of uninterrupted quality time. I've even cleared my work schedule for it, which made my assistant manager, Steph, question my sanity. I haven't taken this much voluntary time off since she was hired. I might take a few hours here and there, but not three whole days, and on a weekend, no less.

But my priorities are different now. I don't feel the need to fill my every waking hour with activity, at least not when

I'm with Lydia. I can slow down, just be in the moment with her. It took Steph pointing it out for me to realize how much Lydia has changed me, and my pack.

My phone buzzes in my hand with another message, this time from Lydia.

Lydi-bug: Did you see? About Seth???
Me: Yeah. Rhett sent me the article. This is fucking wild.

"Wild" is an understatement, but I can't think of anything else. He's gone. Seth is gone, and my pack is free. We can move on, leave the past where it belongs.

It's hard for my brain to wrap itself around, the idea that we finally are rid of that scumbag. We've spent so long under his thumb that I don't know what to do now.

My phone goes off again at the same time someone knocks on my door. As my head shoots up, my eyebrows lift in surprise. Steph is in the open doorway, and over her shoulder, I can spot the familiar face of Officer Lee Nyueng.

"Hey, the police are here and want to ask you some questions. Are you busy?" Steph asks hesitantly.

I shove my phone into my pocket and stand, brushing the front of my chef's jacket out of habit. Not that the stains from years of wear will suddenly disappear with a wave of my hand. Steph steps back and lets Lee maneuver around her before giving me a terse, concerned half-smile and closing the door.

"Mind if I have a seat?" Lee starts with a sigh.

I shrug and motion for him to take the metal folding chair I'd managed to squeeze between two stacks of boxes. I sit back in my beat-up rolling chair and swivel to face him, bringing one of my legs up and resting my ankle on my knee.

"So I'm assuming you've heard the news? About Seth Douglas?" Lee asks, pulling out a small notebook and pen from a front pocket of his tactical vest.

"Just read the article. I'm still sort of waiting for someone to yell 'gotcha,'" I reply with an ironic chuckle, running a hand through my hair before crossing my arms over my chest.

"What do you mean?" he asks quickly, looking up at me from beneath a lowered brow, pen poised over the paper.

I shrug again. "After all the shit we've been through with him, it wouldn't surprise me if he found a loophole out of death. He managed to find one in everything else we threw at him."

Lee snorts a laugh. "Yeah, I get that. But I can assure you it's real. I wasn't at the scene, but I saw the pictures. We're still waiting on some of the tests to confirm it, but between the registration in the car and wallet we found... yeah, it was Seth in there."

"Was it bad?" I ask, morbid curiosity taking over.

Lee gives me a long look. "I can't discuss particulars of an ongoing investigation, but yeah. It was bad."

I try not to let my imagination run away from me. I've seen enough from TV and movies to picture what a burnt-to-a-crisp body looks like.

"Speaking of the investigation, I do have to ask. Where were you yesterday into this morning?" Lee asks, interrupting my thoughts.

I blink at him for a moment as understanding dawns. "You think I had something to do with this? The paper said it was a drunk driving wreck," I throw back, not able to keep the indignation from my voice.

Lee holds up his hands in a surrendering sort of gesture. "I'm just trying to do my job, Mr. Klausen. Until we know more, we can't rule anything out. Your pack has had very public bad blood with Mr. Douglas, and would benefit the most from his sudden disappearance."

I swallow a growl of irritation, but I know he's right. From an outsider's perspective, I can see how this could look bad. But I know we had nothing to do with this.

"Yesterday I was at work until close, and I hung around with my team for a drink before going home. I drove straight there, and didn't leave again until this morning. I came straight to work, and have been here ever since," I explain, forcing myself to remain calm.

"Can you be more specific with times?" Lee prompts, scribbling notes on his pad.

I sigh and look up at the ceiling as I try to remember. "We closed at eleven, last customer was out not long after that. I wasn't looking at the clock, but I know the crew and me all left at the same time, and I personally armed the security system before locking up."

"Can anyone confirm what time you got home?"

I nod. "We have a security guard and a key fob scanner at the entrance to Bristol Point. They keep track of who comes and goes and when."

"Just the one security guard?"

I chuckle. "Just the one, because there's only one entrance."

"There's no secondary way to leave? No service entrances or—"

"Listen, Lee. I can get you the logs of when I clocked in and clocked out, when I set the alarm to this building, and the records of when I got home and left. But if that's not enough, I might have to get my lawyer involved," I snap, narrowing my eyes at him.

Lee looks up at me and blinks, genuinely surprised. "Nah, man. It's not like—I get it. I don't think I'm stretching if I say that a lot of people aren't sorry this happened. I just want to make sure y'all don't have to hear from us again, you know what I mean?"

Sighing, I rub my eyes. "Yeah. But look, we're all accounted for. I've told you where I was. Rhett is literally in another state right now, with an ankle monitor. Lydia has a body-guard with her at all times. Lex and Mateo were on the road to Savannah after end-of-business yesterday. They'll have their toll pass records to prove that."

Lee nods and makes a note. "I heard about Mr. Cooper's arrest. I could tell he has a temper, but..." Lee trails off with a low whistle.

"He was acting in self-defense and to protect Lydia from her abusive ex," I grumble through gritted teeth.

"Hey, don't get me wrong. Scumbag abusive alphas need to be put in their place sometimes. Too bad this one's place wasn't six feet under," Lee returns, tone darkening slightly.

I give him a genuine smile for the first time. "Yeah. But Rhett's not a murderer. None of us are, even if the people who hurt us deserve it."

Lee nods and goes quiet as he finishes his notes. He reads through them once before sliding the notebook back into his vest. Pulling out a business card, he hands it to me before getting to his feet.

"My email address is on there. When you get a chance, send me anything you've got. I think you're solid, but my boss will want a paper trail," he says with a sigh.

I smirk and nod, putting the card on my desk and getting to my feet. I walk him to the door of my office and open it for him.

"Thank you for your time. With any luck, this might be the last time you see me," Lee says with a light chuckle.

"Don't take this the wrong way, but I sure as hell hope so," I return with a laugh of my own.

Lee sticks out his hand, and we shake once before he finally turns and leaves. I exhale heavily and turn back to my desk. I want to blow this off and spend the weekend with Lydia like I'd planned, but I know I can't. Once we're cleared and the investigation is over, then I never have to worry about Seth again. I might as well do everything I can to expedite the process.

CHAPTER EIGHTEEN

Mateo

MY BEACH HOUSE USED to be a secret place, a retreat, an escape from the mask I have to wear as the face of the St. Clair Foundation. I'd brought Lydia here not that long ago, to get away from the madness, only to have it encroach on us anyway. And now my private place has been invaded again.

Lex is sitting at the head of the dining room table, looking for all the world like she is a queen and this house is her castle. Meanwhile, three alphas I've never met are scattered throughout the living area. I'd been introduced to them as Gideon, Delano, and Hunter, but I haven't been given more information beyond their names. It's impossible to not see the familial connection between Lex and Gideon, though. If the Ice Queen ever had a twin, it would be Gideon. Even their scents are similar: spicy and citrusy, and while Lex has notes of mulled wine to her, Gideon is all smoke. Almost like someone set an orange grove on fire with cinnamon sticks as kindling. He's posted up by the door, leaning against the wall with his arms crossed. His eyes stay fixed on Hunter's back as he unpacks supplies from a black bag. The somber undertaker in every sense of the word; Hunter's hardly said a word since the trio arrived a little over an hour ago. In contrast, Delano hasn't stopped his incessant, inane chatter as he digs through every cupboard and cabinet he can find.

"...but anyway, I prefer gasoline in most cases. If you're going to do something, you shouldn't half ass it, and nothing gets the job done like the classics," he's saying, though I've long since lost the thread of what he'd been talking about.

"Dee, enough," Gideon snaps, rubbing at his temple.

At least I'm not the only one he's annoying.

"God, where do you keep your fucking booze, Matty?" Delano sighs dramatically, slamming the last of the kitchen cabinets closed.

"There isn't any here. This is a vacation rental most of the time," I drone, words clipped.

"Fucking lame, bro. You didn't even bring any liquid courage for your weekend trip?" he asks, turning an incredulous stare in my direction.

"Just because you can't go three hours without a drink doesn't mean no one can," Hunter grumbles, holding a vial and a syringe up to the light.

Delano turns to glare at Hunter, not that he notices, and then saunters out of the kitchen, hands deep in his front pockets as he glances around at the walls and ceiling. Despite myself, I take the opportunity to look him over. His blood red hair is pulled back in a topknot, exposing the shaved and tattooed sides of his scalp. The ink continues down his neck and under the fabric of his loose Henley, and I can't deny the beauty of the artwork on display. His ears are gauged slightly, his plugs maybe the size of a dime, and based on the way his jaw moves, I'd be willing to bet his tongue is pierced too.

A low growl from across the room draws my attention, and I snap my eyes to Gideon. No longer looking bored, his hazel eyes narrow in a possessive glare. I snort a chuckle and smirk at him.

"I'm all set, if you're ready to begin," Hunter says, interrupting whatever Gideon may have been about to say.

"I've been ready for months." I sigh, getting to my feet and crossing to the kitchen.

Delano steps into my path and looks me up and down. We're the same height, so I have no problem looking him in the eye as I stand my ground. This close, I can detect traces of citrus and smoke among the phosphorus and salt pouring off him, swirling together to smell like a freshly struck match, igniting a driftwood beach fire. This close, his light gray eyes are almost unnaturally bright, a keen intelligence in the depths.

"I could stick around, and we could get to know each other a little better," Delano nearly purrs.

Another growl sounds from across the room, but I don't back down. A year ago, Delano Argentieri would have been exactly my type of mistake. We would have destroyed each other, my lightning and his wildfire clashing over and over again, obliterating everything in our path for the sake of having a good time.

But not anymore.

"My dance card's full," I reply simply, rocking my weight onto my back leg.

Delano sucks his teeth and runs his tongue along his bottom lip. Just like I'd suspected, a silver piercing flashes in the light. "Shame. You seem like the type to—"

"If you're done flirting, we're here for a reason," Lex drawls pointedly, cutting across whatever Delano was about to say.

He turns and looks at her with no small amount of surprise on his face. I can't say I'm not a little surprised either. There's something in her expression as she glares at Delano that I don't expect: possessiveness. I'd seen that look on her face whenever someone got a little too friendly with Lucas, and more recently Lydia, but it's never been directed my way. But I'll have plenty of time to ponder that later.

I step around Delano and continue into the dining room, sitting on Lex's right. We both roll up our sleeves to expose our upper arms as he brings the vials closer. I don't know what I'd expected, maybe something in a radioactive shade of green or even blue, but the liquid in the syringes is clear. If I didn't know better, it looks like Hunter is about to give us a flu shot, not administer a bond breaking drug of questionable origin. But beggars can't be choosers, and I'd do anything to be rid of this bond for good.

"You're going to feel some burning, but that should go away after a few minutes. Over the next few days, you're going to be more... irritable, maybe even slightly manic. That's normal, and part of the process. If you're going to have a bad reaction, it'll happen within the first hour or so," Hunter says, words detached and clinical.

"What's a bad reaction?" Lex asks.

"Your body locks up and you stop breathing. Or you start ripping off people's faces," Delano says with a laugh.

I look at him with alarm, and find him in the chair I'd vacated.

"How could you possibly know that?" Lex throws back.

Delano only laughs and taps the side of his nose with a long finger. "Plausible deniability, dollface."

Hearing him call her a pet name twists something in my chest, and I manage to contain my reaction to a glare. She's not his dollface, or his anything.

"This isn't the first time we've done this," Gideon adds, almost no inflection in his words.

I want to question him further, but Hunter looks up at us expectantly. I turn my gaze to Lex, and I can read the question in her eyes.

You want to go first?

"After you, Prime Alpha," I reply, trying for irreverent, but the words stick in my throat.

This is it. We're doing this. Hunter puts on some gloves and sanitizes the injection site on Lex's arm with a little alcohol wipe. I watch her face as the needle goes in, and her only reaction is a slight wince. And then it's my turn. I close my eyes for just a moment, and before I can truly process what's happening, it's over. A slight prick and then it's done. Years of trauma are finally behind me. After this weekend, Seth Douglas will be nothing more than a bad memory.

I'd thought I would be able to feel the drug working, maybe some ripping or shredding in my chest or head, but as we sit at the table and the minutes tick by, the only thing I feel is the burning Hunter mentioned. My upper arm feels like I have a very bad, very localized sunburn, and I rotate my shoulder as the pain ramps up a little. Lex looks at me, flashing a look of concern, but I give her a little reassuring smile.

"Feel like clawing my face off?" I joke with a little chuckle.

"No more than usual," she returns, not missing a beat.

"We'll stick around for a while longer, just to make sure," Hunter says, packing up his bag again.

"I'm sure you have better things to do," Lex says dismissively.

"Of course, we do. But Uncle Leo isn't paying us to do a half-ass job," Gideon adds from the door.

I snort at his words, trying to imagine Leopold St. Clair playing catch with a child Gideon, or taking him fishing, or doing any of the other things my uncles did with me growing up. But I can't make myself imagine the man wearing anything other than a three-piece suit, which only adds to the humor.

"What's so funny?" Gideon snipes, glaring at me.

"Just thinking about your 'Uncle Leo,'" I reply, finger quoting the name.

"What else am I supposed to call him?"

"I call him 'that bastard,' and everyone usually knows who I'm talking about," I say with a satisfied smirk.

His face goes a little red in his temper, and I catch Lex pressing her lips together as she tries not to laugh. That's not the worst thing I've ever called her sperm donor, and it's certainly not even close to the worst things *she's* called him. Gideon looks at his cousin, waiting for her to defend her father, but when she doesn't, he turns back to me.

"Come on, Gid. We both know Leo's an asshole. They just have the balls to say it," Delano tosses from the living room.

Hunter grunts his agreement, moving to sit on the couch and pulling out his phone. Gideon puffs out an annoyed sigh, but doesn't say anything more about Leopold. Lex stands and starts to move around the kitchen, straightening the appliances and wiping the already sparkling surfaces with a towel. Watching her buzz around doing busy work grates on my nerves, and it's only due to my practice in holding my tongue around clients that I manage to not tell her to sit down again. My leg bounces under the table, and I drum my fingers on the wood, staring out the window toward the ocean.

The sun is going down, and the wind is kicking up, shifting from blowing in off the water to off the shore. It's still warm, but with October on the horizon, I know it won't last for long. We've avoided direct hits from hurricanes so far this season, but I'll have to make sure the property manager battens down the hatches after we leave. It'd normally be done by now, but between the few late bookings we had, and now this little getaway, I think I'm going to drive that poor girl to insanity.

But not if Lex drives me to madness first. She's now dusting the knickknacks on the living room walls, climbing on furniture to clean the higher sections. I reach the end of my patience as she balances precariously on the back of one of the couches, one wrong move away from tipping the whole thing over.

"Get the fuck down. I pay housekeepers for a reason," I snap.

Lex throws me a cold look over her shoulder. "They aren't doing a good enough job. Have you seen the cobwebs up here?"

I roll my eyes. "You're going to break your goddamn neck trying to get rid of imaginary cobwebs. Get down from there," I throw back.

"They are not imaginary, and I'm not going to fall," she retorts, a growl at the edge of her words.

"If you don't get down, I'm going to—"

"Oh, my God. You two are like an old married couple," Delano groans.

Lex and I both turn on him with matching glares.

"No one fucking asked you."

We speak at the same time, our growls a near perfect harmony that makes Delano blink in surprise before he bursts out laughing. Clenching my fists, I get to my feet and start looking around the kitchen for ingredients. I happen to glance at the clock, and it's only been ten minutes since the injection.

This weekend is going to be the death of me.

CHAPTER NINETEEN

Rhett

Luc: Just got done speaking with Lee. He didn't say we're under investigation, but he's still asking for alibis.

Me: I can send him my bond officer's phone number.

Luc: Good plan.

Luc: Lydia and I can try to video chat later.

Me: I'll have to check my calendar, see if I can squeeze you in.

Luc: Tell your new pack they'll have to wait. Your beta and your omega need their sir tonight.

Me: Well, when you put it like that...

I CHUCKLE A LITTLE at the banter, not responding to the series of suggestive emojis he sends next. Pouring myself another cup of coffee, I head back to the dining room table, where I've spread out my files. The one good thing about being on house arrest is that it's given me time to really deep dive into the projects I've been neglecting. Ted brought me my work laptop and a few boxes of documents I requested, and it's been a treat to have the time to fall down research rabbit holes. If I didn't have work, I'm sure I'd be climbing the walls after nearly three weeks of isolation. But the distraction has been lovely.

As I shuffle through copies of the photos my team had dug up of the Magnolia Garden Theatre, I compare them to the pictures of the building in its current state. I want to start drafting building plans, but it's much harder to do without my supplies. I'd considered ordering a table and the proper writing utensils, but with any luck, I'll be home by the end of the fortnight, so it hardly seems worth the expense.

I smile to myself as I sip my coffee. I don't know where Lex found Theodore Calhoun, but I will be sending that man a fruit basket on every holiday for the next decade at least, including the stupid ones like Arbor Day. He's done everything in his power to kill the case against me, and it seems like it's working. Every day that the grand jury doesn't turn in an indictment is a day closer to me getting off free and clear.

Circling a support beam in one of the current condition pictures, I write a note on the back, reminding myself to have the inspector give that a closer look. The discoloration on the wood might not be anything, but after sitting empty and derelict for nearly forty years, it could be anything from water damage to termites to mold. I'm looking at another beam in the area when a buzz on the intercom pulls my attention.

I set my coffee down and go to the box on the wall by the front door, checking my watch. It's probably my dinner delivery. I've been trying out all kinds of new places, and sending Lydia pictures and reviews of everything. Between her suggestions and the internet recommendations, I'll be genuinely surprised if I come out of this forced isolation without gaining twenty pounds. I don't bother asking the front desk who it is, and just send a buzz back, the signal we'd worked out so they know to send the driver up. Normally, I'd have to go down and collect my order, but per the stipulations of my bail, I'm confined to the apartment.

A few minutes later, the knock comes on the front door of the apartment, and I saunter over with my hands in my pockets. But my thoughts about my dinner are stopped in their tracks as I open the door and find Jason Anderson on my threshold, looking anxiously down the hallway toward the elevator. At the sound of the hinges, he turns to face me, and I suck in a sharp breath as I see his swollen and bruised eye and cheek.

"Holy fuck, dude. What happened?" I ask, motioning him to come in.

He doesn't answer right away, reaching down to pick up a plastic bag full of takeout containers from the floor before stalking past me. His normally mellow cucumber and juniper scent is gone, replaced with vinegar-tinted rage rolling off him in waves. He finds his way to the dining room easily, having visited me a few times before tonight, where he sets the food down on the table.

"Sorry I didn't text or call. I hope I'm not interrupting anything," he starts, words a little slurred, likely from the swelling in his face.

"No worries. Let's get some ice on that and you can explain why you look like you've just gone ten rounds," I reply, hurrying into the kitchen.

Jason sits at the table, holding a bag of ice wrapped in a towel to the injured side of his face. I gather plates and utensils and bring them back with me, and I dish out portions for both of us. It's a good thing I order two meals' worth of food at a time.

"You don't have to—"

"I know, but I am. So shut up and eat takeout with me," I throw back, no heat behind my words.

Jason chuckles and winces, the hand not holding the ice moving to clutch his ribs. He's quiet for several more minutes, his green eyes—so like Lydia's—distant. I want to push, to find out what happened, but I know that won't help. If he's anything like Lydia, he'll talk when he's good and ready, and not a moment sooner.

"I'm done with them," Jason says at last, voice dark and low.

I don't have to ask which "them" he's referring to. We've talked a lot in the past few weeks, both in messages and in person, and he's answered a lot of the questions I've had about Lydia's family but didn't want to ask out of respect for her trauma. I thought I'd hated them before, but now I'm just waiting for an excuse to ruin their lives. And it seems like Jason might finally be ready to help me.

"Why?" I ask neutrally, digging into my etouffee.

"I've had enough of the head games, and I won't let myself be their pawn anymore. Not when I can actually do something about it," Jason declares, his volume still low but not lacking in passion.

"Good. You deserve better," I say, meaning every syllable.

Jason snorts derisively and takes a slow bite of the food I'd put in front of him. We eat in silence for another few minutes, but then I sit back and look at him a little closer. Most of the damage to his face is hidden under the ice, but based on my experience with combat injuries and the way he winces when he moves or breathes wrong, he's probably got some bruising to his ribs. His knuckles are split open and scabbed over, but they don't seem to be bothering him.

"How'd the other guy fare?" I ask casually, watching carefully for a reaction.

It's hard to see under all the redness and swelling, but Jason and Lydia even blush the same way. It starts from his nose and spreads out across his forehead and cheeks, going down his neck. He doesn't look at me at first, and then he grins sheepishly.

"He uh... yeah, he didn't do so good," he admits, not sounding the least bit ashamed.

"Don't hold out on me, man. What the fuck happened?" I push, keeping my tone teasing despite the undercurrent of anger on his behalf.

Jason sighs and pushes his plate away, having only barely touched the food. He leans back in his chair and removes the ice, setting it off to the side. The swelling has gone down a bit, but it'll probably still be a few more days before he can see out of that eye again.

"Dad got the letter from your lawyer today, the one about Lydia finally being an official member of Pack Saint Clair. He decided to tell everyone over dinner," he starts, looking up at the ceiling unseeing.

I snort humorlessly. "How'd that go over?"

Jason smirks. "Like a lead balloon. Dad is a lot of things, but he's not so bullheaded as to keep fighting a lost battle. He informed us that he's going to let the McLaughlins know tomorrow, and we should let this go and move on with our lives," he says, shaking his head a little.

I blink, taken aback for a moment. After all the shit they've put us through, I didn't expect Samuel Sr. to give up so easily. Jason looks at me and sighs, rubbing the uninjured side of his face a little.

"I think Mom knew the jig was up, but hearing Dad say as much was the last straw. I've never seen her so... unhinged. Just absolutely detached from reality. She started going off about getting Lydia back here, and how she stole from the family and shouldn't be allowed to walk away. I tuned her out after a while, thinking she'd scream until she tired herself like usual. But then she started talking about what it would take to lure her back home, and I couldn't keep quiet. Because I knew how she'd do it," Jason explains, stopping and starting as he picks his words with care.

I nod solemnly, knowing what he's not saying. Diane Anderson used Lydia's kindness and her protectiveness of Jason against her once before. It wouldn't be a stretch to think she'd do it again.

"Where was your dad in all of this? Surely, he wasn't just sitting, letting his mate fly off the handle," I say as the thought occurs to me.

"Oh, you bet your ass he was just sitting there," Jason throws back heatedly. "But that's just how he is. Getting her to stop once she's started is like trying to keep waves on the shore, so he lets her go. As long as she's not embarrassing him, then he'll just smile and nod and say 'yes, dear,'" he spits bitterly.

I frown and sigh. I can't imagine being married to someone like Diane Anderson is easy, let alone being mated to her. From what Lydia's told me, he's an old-fashioned sort of alpha. So, of course, he wouldn't undermine his wife, the de facto authority figure in the family, in front of his children.

Even though they're all adults now, calling her out for being wrong would be a sign of weakness, and for someone like him, that would be unacceptable.

"When I told her to keep me out of her schemes, she started in on me. How I don't care about my family, and that I've been a bad son, and a poor excuse for an alpha my whole life, blah, blah, blah. It was a lot," he goes on, interrupting my thoughts.

He doesn't say it, but there's a flash in the depths of his emerald eyes that I know well. He's trying to play it off like nothing his mother said hurt, but I know it cut him deeper than he's letting on. But he's speaking again before I can reply.

"She hasn't hit me in years, not since I outgrew her and wasn't afraid of the switch anymore, but when I threw back that if she were any sort of decent mother, then her kids wouldn't be trying to get away from her so bad, she came at me, claws flying."

I suck in a sharp breath, conflicted. I would never, ever condone violence against a woman, but I can't deny that I've considered making an exception for that vile piece of work. So I don't have any room to judge Jason's actions. And besides, if he was acting in self-defense, can I really blame him?

"Don't get me wrong. Even though she was trying to gouge my eyes out, I didn't hit her or nothing. I only shoved her back, just to get her off me. But being the drama queen she is, she hit every chair, table, lamp, and picture frame in the goddamn room on her way to the floor, and then she started wailing like I'd cut off her fucking leg. Well, that's when

Adam decided to jump in and..." Jason finishes, motioning to his face and chest.

I can't help the sigh of relief that escapes me. Now that Lydia is part of my pack, Jason is family, so I'll support him, no matter what. But I can't say it's not easier to do knowing he kicked the ass of someone who deserved it.

"He got one good swing, hence the shiner, but I definitely knocked out a tooth, or four, and broke his nose. The only reason he's not bunk buddies with Darren right now is because Dad barked at us to stop fighting. Adam kept running his mouth, the kiss ass. 'I'm gonna press charges' this, and 'you're a fucking coward' that. But Sammy and Ally were there, and between her telling him exactly what she thought of him, and Sammy backing her up, Adam finally left with Mom to go to the ER. And that's when I told Dad that if this is how I was going to be treated, then I'm out."

There's a warm swelling of pride in my chest, and I reach over and gently clap a hand on his shoulder. Jason's smile is shy again, and he shakes his head, almost in disbelief.

"You're doing the right thing, Jace. And like I've told you before, you have a place with my pack, if you want it," I say soothingly.

Jason shakes his head. "I'm done with packs, at least for now. I'd rather be an alpha outcast than deal with the politics again."

I sigh. Tonight isn't the night to explain how packs in the real world actually function. "Whatever you want. But it's the least we can do to give you a place to stay while you get on your feet."

Jason nods and looks down at his plate. I sit back and give him space. He's been through a lot tonight, and it's going to take time for him to adjust to life outside of his family. When I met Lydia, she'd had four years of space to deconstruct and find herself again. I'll do whatever I can to help Jason work through his past.

"If it's not too much trouble, I might stay here for a while. I've got all my stuff and those boxes I was talking about in my car, and I'd thought I was going to drive out that way tonight. But Lydia'll have kittens if I show up on y'all's front door looking like this," Jason says with a chuckle.

I nod and laugh along. Knowing he got the boxes out safely is a relief, but we can deal with them another day. For now, I get up and head over to the fridge, pulling out two cold beers and bringing them back to the table. After I pop the caps and slide one his way, I hold mine up for a toast.

"To freedom," I say, words lifting in question.

Jason picks up his bottle and clinks it with mine. "To freedom. And revenge."

We both drink deep to that. Now that Jason's safe, there's nothing stopping us from dealing with Diane Anderson, once and for all. And I can't wait to get started.

CHAPTER TWENTY

Alexandra

HUNTER, GIDEON, AND DELANO finally leave after we've confirmed that Mateo and I aren't going to have any adverse reactions to our injections. I can't say I'm sorry to see the back of them. After Delano started making eyes at Mateo, I started counting the minutes until these three were gone for good.

Mateo and I made a simple supper, and after the dishes were done, there was nothing to do except wait. I've changed out of my professional clothes and into comfortable sweats before curling up on the couch. Mateo is in his armchair, flipping through the channels on the television, but not able to settle on anything. It only takes a couple of minutes of this for me to lose patience.

"If you can't pick something, then just turn it off," I snarl, looking out the window to admire the view of over the ocean.

"Not my fucking fault there isn't anything good on," Mateo volleys back.

I scoff and roll my eyes, not in the mood for this. I want to sleep, but my body's buzzing. Only there's no outlet for my nervous energy. We'd been told to avoid contact with anyone, just to be safe. We've already established our alibi, and while the drugs are doing their job, things would be a bit touch and go.

Thankfully, a distraction comes in the form of my phone pinging. I quickly swipe it open and read Lucas's text.

Luc: Guess who just showed up at Alice's.
Me: You know I detest guessing games.
Luc: You're no fun.
Luc: It was Lee Nyueng from the EPD.

I blink at the messages, willing my heart to calm. We'd left him out of the loop for this exact reason, I remind myself. He has nothing to worry about, and doesn't need to lie to the police.

Me: What about?
Luc: He wanted my Christmas goose recipe.
Luc: Why do you think it was here?
Luc: Seth's accident
Me: What did you tell him?
Luc: That I had nothing to do with it, that none of us did. I sent him my time clock records and I'm having the gate guard put together the report of our comings and goings.

I sigh in relief, and Mateo shoots me a curious look.

"Luc got a visit from EPD, asking for alibis," I relay.

Mateo's face goes pale for a moment, and he swallows. "He's set, right? Lydia, too?"

I nod. "I told Caleb to keep Lydia at home as much as possible while we're out of town, and he's done his job. Lucas has a paper trail to confirm his story."

Mateo relaxes and then goes back to flipping channels. My nerves only manage to get through five clicks before I'm on my feet, ripping the remote out of his hand and shutting off the television. Mateo sputters some outraged nonsense, but I take the remote back to my seat and tuck it under me before looking out the window again.

"Don't think I won't move you to get that back," Mateo snaps at me.

I growl low at him, but he doesn't move to challenge me. All the better. I don't feel like getting into a fight with him right now, at least not a physical one. He has at least a hundred pounds on me, and I know how often he and Rhett work out. I'd still put up a fight, but I don't like to lose.

"Rhett is going stir crazy," Mateo says, out of the blue.

I chuckle to myself. That's a bit of an understatement. One of the things I love about Rhett is his seemingly endless energy and drive. Being trapped in one place, no matter how nice, is like caging a tiger. We'll have to run him once he's free.

"Ted says that the case isn't going well for the prosecution. Without Lydia's testimony, it's all he said, she said, and the grand jury is skeptical. If they don't settle on an indictment in the next two weeks, the case will have to be dismissed," I say, a little wistful.

Rhett, Ted, and I have been discussing options for plea deals if the grand jury decides to indict, all with the goal of getting Rhett back to Georgia post haste. A refusal would be the best-case scenario, but I'm not going to put all my eggs in that basket.

"Lydia's heat is coming up, and I don't want her to go through it without him," Mateo comments.

I turn to look at him curiously, and I find him staring unseeing into the middle distance, as if lost in thought. Though I understand his concern this time. Lydia's heat has been on everyone's minds, for better or for worse. It'll be the first time we've gone through an omega's heat since Seth.

"I don't want to go into a rut again," Mateo says, drawing me out of my thoughts.

I snort in agreement. Even if mine wasn't the full thing, seeing Mateo and Rhett undone by the need to claim and bite and fuck isn't something I'm likely to forget.

"I'll make sure everyone stays safe this time," I say with finality.

"I know. But you shouldn't," Mateo returns flippantly.

"What's that supposed to mean?" I snap, temper on a razor's edge.

Mateo shrugs. "If you're caught up in keeping order, you're not going to be able to enjoy yourself."

I blink at him, equal parts annoyed and defensive. "Do you not want everyone to be safe?" I return heatedly.

Mateo throws me a harsh look. "That's not what I said. But whatever. Forget I said anything."

I stare with my mouth slightly agape as he settles into his chair and crosses his arms over his chest, trying to end the conversation. But like hell would I let him do that, not after throwing around a serious accusation like that.

"Lydia's safety and comfort is the number one priority, and if that's not the case for you—"

"Don't. You. Dare. Accuse me of not wanting to protect her," Mateo growls, voice dropping nearly a full octave.

"Our enjoyment shouldn't ever come at the expense of her mental and physical well-being," I finish, lifting my chin a little.

"God, you can't be serious right now. I'm not going to hurt her, Lex. No one is going to," Mateo nearly shouts, throwing his hands up in exasperation.

"You were the one who was just bitching about not wanting to go into a rut again," I return, voice rising to match his.

"Yeah, because I want to remember the moment I bond with her this time!"

I blink and go quiet for a long, tense moment. Understanding comes in waves, each more unsettling than the last.

"What... what do you remember of... the incident?" I ask hesitantly.

Mateo sighs harshly before running his hands through his hair and sitting up with his elbows resting on his knees. He's looking at the floor, eyes wide and distant. I let him think, swallowing hard. Those four days in our suite at The Valencia still haunt my worst nightmares, no matter how hard I've tried to push them down. Watching my pack mates, if not in truth but in my heart, hurt each other over an omega and not be able to do anything to stop them or calm them down, all the while Seth had me trapped in that haze of need. Even now, my blood runs a little colder at the memory of their faces, so twisted with alpha rage, and unrecognizable as the men I'd grown to trust more than my own blood relatives.

"I remember getting out of the elevator, and everything smelling like sticky sweet cherries. And there are flashes. Throwing a vase or something across the room. Lucas cleaning my knuckles in the bathroom. But for the most part... I only remember feeling like I was drowning in rage and need, and I was only able to get my head above water to breathe for a minute or two at a time. The next solid memory I have is waking up on the living room floor, buck naked, with a headache and a busted lip."

Mateo's voice is flat, detached, and his soft brown eyes are shadowed with ghosts I know all too well.

"I remember it. Every moment. Every time he'd look at me and I wasn't able to resist him, even when I really wanted to. I couldn't get us out of there, couldn't do anything—"

"Don't do that to yourself, Lex. You are just as much of a victim in this as the rest of us," Mateo interrupts.

I shake my head, fighting the lump in my throat. He doesn't understand, will never understand. He doesn't have to remember Lucas begging Seth to stop, to let us breathe and take a break. He doesn't have to live with the memory of what Seth did to us, all of us. Seth never touched my beta, but Lucas was violated just as much as any of us. And I should have been able to do something to stop it. I couldn't protect them, and now I'm here, fighting back tears as Mateo stares at me, waiting for a response.

"It's not your job to protect us all the time," Mateo says, voice maddeningly gentle.

"Yes, it is. You chose me as your Prime Alpha, and it's my job to take care of this pack," I snap, looking out the window again.

"But if you're busy protecting us, then who's protecting you? Who's making sure you don't run yourself into the ground, trying to do everything?"

"I don't need protecting," I murmur, not looking at him.

"Bullshit! You're a fucking human being, Alexandra, and you deserve to be protected and loved as much as anyone else," Mateo shouts.

His sudden anger makes me jump, but I don't look at him. I'm hanging on by a thread, though I blame the drugs for that. I know my place, know my role in this pack. I stand in front of my chosen family, and I'll do that no matter what it costs me personally. They deserve the best I can give them.

"I can handle myself. I always have," I finish, setting my shoulders.

"I thought we were past this, but here the fuck we are again," Mateo drawls sardonically.

"Past what?" I ask with a tired sigh.

"You shutting us out. No more secrets, no more hiding, no more lone wolf bullshit," Mateo explains pointedly.

My head snaps back to look at him, but immediately I wish I hadn't. His soft brown eyes aren't angry, but disappointed, and that cuts me to my core. I want to look away again as the burning starts in the backs of my eyes, but the challenge in the set of his brow stops me. I swallow and take a deep breath. It's all too easy to push down my emotions, tucking them away where they can't escape and be used against me.

"I'm not shutting you out—"

"Like hell, you're not. I say one thing that hits a little too close to home, and you're suddenly the Ice Queen again," Mateo volleys, cutting across me.

I roll my eyes, anger surging up to replace the tightness in my chest. I can handle anger, can turn it into something useful.

"Why do you suddenly care? It's not like you're around all that often to do any protecting yourself," I snipe.

"That's not true," Mateo retorts weakly, breaking eye contact and shifting in his seat, like he wants to stand, but decides at the last minute to remain seated.

I roll my eyes again, not that he can see. "Before Lydia came along, we were lucky to see your face once a week. You were too busy doing whatever the fuck you wanted while I had to handle the hard work at home."

"I wasn't doing whatever I wanted. I was out with clients, doing tours, doing my *fucking job*, all the while having to fight off the amateur paparazzi and the gossip rags. Not to mention the monster himself," Mateo shoots back, hands clenching and releasing where they hang between his knees.

I turn my body to face him more fully, straightening my spine. "But when it came down to it, you chose to fuck off rather than come home and be with your pack."

"Like you're one to talk. You buried yourself so far into the Wickland House project, and then Bristol Point, and left the rest of us to fend for ourselves!"

Mateo is on his feet now, pacing away and giving me his back. My primal mind roars at the dismissal in the gesture, and I growl deep in my chest. He doesn't turn at the challenge, running his hands through his hair. The flex of his muscles under his shirt draws my eyes, but I push the flash of feeling aside, letting it join the rest of the emotions in the back of my mind.

"I was doing my job, the same as you," I snarl, lifting my chin defiantly.

He lets out a single humorless chuckle, throwing his head back before turning back to me, eyes narrowed in a glare. "You're always just 'doing your job.' Because it's work first, no matter what. I should have known from the beginning you would always be in it for yourself."

I get to my feet and advance a step in his direction, but he stands his ground, spine curling defensively. Not that I care at this point. This is years of things unspoken between us finally coming to the surface. And if he wants to go there, then I can, too.

"Everything I've done has been in the name of protecting us, protecting this pack, and making sure we could survive and thrive. I was the one who backed you and Rhett when you had no clients, no experience. Just a dream and a half-baked plan. I used every tool in my arsenal to make sure you got what you wanted. But it was never enough for you, was it?" I shout.

His laugh is more like a snarl, and the ugly twist to his mouth stokes the furious flame in my gut. "I never asked for any of that shit, Lex. I thought you wanted business partners, not charity cases. And if we were so pitiful and in desperate need of your help, why the fuck did you even bother?"

"Because I believed in you!"

"No! You saw us as a means to your own ends! Rhett had the education to make your visions viable, and I've just been the pretty face you parade in front of investors to make sure you have the funds you need to do all the things you want to do." Mateo points an accusatory finger in my direction as he speaks, his face contorted and flushed in his anger.

I can't help the affronted gasp as I reel back from him. "That is not—I have never once—"

Mateo laughs again and spreads his arms wide in triumph. "Then how the fuck do you explain what you did with the Wickland House funding? You went behind our backs and did what you allegedly 'had to do,' but guess what? You didn't have to do any of it! We could have found another project to work on, one that wouldn't have saddled us with a fucking sociopath omega hellbent on destroying us."

I'm too stunned to speak as I take in his words, each hitting me like a blow. My guilt surges back to the surface, and I can't respond. Because he's right. I wanted Wickland House so badly, and I couldn't stand the thought of not getting my way. And everything that's happened since is my fault.

I turn away, not willing to let him see the tears threatening to spill over. Breathing through it, I try to force my mind to think of anything else to get my emotions under control. I can't let him see how deep he cut. I need to get it together.

"Even now, you're hiding from me. What are you so fucking afraid of?" Mateo throws at me.

"I'm not afraid," I protest, but even I can tell there's no power behind it.

"Horse shit. You're terrified of being the person your father tried to make you into," Mateo accuses.

I flinch away, but then defensive anger surges up again, giving me back control. I let my face go blank, no emotion for him to exploit as I turn back to face him. The shift knocks him off balance, and he blinks, staggering back a step. Good.

"And who would that be?" I ask mildly.

Mateo recovers quickly, motioning at me with an open hand. "This. This cold, calculating bitch who would rather die than admit she gives a shit about anyone or anything," he says emphatically.

I roll my eyes. "If you've felt this way, why didn't you leave? Rhett would have gone with you, and Lucas, too. If I'm such a terrible person, then why did you stay?" I ask, words a flat, low monotone.

There's silence for a long time, and my heart cracks for a moment before it hardens. He wants to leave, and why not? He'll be able to get his life back after this weekend, and there won't be anything tying him down. I turn away, suddenly exhausted. But then suddenly a gentle hand on my shoulder turns me around. I look up into Mateo's face, the anger gone, leaving behind a swirling pit of emotions in his fawn-colored eyes.

"Because you're not a terrible person, Lex. I've never thought you were. You are probably the best of us. Hell, if you were a terrible person, you would have admitted to the fraud and just paid the fine, and called it the cost of doing business. And no matter how hard you try, you can't be the person your father wants. You have such a good heart and strong conscience that it ate you up inside, and you care so much about us, even if you don't always show it," he says, voice softer now.

Shaking my head, I try to look away, but he grabs my chin between his thumb and forefinger, pulling my eyes back up to meet his. I'm not prepared for the warmth of his little smile, or the intensity of his stare, and I choke out a sob. I was prepared for the anger, but this acceptance and forgiveness is too much. The guilt and fear and heartache break free of the box I've been putting it in for the last three years, spilling down my cheeks in unstoppable waves.

"I'm sorry. For all of it. I didn't... I can't stand the idea of letting any of you down. I try so hard..."

As my words die in choking sobs, Mateo gathers me up in his arms without hesitation, and pulls me tight into his chest. I return the embrace just as fiercely, unable to help myself. His touch grounds me, especially the hand that runs up and down my spine. He smells like lemons and sunshine, and all the good things I don't know if I deserve. I take deep, gulping breaths of it while I can, closing my eyes and basking in his warmth. We sway gently on the spot, not speaking until my tears stop. I swear his lips brush the top of my head, my stomach flipping a little, but I brush it off. My imagination is getting away from me again.

"I'm sorry, too. I ran because... because I couldn't go any-where in Everton without thinking about him. And I didn't want to burden y'all with what was going on in my head. But I never actually wanted to leave, not permanently. You and Rhett mean everything to me. With Lucas and Lydia, we're going to be a family," he mutters, and now I can't deny the feel of his lips brushing my hair as he speaks, or the flutter in my belly it brings.

I can't help the little smile that forms as he speaks, the im-age of all of us together after everything we've been through warming my heart. We fall silent for another moment, hold-ing each other as the sound of crashing surf fills the air. I have to think about the last time I let someone do this, and it makes my stomach drop to realize that it's been months... maybe even years. But this feels... right. Safe. And even as I fight the instinct to melt into him, I can feel something else in the air, like the final notes of a symphony, suspended in that liminal space before the conductor drops his arms, and the audience erupts in cathartic applause.

Mateo cracks the silence as he clears his throat and shifts slightly. Not letting me go, but adjusting his weight. I brace myself, not sure what I'm expecting him to do next.

"If we're clearing the air, I do have one more question, and it's been bugging me for years," he says suddenly.

But that sure as shit isn't it. I lean back to look up at him, brow furrowed in question. His eyes are darker now, and he's smirking. I almost pull away, but if I'm being honest with myself, I don't know if I could leave his embrace if someone paid me to right now.

"The last night of the conference, when we were in the hotel bar, and we invited you back to our room, you said you never mixed business with pleasure," Mateo says.

I flush hot and look away, pursing my lips to hide my smile. I remember that night, and I can't say it doesn't rank pretty high on my list of regrets. At the time, I was too worried about people using me for my name, and I didn't want anyone to accuse me of using my feminine charms to get what I wanted. But even then, it was a flimsy excuse. Rhett and Mateo didn't have any influence, and we'd already agreed that we should work together. The chemistry was there then, and hasn't diminished in the slightest over the last decade.

"I'm not sure what question you're asking," I say slowly.

"Well, I'm calling bullshit. You most certainly mix business with pleasure, with both Rhett and Lucas. I guess I'm asking... was—is it me you don't want to fuck?"

I look up at him in surprise, caught completely off guard. His face is so open, so vulnerable, and he's never looked more beautiful. His arms are steel bands around my waist, no room for escape from his question. My heart beats wildly, and I blink a few times as I try to get my brain to form a response. Every moment of my silence that passes, I can see the heat filling his eyes, challenge and invitation mixing together. My skin breaks out into goosebumps, and our chests brush each other with each breath. The last note of the symphony we've been dancing to for years fades, leaving only the undeniable truth. One that I've denied for too long, but no more.

Reaching up, I grab him by the back of the neck, pulling his lips down to meet mine.

CHAPTER TWENTY-ONE

Mateo

I FREEZE FOR A moment as my lips meet Lex's, but then something switches in my mind. One of my hands tangles in her hair, loosening the messy bun she'd thrown it in earlier, while my other hand pulls her tight to my chest, fingers digging into her side. I feel her trying to pull away, but I can't let her go. She tastes like bay laurels and liquor, and I'm drunk off the first taste. When she breaks for air, I kiss down her neck, the salty taste of her skin making my cock hard. She sighs, clinging to my shoulders for dear life.

"It was never about business and pleasure, Mateo. I have needs, and I didn't know back then if either of you could handle me. Rhett has proven himself, but you don't play like we do. Or at least you claim you don't," Lex nearly purrs, her body pressed to mine.

"Just because I'm not into whips and chains, that doesn't mean I can't handle you," I retort into the juncture of her neck and shoulder, hackles rising at her challenge.

I grip her tighter and try to walk us backwards toward the couch, but she doesn't move. We're kissing again, lips moving together, but she won't yield. I growl low in my throat, and she growls right back. Then her hands are in my hair and she's yanking my head back hard, but the pain is secondary to the sudden throbbing in my jeans. Her teeth scrape the column of my throat, catching on my Adam's apple for a moment before she tries to claim my mouth again. Her laugh, low and sensuous, only adds fuel to the fire in my lower belly. Moving before she can stop me, I grab her wrist and pull her fingers from my hair. The motion puts her off balance and I use the momentum to my advantage, dropping my opposite shoulder and hauling her off the floor and across my back.

I only manage a few steps toward the master bedroom before she recovers and starts scratching and kicking. An elbow to my back makes me grunt, and I stumble sideways as I cough. Using my moment of weakness, Lex manages to wrap her legs around my waist, forcing me to let go of her arm as her weight shifts, and I grab her under her thighs so she doesn't fall. Her hands are back in my hair, and then we're kissing again, a vicious meeting of lips and tongues and teeth, like we're trying to devour each other and can't get our fill.

Her legs grip me tight, but I stumble forward until her back meets the wall of the hallway leading to the master bedroom. She's grinding her core against my crotch, and I dig my fingers into her hips, matching her rhythm, then pressing her forward and trapping her body with mine. With her ankles locked behind my back, I reach up and grab her throat, pinning her head against the wall. We finally break apart to breathe, but her hands don't stop moving through my hair, down my neck, and across my shoulders, nails scraping hard.

I almost lose myself in the sight of her, wearing my hand like a necklace made of the finest diamonds. Her chin lifts, hazel sparks in her eyes as she waits for me to make my next move. Her lipstick, that signature crimson war paint, hasn't moved an inch.

"If you think I'm going to be your obedient little fuck toy, you've got another thing coming, princess," I pant, squeezing her elegant neck a little tighter.

"Promises, promises, Mateo. I hope you can cash the checks your mouth keeps writing," she purrs, completely undeterred.

I growl and pull her away from the wall, striding toward the bedroom with purpose. Careful of her head on the door-frame, I slam the door closed with a solid kick behind us. The room is dark, but I find the bed with ease. It takes more of my strength than I would have anticipated to get her to let go, but when I do, I send her flying backward onto the mattress. I whip off my shirt before she even hits the covers, and then I'm pouncing on her while she's stunned.

My hands find her breasts and squeeze hard, kneading the soft flesh as my mouth finds hers again. She's not wearing a bra, so my palms brush her nipples even through the material of her shirt. I swallow her moan, positioning myself between her thighs and grinding my rock-hard length against the apex. Her nails drag down my back, adding a bite of pain that makes me hiss and draw back slightly. She hooks one of her legs around mine and leverages me onto my back, pulling my hands from her tits and pinning them above my head. Sitting up slightly, her dark hair cascades around her gorgeous face, her lips pulled up in a smirk as she rolls her hips.

I curse at the bolt of pleasure zipping up my spine, matching her rhythm even as she tries to maintain control. I use that moment of distraction and twist my hands free, one of them going back to her throat and the other into her hair. Flipping us again, I bite her lower lip as I press her hard into the mattress. She's smirking as I pull away, but it fades to a gasp as I roll my hips, the rough material of my jeans hitting her right on her clit. Her eyes roll back for a moment, and I smirk in triumph.

"Feels good, doesn't it, princess?" I purr, letting her hair go and trailing my hand down her chest.

She's too lost in her pleasure to notice when I take fistfuls of her shirt and pull hard, tearing the material and revealing her bare chest. She gasps, eyes flying open at the sound. My mouth descends on her right nipple, sucking hard and biting. She bucks, hands threading into my hair and holding me to her breasts. But then I ease off, teasing licks across the swells, down to the valley between, and then back up to the other.

"Fuck me," she groans, trying to flip us again, but I use my weight advantage to hold her in place.

"That's the plan, Lex," I retort, unable to keep from laughing even as I bite her other nipple hard.

It feels good to sink my teeth into her soft flesh, and judging by the little sounds she's making, she's enjoying herself, too. I drag my nails down her stomach, teasing the skin along the hem of her leggings. She's lost in the feeling of my mouth on her breasts, and I want to keep her there. She deserves to let go, and if I have to exert every ounce of dominance and willpower I have in me to get her there, then I will do it gladly. But she recovers quickly, snarling low in her throat. I look up at the sound, and watch as she cocks her hand back, as if going to slap me. But I'm faster. My hand darts out, wrapping my fingers around her wrist and pinning it to the bed, and grabbing her slender throat again, and squeezing.

"None of that. Not a fucking chance," I snap, sitting up slightly.

"Don't like being smacked around by a girl?" she taunts breathlessly.

"No, and if you want to talk shit, I'll find another use for that fucking mouth," I retort.

Lex laughs, the sound grating on something I didn't know existed inside of me. It's like a switch flips and I feel this overwhelming need to see her submit to me. I use my grip on her throat to drag her to the nearest edge of the bed, shoving her down to the floor while my free hand frees my aching cock from my jeans. I only shove my pants and underwear down enough to allow it to spring forward, already throbbing and leaking.

"Suck," I order, pulling Lex up until her face is level with my erection.

Now that my eyes have adjusted more to the darkness, I can see her looking up at me through her lashes, eyes wide. I shift my grip from her neck to her hair, pulling hard enough that she gasps, and I press my advantage. The warmth of her mouth, the wet slide of her tongue on the underside of my cock, makes my knees buckle, and I curse again. Lex closes her lips around me, bobbing eagerly up and down my length without any prompting. She takes me farther and farther down her throat until her lips are brushing against my swollen knot. Then she has the audacity to look up at me again, and something between a growl and a purr spills from my throat.

"Just like that, fuck. Such a good girl," I babble mindlessly as she retreats, swirling her tongue around the head.

Lex pulls back with a gasp, panting hard. Her hands take over where her mouth had been, stroking in tandem so my entire length is stimulated at once.

"I'm not your fucking good girl," she says once she's caught her breath.

I laugh outright, but the sound is cut off by a guttural groan as she squeezes my knot, hard. With no warning, my balls tighten, and my spine tingles. I grab her wrists and yank her to her feet before she makes me cum before I'm ready. Her smug little smirk sets me off again, and I stand up, spinning around and shoving her face first into the mattress, bent over. I rip her leggings down, along with her lace panties, and immediately bury my face in her dripping cunt.

Whatever protest she was about to make dies in a long moan at the first long stroke of my tongue over her slit. She's absolutely soaked, and I drink down every drop of her fruity sweet juices. There's a tart aftertaste that I've never experienced with Lydia, but it's not unpleasant. If anything, it makes me want more, to quench my thirst with her essence until she's limp and boneless and pliant. To that end, I move my mouth to suck on her clit, sliding two fingers deep into her fluttering pussy, hooking them as I feel that rough patch of nerves that sends her screaming.

"Don't stop. Don't you dare fucking stop," she whines, hips thrusting back onto my face and fingers.

I grin to myself, slowing my fingers and curling them purposefully. She gasps and arches her back, and I move to hold her down with one forearm across her lower back. Her feet can't quite touch the floor, so she has no leverage to get anything more than I'm willing to give. And right now, that's only one thing.

"Beg," I growl, twisting my fingers cruelly, letting her dangle on the edge.

"Not a fucking chance. Fuck—give it to me," she cries, hands struggling for purchase on the duvet cover.

But I press her down harder, ghosting my thumb over her clit and making her shriek before backing off. Her skin is slick with sweat, and she's fighting like a rabbit caught in a snare, but I hold on. I will get this from her, no matter what. I slap her ass hard, the crack ringing through the darkness and making her pussy clench on my fingers.

"If you want to come, you're going to have to beg me for it, princess," I taunt, adding a third finger to stretch her even farther.

Her juices run down my wrist, and her thighs are shaking, but she doesn't speak. She only lets out guttural, animalistic whines. I know she's close, but I keep my thrusts slow and deliberate. The rush of power makes my head spin and cock throb, and I purr in my chest.

"Fuck you, Mateo. Fuck you right in the ass with a cactus," she spits, flopping limp on the bed.

I laugh outright, spanking her again, harder still. She gasps and shrieks, and I do it again and again. I won't have her give up on me that easily. Daring to circle her clit with my thumb, she moans long and low, pushing up her torso backward, nearly in half.

"Don't stop... p—Mateo, I'm—"

"You know what to say, princess. One little word, and I let you come, and I won't stop making you come for the rest of the night," I say, words dropping to a frantic murmur.

For a moment, I think she's about to call me names again, insulting my manhood, or worse, tell me to stop. But as her hazel eyes meet mine, and I see the tears lining the edges, something shifts between us and understanding dawns. She's afraid to let go, to give me that power because she doesn't know what I'll do with it. Little does she know that I've always been there waiting to catch her. So I give her a smile and a nod, and finally, she yields.

"Please," she breathes, closing her eyes.

I drive my hand deep into her clenching channel, pressing hard and fast against her sweet spot. She screams as she shatters, muscles tightening so hard around my hand that it takes most of my strength to move my fingers and keep her coming. I stand up, even as I keep fucking her with my fingers, and she's too blissed out to notice or protest. She's squeezing me so hard that I'm not sure I'll be able to withdraw, but my instincts are screaming for me to claim her, to fill her so completely that she'll never be able to get me out from under her skin. There's only the briefest pause between pulling my fingers free and sliding the entire length of my cock into her spasming cunt, and she screams a string of profanity so strong it'd make a sailor blush.

"That's it. Take my dick in that pussy. Fuck, you are so tight," I groan, thrusting hard and fast.

She pushes back, our hips slapping together obscenely as we both ride waves of pleasure. She's tight and warm, the feeling of her nearly taking the strength out of my knees. My knot brushes her outer lips each time, her arousal coating me until it soaks into my clothes. I don't know if she ever stopped coming after her first orgasm, but she screams my name as her pussy clenches tighter. Bringing my hand down on her ass, she moans, bucking at the sensation. I spank her over and over, not sure where the impulse came from, but enjoying her reaction too much to care.

Instinct takes over, and I grab her by the waist and drag her up onto the bed, never withdrawing. I need to cover her, to make her mine in every way that matters. She doesn't protest, merely going limp in my arms, too drunk from her release to care. I flip her onto her back and push her thighs to her chest, spearing her again on my cock. She lets me rut into her, eyes staring unfocused as she continues to writhe and moan beneath me.

"Look at me," I bark, the growl making my bones rattle.

Her head flops over until her eyes lock with mine, a little clarity coming back. I let one of her legs fall to the side, putting my hand around her throat again.

"You were made to wear my hand around your neck, Alexandra. You were made to be fucked like this," I whisper hoarsely, spine tingling as my orgasm approaches.

She doesn't respond, only whimpering as my angle shifts and my pelvis grinds into her clit with each thrust. She swallows against my fingers, and I kiss her again, dragging her lower lip between my teeth.

"You want my cum? Want me to breed your greedy pussy like it deserves?" I snarl, leaning down to press my forehead to hers.

She nods, but that's not good enough for me right now. I slow my thrusts, driving deep and hard, making the bed shake. Gasping, her eyes roll back into her head. But I squeeze her throat and bring her focus back to me.

"Say it, princess. Tell me you want it," I demand, hanging on by a thread.

She growls, the fight coming back into her eyes at last. "Fuck, yes! Give it to me! Do it, you fucking—"

She doesn't finish whatever she'd been intending to say, screaming as I slam home, my knot slipping inside of her channel and swelling to lock in place. I roar as my entire body thrums from the intensity of my orgasm, each pulse of my cock shooting cum deep inside of her.

We're silent for a long time, and as I become more aware of myself again, I realize that my knot is being squeezed tighter than I've ever felt before. Lydia's body is soft and accepting, which allowed some freedom of movement even after my knot locked into place. But right now, I'm not sure I could move an inch if I tried.

"Holy shit, Matty. Fucking... wow," Lex pants.

"Let's get... yeah, my legs are shaking," I reply with a breathy laugh.

"I know, right?" she replies, voice lighter than I've ever heard before.

It takes a minute to maneuver, but I eventually manage to scoop her into my arms and get us into bed, lying us on our sides. I want to hold her, but I'm not sure if that's the right move. She's never been a touchy-feely person before. Does she do after sex cuddles?

"I can practically hear you thinking from here. Just fucking put your arms around me, you colossal dork," Lex sighs, half joking, half exasperated.

I chuckle nervously as I pull her to my chest, and we're quiet again. A million thoughts race through my head, but I can't pin them down. And it doesn't help that her pussy is still pulsing, and each clench and release on my knot scrambles my brain all over again.

"Let me save you some anguish. This can mean something, or it can mean nothing. We can let our alpha bits calm down, clean up, and then go to bed in our separate rooms, and pretend like this never happened," she goes on, not looking at me.

I swallow, my heart twisting unexpectedly. "Or...?" I prompt.

"Or we can sleep in this bed tonight, maybe have some lazy morning sex, and figure out what comes next over coffee. And let the pack know. Either way, we should tell them," Lex finishes with a resigned, contented sigh.

I think for a moment, but I know my heart has already made its decision. I tilt her chin up so she can see the honesty in my eyes as I speak. "I don't want this to mean nothing, Lex. And I don't want to pretend it never happened."

Lex smiles, a genuine thing that lights up her whole face and makes my heart skip a beat. "I was hoping you'd say that."

My heart melts a little, even as my knot deflates, and her pussy finally unclenches enough for me to withdraw. She moves to sit up, but I pull her back down and kiss her again, gently this time. I cup the side of her face as we break apart, stroking her cheek lightly.

"Don't get all mushy on me now, Mat. Or I'll think you aren't the beast who just fucked me silly. And I *really* liked him," Lex teases, her lips brushing mine as she stays close.

"Lucky for you, I'm a man of many talents."

She laughs and pulls away fully. I recline back and watch her shed what's left of her shirt and pants before moving to turn down the covers. Shucking my damp and sticky clothes, I slide under the blankets and pull her back to my chest, closing my eyes.

If you'd told me yesterday that I'd be falling asleep next to a naked and fully sated Alexandra St. Clair, I would have laughed. But now that it's happened, I can't believe we didn't try this sooner.

CHAPTER TWENTY-TWO

Lydia

MY PHONE GOES OFF in the middle of Lucas and me cooking brunch. Caleb and Gabby are in the sitting room, and their bickering reaches us even across the open floor plan. I catch something political and know it's best to stay out of it. I'm switching out a batch of toast as a message chimes on my phone, and I glance at the screen. A grin splits my face as I see Mateo's name pop up.

Mateo: Good morning, baby. Do you have a second to talk?

I swipe my phone from the counter and dial his number, and he picks up on the first ring.

"Lydia! I didn't expect you to call so soon," he exclaims happily.

"Hey, good morning. I'm cooking with Luc, but I can spare a few minutes to chat. What's up?" I ask, leaning forward to rest my elbows on the counter, my back to the room.

"Just wanted to hear your voice. I miss you," he coos, and I roll my eyes.

"Matty, it's been less than two days," I scoff.

"I know, but still," he retorts playfully.

"If you're that lonely, you and Lex could always work out some tension," I tease, smirking.

Instead of the usual immediate denials, I'm met with the world's loudest silence. I blink several times, waiting for him to respond.

"Mateo, you and Lex..."

"Look, it's not like we planned it or anything," Mateo grumbles when I trail off.

I let out a whoop of triumph, drawing the attention of everyone in the room.

"I fucking *knew* it!" I crow, laughing my head off.

"Lydia, have you lost your damn mind?" Gabby asks, sounding both amused and concerned.

"Matty and Lexi sitting in a tree. F-U-C-K-I-N-G," I sing, doing a little happy dance.

"Jesus Christ. What are you, eight?" Mateo groans, and I can almost picture the exact shade of red he's probably turning.

"Wait, what? No, they didn't!" Lucas chirps, perking up.

"Wait, who's doing who now?" Gabby shouts from the sectional.

"I thought you said you're cooking with Luc. Who else is over there?" Mateo asks sharply.

"Gabby," I tell him, pulling the phone away from my face for a minute. "Lex and Mateo finally boned," I shout, throwing the hand not holding my phone into the air in celebration.

"You're shitting me. Really?" Lucas nearly shouts, turning to face me with a wide grin and excited eyes.

"That's the word on the street. Mateo and Lex finally caved and danced the horizontal tango," I say in mock seriousness, smirking to myself as Mateo coughs.

Lucas bursts out laughing, nearly dropping the pan of eggs he was stirring. Gabby joins him in his mirth, and I smirk as I put my phone back to my ear.

"Did you have to make it sound like that?" Mateo sighs, exasperated.

I'm about to respond, when Lucas motions for my phone, still laughing. Intensely curious about what he might have to say, I hold it out eagerly.

"I gotta know, Matty. Did she—" Lucas cuts himself off, laughter bubbling up again until he's breathless. He tries to start the sentence several more times, losing it before he can finish the thought, but he finally manages to pull himself together long enough to speak. "Did she top from the bottom, or—"

Whatever Mateo says in response sets Lucas off again, and he can barely breathe as he hands the phone back to me, wiping the tears from his eyes. When I put the phone back up to my ear, Lex's voice sounds in the background, even if her words aren't clear enough for me to understand. But I don't need them to recognize the annoyed, exasperated tone she's using.

"What? It's the truth!" Mateo is responding, and I laugh.

"So do we need to hire a contractor to patch the holes y'all put in the walls? Is the bedframe still intact, or do we need to order a new one?" I comment through my chuckles.

"We shouldn't leave you alone with Lucas anymore. He's a bad influence," Mateo groans, but it lacks any real heat.

"Speaking of not leaving us alone, do you think you'll be back by Monday?" I ask, moving back to the toaster as it pops again.

"I hope so. And then I've got something to show you," he says excitedly.

"Oh? It better not be a surprise, because you know we've put a moratorium on those," I say in a mock stern voice.

Mateo laughs again, and my heart melts at the sound. My skin prickles a little, my pussy clenching on air. God, I need him to get back here.

"It's not a surprise. Well, not a new surprise. I want to show you the building you never got to see," Mateo says.

I blush a little, a flash of old guilt coming forward. I push it aside, done feeling sorry for myself.

"I'm sorry to cut this short; we've got to go do a thing. If everything goes smoothly, we'll be back tomorrow night, and then I can show you The Garden the day after, okay?" Mateo says distractedly.

I agree and we say our goodbyes, and when we hang up, I'm left feeling more relaxed than I'd thought I'd feel. Ever since Rhett introduced me to the concept of polyamory, I keep having these moments of revelation, like pieces falling into place that I didn't even realize were missing. I'd sensed tension between Mateo and Lex, but I'd never pushed them to explain it or solve it. And knowing that my pack mates are working things out settles a little slice of my soul. I'd have to ask Sylvie about this the next time I see her.

"You owe me $100, by the way," Gabby is saying from the sitting room.

I look up at her, confused, but realize she's not talking to me when Caleb scoffs loudly. "That wasn't a real wager," he protests.

"We shook on it and everything! You two-timing—"

"What was the bet?" I ask, cutting in before Gabby can work up a full head of steam.

She gives Caleb another glare and then gets up and saunters over to sit at the kitchen island counter. "I'd bet him that your pack would become one giant queer fuck puddle by the time you went into heat again. The Albanian Asshole—"

"I'm not from Albania!" Caleb interjects loudly, accent coming forward a little more.

Gabby rolls her eyes before continuing. "*He* said that would never happen because Mateo and Lex would never knock boots. He was stupid enough to doubt me and my absolutely infallible sexual tension detecting skills."

"I can't believe you're placing bets about our sex lives," I scold, but my smile betrays me.

"The conditions haven't been fully met, anyway," Caleb protests, either not hearing me or ignoring me.

As Gabby pauses to think, Lucas and I share a look. It's up to him if he wants to rain on Caleb's parade, and judging by the spark of mischief in his steel-blue eyes, he's more than happy to stir the pot.

"Hate to break it to ya, my guy. But you're going to have to pay up," Lucas drawls, his voice full of fake remorse.

Gabby gasps dramatically, slamming her hands on the counter. "You. Did. NOT! You and—and you—babe, you knew—"

I snort and continue plating toast. "Oh, I've known. And witnessed," I reply cryptically, trying to hide my blush.

"And you didn't fucking tell me! You bitch!" Gabby exclaims, trailing off into laughter even as Caleb groans from the couch.

"What can I say? It's not my fault that no one can keep their hands off me," Lucas snarks, striking a pose to flex his muscles.

I scoff and laugh, about to protest, but my phone pings again. This time, with a message from my brother.

> **Jason: Hey. What are you doing this week?**
> **Me: Apartment hunting with Gabby. Why?**
> **Jason: No reason.**

I roll my eyes and show the messages to Gabby, who's sulking a little now. Her mouth pulls down in a little frown of confusion before she looks back at me.

"What's going on with him? He's been super cryptic with me lately," I ask, shoving my phone away and moving to find plates.

Gabby shrugs, but stays uncharacteristically silent. And as I turn back to her, I realize she's blushing.

"Spill. What the hell has he told you?" I demand, setting the plates on the counter next to Lucas and rounding on her.

She opens her mouth like she's about to start speaking, but then closes it again. I give her a hard stare, but she looks away, blushing deeper now.

"He's been going through it, and he doesn't want to worry you, okay? It's not like he's hurt or anything," Gabby groans, words tumbling out as she can't keep them in any longer.

I sigh, not sure how to respond. I don't like him keeping me in the dark, but I'm glad he's talking to someone. Things down there can't be easy after the mess I left behind. I wish I knew how to fix it, or to get my family to go away and leave me alone. Unlike other members of my pack, I don't care enough about them anymore to want to see them ruined or disgraced. I just want to live my life without having to look over my shoulder all the damn time.

"I know that look. Don't start feeling guilty for shit that doesn't have anything to do with you. Jason's a whole ass adult and can handle his business without his big sister trying to interfere," Gabby says sternly, even going as far as to wag a finger in my face.

I purse my lips, knowing she's right. I want to help, but doing anything right now would probably hurt more than it would help. He'll tell me when the time is right, I'm sure.

"So how many times do you think Lex and Mateo are going to fuck before they get back?" Lucas says, masterfully changing the subject.

We move to the dining table, Caleb joining us to eat. Gabby and Lucas go back and forth, wildly speculating about Mateo and Lex's hook up, and I let myself get lost in their banter. I can't let go of the nagging worry in the back of my mind, but I can push it far enough back to not let it spoil the day. And that's good enough for now.

CHAPTER TWENTY-THREE

Lucas

THE MORNING AFTER MATEO and Lex returned from their fuck-cation—or business trip, as they keep trying to call it—I'm lounging on one of the sofas in Lex's boudoir, watching her as she gets ready for work. I'm in sweatpants, sans shirt, and I can feel the watery rays of autumn sunlight hitting the backs of my arms where they're spread out on either side of me along the back of the sofa. This is a late start for Lex, but she did wear both of us out pretty thoroughly last night.

"Have you talked to Rhett recently?" I question, raising my voice so she can hear me from her position at her bathroom vanity.

"Not since last night," she responds evenly.

I hum, thinking back to my last conversation with my absent alpha. When Lydia and I tried to initiate a video call Saturday night, he'd declined with a flimsy excuse of being too tired from working out. We'd both known it was bullshit, but decided not to press. Rhett is trapped in an apartment with only a treadmill for exercise equipment. Rhett is a bit of a gym rat, but he's not a runner. So when I'd called him again the next day, I didn't let him off the phone until he fessed up.

And that's when I found out that Jason, Lydia's brother, has been staying with Rhett for the last few days. Rhett's loyalty to this pack is unshaking, so it's not like I suspected anything untoward, especially considering that Jason is painfully straight. But I didn't like that he was trying to hide it. But Jason insisted that he wants to talk to Lydia in person and explain everything. So he'll be heading our way this week, and they made me promise to not tell Lydia.

They failed to make me promise I wouldn't tell Lex. Because like hell was I going to let her be caught unaware in this mess.

"Rhett promised to tell me when Jason leaves," Lex continues, words almost patronizingly calm.

"I don't like Lydia being kept in the dark. We all know how well that went over last time," I throw back.

"I know. I said as much, but Jason said he'd take full responsibility for us not telling her."

Good. I don't want Lydia to think we're backsliding. Not after all the progress we've made.

Lex struts out of the bathroom in nothing but her short silk dressing gown, heading toward her extensive collection of clothes. I follow her movements with my eyes, licking my lips as the curve of her ass peeks out from the bottom hem when she reaches for an upper shelf. Her scent is everywhere in here, but a fresh wave of spicy orange notes hits me when she catches me staring.

"Has Lydia mentioned of any heat symptoms?" Lex asks, turning back to her clothes.

I have to make an effort to ignore the growing hardness in my sweats as I clear my throat. "Not to me. But she's been... extra eager for attention, and not just sexual attention."

Lex hums thoughtfully, pulling out two dresses and making a show of trying to choose between them. The one in her left hand is an eggplant-colored vintage style wiggle dress, with a square neckline and little cap sleeves. The other is a more modern sheath dress, black with a sheer illusion neckline.

"Go with the black one," I rasp, the words spilling out of my throat before I have the chance to catch them.

Lex throws me a look, a knowing twinkle in her eyes. Lex could wear a literal potato sack and still be the sexiest, most powerful woman on the face of the Earth. But seeing her in black, like she's already dressed for your funeral before she's even laid a finger on you, makes the wires in my brain cross. I can never decide if I should kneel at her feet in submission, or if I should bend her over the nearest horizontal surface, pull her hair, and make her scream my name.

"I'll need your help with something. Do you mind?"

Lex's purr pulls me from my fantasies and back to reality, only to make me question if I've died and gone to heaven. She's slipped into her usual garter belt and lacey underwear, along with some black thigh-highs attached to the end of clips. But she's holding a long-line bra to her chest, a demure expression pulling on her red-painted lips. I sit up straighter and try to adjust my raging hard on as subtly as I can, nodding. Her smile is pure deviousness as she slowly spins to give me her back, pulling her hair over one shoulder. I can't help myself; I let my eyes wander down her back, over the fully exposed cheeks of her peachy ass and...

Fuck me, she's wearing the tights with seams.

I'm throbbing in my pants now, and the situation only gets worse as she drops to sit on my lap, wriggling a little to get comfortable. I know she can feel me through the thin material, but she declines to comment. I'm taking several deep breaths to try to control myself when she clears her throat pointedly.

"I do have to get going soon, Luc," she comments.

I growl a little in my throat. Oh, *now* she suddenly remembers she has to work.

I start on the little hook-and-eye closures, which are God's curse unto men. I hope whoever invented this type of bra closure is burning in their own private pool of lava in Hell.

"With Lydia's heat, I know we haven't really talked about it in a while, but..."

My hands pause as Lex trails off, suddenly hesitant. I stay quiet, knowing my silence will do more good than trying to question her. I'm rewarded when she sighs and looks over her shoulder at me.

"I still want you as my bond mate. You and Lydia are... you're my whole world."

Her eyes are bright, the hazel reflecting olive green in this light. The naked emotion in the depths startles me for a moment, but I mentally shake myself.

"I still want you, too, Lex. I know we've been through a lot, but that's never changed. I love you just as much today as I did when you asked me the first time," I reply emphatically.

Her answering smile makes my whole body flush with joy. Alexandra's smiles are as rare and precious as diamonds to me. She turns back around, and I finish with her bra. She adjusts it slightly, and I expect her to get up and finish getting dressed, but she spins until she's straddling me. I automatically put my hands on her hips to hold her steady, and she rests her hands on my neck, thumbs stroking the stubble on my jaw.

"Do I need to look into the logistics? I want to make sure we're prepared before we go in, so we don't get lost in the heat of the moment," she starts seriously.

I blink, and it takes me a minute to figure out what she means. But then I grin as I grasp her meaning.

"Lydia has been spending a lot of time with Caleb's mate, Sylvie, getting omega lessons. They've told me what we've got to do to make a bond stick between us," I say, voice dropping to a husky purr.

She cocks her head and waits for me to go on. I glance down her toned stomach, and then back up over her amazing tits and then to her face, letting my eyes drag in a slow tease while the tension builds.

"When Lydia goes into heat, she'll need to come a few times, to make sure she's fully under. I'll take care of that, and I'm going to make sure to get plenty of her scent on me. Then, the next time she needs to be fucked, either you or Rhett can knot her."

I keep my voice low so she has to lean in close to hear me. My mouth waters as I take deep inhales of her fruit and spice scent, and it takes most of my control to stop myself from grinding my cock into her hot, dripping core that's poised just right over me. She watches my face closely, the faintest blush rising on her cheeks. But like the good Domme she is, her face gives nothing else away.

"Once one of y'all is locked in, you're going to want to bite her, to claim her. That's when I'll step in, and she'll redirect you to bite me instead," I finish.

Lex nods thoughtfully, and I grip her hips a little harder, adjusting myself under her, hoping to gain any sort of momentary friction. But she moves with me, and I bite my lip to keep from groaning.

"Is the knot necessary? Or can we both bite you at the same time?" she asks, seeming genuinely curious.

I shake my head. "The knot makes the alpha and the omega release bonding pheromones. Having Lydia's scent all over me will trick the primal part of your brains into thinking you're marking an omega, as will Lydia's purr."

Lex nods and looks at me for a long moment. My mind quiets as I look into her eyes, trying to read her expression. There's something there, a light I haven't seen since...

I don't get to finish my thought as she leans in and gives me a tender but brief kiss. I melt under her, yielding without a second thought to the alpha who changed my life. When she pulls away, her little smile makes my soul sing. I almost whine at the loss of contact as she gets up, but then I'm treated to the view of her ass as she walks away, and I'm much less upset. I let out a longing sigh as she slides into her dress, pulling up the back zipper with practiced ease.

"I'm going to put in an order for nesting materials. Can you ask Lydia to text me if there's anything in particular she wants?" Lex asks, backed turned as she bends down to pick out a pair of shoes.

I hum absently, enjoying the fuck out of the way Lex's backside looks in this dress. It's clinging in all the right places, and my *God*, do I need to take a cold shower.

"Hopefully, we can make it through the next week and a half without incident. Rhett has made it abundantly clear that he does not want her to try to hold back and hurt herself in the process."

Lex is still talking, but I'm hardly paying attention. My hand has drifted to the crotch of my sweats, and I swallow a groan at the damp patch I feel, too big to just be from my leaking dick. I glance down and see the outline of my cock as the material sticks to it, and I give it one slow stroke, looking back toward Lex.

But I jump as I realize she's right in front of me, brow pulled down in a stern expression. I swallow, eyes wide.

"These buckles always give me trouble. Would you be a dear and help me?" she asks, the innocent tone of her voice clashing with the hard glint in her eyes.

I nod and go to bend down. But then, she lifts her foot and plants the sole of her strappy pump in the middle of my chest, pushing me back. She raises her chin, as if daring me to challenge her. But instead, I simply do as I was instructed and buckle one shoe, and then the other.

"If you can keep your hands off yourself until I get home, we can start prepping you to take a knot tonight," Lex drawls.

I spot the loophole in her order, but keep my expression contrite for the moment. Tenderly, I reach up and hold her calf and ankle before kissing the top of her foot.

"Yes, Domina," I mutter submissively, even lowering my eyes to add to the effect.

Lex purrs a little, and I let her leg down. She doesn't stick around the pack house for much longer, needing to get to work. I watch out of the front window as she drives off, waving slightly as I catch her eye. I wait until I'm sure she's gone before bounding away down the basement stairs.

Lex may have ordered me to not touch my dick until she gets home, but she failed to include others in her instructions. And thankfully, Lydia's impending heat has made her insatiable, even at ungodly hours of the morning. Even if I have to elbow Mateo out of the way to get my turn with our girl.

CHAPTER TWENTY-FOUR

Lydia

Rhett: Good morning, my love. Do you have any plans for today?

I ROLL OVER AND read the message through bleary eyes. At my movement, Lucas snuggles closer to my back, clinging tighter in his sleep. I smile a little as I realize who it's from, quickly typing out a reply.

Me: I'm going to see an apartment with Gabby and Wila in the morning, and then Mateo's picking me up for lunch. He wants to show me The Garden today.
Rhett: Excellent.
Rhett: Would you like to play a game with me, little one?

My body reacts almost instantly, flushing hot with desire, my clit throbbing a little. Lucas breathes in as my scent shifts, burying his nose in my hair. With each passing day, my body is getting more and more sensitive, and my libido is out of control. I can hardly be alone in a room with one of my pack mates without jumping them. Thankfully, they've all been more than agreeable to my increased needs. Even now, half asleep, I can feel Lucas's cock waking up and pressing against my bare ass.

Me: What sort of game, sir?
Rhett: I was going to wait and save this for Christmas, but I think today is the perfect day for you to try out a new toy for me.
Me: Oh? What kind of toy?
Rhett: You'll see. After you get dressed, head up to my room and call me. The game starts now, so remember our rules.
Me: Yes, sir. My safe word is red if I want to stop, and yellow if I need a break.
Rhett: Good girl. And what is our rule about coming?
Me: I have to ask for permission, and wait until you grant it.
Rhett: Such a perfect, obedient little omega you are for me, sweet girl.

I preen a little from his praise, and I hear a husky chuckle behind me.

"How's our sir doing, sweetheart?" Lucas purrs in my ear.

"He's good. We're going to play a game today," I reply, glancing at the clock. It's still morning, but not too early. My sleep schedule has been all out of whack since I stopped working.

Lucas hums, grinding his cock against me. "I should make sure you're good and ready for whatever he has in store for you."

I gasp as his fingers trace over my hip and slide between my legs. I'm already dripping for him, and he slides two fingers inside me with ease. As I hitch my leg back over his hip to give him better access, my mind floats in a sea of sensations. But as I draw closer to my peak, my eyes fly open, and I grab Lucas's wrist. He freezes, sensing the sudden tension in me.

"What's the matter?" he asks seriously.

"I—Rhett said we're already playing. I have to ask—"

Lucas's growl cuts me off, and I try not to whine as he pulls his fingers out of me. My walls clench involuntarily, my body reluctant to let him go, even if my mind knows better. But then I yelp in surprise as he rolls me over onto my back and settles himself between my thighs. And then, in one languid thrust, he's seated his cock to the hilt. I moan long and low, relishing the feeling of his thick, rock-hard cock stretching me open.

"Go on, then. Ask him," Lucas taunts, starting a slow but steady pace as he withdraws and sinks back into my heat.

I nod, hands fumbling over the sheets until I finally find my phone. My fingers shake as Lucas angles his hips just right to hit that rough patch of nerves on my upper wall, and it takes me twice as long to get the message out.

Me: Please, sir. I want to come so bad. Please let me come.

I expect a swift reply, but each second drags like an hour as Lucas pounds relentlessly into me, hips grinding on my clit with each forward thrust. My whole body is shaking as I struggle to hold myself back. Finally, my phone goes off, not with a message, but with a call. I answer and put it on speaker.

"Little one, what are you—"

"Fuck, please, sir. Lucas is fucking me so good, and I need to come. Please, sir. Please let me come on Lucas's cock," I beg, words becoming more garbled as I nearly sob from the pressure building in my belly.

"Luc? Is she being good and not coming?" Rhett questions, not missing a beat.

"Yes, sir. Fuck, she's so tight. You feel so fucking good, squeezing like that," Lucas says, first to Rhett, then to me.

"I had plans for you today, little one. If you come now, you're going to have to wait a long time for your next one," Rhett says, voice full of warning.

"I understand, sir. Please, please, please, I want to come so bad for you!"

A tear leaks down my face, but Lucas is there, kissing it away.

"Don't say I didn't warn you. Now, come all over our beta's cock," Rhett commands, just the edge of a growl to his words.

I shatter completely, a scream of pure bliss tearing from my throat as my pussy pulses and gushes my release. Lucas is right there, whispering in my ear, telling me over and over how good I feel, how perfect I am, and it drags the warm rush of release out into eternity. I'm so far adrift that I don't even hear Lucas's moans, but I feel him drive deep into me and then hot ropes of his cum fill me. We sit there panting for a moment, and I only remember Rhett is still on the phone when he clears his throat.

"God, I miss you both so much," he says, almost under his breath.

Another tear slips from my eyes, and Lucas wipes it away. "I miss you too, so much. I want you home," I reply, a little whimper in my voice as my lower lip quivers.

"Soon, love. I promise I'll be home soon. But you've got a busy day. So how about you both take a nice, relaxing shower and get yourselves ready, yeah?" Rhett suggests warmly.

I nod, but then remember he can't see me and agree verbally. He makes us promise not to get up to any more shenanigans, and after we say our 'I love yous,' Lucas finally slides his softened cock out of me, then rolls over to cuddle me into his chest. I have to hold back the urge to sob, my heart aching even as my body sings with satisfaction. Not having Rhett here to hold me after moments like this doesn't get any easier. Lucas understands in a way I'm not sure Mateo or Lex do, how hard it's been to not have Rhett around. I know the only thing that'll finally heal this hole in my chest is having Rhett's arms around me again.

I want to wallow more, but my phone buzzes in my hand with a message from Caleb, letting me know he's on his way to pick me up and take me to meet the Fitzgeralds. Well, I guess it's time to figure out what Rhett's surprise is.

I flush as I shift uncomfortably in the front seat of Caleb's SUV, but it doesn't make things any better. It turned out that Rhett's surprise was a small, remote-control vibrator. He'd walked me through lubing it up and proper positioning, but I didn't have time for him to explain any of the other features before I had to throw on some clothes and leave. I can feel it every time I move or walk or breathe, pressing against my clit and G-spot perfectly. My underwear keeps it in place, but it's already a soaked mess. I'm glad I'd opted for a skirt today rather than jeans, or I'd be walking around looking like I wet myself.

My scent is strong enough for even me to notice it, which usually never happens. When you live constantly surrounded by your own perfume, you go nose blind to it pretty quickly. But there's a heavy coating of honey and earthy rain filling the cabin and overpowering Caleb's usual cedar and snickerdoodle scent.

"So I take it your heat is almost upon us?" Caleb questions awkwardly as we sit at a red light.

Flushing, I turn away from my bodyguard. Though, now that I think on it, with Darren still recovering and Seth dead, is he still on Lex's payroll?

"I think so. I'm not nesting, but... yeah. Do you need..." I trail off, biting my lip.

I should have thought this through. Caleb is an alpha, even if he's happily mated. Having the overwhelming scent of unbonded omega about to go into heat in his head can't be comfortable.

"I've been speaking with Ms. St. Clair. With Sylvie being so close to her due date, and with your heat, we've made the call and terminated the contract with my employer. Today's going to be my last day," he says solemnly.

I frown and look at my lap, a sudden sadness filling my chest to bank the heat in my belly. Caleb may have only been my bodyguard at first, but he's grown to be so much more than that. He feels more like an older brother, a friend and confidant, when I needed one the most. I'd like to imagine that, if circumstances had been different, Sam and I would have had the sort of relationship Caleb and I have now. And I've been learning so much about what it means to be an omega from Sylvie. But I don't want it to be awkward when Caleb has to move on and is assigned another "baby," as she calls them.

"They weren't happy about losing someone with my sort of experience. But the offer Ms. St. Clair put on the table was too good to pass up. The benefits package alone—"

"Wait, what?" I sputter, whipping my head around to face him, blinking rapidly.

The smug bastard has the audacity to smirk as he watches the road, carefully executing the last turn into the Wickland House parking lot.

"Sorry, I thought she told you. I'm being brought on to take control of the security across all the St. Clair Foundation properties," he says, winking at me.

I open and close my mouth a few times as I process that information. "Does that mean you're not going to be my bodyguard anymore?" I ask, spitting out the first coherent sentence I can think of.

Caleb sighs and shakes his head as he pulls into a parking spot. "Unfortunately, *voyin*, it does mean I have to step away from that role. But I'll still be watching over you, just not from your side."

He looks over at me, his gunmetal gray eyes bright with emotion. Before I can stop myself, I unbuckle my seatbelt and throw myself across the center console, wrapping my arms around his neck in a tight embrace. He's only stunned for a moment before he returns the hug just as fiercely. We linger for a long moment, and I let myself enjoy the feeling of being held like this. His bulk has always meant safety to me, and I've grown so used to him being there, I don't remember how I lived without a constant companion.

"I'm going to miss you," I whisper into his ear.

Caleb chuckles, and I sit back as his arms drop from around my ribs. He doesn't let me go far, kissing my hairline and sending a rush of fondness through my chest.

"Oh, if you think you're getting rid of me that easily, you're sorely mistaken. Sylvie doesn't go a day without asking after you. And you wouldn't leave a pregnant omega out in the cold like that, would you?" he teases, pinching my cheek slightly.

I brush his hand away with a laugh, sitting back in my seat. Shoving his shoulder, he makes a show of acting wounded, just like a good big brother would do. I roll my eyes and am about to respond when I see Gabby and Wila exit the front doors of the hotel.

"Tell Sylvie I'll be over tomorrow. If I can find a ride," I say with a laugh, picking up my bag and turning to leave.

"None of that. Your days as Miss Daisy are over. It's time for you to get behind the wheel again, *voyin*. I know you can do it," Caleb chides.

I swallow a little bit, pushing down the momentary pulse of panic that rises at the mention of me driving again. But that's a problem for future Lydia. I give Caleb a furtive smile before sliding out of the SUV and heading toward my best friend.

I'd been distracted in the car and had nearly forgotten about the toy inside of me. But walking makes me all too aware of it once again, and I have to swallow a moan. If Gabby notices anything weird in my expression, she doesn't say anything. But there's a sparkle in Wila's chocolate eyes that I don't like.

"Well, let's get this show on the road. I've got a good feeling about this place," she says, clapping her hands together and striding off toward Gabby's beat-up old hatchback.

Gabby and I roll our eyes, having no choice but to follow her. After the customary shuffling of takeout wrappers, empty soda bottles, and other debris on the floor of the car, we're off. Conversation is light as we maneuver through traffic, and I'm finally able to relax for a moment.

That is, until the vibrations start.

I jump nearly out of my skin as the first pulse zings through my clit and straight up my spine, and I disguise my yelp in a cough. The frequency of the buzzing is low, and so quiet that I can't even hear it. The pulse of the toy rolls over my clit, getting stronger and backing off like waves crashing on the shore. I fight to keep it together, to not pant and moan and grind my hips into the seat for more friction. The vibrations grow more intense with each cycle, and my walls clench around the bulb of the toy inside of me. The edge is in sight, the tingling in my toes taking over as my orgasm nears. Closer and closer, just out of reach—

And then, as suddenly as it started, the vibrations stop. I'm still reeling from the sudden loss of stimulation when my phone goes off in my bag. I dig for a moment before pulling it out and finding a new message.

Rhett: I hope you enjoyed your morning with Lucas, little one. Our game has officially started. So behave yourself today, and enjoy yourself as much as you can. I'll be by

my phone all day, so if you need to ask me anything, don't hesitate to send me a text. I love you.

Chapter Twenty-Five

Lydia

After the first show of force, I'd expected Rhett to toy with me all day. But instead, I'm left with only the strange sensation of the toy shifting around inside of me as I tour the first two apartments Gabby had lined up for us. The anticipation of not knowing when the next burst will come drives me nearly to insanity, and I can't help myself.

Me: Is the game over, sir?

Simple, not overly needy. Because I still want to play, but I can't stand the suspense. Thankfully, Rhett doesn't keep me waiting.

Rhett: You're out with people who haven't consented to playing.
Rhett: But do let me know when Mateo has picked you up, yeah?

I huff a sigh, but relax despite myself after sending back a brief 'yes, sir.' Rhett's views on consent continue to surprise me, though they really shouldn't at this point. I'm still a little annoyed that he chose not to inform me of this decision, and left me an anxious mess for the better part of the morning. Knowing that I have some time before he starts up again in earnest, I rejoin the conversation happening in the front of the vehicle.

"That last one would have been perfect," Gabby moans.

"It's too far from the major traffic routes. And did you see the state of the bathrooms? I'm sorry, but salmon sinks and toilets died in the 70s for a reason," Wila sniffs.

"It's retro!" her granddaughter protests, but Wila doesn't deign to respond.

Luckily, we pull up to the last place for the day before the fight can continue. Gabby parks on the street outside of a four-story building, the two display windows that frame the store entrance covered in white plastic, and a "For Lease" sign hanging in the left one. There's a door to the right of the opposite window, with a matching "For Rent" sign tacked to it.

"The leasing company is willing to cut us a deal if we want the retail space and the apartment," Gabby comments, taking the lead toward the entrance.

She enters a code into the lockbox hanging from the handle, extracting several keys from within before unlocking the door. Wila gives me a look, and I suddenly realize where Gabby inherited her Sigh of the Long Suffering. I smother a giggle under a cough and follow Wila inside.

This retail space is bigger than I'd anticipated, completely empty of any displays or refrigerator units. Looking around, the walls are still bare of paint, the floor covered in plastic drop cloths. The only thing breaking up the area is a long countertop in the back that spans almost the entire width of the room, centered with enough space on either side for the tellers to come around from behind it without having to vault over it. The wall behind the counter has built-in shelving, and a door, which I presume leads to the stockroom and workspace.

Gabby has been rattling off numbers, but it's all Greek to me. Wila, though, looks distinctly impressed. As she takes everything in, there's a brightness to her eyes that I haven't seen in a long time, not since before the fire.

"And the best part: even though we're on State Street, we're out of the B.O.A. territory," Gabby finishes with a smug flourish.

I contain my laughter to a snort, but Wila perks up. The Business Owner's Association has been a thorn in her side for as long as I've known her. The endless string of meetings and phone calls is bad enough, but she's been obligated to follow their rules about what she can display in her windows, even when it doesn't truly reflect the types of products and services she offers. Because, yes, while the shop did do a fair number of walk-in arrangements, the vast majority of the business comes from special events like weddings, funerals, and parties. It didn't benefit us to display Easter baskets and leprechauns during peak wedding season, but the B.O.A.'s rule was gospel.

I look around again, spinning in a slow circle as I try to imagine what this place would look like when it's complete. But even as I do, something nags at my heart, a hollow feeling like I'd imagine a kid with diabetes might get on

Halloween. I could dream all I liked, but now that I'm part of Pack St. Clair, this store isn't my future.

"Let's go look upstairs. I think you're going to love this," Gabby says, bouncing excitedly on her toes.

"Y'all go on ahead. I want to take a better look around, do some measuring," Wila says distractedly, already walking off toward the backroom.

Gabby hardly waits for the words to come out of her mouth before she's taking my hand and dragging me out of the front door, through the side door, and up a narrow but well-maintained staircase.

"Is it too soon to be grateful we don't have furniture to move? Because could you fucking imagine trying to get a couch up these?" Gabby laughs as we stop on the landing.

I chuckle nervously, not giving more of a response than that. She uses one of the other keys to unlock the door and it swings open on smooth hinges. Stepping inside, I suck in a sharp breath. The place is already furnished, but the atmosphere is so comfortable. Like the rest of the building, everything feels brand new, but with an air of inexplicable coziness.

"Yeah, I know. It feels like the one, doesn't it?" Gabby sighs, stepping around me to flop down onto the overstuffed couch.

I nod and join her, sitting more carefully to avoid any awkward jostling. We're quiet for a long time, but neither of us moves to explore the place any further. She lets out a deep, relaxed breath, leaning over to rest her head on my shoulder, and I immediately tip my head so my cheek sits on the top of her intricately braided head. Her scent of caramel candy apples is touched with cinnamon, and I let myself sink into it.

"Gran's trying to put it off for as long as she can, but she's only delaying the inevitable," Gabby whispers in the quiet.

My stomach drops, and I tense, waiting for her to go on. The relaxed bubble around us seems to close in, slipping away with each passing second.

"You've got a pack now, babe. And with any luck, you're going to have a gaggle of bond mates before Halloween. And we both know you weren't meant to work retail for the rest of your life," she goes on, trying for levity.

My throat closes up, and I close my eyes. I know she's right. Even now, Mateo is on his way here to pick me up and take me to the building he and his pack *bought* me for the express purpose of giving me an event venue to run. I've been willfully ignoring the implications of what that would mean for my job as a florist, but it seems time's up on that act.

"I mean, there's still time. I don't know how long things are going to take, and I'm sure y'all'll need help getting this place ready—"

"It's okay to let us go, babe. I'm so happy you finally found your people, and you deserve this opportunity to do what you've always dreamed of," Gabby interjects, sitting up and twisting to face me.

I twist as well, until we're knee to knee. She reaches for my hands, and I return her tight grip. Her lower lip quivers, but her smile is heartbreakingly beautiful. My own eyes water, and I blink back the tears threatening to overflow.

"I don't know what I'll do without you," I admit, voice barely above a whisper.

Gabby laughs outright. "Nah, bitch. You are stuck with me for life, and that *is* a threat." She lets out a disbelieving noise through her teeth and rolls her eyes, and I join her laughter this time.

When we're quiet, I look down at our hands, years of memories coming back to me in a rush. I want to say something, to thank her for everything she's done for me over the last five years, but no words feel big enough to express what I'm feeling. She picked me up when I was at my lowest and has been in my corner for every step in my healing process. Gabby Fitzgerald is more than my friend; she's my sister, my platonic soulmate.

"I still want to help get things set up here. I can't lay around the house all day; I'll go nuts," I tease with a chuckle.

Gabby groans and gives me her Sigh of the Long Suffering, but her eyes lack any real heat. "I suppose we could let you do that. But you need to get through your fucking heat first."

I roll my eyes and smirk, nodding a little. That's reasonable, I suppose.

"For real, though, babe. You need to stay indoors until you're done pushing out that insane perfume. Like, I don't even like women, and it's making me want to fuck you. You're gonna get jumped if you keep going out in public," Gabby goes on.

I let out a bark of startled laughter and blush red hot, which only makes Gabby laugh, too. We're still a riot of giggles when Wila comes in a few minutes later, hands on her hips.

"Have you girls done anything productive?" she asks sternly.

Gabby and I look at each other, trying to smother our laughter, but the effort only makes us laugh more. Wila, the trooper, just rolls her eyes and goes off to actually look at the apartment.

Not too long after, the decision has been made. This is going to be their new home. Gabby is on the line with the leasing agency as Mateo pulls up, waving at Wila through the windshield. I turn to the woman who's treated me as nothing less than her own flesh and blood for the last several years, smiling sadly.

"Gabby and I talked," I say simply, and it only takes a minute for Wila to understand my meaning.

"You've done damn good work for me, Lydia. And you're going to do amazing things with the St. Clairs," Wila says, words failing for a moment as she clears her throat and takes a deep breath.

I take one of her wrinkled hands and give it a comforting squeeze. She glances down at our joined fingers for a moment before setting her shoulders and bringing her gaze back to mine, jaw set.

"I expect you and that pack of yours to show face for Thanksgiving, Christmas, and Easter, you hear me?" she says, tone matching her expression.

Smirking, I give her a teasing shrug. "We may have to negotiate our holiday schedule. I've been told Christmas celebrations are a bit of a production for them."

Wila gives me a grunt, and I smirk a little wider. The image of Alexandra St. Clair and Wilhelmina Fitzgerald sitting down and haggling over who gets me on which holidays plays in my mind, and I have to admit that I don't know who would come out the victor in that match up.

Gabby ends her call and heads back toward us, and before I can think better of it, I throw myself around Wila's neck in a tight embrace. She doesn't miss a beat and returns it. It only lasts for a moment, but it sets the last little bit of my nerves to rest. Wila and Gabby are family, and always will be. I'm not losing them, and they aren't leaving me behind. We're growing, and sometimes that means embarking on different paths. But I know that nothing will ever come between me, my best friend, and Gran. So as I give them a parting wave from the passenger seat of Mateo's SUV, I'm not filled with the sadness of a goodbye. Instead, my heart is light with excitement for what's going to happen next.

CHAPTER TWENTY-SIX

Lydia

MATEO KEEPS GLANCING AT me out of the corner of his eye as we start toward our destination, ozone and citrus coating my tongue and throat with each passing block. His hand is on my thigh, fingers tracing nonsense patterns on the sensitive inside of my leg. I try not to fidget or squirm, but I've texted Rhett, so the game is truly on now. And it doesn't take more than a few minutes for the vibrations to start, a low buzz so soft that I almost don't feel it at first. But as it builds, I try to keep my breathing even, my stomach in knots as I clench uselessly against the silicone. It only lasts for a few minutes, not enough to push me to the edge, and I sigh when it stops, trying to bring my heart back under control.

"You doing okay, baby girl? You look a little flushed?" Mateo asks in a low purr.

I shiver as the words slide over my skin like ice cubes, and I nod, not trusting my voice. But as I look up at him when we stop at the next traffic light, I yelp as he leans over and grabs me by the back of the neck, kissing me hard enough to bruise. My head spins as he backs off again, settling into his seat.

"I'll take care of you when we get somewhere more comfortable," he says with a wink.

I nod dumbly, swallowing a groan as the bulb pressed against my G-spot starts to vibrate, sending a fresh wave of heat through me. I clench my teeth as I ride it, rising higher and higher. My orgasm builds steadily, and after being stimulated without release all morning, I know I can get there, maybe even without Rhett knowing. I try to rock my hips in little circles, getting a little more friction, a little more pressure. But suddenly, Mateo's growl cuts through my haze, and I whip my head around to look at him with wide eyes.

"No cheating, baby. If you come without asking, Rhett has given me permission to punish you. And it *will* be a punishment, none of this spank and a tickle shit that you secretly love," he says sternly.

I blink, jaw falling open in shock. The toy goes still again, but I hardly notice. I've never seen Mateo like this, but the primal part of my mind doesn't object to the change in the slightest. His shoulders are tense, eyes black with hunger as they look at me from under a stern brow. There's an air of violence to him, one that sets something in me ablaze, wanting to rise to the unspoken challenge. But the desire to please my alphas crashes down on that momentary recklessness, and I nod vigorously.

Mateo's smile is a dangerous flash of teeth, making me shiver again. "That's what I thought. My good little baby girl knows better than to try her luck."

I whimper and tuck my chin, leaning toward him on instinct. I have the sudden urge to climb into his lap, to be cuddled and pet, but I still have enough self-preservation to not try it while he's driving. Instead, I lean as far as I can over the center console and rest my head on his shoulder. He turns and kisses the top of my head, and I smile as my shoulders do a preening little wiggle. His laugh soothes the frayed edges of my nerves, and I let myself indulge in the closeness for the last few minutes of our ride.

When we pull into the gravel parking lot, I look at the building beyond the locked chain-link fence and frown thoughtfully. It's not nearly as bad as I thought it might be, based on the types of projects Lex, Rhett, and Mateo have taken on in the past. The outside looks worn, but there aren't any smashed or boarded-up windows. The marque is yellowed with age but still intact, though I have to wonder at how many of the remaining lightbulbs would still glow at night.

I slide out of the car, my shoes crunching a little on the loose stone as I look up. Rhett told me a bit of the history of The Magnolia Garden Theater last week, so I could have a frame of reference for what I could expect. Still, I have to stop and stare up at the building, in awe of its elegance, even in decay. The brick walls are covered in vines and dirt, but the potential is there. Mateo comes up beside me, fingers looping through mine as we just stand for a moment together in silence. For the first time, the reality of this situation hits me. This building is *mine*. I'm going to be in charge of the restoration and operation of this historic landmark.

I let Mateo lead me through the front, the plywood-patched doors propped open by a cinderblock. There are glass cases where posters would go inside the vestibule, a short flight of crumbling stairs leading up to a second set of doors and into the foyer. Once inside, the air is cool and musty, dust lingering in the beams of sunlight filtering through the dirty windows. The lobby is shrouded in plastic, but I can see the shapes of a ticket booth and turnstiles below.

"Let me give you the tour," Mateo says in my ear, putting a hand to my lower back.

I nod, following his lead. Looking around, I recall what Rhett told me. The Magnolia Garden first opened in the early 1900s, and it was the first building in Everton to have electricity, to light up the stage for all manner of traveling shows and plays. Even now, as Mateo and I wander through the dusty interior, I can see the old-fashioned candle sconces on the walls, still covered in century-old wax, mixed with more "modern" fixtures. When silent movies came along, a new theater was built across town, so business here trickled off. This building still had some use as a venue for live-action entertainment, and based on the dressing rooms and lounges Mateo shows me, it was certainly a place for the wealthy to see and be seen.

But the final nail came when the Broadway-caliber theater popped up in the next town over. It was bigger, state-of-the-art, and only an hour away. So The Magnolia Garden closed its doors in the seventies, and hasn't opened to the public since. It was empty for a long time, but the last couple of decades saw it passed around from developer to developer, each one making incremental progress on refurbishments but never getting much accomplished before the costs exceeded the projected profits. Then they would sell, starting the process all over again, until finally, two months ago, The St. Clair Foundation managed to rescue it. The building itself is on the corner of the block, a prime spot that is easy to find, but not on any major commuting routes. I'm sure if this hadn't been declared a landmark, someone would have torn it down and turned it into a gas station or something a long time ago.

Mateo's hands stay in contact with my skin the entire time, and while I'm aware of it, my mind is too busy taking everything in. Each room we enter is in some state of demolition or repair. But my imagination is in overdrive, each space setting off a chain reaction of ideas, plans, and possibilities. Mateo does his best to describe the necessary structural changes they have planned, but it hardly matters. The place isn't in as bad of shape as I'd feared, and I can already see the skeletons of the event spaces in place. They just need to be completed. I also hadn't expected to see signs of work yet, but there's a certain buzz of activity around, a few workmen outside taking a lunch break, a few more unloading a truck, the sounds of machinery in the distance. A few crew members wave at Mateo as we pass, a gesture he returns with a grin, but I stick as close to his side as I can.

We finish the tour in the theater, which, unlike modern ones, doesn't have the sloped floor and fixed seats. Instead, it's flat, more like a ballroom with a stage at the end. The mezzanine has pillars and arches currently supported by scaffolding, but it offers a perfect view of the entire room. I stand in the center of the empty space and spin in a slow circle, letting my mind paint over the cracks and the dust until the gold leaf shines and the hardwood gleams. I can see it all, how we'd set up the space for a wedding ceremony, and then how it would transform into a reception space while guests mingle on the terrace beyond the door on the west wall. There's a lounge space that could be converted into a kitchen in the rear, and we wouldn't lose an inch of beauty.

"I take it you like it?" Mateo asks, sliding up behind me and wrapping his arms around my waist.

"It's so... I can't believe you've done this," I whisper, voice cracking slightly.

He kisses my cheek, and I can feel his smile against my skin. "You deserve the world, Lydia. This is just the beginning of the amazing things our pack is going to do together."

I'm about to respond when, out of nowhere, the toy comes to life at nearly full speed, both ends buzzing hard enough to make my teeth rattle. Mateo's arms keep me from collapsing to the floor, holding me up as the strength goes out from my legs. I bite my lip hard, whining and shaking. He purrs in my ear, one of his hands sliding down to cup my mound over my skirt.

"Oh, baby girl. Rhett's playing with you hard now, isn't he? Does it feel good?" Mateo breathes, pressing the toy and grinding his cock against my ass.

I nod, gasping as the inserted bulb pulses rapidly, and I swear it moves, almost like it's rotating and stretching me in just the right way. I let Mateo walk us forward until we're under the cover of the mezzanine, not that it does much to block us from view of anyone passing along to the opposite walkway. But at least I'm not convulsing out in the open.

"You want to come so bad, I'm sure. You've been worked up all day, and not able to do anything about it," Mateo continues, the hand not pressed against my core, gathering up the fabric of my skirt until it can slip under.

I nod again, knees knocking together and eyes screwed tight. I fumble for my bag, trying to get to my phone. I'm barely hanging on, and I need to text Rhett.

"Ah, ah, ah, stay with me, baby girl. Stay. Right. Here."

Mateo punctuates those last three words by pushing against the toy hard, fucking it somehow even deeper. I whimper, slumping back against him, mind at war. I told Rhett I'd play by his rules, but Mateo is right here, his purring growl against my back and hands all over me. But I don't want to disappoint Rhett. Not when I promised him I'd be his good girl. I'm momentarily distracted as I feel something against my ear, and I open my eyes at Mateo's touch, and then something rubbery slips into my ear for a moment.

"Hello, little one."

Rhett's voice nearly makes me sob, and I cover my mouth with one hand to muffle the sound, and I adjust the earpiece with my other.

"Mateo is taking the lead, but I'm going to be right here. I can hear you, so don't forget our words and our rules," Rhett says calmly, a balm that washes over me like spring rain.

"Yes, sir. Red to stop, yellow to slow down. And I'll ask before I come," I answer, reiterating the rules from earlier on instinct.

Rhett hums in pleasure, and my stomach does a limp little flip-flop. He's about to say something else, but Mateo takes the earpiece away before I can hear. And he laughs when I let out a noise of indignation. But my irritation slips away as the hand under my skirt slips between my legs. Mateo groans low in his throat, fingers tracing the toy through the fabric of my panties.

"You must be so uncomfortable with your panties soaked like this, baby girl," he coos, fingers slipping below the waistband and peeling them away.

I shiver as cool air hits my soaked thighs and lips, but once my panties hit my ankles, I kick them off carelessly, panting even as the toy slows down. It's not vibrating as hard, but I can still definitely feel the inner bulb rotating in slow circles inside of me. I try to rock in time with the motion, but Mateo presses me against the wall face first, pinning me and shielding me with his body. I have enough room to arch back into him, but I have no choice but to go still.

"Fuck, you're so wet, making a mess all over yourself for your alphas," Mateo purrs in my ear, quiet enough not to carry through the empty room.

I gasp as the tip of one of his fingers slips into my swollen and aching slit alongside the toy, the stretch just on the pleasurable side of painful. His touch is a countermelody to the toy, and my mind is overloaded with sensation. I need more, anything to make this bone deep ache go away.

"Please, I need—please, I'm so—" I stumble over myself, hardly able to form words as the vibrator starts up on my clit again.

Clenching and releasing over and over, my juices drip down my thighs, coating them almost all the way to my knees. The sounds coming out of my body are obscene and inhuman, but that's what I am now. I'm simply a vessel to contain this pleasure, and it's threatening to run over at any moment.

"Tell me what you want, baby girl. Tell me, and I'll take care of you," Mateo says, breath hot on the side of my face.

"Please fuck me, make me come. I need you," I beg, nearly sobbing with built up pleasure.

"She does sound so good like this, doesn't she? What do you think, Coop? Should I give her what she's asking for?" Mateo asks, and the taunting edge of his words makes me whine.

"Please, please, please. Daddy, please—"

As soon as the word slips out, I brace for his reaction. I've never called anyone that, but something about it feels right. But Mateo doesn't play those sorts of games. Will this upset him?

I whine as the hand not between my legs wraps around my throat, the grip not harsh but tight enough to be proprietary. His growl against my back rattles my bones, and I gasp as his fingers abandon my slit and travel back, spreading my cream to my tight rear entrance.

"Say it again," Mateo grits, nearly an octave lower.

"Please fuck me, Daddy," I mutter pathetically, pushing back as he circles and probes, opening me up.

"I will, baby girl. I'm going to fuck your ass and your Sir is going to play with your cunt. We're going to make you feel so good. Because you're our good little omega, and good girls get what they want when they behave and beg so pretty for Daddy."

Mateo's hand never stops, and I'm so keyed up that he can easily slip in one slick finger, and then two, scissoring them to stretch me quickly. I nod, tears trailing down my face, even if I don't know why I'm crying. My emotions are all over the place, but the strongest is love and need for the man behind me. I want his cock, need his praise more than air. I have to stop myself from sobbing outright as he withdraws and starts fussing with our clothes, though I'm distracted as the vibrator starts up in earnest again on my clit. I'm so overstimulated and on edge that I don't even feel close to an orgasm anymore. But I know it won't take long for that to change. Especially not when the blunt head of Mateo's cock presses against my puckered hole.

"Let me in, baby girl. That's it, fuck yes. You are so fucking good," Mateo groans, pressing forward and heaping on the praise as he breeches me.

I have to cover my mouth to muffle my cries as he fills me up inch by inch, the fullness of him and the toy side by side almost too much. He rocks forward and backward, withdrawing and pressing deeper and deeper with each thrust until he bottoms out and goes still for a moment. I don't know how I'm still standing, and I'm grateful as he bands his arms around my ribs and pulls me back into his chest.

"Just hang on and enjoy it, baby girl. Let Daddy take care of you," he whispers tenderly, rolling his hips slowly.

Nodding, I tuck my chin, closing my eyes tight. The toy hasn't stopped this whole time, but now the inner vibrations kick in, along with the stimulation to my clit. There's no rhyme or reason to the pattern of the pulsing, sometimes hard and fast, other times a slow rolling, and the variation keeps my building release just out of reach. Mateo's thrusts get harder and faster, and I don't have the strength to even try to meet his strokes.

"Daddy, I want to come so bad. But I d-don't think I can, please—I'm sorry, Daddy, please—"

My words die as more tears choke my throat, and I'm overwhelmed by everything around me. Mateo shushes me and kisses my cheeks, arms around me, holding me tight and secure.

"You can, baby. I know you can. You've been so good, and you're going to come for me, come all over my cock in your ass."

I gasp loudly as the vibrator turns on full blast, going harder than it has before, and it's like an injection of liquid fire straight into my veins through my swollen, abused clit. And then Mateo tilts his hips just right and stars burst behind my eyes as my entire body throbs with the most intense orgasm I've ever had in my life. Mateo's hand slaps down onto my mouth to muffle my screams, groaning in my ear as I squeeze him tight. A fresh flood of my juice slides down my legs and drips onto the floor, so much that I'm sure that I'm going to be standing in a puddle any minute. I wait for the pleasure to end, but it stretches on and on, every inch of my skin zinging with endorphins.

"That's a good girl, such a good fucking girl," Mateo pants, slowing his thrusts for a moment as I ride the wave.

"Thank you, Daddy. Thank you, Sir. Oh, God, thank you," I moan from behind his hand.

Mateo growls and presses forward until my cheek is flush with the wall. His hand is back on my throat, squeezing as he picks up again, slamming into me hard and fast as he chases his own release. I can only hang on, babbling mindlessly as another smaller wave crests and crashes over me. My muscles clench over and over, and Mateo can't hold out. He pushes in as far as he can without knotting me, and I flush at the rush of warmth filling me as he comes.

We're quiet for a moment, breathing heavily as we come down. The toy slows and eventually stops, and Mateo reaches down and pulls it free. But I'm too far gone in the high to really care. I'm a sticky mess, my nose completely full of lemons and lightning, but it's perfect. I like being covered in his scent.

"You okay, Lydia?" Mateo asks gently, brushing my hair to the side so he can see my face.

I nod dazedly, whining a little as he pulls his softened cock free. I feel empty, even though I don't know if I could take any more filling right now if I tried. The brush of a cloth caresses my ass, and I try to squirm away from him.

"You're a mess, baby girl. Let me clean you up," Mateo chides under his breath.

"I don't wanna," I grumble.

Mateo chuckles and gives a little pinch on the underside of my ass cheek, making me jump and squeak. He finishes up in two more quick swipes and then steps back to let my skirt drop before turning me around. I let him tilt my chin up and melt into his kiss.

"Let's get you home so I can get you dirty again, shall we?" he asks suggestively.

I perk up a little at that, skin flushing hot again. "Yes, Daddy," I reply eagerly.

Mateo shakes his head and kisses me again. His eyes blaze into mine when he pulls away, and despite the thorough fucking I just received, my belly leaps and thighs clench at the look. "I thought it'd be weird, but hearing you call me that... fuck, that hits different."

I smile serenely. "As long as you like it, I'll keep doing it."

Mateo nods. "Only in the bedroom, okay?" he asks hesitantly.

I nod again, snuggling into his chest. He keeps me tucked close as we head back to his SUV, holding my hand as we make our way back to the pack house. It's only later when I'm lying in bed after a few more rounds that I realize I didn't see where my panties ended up. I hope some poor worker doesn't find them.

CHAPTER TWENTY-SEVEN

Alexandra

I PICK THROUGH THE stack of papers in front of me, looking for the document I received this morning, as my phone's ringer cuts through the air. I pause only in my search to press the answer button, putting it on speaker.

"Is that you, Rhett?" I ask, eyes still scanning the papers in my hand.

"Good morning, love. It's always a pleasure to hear your voice," Rhett practically purrs through the line, and I can't help my little chuckle.

"Usually that sort of talk precedes you telling me about something bad you've done," I tease.

"I've been a perfect angel, haven't I, Jason?" Rhett tosses back in mock offense.

"Angels don't get their house guests wasted three days in a row," Jason mutters darkly.

"Not my fault you thought you could beat an Irishman in a drinking contest," Rhett says with a laugh.

"Then how do you explain the other two days?" Jason shoots back, voice rising slightly.

I laugh at their banter, letting out a little noise of triumph as I find the document I'm looking for.

"Your father responded, Jason. Would you like to hear this gracious letter?" I ask, redirecting the conversation.

Jason grunts his assent, and I clear my throat.

"'Dear Ms. St. Clair, we have received the forwarded documentation regarding the pack status of one unbonded omega, Lydia Anderson. After review, we recognize the transfer of authority over the unbonded omega from the Chauvert Anderson Pack to Pack Saint Clair. However, we will need to meet to discuss details that were glossed over in your haste. We will forward additional documentation to your counsel in the coming weeks. Best wishes.'" Can you believe this load of bull?"

I finish reading and set the page down, leaning back in my chair and crossing one leg over the other.

Jason sighs heavily, quiet for a moment, before speaking. "Honestly, considering it's probably my mother behind this bullshit, I'm surprised it wasn't more strongly worded. Though I'm not sure what they mean by 'details,'" he says at last.

Rhett swears under his breath and sighs. I can almost picture how he'd rub the bridge of his nose in frustration. "Is Louisiana one of those states that has alpha dowry laws still on the books? I would have thought they'd all been phased out."

"Explain," I prompt, the word clipped.

"Me mum once talked about how her Pa was expected to have a dowry set aside for when he found a mate. He didn't do it, and me Gran wouldn't have accepted the money even if he had it. Mum might be tough, but she learned how to burn her bras from the best. She ran on about how she wouldn't be putting one together for me or Mia, because we shouldn't need money to attract a worthy partner," Rhett goes on.

"So you think Samuel is going to make us *pay him* for Lydia? Like she's some piece of chattel," I scoff, hackles rising.

"Yeah, I know. I have a few cousins who still practice it, but they're generally considered the family weirdos. They still believe in true mates and celibacy until marriage, like we live in some sort of fairy story and not the twenty-first century," Rhett replies, just as incredulous.

"Don't get me wrong. I was raised with some backward notions, and quote, unquote traditional values, but if you told my father that finding me a partner would mean negotiating an exchange of assets, he would have had a stroke," I snort, amused by the idea of my father having to give something up for me to continue the family name. I would have died a virgin, for sure.

"It's just an idea. We'll have to investigate things to see if that's what they're referencing, but it wouldn't surprise me if it turned out to be true," Rhett adds, laughing at the end.

"What do you think, Jason?" I ask dully, not liking where this is going.

Jason sucks in a breath. "It's possible. Even if he was willing to let it go, Dad still wasn't thrilled about how everything went down. I think that has more to do with his pride, though. He's big on deference to the patriarch, and y'all scooping Lydia out from under him without kissing the ring doesn't sit well. But asking for money has my mother written all over it, but she wouldn't... hmm."

He trails off in thought, and when I go to ask a follow up, I'm interrupted by the beep of an incoming call.

"Hold that thought, it's Caleb," I say quickly.

I press the button for the other line, and the air explodes with sudden sound. A car engine revving, a woman moaning in pain, another voice that sounds like Lydia trying to calm the first woman down. After the shock wears off, I can take in some of the words, even through the sound of Caleb hammering on the car horn like it owes him money. There's a squeal of tires, and more frantic shouting, and I can't stay silent anymore.

"Caleb? What's going on?" I ask frantically.

"*De, na bisa, tviy pokazhchyk povorotu, ty, pavian bez materi!*[1] Sorry, Ms. St. Clair. Lydia was with Sylvie today, and we're headed to the hospital," Caleb says, honest to God shouting. I don't think I've ever heard him raise his voice once in the months since we met.

"Is everything okay? Is anyone hurt?" I press, uncrossing my legs and leaning forward.

"I think so? *Shcho tam vidbuvayet'sya?*[2]"

"Speak English and keep your eyes on the motherfucking road, you asshole!"

I don't recognize the new voice, but it's shrill and thin, and not Lydia. My heart slams in my chest, my skin cold. Lydia can't be hurt, not now. Not after everything we've done to protect her. Caleb would have told me right away if Lydia was hurt, even if he's technically off the clock right now and not obligated to keep to protocol.

"Slow down and explain yourself. What is going on?" I demand, pushing a little of my subaudible alpha back toward him.

But it doesn't seem to have any effect, at least judging by the amount of Ukrainian spilling out of his throat. Another honk, this time from outside the car, and Caleb snarls loud and fierce enough to make me shiver.

"I have to go. We're going to St. Mary's, and I'll—I don't know, I'll text you. Or I'll try."

And before I can answer, the line goes dead. He hung up on me. Caleb Novak, the consummate professional, the soldier I chose for his calm, unshaking control in stressful situations, hung up on me. I'm too stunned to speak, even when my phone switches back over to Rhett and Jason.

"What's going on, Lex? Is everything okay?" Rhett presses.

I blink, trying to get my throat to work. "I... don't know. Caleb is on the way to the hospital. He has Lydia with him, and his mate. But he didn't say why or what's going on."

As I scramble for my keys, my bag, my cell phone, I can barely hear anything over the sound of blood rushing in my head. I need to get to the hospital and figure out what the hell is going on. And then maybe dock Caleb's pay.

"Lex, wait a minute. What's—"

But Rhett's frantic question is cut off by another incoming call. I don't even look at the caller ID as I slam my finger on the button.

"Caleb, you better fucking—"

"Now hold on there, just a minute. What's going on, Lex?"

My heart skips a beat at the sound of Ted's voice, and I flush hot as I realize who I'm talking to. "Sorry, there's something going on with Caleb Novak, my head of security. He's got Lydia with him and they're on their way to the hospital. I don't know why, and I was hoping you were him calling me back," I ramble, rifling through my bag to make sure I have everything I need.

"Well, shit, that's not good," Ted puffs simply.

The only thing that keeps me from snapping at him is the knowledge that this man is the only hope I have for reuniting my pack before the new year arrives. I take a deep breath and recenter, pressing down my emotions to be dealt with another time.

"I assume you had something you wanted to tell me or ask me?" I ask calmly.

Ted chuckles, a noise that drags on my fragile nerves like broken glass. "I just got the word from the Orleans Parish DA. The grand jury is refusing to indict. Rhett's coming home."

I sag, hand to my chest. Closing my eyes, I send a prayer of thanks to every higher power I can imagine.

"Now it'll probably take until Monday to get someone out to get that ankle monitor off him, but after that—"

"No!" I practically shout, sitting straight up. "I want him on the plane and in the air before midnight. You hear me, Theodore Calhoun? He's been away from his omega for nearly eight weeks, and she's being rushed to the hospital as we speak. He. Comes. Home. *Tonight.*"

"Yes, ma'am. I'll do what I can," Ted says, and I can practically hear him swallow.

"You do whatever you have to, pay whomever you need to. I mean it."

I get to my feet and lean over the phone, and as if he can sense it, he gives me another quick "yes, ma'am" before hanging up. I switch over to Rhett and Jason, sighing.

"Ted's going to call you in a minute. I'm heading to St. Mary's. I'll text you when I know more," I drone, shifting my weight from one foot to the other.

Rhett grunts out an acknowledgement, but I don't have time to talk him down. Instead, I hang up and stride out of my office and out to my car.

---

1. Where is your turn signal, you motherless baboon!
2. What's going on back there?

CHAPTER TWENTY-EIGHT

Rhett

I END MY CALL with Ted, a bittersweet warmth filling my gut. I'm free. They're dropping all charges due to failure to indict. I'm going home. I should be over the moon, shouting and dancing because I'll finally be able to see my pack again. But instead, all I can feel is overwhelming anxiety over the situation with Lydia.

I've tried calling her several times, but she's not picking up. Does she not have her phone? Or is she too hurt to answer? I have to slam the door in my mind that cracks open with those terrifying questions. I promised myself I wouldn't go back there, to that place of anxiety and desperation. A spot above my heart aches, and I massage it slightly, trying to sense anything. Lydia has me convinced now about this "pseudo-bond," despite my early skepticism. But the longer we've been apart, the less I've been feeling that longing, the random flashes of emotions that don't relate to anything I'm doing. And in this moment, I can't tell if I'm not feeling anything because the bond is so fragile, or if there's really nothing to feel.

Trying to distract myself from that dangerous line of thinking, I fire off a text to Lucas, asking if he's heard anything from Lydia. I wander around the apartment, trying to gather as much of my stuff as I can onto the bed I've been sleeping in. I want to be ready to sprint out of here as soon as this monitor is cut free from my ankle. But I can't get much accomplished while I'm constantly checking my phone for a reply.

The minutes drag like decades, but no one is answering me. I remember latently that Lucas has work right now, and probably isn't answering because he's actually doing his job. But Lex still hasn't texted, and I know she would have reached the hospital at this point.

"Dude, you have to sit down. You're driving me crazy," Jason snaps from the kitchen island.

I growl at him, my patience too short to deal with him, too. Not that he has a whole lot of room to judge me and my coping mechanisms. His face is placid, but he keeps fidgeting, messing with the couch cushions, straightening the coasters in their little holder on the end table, refolding the kitchen towels. I swallow the sharp words threatening to come out, not willing to start a fight when we both have better things to worry about. I keep refreshing my phone, waiting for someone to tell me what's going on. I feel so useless, like I have for the last two months. My omega needs me, and I can't leave this fucking apartment.

Finally, I get a message from Lex in the pack group chat.

Lex: Lydia's fine. Sylvie went into labor.
Me: Thank God she's not hurt.

I relay the information to Jason, and his shoulders slump in relief. He slides into a dining room chair, pulling out his phone. I return my attention to my own device as it buzzes again.

Lex: Sylvie won't let her leave, not that Lydia wants to go anywhere.
Mat: What? Why?
Lucas: Sounds like an omega thing. It's in their nature to protect and care for other omegas, especially during the birth process. So we probably won't be able to get Lydia to leave until after the baby's born.
Lex: Well, she may not have a choice.
Lex: She's starting to go into heat.

I swear under my breath, running a hand through my hair. The others go back and forth, figuring out how to best proceed, but my mind is elsewhere. I fight the urge to call Ted again and tell him I'm going home, with or without getting my ankle monitor removed, but Jason's voice pulls me from my thoughts.

"Look, I'm going to go through with our plan. I'll take my time and let you get home and get settled in, but I need to leave tonight. Sammy isn't sure he can cover for me for much longer." Jason sighs.

"What's going on? Have you heard something?" I ask, abruptly focusing.

Jason shrugs. "They've figured out stuff's missing, but they are having a hard time pinning down exactly what I took or what it means. But I should get it out of their reach before they do. You know what I mean?"

I nod thoughtfully. I'd looked over the documents and files, and while I consider myself to be pretty finance savvy, the sheer amount of information contained in the spreadsheets was overwhelming without his explanations. Lex wanted us to send copies of the files, but sending massive amounts of encrypted files from my computer to hers via a highly secured line seemed a little suspicious. Jason has the boxes loaded back in his car and is going to drive them to Everton, and then the forensic accountant can get to work.

If Jason's this worried and wants to leave, I don't think it would be smart to stop him. There's really nothing to keep him here any longer, especially now that I'm leaving, too. The company over the last week has been a welcome change, but it's time for us to get him safe. We can protect him better in Everton when he inevitably faces the backlash of his formal petition for pack severance. After a long pause, I nod and pull out my wallet. Sliding out a thick white plastic card, I hold it out for him to take.

"This is the access card for the elevator to my pack's suite at Wickland House. I don't know what the situation is going to be once I get home, and I don't want you to not have anywhere to go while things get sorted," I explain.

Jason gives me a withering look, a smirk pulling at his lips. "Don't want me crashing the party?" he teases.

I roll my eyes. "I was trying to not make it weird for you and your sister, but hey, if that's what you're into, I'm not one to kink shame—"

Jason takes a swing at me, but I dodge easily, laughing. I like Jason a lot, especially after having spent the last several days with him. He's still got some work to do in deconstructing all the dogma his parents put in his head, but Rome wasn't built in a day. We haven't talked about his plans for his future after he gets released from his pack, but I do hope he'll stick around Georgia. I know Lydia would love having him close by, and we could find a place for a sharp mind like his within the St. Clair Foundation.

My thoughts are interrupted as my phone buzzes in my hand, and I let out a snort of annoyance. It's just Ted informing me that he's found someone to remove the ankle monitor, but they won't be able to come out for another hour or two. I have half a mind to cut it off with a pair of kitchen shears, but it would be stupid for me to come this far only to trip at the finish line. I've gone this long. I can manage a few more hours without ripping my hair out by the roots.

I contain my manic energy and channel it into packing, at least while Jason finishes gathering the last of his things. One bro hug later, and he's off into the afternoon sun. He'll drive a few hours, hopefully getting across the Mississippi border before stopping for the night. Once the door closes behind him, I'm left alone with my thoughts and anxieties once again. It's only a few more hours, I tell myself. I can do this.

My suitcases are packed, boxes of my work piled on the table and taped shut, ready for the trip back to Everton. The group chat hums constantly, everyone doing their part to prepare. Lucas is with Lydia, monitoring her and making sure she's safe. Lex is out running errands, making sure we have plenty of easy meals and snacks in the house, as well as bottles of electrolyte-filled beverages. Mateo is helping her for now, but will be there waiting for me at the airport as soon as the plane touches down. I have nothing left to do but wait and pace and wonder if my omega will be there for me when I'm finally set free.

CHAPTER TWENTY-NINE

Lydia

I'VE BEEN TOLD ALL my life that it's not a mortal's place to question God's timing, that things happen when they're meant to, and we should just do our best with what we're given. I haven't believed anything like that in a while, but the events of today really hammer home that Sky Daddy is a petty bitch with a malicious sense of humor.

I'd been spending the day with Sylvie, helping her get the last few things settled in the nursery. Clothes were folded, pillows fluffed, diapers stuffed in every available space. I'll admit that her nesting has only enhanced my own urge to do the same, but I keep pushing it off. My pack knows that I'm close to my heat, and have been doing everything in their power to make sure I'm comfortable. Only I have been shoving down all my urges for days in an effort not to alarm them. I know the moment Rhett is released, however, I won't be able to hide how close I truly am.

But all my work and effort were thrown out the window the moment I heard the sudden gasp and splash on the kitchen tile. My senses flooded with cinnamon and sugar, and something deeper that punched me right in the gut. Sylvie's water broke, and the world fell into chaos.

Now I'm sitting in a delivery room in St. Mary's Hospital, clutching her hand as she breathes through another contraction. We've been here for a few hours, and I haven't been able to move more than an arm's length away from the bed without my mind screaming panic at me. I have this overwhelming need to be by her side, to soothe her and protect her and the baby. I've never felt like this about someone before, but I don't have the mental capacity to look at those feelings too closely at the moment.

The contraction subsides, and Sylvie sags down into the pillows. I reach over and gently wipe the sweat away from her brow, brushing back a few loose strands of her cotton-candy pink hair. She smiles weakly up at me, nuzzling my palm slightly.

"Your pack must be losing their shit, girlie," she jokes, laughing breathily.

I shrug. "They'll be fine. I'm staying with you," I say in a tone that brooked no argument.

"I know. And I'm glad you are. Caleb's useless."

We both laugh, and I glance over my shoulder at my bodyguard. He's sitting in a chair, elbows on his knees, hands steepled and pressed to his lips as they mutter softly in his native language. His eyes are closed, but I can see them moving back and forth beneath his eyebrows. I didn't think he was particularly spiritual, but the birthing process does strange things to people.

A sudden pang of white-hot pain shoots from my lower belly, up my stomach, and into my lungs, and I have to hide my wince. I know it's just the first warning sign of what's to come, but I won't let Sylvie worry about me. She needs to stay calm, to keep that baby safe. I look up at the monitor, watching the rapid but steady pulse of their heartbeat.

"Still hoping for a boy?" I ask conversationally, stepping away to pour a glass of ice water.

Sylvie snorts and Caleb growls. They'd intentionally decided not to learn the sex of the baby, and it's been a point of contention. Caleb is convinced it's a boy, but Sylvie insists it's a girl. Something about a ring test or another old wives' tale. I know they'll be great parents either way, but it's almost too easy to tease them.

A nurse comes in to check on progress, and I hover close, smoothing down her blankets and generally fussing. My skin itches and I feel like I'm dripping sweat, but I can't leave. The farthest away I can tolerate is the connected bathroom, but even then, I'm restless and slightly manic. The ache in my gut grows steadily, but I can ignore it, at least for now.

I don't know how long we've been there when the door bursts open and I nearly collapse from the wave of mulled wine that crashes over me. Lex strides into the room, looking royally pissed off. Her hazel eyes flash, taking in Caleb, who's now perched on the edge of Sylvie's bed, holding her hand and then me, with my chair placed as close as I can get without being in the way. Her shoulders relax ever so slightly, but she's still frowning.

"Ms. St. Clair, I—oh, God. I'm so sorry, I forgot to call you back—"

"Yes, you did," Lex snaps, cutting off Caleb's rambling apology.

She crosses to me, tilting my chin up with a finger so I can't look anywhere but her eyes as she assesses me. I swallow hard, hands twitching in my lap as I hold back the impulse to drag her close and never let her go. She doesn't miss my slight wince as my belly turns painfully, and I flush hot.

"You need to come home, sweetness," Lex says softly.

My eyes go wide, and I look to Sylvie, throat tight. "I can't. I need to be here—"

Lex growls a little under her breath, and I whimper, shaking my head. I want to give in, but the idea of leaving Sylvie and the baby right now, when they both need me, is too much to bear. My mind is consumed with worries for her comfort and safety, as well as the safety of the baby. I can't go more than a few minutes without touching her, soothing her in some way. And the idea of leaving her side makes my heart throb painfully in my chest.

"Your pack needs you, too. And it's going to get more dangerous for you to be here the longer you let this go on," Lex reasons.

I know she's only looking out for me, but I can't fathom leaving. I jerk my chin away from her grip and move to sit on the bed opposite Caleb. Sylvie looks up at me wearily, smiling as I push her hair back from her damp forehead. I purr a little and both she and Caleb seem to relax, which settles something in my chest.

Lex lets out a frustrated huff, and I hear her shoes on the floor as she moves to stand behind me. Her hand is cool against the back of my neck, and I close my eyes as she rubs slightly, tension leaking away under her touch.

"You can stay, but under a few conditions," Lex starts, speaking into my ear.

I nod, already agreeing before I even listen to what she has to say.

"I'm going to send Lucas to stay with you. He'll keep an eye on you, try to keep things from escalating too quickly. But if he says you're at the point of no return, you will listen to him and come home immediately. Do you understand, lovely?"

Lex's voice takes on that strange, unrelenting quality that runs straight to the primal part of my mind, melting it like ice cream on pavement in July. I nod mindlessly, not hesitating for a moment. I know I can handle myself, but if having our beta here will make her feel better, then so be it. And if push comes to shove, I know I can convince Lucas to let me stay. Lex kisses me softly before she turns to Caleb and gives him a stern, assessing look. Not that he notices. His attention is entirely focused on Sylvie, helping her to breathe through a contraction. She gives up after a minute, then kisses me one more time before heading out of the door.

Not long after, I get a text from Lucas, letting me know he's in the Labor and Delivery waiting room and to keep him posted. I only manage a quick, one-word reply before I'm drawn back to Sylvie and helping her sit up. She wants to walk, and I don't want her to fall and hurt herself. But she's willing to try anything to get this baby moving.

***

The sun set a long time ago, leaving the only artificial lights overhead to illuminate the space. Every second that ticks by drags on my nerves, leaving me feeling raw and hot and uncomfortable. I've shed my t-shirt, leaving me only in a sports bra and flimsy tank top, but it hardly matters. My skin is damp, and sensitive to every brush of air or accidental touch. My legs ache, and the sticky mess on my inner thighs grows to almost uncomfortable levels. But I can tolerate this. It's nothing compared to what poor Sylvie has been going through.

We're on the tenth hour of labor, according to the doctor, and they're almost ready for her to push. Even with the pain medication, she moans and groans with every contraction. They're nearly constant now, with only brief gaps for her to catch her breath. But I'm right there with her, holding her hand and letting her crush it in an effort to channel her rage and pain into something else. My floral scent is masking most of the other scents in the room, and it's strong even to my nose. But I keep purring and pushing out the calming pheromones for Caleb, which in turn allows him to keep his head enough to use his alpha voice to help his mate. I can't imagine what sort of state they would be in if I weren't here.

"All right, Mrs. Novak. Feet up in the stirrups. We're ready for pushing whenever you are," the doctor, a serene female beta whose name escapes me, says as she pulls a stool toward the end of the bed.

"I was ready an hour ago, but y'all wanted me to pump the brakes," Sylvie grumbles, not as softly as she thinks, judging by the nurses' chuckles from behind me.

There're a few moments of shifting to get her into the right spot, but we finally get to where the doctor wants. Caleb is on Sylvie's right, me on her left, both of us clutching her hands tight. Caleb leans down and kisses her forehead, whispering something I don't quite catch, but that makes Sylvie smile wanly. But the moment is cut short as another contraction wracks her body.

"Push now! Ten seconds, you can do it!" The doctor counts slowly, interjecting praise and encouragement until the time is up, and Sylvie collapses back against the pillows.

"Again! Come on, you've got this," a nurse says from over my shoulder.

I purr harder than I've ever done before in my life, my stomach clenching over and over, almost in sympathy with the omega before me. Caleb can't take his eyes off Sylvie, but I glance down at the doctor, catching the worried furrow of her brow and the serious frown pulling down her lips.

"Okay, relax, baby. You're doing great. Take a breather and wait for the next one," the nurse behind me soothes.

Caleb strokes Sylvie's face, but I'm still focused on the doctor. The longer she's quiet, the harder my heart kicks in my chest. There's a noise from the hall, and it muffles whatever the doctor says to the nurse at her side, but the blanching on the young man's face, followed by his scampering exit from the room, says enough.

"What's going on?" I demand loudly.

"Nothing to panic about. I'm calling in my colleague to assist me. It seems like baby's shoulder might be a little stuck," the doctor says, voice way too light for my heart to take.

"What do you mean 'stuck?'" I ask, voice rising in fear.

Caleb and Sylvie look up at that, Caleb's alpha growl making the whole room go quiet. The doctor takes a deep breath and I think she tries to smile, but the paper mask over her face doesn't help.

"It's going to be okay. I've handled this sort of presentation before. I just want to make sure we're prepared for anything.

We're going to keep Mom and Baby safe," she replies, unshaken.

A moment later, another doctor, a man this time, flies in through the door, his white coat flaring like a cape behind him. There's a rapid exchange of medical jargon between the two doctors, but I don't process any of it. The male doctor's eyes find mine, narrowing in a glare.

"Why are you here?" he spits harshly.

I blink at his sudden angry tone, but recover quickly.

"My friend needs me," I reply simply, not letting this man judge me or intimidate me.

"You're about to go into heat. You're not helping—"

"How about you focus on the lady giving birth, asshole? She stays," Sylvie snarls, trying to sit up onto her elbows, but not making it as another contraction hits.

"Don't push right now! We need you—"

"Can't fucking stop if I tried, Molly," Sylvie cries over the female doctor.

Molly swallows and gives her colleague a harsh look before snapping out instructions. He rolls his eyes, setting my teeth on edge, but decides to cooperate. Trading places with Molly, he positions himself to catch while the other doctor helps Sylvie pull her knees to her chest, instructing Caleb and me to hold on to her and keep her there.

"Next contraction is going to hurt like hell, but you're going to push, hard. And don't stop until we tell you, okay?" Molly says seriously.

Sylvie swallows, shaking, but I nuzzle her head with my nose, trying to comfort her as best as I can. She returns the gesture before turning to Caleb.

"I'm right here, *kohkanny*. You're so strong and brave. I love you so much," he gushes, kissing her forehead, cheeks, and finally her lips.

I look away from the tender scene, but it only lasts a moment as Sylvie's whole body locks up with an intense contraction. She screams, a wordless cry of pain and effort, and it only gets louder as Molly pushes down on the still-swollen part of her lower belly. All the nurses and doctors are chanting for Sylvie to push, push, push. She's crying, and then suddenly I'm crying, my skin flushing hotter than ever before as I struggle to keep Sylvie in position. The moment stretches on and on, and I swear it'll never end, that I'm going to be stuck in this exact point for eternity. But then, something intangible shifts in the air, a relaxing exhale. The whole room goes quiet, and then the world is shattered by an infant's first wailing cry.

"It's a girl! Congratulations!"

Nurses take over for Caleb as the baby is placed on Sylvie's chest, covered in fluids and still screaming. I can't look away from her tiny face, screwed up and furious. She's here, she's safe. Sylvie did it.

My omega mentor looks up at me, tears streaming down her face. I reach over and push her hair back and rest my forehead against hers.

"Thank you, Lydia," she whispers.

I smile and back away, letting a nurse take my space to see to the new mom and her baby. Breathing deep, my heart skips a beat as I smell her for the first time. Peaches, and maybe something a little woody. It's delicious and precious and makes every fiber of my being cry out with a need to protect and care for this fragile new life.

That is, until my body shakes and I flash hot and cold, panic rising in my throat like bile. The room is crowded, too crowded. Too many people, none of them my pack. As if sensing my distress, Caleb looks up with alarm. I swallow, frozen and shaking.

"Go to the waiting room, *voyin*. Your work here is done."

The command is firm but soft, a hint of his bark coloring the edges. But it's enough to get my legs to move, and I bolt out of the room.

CHAPTER THIRTY

Lucas

THE PA SYSTEM CHIMES, and for what feels like the hundredth time in the last six hours, the Nursery Lullaby song plays. Another baby has been born.

Sitting in a Labor and Delivery waiting room and having no vested interest in any of the families in the rooms beyond has been a strange experience. I've been dragged into multiple celebratory huddles, been handed half a dozen cigars wrapped in pink and blue ribbons, and had my heart ripped out as a family received the worst news of all. It's been an emotionally draining roller coaster, and all the while, I've had to deal with the swift undercurrent of anxiety for my omega.

I've been sitting with Caleb's parents and Sylvie's father and stepmother for the better part of the last two hours when I finally catch my first whiff of Lydia's scent. Honey and lilacs drift toward me only moments before I see her rushing down the hallway in my direction. She's only in a tank top and thin leggings, a shirt clutched in one hand as she looks around frantically. I get to my feet, taking two steps toward her before she finally sees me and barrels in my direction. When she collides with my chest, it knocks the wind out of me for a moment, and I struggle to breathe as she wraps her arms tight around my ribs. She's rubbing her cheek against my sternum, whimpering. It's only when I put my arms around her that I realize how hot she is to the touch.

"You're okay, sweetheart. Let's go home," I whisper, kissing her head and rubbing her back.

"Need you," she mutters, pressing her body as close as she can without physically fusing with me.

"I know, but we need to get you back to your nest. Then I'll take care of you, okay?" I say gently.

She huffs but nods, and I relax a little. She's not as far gone as I'd feared. If I can reason with her, then there's still time. She has to be conscious enough of her surroundings for our plan to work. Though, if it came down to it, I'd skip my bonds if it meant keeping Lydia happy and safe. But I know she'd regret not doing it after the fact.

I disentangle her arms from around me enough to start walking toward the bank of elevators. I'm trying to remember where I parked as the doors slide closed, but I'm distracted as Lydia pulls my mouth down to hers by the back of my neck. I've been half hard since I first caught her scent, but now I'm sitting up at full attention as she kisses me like I'm her last meal. I lose myself in her touch, her taste, moaning and spinning us so her back is pressed against the metal wall of the car. She tries to hook a leg over my hip, but I push her back down with a growl.

"Please, Luc. I'm so empty, and it aches so bad," she whines, nails digging into my shoulders.

Thankfully, I'm saved from having to answer by the bell chiming, and the doors opening onto the lobby level. I grab her hand and pull her behind me as I stalk through the space, and out into the parking lot. It's dark, but well lit, which ruins my plans. But I can make do. She's going to be a mess if I don't do something to take the edge off, and she could hurt herself in an effort to get relief. So instead, I make a beeline toward my bike in the corner of the lot. There aren't any cars around, which is both a blessing and a curse. No one to watch, but nothing to give us cover. When we reach my bike, I spin her around and set her on the seat sideways before stepping in between her legs. She parts them automatically, clawing at me, trying to get to my skin through my clothes.

"If you're good for me now and when I'm driving, I'll give you the fucking you've been craving when we get home. Deal?" I ask hastily.

She nods, head falling back between her shoulders as she moans, not in pleasure, but in pain. My heart flips, and I don't waste another moment. I slide my hand below the soft waistband of her leggings, and I have to bite my lip to contain my groan as I realize how absolutely soaked she is. I can work two fingers into her tight heat without any prep, and I twist my wrist until I can press my thumb to her swollen clit.

She shouts at the sudden intrusion, hands flying to my shoulders as she hangs on for dear life. I pump hard and fast, and it's not long until she's clenching down and gushing more cream over my hand. But I can't stop. The pleasure written on her face is a drug, and now that I've had a hit, I can't quit. Her ankles lock behind my legs and she melts backward, arching her back and breathing hard, sweat beading on her chest. I lean forward and lick a long stripe up her cleavage and neck, tasting the earthy rain and vanilla of her arousal on her skin.

"Oh, God, Lucas. Please don't stop," Lydia pants, clinging closer to me.

"One more for me, greedy girl. You get one more and then we're going home to our alphas," I snarl out through gritted teeth, adding a third finger to stretch her, just like she loves.

The pain of her nails digging into my back is nothing; inconsequential to the feeling of her channel milking my fingers, dragging me in. It only takes a few more flicks of my thumb, a few more hard, deep thrusts of my hand to send her crashing into another climax. I wrap an arm around the back of her neck and pull her forward to bury her face in my shoulder to muffle her cries of ecstasy. I slow my thrusts, working her through the orgasm, until she finally stops shaking. When I withdraw, I move to lick my hand clean, but I blink in surprise as Lydia snatches my wrist. I don't fight her as she pushes my hand to my throat and chest, working with her to spread her release all over my skin.

"Mine," she breathes, so low I'm not even sure if she meant to say it out loud. "Yours," I echo, nuzzling her throat to cover myself in more of her.

When my hand is dry, she nods a little to herself, sitting back to look at me. Her eyes are a little clearer, but her skin is still flushed. I take off my riding jacket and start to put it on her, but she whines and fights me.

"You don't have to zip it. But your arms need protecting from the wind and bugs," I say, trying to stay calm.

"It's too hot," she grumbles.

I chuckle, but shake my head. "I know, sweetheart. But it's just for a few minutes."

She sighs, but doesn't protest anymore, letting me help her slip her arms into the leather jacket and put on her helmet. Then I put my own on, making sure the Bluetooth connection is on between us before climbing on. Lydia shifts into position behind me, pressing a little closer than usual. With a rev to the engine, I take off into the night, heading back toward the pack house.

Her body heat radiates into my back, sweat gathering below the material of my shirt, running down toward my waist with each passing moment. I speed up a little, pushing over the speed limit to get home before it's too late. The buildings are a blur, and I'm acutely aware of every place we touch, especially her hands. She can't keep them still, running them up and down my abs, going lower and lower with each pass.

"If you want to make it home in one piece, don't distract me like that," I comment, but I only half mean it.

She hums, sensing my lack of conviction, only growing bolder with her touches. It takes every ounce of concentration I have to keep from swerving into oncoming traffic as she cups my cock through my jeans, stroking it firmly.

"Have I ever told you how much I love the way your cock feels in my pussy? You're so thick and just the right length to fill me up," Lydia purrs, pressing her breasts to my back as she continues to work me through the material.

I rev the engine and execute a passing maneuver that I would normally never attempt with a passenger, but *fuck*, I need to be inside of her, in any way she'll have me. She squeals as the motor roars, and I smirk to myself. There's barely anything between her core and the bike, and I know she can feel everything. Her hand tightens on my cock, and

I groan low in my throat. Fine. If she wants to play a tease, I can play right back.

Now that we're in the suburbs, I open up the throttle and really let go. Lydia's gasp is like music to my ears, and I revel in it. I know it's bad for the engine, but I don't shift down a gear, keeping the RPM higher so she can feel the intense vibrations through the seat.

"Oh, God, Lucas. That feels so good," Lydia moans, shifting slightly to rock against the seat.

"Hold still, sweetheart. We're almost home," I soothe, taking another reckless turn.

Lydia leans with me, and her breathless, wordless cries of pleasure spike. I keep a steady pace through the twists and turns, and Lydia forgets all about my cock, clutching my waist tight as she rolls her hips as much as she can. I push us faster, faster than I've ever gone with a passenger, but she's so close, and I need her to finish before we get home. We're running out of space and time, but as I make the last turn onto the straightaway leading up to the Bristol Point gates, Lydia screams as she crests her peak.

I slow down smoothly as we approach the security booth, Lydia's whole body shaking against me. Her helmeted head is pressed to the spot between my shoulder blades, and I can hear her taking deep, slow breaths. She whines a little as I take off again, but I keep it slow, hoping I'm not overstimulating her too much. I don't bother looking for any other cars in the garage, heading right down to the lower doors of my personal workspace.

I hardly have time to shut off the engine before Lydia is throwing herself off the bike and onto her knees next to it. Her helmet comes off, and she tosses it carelessly off to the side, flipping her hair back as she reaches for my belt. I get my leg over to sit sideways on the seat in time, but I don't get much farther, as her fingers already have my jeans open and pushed down just enough to free my leaking cock.

My brain stops functioning the moment her mouth closes around my tip. Her moans vibrate up and down my shaft as she sucks, bobbing her head as she takes more and more down her magnificent throat. I gently thread my fingers into her hair, holding it back out of her face, but not making any moves to control her pace. I can only hang on, my eyes rolling in the back of my head as she takes me all the way, her throat muscles squeezing around me hard. I'm so close, and I try to hold back, but she won't stop. Her tongue swirls around me on every stroke, licking and sucking and moaning. My chest heaves as my spine tingles and my balls draw up, ready to spill.

But then the door bursts open, and my attention snaps to the figure of Alexandra St. Clair standing in the frame, wearing nothing but her signature red lipstick.

CHAPTER THIRTY-ONE

Alexandra

THE SECURITY GUARD AT the gate gave me enough warning for Lucas and Lydia's arrival, but I'd expected them to come to Lydia's room right away. I've been waiting on one of the lounge couches outside of her room, not wanting to enter her nest without her permission. But the minutes ticked by, and they don't come out of Lucas's garage, so I decide to investigate.

As I walk down the hall toward the closed door, a wall of scent hits me out of nowhere, and I have to lean sideways for a moment to adjust to the sudden rush of blood between my legs. My pussy clenches on air, and my heart flip-flops. Lydia's muffled moans come through the wood, and I have to shed the short silk robe as a sudden flash of heat explodes across my skin. Swallowing, I try to breathe through it, but the longer I stand there, listening to the wet sounds of some sort of sex act, the harder it gets. I can't stop my hands as they slide across my stomach to cup my breasts, tweaking my nipples as my eyes slide closed. Lucas is getting louder, the sucking more vigorous. I have to see what they look like, my two lovers chasing pleasure together. I can't stand it a moment longer.

I whirl around, not bothering with my robe, as I fling the door open. I freeze as Lucas's head whips around to me, face flushed, and his normally blue-gray eyes swallowed by his blown-out pupils. He's leaning backward against his bike, pants loose around his hips as Lydia kneels before him, mouth worshiping his cock. He tries to speak, to explain, I'm sure, but his words die in a long moan as Lydia sucks him all the way down, visibly swallowing around his length.

"Fuck, sweetheart, I'm gonna—"

Lucas doesn't get to finish before the hands in Lydia's hair tighten and his hips buck. Lydia moves with him, letting out a long, satisfied hum as she swallows his cum. My pussy aches at the sight of them, the way Lucas's hair falls over his forehead as he hunches forward, the pink flush to Lydia's hollowed out cheeks. As she slides back, dragging our beta's cock from her mouth painfully slowly, her eyes find mine, not leaving even as she lets a few strings of salvia hang in the air, licking her lips once they break.

My growl shakes my entire rib cage, and I stride across the room, shoving Lucas's hands away before pulling Lydia to her feet and devouring her mouth with mine. She tastes like honey and chocolate and smoke, and I need every drop. She melts against me, pliant and perfect.

"Table, now," I snarl, pulling away from the kiss long enough to give the order.

Lucas moves first, scrambling around us to clear the work-table, and I walk Lydia backwards in his direction. He lifts her back until she's spread out on the table like a feast. But a feast that is wearing far too many pieces of clothing.

"Off, all of it," I command.

"Yes, Domina."

The reply comes from both of my lovely submissives, and I can't help the proud lift of my chin as they shed their layers. Lydia reclines back, arms stretched out above her head and a coy smile on her face. What a sly little temptress she is, my lovely omega. But I will have her as I desire. So I spring forward, grabbing her knees and pushing them apart until her dripping cunt is fully exposed and I dive in face first.

Lydia's back arches, and I have to use more strength than I'd assumed to hold her down as she writhes and squirms under my tongue. But I move with her, drinking her essence deep until the only thing I know is honey and vanilla and lilacs. I swirl my tongue around and around, thrusting and flicking and sucking her down. She tastes perfect, as sweet and delicious as that first taste from Rhett's fingers promised.

Hands grab onto my hips, guiding me and Lydia forward until her head hangs off the far edge and I'm kneeling on the table, my ass in the air. I moan as Lucas's lips close over my clit, sucking hard, just how I like. He alternates between sucking my pleasure bud and licking my entrance, even going as far as to drag his tongue back to my ass, circling it and thrusting with a hint of pressure. I mirror his movements on Lydia, and her screams of pleasure fill the room, her release gushing over my chin and mouth. I don't slow, don't relent as I reach behind me and hold Lucas's face to my pussy when he sucks and flicks my clit. Lydia's hips roll as I build her up to another release, and I can feel my own cresting. Lucas understands my silent command, sucking harder and thrusting two fingers into my pussy to push me over the edge at the same moment as Lydia falls.

"I need you, Alpha. I need your knot, need more. More, please," Lydia moans, her nails scraping on the wood as she struggles to hold on.

Lucas pulls away with a deep inhale, working to catch his breath after so long holding it. He moves to kneel at Lydia's side, cock almost fully hard again. He looks at me, silently asking for permission. I bite the inside of my lip and glance at the clock on the wall behind him. Mateo should have gotten to the airport by now, but who knows if he's picked up Rhett yet. My heart aches from the need to fuck Lydia into the table, to bury my knot into her sweet cunt until she's truly mine. But doing so could snap the last thread of her sanity, and we need her to focus.

"Domina, use my cock to pleasure your omega. She needs to earn your knot, doesn't she?"

Lucas is looking at me pointedly, and I know we're thinking the same thing. Lydia whimpers and rolls onto her knees, bending at the waist until her forehead touches the wood in supplication. Lucas gives me a nod of consent and a slow blink. I've got to hand it to him; he really knows how to play to an omega's instincts.

"Please, Domina. I'll show you how good I can take a cock. Please let me. I'll be so good for you, please, Domina, please," Lydia begs, nearly hysterical.

I hum a little, letting the primal part of my mind slip forward. Backing up off the table, I drag Lucas's wheeled chair into position, draping myself across it like it's my throne. Lucas drops to sit on his heels, head bowed like the good little boy I know he can be. Lydia doesn't look up, waiting for my judgment.

"Very well, my lovely. My little slut of a beta is already hard again for you, so show me how well you take his big cock in your holes. Fuck my omega's cunt, and don't hold back," I order, lifting one of my legs to hook over the arm of the chair as I lean back and watch the show.

Lucas moves into position behind Lydia, taking her hips roughly in his hands and pulling her up to meet his thrusting cock. She screams as he impales her on this thick length, and he takes off, setting a brutal pace. He's already come once, so his already impressive stamina should hold up long enough to give Rhett and Mateo time to get back to us.

"Thank you, Domina. Thank you for letting him fuck me," Lydia moans, words choppy as she bounces against Lucas's hips.

"Play with her ass, too, slut. We need our omega to be ready for all the dick she's going to get over the next few days," I say, ignoring Lydia and speaking to Lucas.

He nods, eyes sparking with joy as he gathers some of her dripping juices off the table and spreads them around her asshole, not once breaking his steady rhythm. I let my fingers trail down my stomach, over the neat patch of hair on my mound, until I find my swollen clit, still slick from Lucas's mouth. My omega screams her pleasure as Lucas works one, then two fingers into her tight rear, twisting his wrist in counterpoint with his cock, opening her up and shattering her all at once.

I purr in my throat as Lydia reaches between her legs and gathers more of her cream, pushing herself up until she finds Lucas's chest and smears the fluid across his tattooed muscles, marking him, claiming him. The primal part of me preens, content that my lovers are so deeply connected. Lydia's moans turn to a chant of 'mine, mine, mine' as she digs her nails into his skin, not quite deep enough to draw blood, but enough to leave long red streaks on his forearms, biceps, legs, anywhere she can reach.

"On your back, slut. Ride him, Omega," I snap, fingers moving faster on my clit and occasionally dipping into my entrance to gather more of my own wetness.

They scramble to obey, and to my surprise, Lydia doesn't take him back into her pussy, but lets him slip into her ass as she squats down slowly. But once he's fully seated, she adjusts her legs and bounces. He helps her move, hands digging into her hips. Her head is thrown back, eyes closed as one of her hands squeezes a breast, pinching and tweaking her rosy nipple, and the other is between her legs, three fingers deep in her spasming cunt.

I can only watch as they move together, racing toward a finish line that's just within reach. My own hand rubs hard, fast circles around my clit, my breathing fast as I try to keep pace with them. When Lydia peaks, her whole body shakes and she moves her hand just in time for a stream of her release to coat Lucas's chest and face, pulsing over and over as he drives his cock deep into her ass. She collapses forward slightly, hand on his pecs as she grinds her hips in circles, sending him shouting into his own expletive filled orgasm. Watching them fall apart is enough to trigger my peak, and I moan and gasp through it, working my clit until I can't stand it and collapsing back into the chair.

There's silence for a long while, the ticking clock filling the air until suddenly, there's the crunch of car tires in the driveway, reaching us from up the hill through the still-open garage bay door Lucas pulled in through. Mateo and Rhett are home. And neither of them bother to park properly, killing the engine in the driveway and bursting through the front door and into the foyer.

"Your sir is home, sweetheart. Domina will tell him how good you've been for us, won't she?" Lucas coos, tilting his head back to look at me.

I can only swallow and nod. Seeing Lydia's face light up like a Christmas tree brings a smile to my lips, and I get to my feet and pace toward the table. She looks up at me, and I'm relieved to see a glimmer of clarity still left in their emerald depths.

"Let's get you to your nest, my perfect omega."

CHAPTER THIRTY-TWO

Rhett

MY LEG BOUNCES AS the plane taxis into the hangar, beyond ready to be done with this trip. It's nearly midnight, nearly twelve hours after I'd been given the good news that I had my freedom back. The delay had been mostly getting clearance to fly from the FAA, but that's all behind me now. I'm back in Georgia, and minutes away from reuniting with my pack.

I don't even bother with my bags as I bound down the airplane stairs, looking around for a car, a taxi, fuck, even a Penny-farthing bicycle to get me on my way home. Thankfully, Mateo's SUV rounds the corner before I have to steal one of the baggage carts, stopping short of hitting me. He doesn't even put the car in park, and I have the door open and I'm climbing inside. I turn to look at my best friend, the closest person I have to a brother, and exhale. The interior of the vehicle is drenched in lemonade and fresh cut grass, a scent so familiar that it brings tears to my eyes. I can't help myself, and I lean across the console and grab him in a tight hug.

"Yeah, I missed you too, Coop," Mateo says into my ear, hugging me back.

I laugh briefly before settling back in my seat and buckling my seatbelt. Mateo takes off with a slight squeal of his tires, but I can appreciate his haste.

"So, how was the trip?" Mateo asks conversationally.

I roll my eyes and scoff at him. "Absolutely delightful. So relaxing," I retort sarcastically.

Mateo barks a laugh as we exit the airport gates and turn onto the main road, and Mateo lays on the accelerator, taking the dark twists and turns with practiced ease. No one else is out at this time of night, and the headlights illuminate the trees flashing by. It almost feels unreal, like I'm floating in a dream.

"Not that I'm condoning your stupidity, but if you're going to get arrested for assault, at least finish the job next time," Mateo jokes, rolling through a stop sign.

"Don't think I didn't consider it, but he's not worth catching the attempted murder charge," I throw back.

"It's only attempted if you're a quitter," Mateo growls.

We share a dark laugh, but our conversation dies as Mateo races toward home. A few minutes later, we're through the security gate, and gliding around the winding roads of Bristol Point. The houses are dark, the streets quiet, adding to the liminal feeling of this entire day. Even as we pull into the driveway of the pack house I built for my family, I half expect to jerk awake back in my lonely bed in that apartment in New Orleans again. I'm floating as Mateo and I bolt toward the front door, not even bothering to park in the garage. And as the front door opens, and the familiar smells of mulled wine, pine smoke, lilacs, sugar, and spices fill my senses, my eyes burn with tears. I'm home. I'm truly home.

But I don't get to dwell for long on those feelings as a noise from the lower level reaches my ears, a moaning scream of pleasure that goes right to my cock. My omega.

I don't even bother taking off my shoes as I dash through the house, leaving Mateo to follow behind me as we rush down the stairs and into the lounge. I stop short in the open doorway to Lydia's room, frozen in place by the sight before me. Lucas is on his back, completely naked, his pale skin shiny with sweat and who knows what else. Lex is straddling his waist, tits bouncing as she fucks herself down onto his cock, and Lydia is kneeling over Lucas's head, eyes closed and mouth slightly open. I jump as Lucas's hand comes down on Lydia's ass with a sharp crack, making her moan again.

"I won't ask again, Omega. When I tell you to sit on his face, I don't mean hover. I mean *sit*," Lex snarls, pausing long enough to reach out and shove Lydia's shoulders as she whines but relents, finally lowering her dripping slit down onto Lucas's waiting mouth.

My growl rumbles up from my chest, making my whole body shake with a sudden, unstoppable hunger. My cock is rock hard, pressing painfully against my zipper, and I take two long strides into the room, stopping at the edge of the massive bed. Lydia's eyes pop open, and her face instantly brightens as she looks up at me. She tries to move toward me, but Lucas has his arms banded around her hips, keeping her locked in place. I lean forward, but I have to stop. I will do this the right way, so help me God.

"May I enter your nest, little omega?" I purr, hands twitching at my sides.

She moans, legs shaking and hips rolling as her face twists with pleasure, and a wave of honey-vanilla arousal coats my tongue like syrup. She nods frantically, arms reaching for me even if she can't move away from Lucas's relentless tongue.

I don't waste another moment, stripping down to my skin before climbing up to her side and gathering her in my arms. She's hot to the touch, but I don't care. My kiss is tender, soft and exploring. I'd nearly forgotten how sweet she is, how she yields for me with the slightest push. Her little fingers dig into my hair, pulling me closer. Lex commands Lucas to let go, and Lydia climbs off his face to fully face me, melting into my embrace. She was made to be held, designed to fit perfectly against me. Every soft curve of her body is exactly where they need to be, and I let my fingers rediscover each and every one.

"Rhett, I—I can't believe you're here," she breathes when I pull away to kiss down her neck.

"Nothing was going to stop me from being here for this, my love," I mutter against her skin, cupping her delectable breasts in my palms, gripping them just right for her to arch and moan.

"I've missed you so much," Lydia says, voice cracking with tears, and she wraps her arms around my neck.

I adjust her in my arms, gripping her tight around the ribs so she can press her face into my neck as I bury my nose in her hair. Her smell, the feel of her skin under my fingers, is like heaven on Earth, and I swallow the sudden lump in my throat.

"I missed you, too. But I'm home now. I'm here," I soothe, closing my eyes tight for a moment.

Looking up, I see that Lucas and Lex have adjusted their position, and they're now lying on their sides, Lucas behind her, holding up one of her legs as he languidly thrusts up into her. I smile at my beta, a soft thing that I reserve just for him, and he nods. I don't know what I did to deserve such an understanding partner, but I make a promise to myself to thank him very thoroughly for his patience later. But for now, Lydia's breathing against me is becoming ragged, her little whimpers cutting straight through me.

"I've got you, love. Let me take care of you," I whisper, gently pulling her arms apart and easing her down onto her back.

As she relaxes into the mattress and I take her in, I have to stop as the gravity of this moment hits me. We're really doing this, finally sealing the bonds we've held in our hearts for so long. Everything is in place, and my heart is so full that it nearly chokes me. Lydia looks up at me, reaching out and lacing her fingers through mine. She's smiling, eyes glassy with happy tears, like she can already feel what's going on in my head. With her other hand, she reaches out toward Lex and Lucas, palm up in invitation. I glance their way and catch the tail end of Lex kissing our beta deeply, brushing his cheekbones with the tips of her fingers when she pulls away. Then she fully exits the nest, leaving me, Lydia, and Lucas alone. The world shrinks as the man I love more than the air in my lungs comes up and leans into my side, wrapping his strong arms around me.

"Welcome home, Rhett," he whispers in my ear, kissing my cheek.

I don't let him go far, cupping the back of his head and covering his mouth with mine. He moans and melts into my side, parting his lips for me to taste him. His s'mores and pine smoke flavor explodes over my tongue, and my heart kicks hard in my chest. Lucas has been at my side for so long, and he's been my rock, my comfort, my joy. Kissing him is like hearing my favorite song on the radio, and the world is brighter now that I'm back in his arms. We pull apart and I look into his eyes, trying to find the words to tell him how I feel, but he just smiles.

"Yes, Rhett. If you'll still have me, I will be your bond mate," he says.

I can't help the bubble of laughter that bursts from my throat, and I press my forehead to his. "Of course I'll still have you."

"Oh, good. For a second there, it looked like you were going to—"

I cut him off with another heated kiss, and I can feel his grin against my lips. Bratty little shit stirrer. This time when we pull apart, we both turn to look at Lydia at the same time, and I suck in a sharp breath as I watch her slowly toying with her clit. She's smirking, and I roll my eyes. It seems like Lucas's attitude is infectious. Reaching over, I pull her hand away, moving forward to press my cock into her slick fingers. She understands my silent instruction, stroking me from root to tip and coating me in her juices. I shudder and gasp, overly sensitive from having gone so long with no one's touch but my own. Lucas settles down on his side next to her on the bed, and Lydia opens her legs even farther as I lean forward to settle between them. Her inner thighs are slick with her essence, and as I line up my tip with her entrance, her heat radiates off her skin like a furnace.

My thrust forward is slow but steady, and I nearly lose control at the feeling of her warm, tight cunt gripping me. She's so wet that I can slide all the way inside on the first thrust, my knot pressing against her outer lips as I bottom out. She sighs and arches, and I set a slow pace, enjoying the feel of her for the first time in weeks. I know I won't last long this first time, but I want her to come at least once before I burst. I sit back slightly, angling my hips so I can drive hard into that patch of nerves on her upper wall while rubbing circles on her clit. She meets me thrust for thrust, building tempo with each cycle until the sound of flesh meeting flesh fills the air. Lucas is there, mouth on her breasts, biting and licking to enhance her pleasure.

"I'm close, I can feel it. Please—"

Lydia clenches hard as she peaks, but Lucas scrambles to straddle her waist, facing me. He doesn't put any of his weight on her, but the position makes me pull back. Something flashes through me, a predatory urge to push him out of the way and snap at him. He's coming between me and my omega, and I need to get to her. My jaw aches and there's a feeling building inside of me, starting in my lower belly but spreading fast.

Mine. Claim. Bite. Mate. Claim. Mine. Omega. Mine.

"Alpha, I'm here. My pussy is so wet for you, and I can't stop coming all over your thick cock. Please give me your knot. I need it so bad."

Lydia's voice has an otherworldly hum to it, and my mind goes blank for a moment, and then the primal part of me lunges forward, latching onto her command. My omega needs her alpha, needs a knot. My hips slam forward over and over, harder and faster, until my spine tingles and my balls ache and pull up. I push forward one more time, my knot slipping inside of her channel with almost no resistance before it swells and locks in place. I roar my release as my whole body comes alive with pleasure, nerves firing and wires crossing as load after load of my cum fills my omega's pussy. My knot pulses and throbs in time with my racing heart, and I go a little lightheaded for a moment before the instincts are back.

Claim. Mate. Mine. Omega. Claim.

"Your mate is here, Alpha. Look at him."

Lydia's purr rattles my bones and I obey, looking up into my beta's eyes. He leans in, and he smells so good, like graham crackers and honey and sugar and smoke. My teeth throb with a dull pain, and I gather him in my arms. Yes, he's mine, too. I need to claim him.

"You are mine, Rhett Cooper, and I'm yours," Lucas whispers, bending his head back to expose the long, pale line of his throat.

I strike before I'm fully aware of what I'm doing, my teeth digging deep into the flesh of his throat. I clamp down hard, until my mouth fills with fluid, sweet and sharp, but absolutely delicious. After swallowing a few mouthfuls, I pull away to lick at the wound. Over and over, I whisper to him, affirming the connection between us. And I can feel it, like threads weaving together, twisting around and around until a thread becomes a braid, and the braid becomes a rope, and that rope becomes a line, an anchoring tether so real that I expect to see a physical thing between us when I pull away to look at his face.

The first little tug from the other side makes me gasp, and I pitch forward slightly before catching myself. Light, bubbly amusement fills my chest, and I know instinctively that it's not mine. There's another little pulse in my chest, warm and comforting. Love. I send the feeling back, and Lucas smiles brighter than all the stars in the galaxy.

"I feel you," he breathes, touching his chest.

My lower lip wavers as I nod. I'm so full of emotion, so overwhelmed by everything that's happened today, and it starts to crash down on me. My chest struggles to expand, and I fight to breathe, panic on the edges of my senses. But then there's Lucas, smoothing away my raw edges and filling me with comfort. A tear slides down my face, happiness filling me nearly to the brim. Lucas moves off of Lydia, and I look down at her again. She's smiling, blissed out in her own way. I lean forward to bite her too, but she puts a hand to my mouth, stopping me.

"Lucas first," she whispers, words slurring together slightly.

I nod and sit back slightly. She wants to make sure Lucas gets his bonds first, and a burst of affection spreads through me, enhancing my own awe for the kind omega in my arms. My knot has deflated enough for me to slip free, so I collapse down at her side, gathering her to my chest and kissing her everywhere I can reach. I try to speak, but nothing seems right, no words big enough to express what's going on in my head.

"Thank you, Lydia," Lucas says, sliding up behind her and cuddling close.

As I look up into his face, the gratitude rolling off him takes my breath away. Gratitude and love. I had no idea he felt so strongly about Lydia, but then again, I shouldn't be surprised. The soft, compassionate, beautiful omega in my arms is impossible not to love. Lucas meets my eyes, his serene smile making my heart melt all over again.

Lydia nods sleepily, and I don't stop her from falling asleep in my arms. Lucas and I share a glance and a smile before we turn to Mateo and Lex. Lex is wearing her short silk robe, and Mateo is down to his boxer briefs, and to my surprise, she's sitting in his lap as he lounges in an overstuffed bean bag chair. And even more surprising, his hand is between her thighs, toying with her pussy, fucking her deep and slow with his fingers. They're lost in their own little space, with him so focused on her pleasure that he doesn't seem to notice his audience at first. But as Lex sighs with release, relaxing against Mateo's chest, he looks up and shoots us a wink.

Mateo gathers Lex in his arms with ease and carries her over to the bed, settling her beside us as she recovers. He leans in and brushes a piece of Lydia's hair from her face, looking her over with such adoration that I have to look away. And as he settles nearby, he keeps a hand in contact with Lydia's skin, still warm but not quite as hot as it was a few minutes ago.

"She's asleep, then?" Lex whispers.

I nod, then realize Lucas is passed out, too. I look back to Lex and Mateo and smile. Their scents are faint compared to the thick layer of honey and vanilla in the air, but the familiarity of them helps to settle the last restless parts of my heart. I'm home, back with my pack. We're safe, and together, like we were always meant to be. It doesn't take long before we're all snuggled in Lydia's nest, all touching each other in some way.

Surrounded by my pack, I close my eyes and let myself relax and sleep deeply for the first time in months.

CHAPTER THIRTY-THREE

Lydia

THE ROOM IS DARK when I come to again, and I groan, trying to stretch into a more comfortable position. But I'm pinned down by far too many limbs. The last few hours come back in flashes, and my body flushes as the memories replay behind my closed eyes. I'm surrounded on all sides by deep, even breathing, and the combined scents of my pack. My heart feels lighter than I can remember as I detect the distinctive whiskey, leather, and dark chocolate in the mix now. He's home, and clinging tighter than a barnacle to my side.

Feeling nature's call, I struggle for a few moments to extricate myself from the pile in my nest and stagger across the room to the open door of my attached bathroom. I'm washing my hands when a wave of heat crashes over me, almost sending me to my knees. Clinging to the edge of the sink, my legs shake and my stomach rolls. I throw my hair up in a messy bun to get it off the back of my neck, but it doesn't stop sweat from pooling in between my aching breasts, along my brow. Stumbling backward, I try to stay upright as I blindly reach for the doorframe. I need to get back to my pack, need my alphas, my beta.

Another cramp flashes through me as I cross the empty space between the bathroom and the bed, and I lose all strength in my legs. I thump to the floor, rolling onto my back as my pussy clenches over and over, each muscle contraction so painful that I feel like I'm going to vomit. Reaching down, I rub my clit, trying to get any form of relief. I just need a moment and then I can make it back to bed. But the orgasm that builds won't crest, even as I fuck three fingers into my dripping core. But I can't go fast enough, deep enough, hard enough. I need more, more—

"I'm here, lovely. Alpha's here," a feminine voice whispers from above me.

A cool hand brushes my hair back from my eyes and I crack them open to look up into the hazel orbs of my prime alpha. I can't stop touching myself, not even as she leans in and kisses me, moving to kneel between my bent knees. Her slim fingers take over, and I moan loudly, her touch electric on my overly hot skin. Madness lurks at the edges of my mind, and I fight to hang on. There's one more thing that has to be done before I can give in and fall into the pit of need waiting below.

"Does my omega need her alpha to make it better? To make this tight little pussy feel good?" Lex purrs, nuzzling her face against my mound as she thrusts four fingers into me, adding just the right hit of pleasure-pain.

I nod and whimper, losing my words as her primal nature calls to mine. I roll onto my belly and rise up onto my knees, chest low as I present myself to her. She hums in satisfaction, slipping her fingers back into my slit with a wet squelch. I rock back in time with her thrusts, my climax rising again, but not peaking.

"Lex," a new voice calls.

I look up to see Rhett tossing Lex something, though it's hard to tell exactly what it is in the darkness. Moonlight filters through the frosted windows, and I realize the boys are awake. Lucas lay draped over Rhett's lap, mouth full of our alpha, one of his hands wrapped around Mateo's cock, pumping slowly. I moan in appreciation, but it turns into a whine as Lex's fingers slide free, and I'm left empty again.

But then I'm thoroughly distracted as Lucas shifts onto his hands and knees, Rhett rising up behind him with a bottle in his hand. Lucas groans as Rhett inserts two lubed fingers into his ass, but the noise is cut off as Mateo brings Lucas's head down and begins to fuck his throat. I flush and stare, mouth agape. Rays of silver paint their flexing muscles, all shiny with sweat, and they look almost like marble statues of Greek gods, caught in this moment of primal delight. I crawl toward them, needing to touch, to lick, to bite any part of them I can reach. I only make it to the edge of the mattress before firm hands catch my hips and hold me still.

"You can watch our boys play, but your cunt is mine, Omega," Lex growls, nails digging into the soft curve of my waist.

I nod, entranced by the vision before me. Mateo looks down at me, and our eyes connect, heat blazing between us. He slows his hips, each movement deliberate and sensuous. He's putting on a show for me, and the performance captures me entirely. Lucas moans loudly, the wet sounds of his mouth obscene in the best way, and Mateo purrs in approval.

"Don't worry, baby girl. You'll get your turn to choke on my cock soon enough," Mateo coos, pushing Lucas's head down sharply, making him gag for a moment before it's replaced with a muffled curse.

I drag my eyes down Lucas's body, the colors of his tattoos muted in the moonlight, but no less beautiful. His cock hangs heavy and leaking between his legs, bouncing slightly as Rhett pushes his hand into his ass over and over. The rippling muscles make me clench and whimper, and I want to touch them, taste them, join them. I want Lucas to fuck me as he's being fucked, and we can share Mateo's cock, taking turns sucking him deep, just as he likes.

But I lose all sense of reality as the thick head of Lex's strap-on cock breaches me for the first time. It's bigger than the one she used on me at Wickland House, or any of the toys she's used on me since, but my God, it feels good. It fills me in a way I didn't know I needed, the silicone soft and so realistic that I don't know if I could tell it apart from Rhett's or Mateo's if I were blindfolded. Once she's deep enough for the head to push on my cervix, Lex lets go and pounds into me with hard, sharp thrusts that I can feel all the way in my diaphragm.

Lucas locks eyes with me, shifting slightly toward me as Rhett lines up his cock. Mateo sits back and strokes himself as he watches, purring long and low in his chest with primal satisfaction. Lucas's eyes are a bright spot in the darkness, his mouth pulling into a perfect 'O' as Rhett fucks into him slow and deep. The world falls away, and I reach out a hand to lace our fingers together.

"I love you, Lucas," I whisper, giving in to the urge to speak the words aloud.

"Love you, too, sweetheart. Are you going to be able to hold out?" he replies softly.

I gasp as Lex brings her palm down on my ass, the sting of it adding to the roiling pit of liquid fire on the edges of my senses. It's creeping higher and higher, dulling pain and heightening pleasure and desire. I haven't felt like this in years, but I know the signs well enough. I can fight it for a little longer, but very soon, I'll be fully in the throes of my heat. But I have to hold off for one last task, and then I can fall and let my pack get me through. I nod and gasp as Lex spanks me again and again, her growl and purr mixing constantly now.

Lucas sets his jaw and turns back to look at Rhett. "I need to be closer," he says simply.

There's a moment's silent exchange, and I have enough brain space left to wonder if they are speaking without words across their new bond. But Lex grabs me by my hair, and I lose myself as my orgasm finally crests, a slow thing that goes straight through me, building that strange feeling in my core, the one that wants to reach out and latch on to the alpha fucking me like the world is ending.

"Alpha, please," I whimper, trying to purr but failing as my arms shake and I struggle to hold myself back from falling.

"Take my fucking cock, Omega. You're mine, and you'll take my knot in this tight hole, take my mark like the good little girl you fucking are," Lex snarls, words vibrating with her alpha bark.

Shaking my head, I clear my throat and reach blindly for Lucas. I can feel the call, the tether reaching out from the primal part of my mind toward Lex, demanding I obey. But I can't. Not when Lucas still needs me to focus. And then he's there, my beta and his clean cotton smell, soothing me and our alpha, tempering the burning in my soul long enough for me to focus and find my purr.

"Yes, Alpha. We're yours. Give your omega your knot, and your beta you mark," I murmur, low and soothing.

Lucas's arms support my upper body, and I lean my damp forehead against his chest, feeling his heart beating wildly against me. He tucks me in close, shifting to put himself between me and Lex, but she growls dangerously.

"Mine. Move, now," Lex snaps, a true alpha bark aimed at Lucas.

"I'm yours, Alexandra St. Clair, and—"

"My omega, not yours," she cuts in, barking again.

"I'm yours, Alpha. Show me with your knot, make me yours. Make Lucas yours," I push, purring harder even as my body goes into overload, orgasm almost constant now.

Lucas's soothing pheromones grow stronger, and I sigh, relaxing into his hold, closing my eyes to focus on my purr. Another set of hands is there, petting my hair, stroking my back. Lex's vicious snarl at the newcomer is met by another alpha's growl, and I recognize it as Mateo.

"Lucas has been patient with you long enough. You want to mark him, don't you, princess? Or are you scared?" Mateo taunts.

I look up at him, confusion cutting through the haze of sex in the air, and Lex goes still. The cramps start almost immediately, the pain flaring as I feel the madness pulling at me, growing harder to resist with each passing heartbeat. The world is fading in and out, and it takes everything in me to focus on my purr, on pushing the bonding instinct from me to Lucas so he can finally have what he's been waiting three years to have.

"Lucas, I—no, I need—Lydia needs—"

"I'm okay, Alpha. Lucas needs his alpha," I whisper, words thinning, even to my own ears.

"Knot her, and claim me, Lex. Please," Lucas says, transferring my weight to Mateo as he approaches Lex.

I whimper, rocking back onto her cock without fully meaning to. But I need something to fill this ache inside of me, and it only fades when there's pleasure to replace it. I lose track of time for a moment, and I'm not even sure how or why, but stars burst behind my eyes as Lex's knot finally slides into place and locks inside of me.

"God, you're so fucking beautiful," Mateo whispers reverently.

Smiling under his praise, I nuzzle my cheek to his bare chest, my hand drifting toward his cock. It's fallen to half mast, which offends me on a strangely deep level, so I drop my back and suck him deep down my throat. And as I taste his sharp metallic arousal on my tongue, the last drop falls into the pool of lava inside my mind. My body melts, and I let myself fall as animalistic need consumes me at last.

CHAPTER THIRTY-FOUR

Lucas

LEX IS LOCKED WITH Lydia for a long time, but I hardly notice as my alpha licks and sucks at the bite mark on my left pectoral, right over my heart. As with Rhett before her, I can feel the bond between us strengthening and solidifying with each thump of my heart against my ribs until it almost feels like a tangible thing, something I can picture wrapping my hand around and tugging. Lex giggles at my experimental pull on our bond, and there's a little effervescent bubble of joy floating back to me.

Rhett comes up beside me and kisses his bond mark, and I shudder as a rush of feel-good chemicals flood my system under his touch. Lex looks up at us, blinking with wide eyes.

"You felt that?" I ask huskily as Rhett trails his hands down my chest.

She nods, humming as she leans in and captures my lips with hers, finger tracing her bite. I moan into the kiss at her touch, and then again as Rhett licks his mark, hand circling my throbbing cock and stroking it slowly, spreading my precum around the head with his thumb. Lex is able to disengage with Lydia, and moves to kiss me more fully as Mateo scoops Lydia into his arms and takes her back to the nest.

I cast a quick glance in their direction. Judging by the glazed look in her emerald eyes and the thick honey scent in the air, Lydia is fully in heat now. I'm glad she was able to hold out, but I do have to wonder how that's going to affect the next few days, mostly if she'll stay in heat long enough to bond with all three alphas. We'll have to be smart about this and stay focused, which are two things I'm sure these alphas will be more than capable of with such a lovely, breedable, submissive omega like Lydia within arm's reach.

I don't get to watch them for long, my attention redirected back to Lex as she trails kisses down my chest until she's wrapped her lips around my cock, sucking while Rhett strokes. I can feel their pleasure as they touch me, and it stokes the fire in my stomach. They moan and Rhett presses his cock between my ass cheeks, not penetrating, but just grinding there. It's like a feedback loop of carnal delights, the three of us connected at the most fundamental level, and it only feels right to solidify that with our bodies.

"You want my cock, pet? Want me to fuck you into the floor?" Rhett purrs into my ear, squeezing my balls as Lex takes me all the way down her throat.

"God, yes. Fuck, that's so good," I pant, eyes sliding closed as I give in to the sensations and feelings flying back and forth across our bonds.

Lex's mouth makes a perfectly obscene popping sound as she releases me and comes back up to look me in the eye. There's a spark there that makes my blood boil, especially as her primal dominance rises until she's half-purring, half growling as I refuse to break eye contact.

"No, he doesn't deserve your cock, my love. He's been so greedy with our omega, getting to fuck her over and over while we had to wait. He needs to pay us back for our patience," Lex coos, low and dangerous.

I swallow, bucking as Rhett squeezes my sack just a little too tight, adding a bite of pain I didn't realize I've been missing. And the idea of playing with my Sir and my Domina has never sounded so good.

Dropping to my hands and knees, I present my ass for them to use as they see fit. Rhett chuckles, rubbing the cheek with a soft touch.

"Safe words, pet," he whispers.

"Red to stop, yellow to slow down, sir. Please make it hurt. I've missed you so much," I reply, words tumbling out before I can stop them.

Lex laughs, and the first crack of her hand on my ass stings, but in the best possible way. I thank her for it, like I've been conditioned to do, and another blow follows, this time from Rhett. I lose myself in their strikes, my mind floating with endorphins, and I know they can feel how good this is for me, because I can feel how much they enjoy my submission. My impulse to disobey, to make them work for it, vanishes as I realize how intense their love is when they have me like this. My ass is on fire, but my cock is hard and aching, balls heavy as I struggle not to touch myself.

Rhett brings both of his hands down onto my ass in a final blow, the hardest yet, and I cry out, cock throbbing with the need to be touched. He pulls me up to make room for Lex, but I catch a glimpse of the shiny patch of dampness my precum made on the carpet during that impact play. The ache is building, and I know I'm probably tomato red, but I don't care. These two could beat me black and blue if it made them feel half as good as I know they feel right now.

"Such a good pain slut for his alphas. You took your penance perfectly, and you deserve a reward now, don't you think?" she purrs, rubbing two fingers along her soaked entrance.

I nod mindlessly, unable to tear my eyes from her fingers. "Yes, Domina. Thank you, Domina," I drone.

Rhett chuckles behind me, pushing me off balance, so I'm leaning over her now. She guides my cock to her pussy, with Rhett pressing hard in the middle of my back, urging me to sink deep into her hot, tight core. Groaning, I go still as a wave of intense pleasure rockets down the bond from Lex, making my cock jump inside of her. I stay still as Rhett's slick fingers probe between my cheeks, circling my puckered entrance, and a single digit slides in with no resistance.

"Someone's been preparing for this, haven't they." He chuckles, adding a second finger with the same ease.

"He has, my love. He should be worked open enough to take a knot, if we think he deserves one," Lex answers for me.

I groan at the mere mention of being filled so completely, and both Rhett and Lex mimic the sound as they feel my longing for it. Rhett doesn't waste any more time, withdrawing his hand only to replace it with the blunt head of his cock. He pushes forward slowly and inexorably until he's fully seated save for the swell of his knot, which presses against my fluttering hole tantalizingly.

"Fuck, you feel so good," Rhett gasps into my neck, nipping at his bite again.

I buck at the burst of endorphins, making them both moan. Rolling my hips as much as I can, I fuck myself back onto Rhett's throbbing cock and into Lex's drenched pussy. They manage to stay still for a few moments, letting me do the work at first before they can't take it anymore. We writhe together, the physical joining of our bodies nothing compared to the ricocheting emotions careening along our bonds. My satisfaction of being so completely filled and surrounded by two of the people who love me, their awe of the depths of my feelings, my acceptance of their need to dominate me, Rhett's love, Lex's love, my love. All those things mixing together until I can't tell who is feeling what. We are one person, one mind, one body, one soul.

The moment of release is a chain reaction, set off by Lex's pussy tightening and locking down around me and her back arching as she yells out our names. I crumple under the weight of her orgasm, my balls drawing up at the same time as Rhett presses forward, his knot slipping inside of me and swelling as he roars, and I feel the hot flood of his cum, so much that it leaks out from around his cock and down my crack. My cock pulses over and over, and I come harder than I ever have before in my life, pouring what feels like every drop of myself into the alphas surrounding me.

We sit there, slowly coming down from the high, just breathing and feeling. A noise pulls my attention, and I look over in time to see Mateo groan and flop backward onto the bed, holding the back of Lydia's head as she sucks him dry, and I smirk. I'd nearly forgotten about them, but I'm glad the voyeur got a good show. Once he's spent, she crawls up his body and lays on his chest, passing out almost immediately. I yawn in solidarity, and after Rhett is able to withdraw and

Lex is able to let me slide free, the three of us stumble back to bed, letting them wrap me in their arms as we fall asleep again.

The sun wakes me up, and I manage to extricate myself from in between Rhett and Lex to use the bathroom before glancing at the clock. It's nearly a quarter to ten, and it's been well over twelve hours since any of us ate anything. So after pulling on a pair of basketball shorts, I sneak as quietly as I can out of the room and up the stairs. The house is quiet, a stillness and peace to the air that I haven't felt in a long time. Not since before Seth came into our lives.

As my mind drifts to that sack of shit, I sigh. I'll have to talk to Lex after everything is over. I don't know how she thought we wouldn't notice the weird timing of everything, but something doesn't add up. The Valencia might have some bad memories attached to it, but to sell it so suddenly, and to her father? And then Seth has a tragic fatal accident a few days after the sale is finalized, and the two people who have the strongest motive to kill him are conveniently out of town when it happens. I may have been born at night, but it wasn't last night. And the worst of it all is that Lex is clearly trying to hide whatever she did.

I set about cooking some nutrient-dense finger foods, contemplating everything that I know and trying to puzzle out how I'm going to approach Lex without coming off like an asshole. I'm rolling dough out for biscuits when arms slide around my waist, and I breathe in mulled wine and orange peels. My body tenses for a moment before leaning back into her embrace, shivering as Lex kisses Rhett's bond mark softly.

"What's on your mind?" Lex mutters in my ear.

I shrug and sigh, not really sure how to put my worries into words. After Lex's behavior right after we got back from New Orleans, it doesn't seem entirely out of the realm of possibility that she'd pay to have Seth killed. And yeah, it's worked out for the best, but could I really condone this type of behavior?

"I can feel you, Lucas. So I know you're worried about something. Is it something with Lydia?" she pushes, turning me around to face her.

Looking up into her hazel eyes, my will crumbles. But before I can speak, the basement door opens again, and Rhett trots into view, brow furrowed slightly.

"I felt you, Luc. What's wrong?" he asks quickly, striding over to me and Lex.

I sigh again, growing annoyed. I didn't want to do this now, least of all with Rhett here. Lex might shut down altogether, and I can't not know if she's an accessory to murder.

"I was about to ask Lex how long she was going to lie to us about what happened with Seth," I grit out, not bothering to beat around the bush.

I look at Lex as I speak, and the momentary flash of panic I feel through our bond is confirmation enough. She is hiding something, even if her face is the picture of shocked innocence.

"I don't know what you're talk—"

"Don't try to lie, Lex. I know something's screwy. Or you're going to try to tell me that you decided to sell The Valencia to your father on a whim?" I throw back, rolling my eyes.

"Wait, you sold The Valencia?" Rhett interjects, turning his shocked stare onto her.

Lex stumbles for a moment, and there're several flashes of emotions, all passing too quickly for me to really identify other than the undercurrent of fear. I reach out and take her hand, pressing my lips to the palm tenderly.

"Whatever you did, I don't care. What really hurts is you hiding from us again," I say emphatically.

Lex's eyes water, and she looks away, pressing her lips into a thin line. I push support and comfort down the bond, and I can feel Rhett doing the same, using my connection with Lex to show her he still cares about her and isn't mad, just concerned. Lex chuckles ironically, a tear slipping free.

"I'll never get used to that," she mutters, wiping it away before either Rhett or I can.

"What? Feeling that we love you regardless of the stupid decisions you make?" I tease, and I'm rewarded with her true smile.

"Yeah. And it's not as bad as you're probably thinking. Seth's not dead," she says.

Rhett and I look at each other, and I swallow roughly. Until this moment, I thought Lex paying for someone to murder her ex was the worst-case scenario. I hadn't considered that she would fake his death, and somehow, that's worse.

"So he's still out there, and could come back at any moment?" Rhett presses, and his panic simmers just on the edge of our connection.

I push a wave of calm in his direction, even if I'm not really feeling so calm myself. I swallow as I absorb, trying to think of what to say next. A pulse of deep shame comes from her, and I reach out and pull her into my chest.

"It's not like that, Lex. I just worry that he's never going to leave us be, that's all," I soothe, holding her tight to my chest.

She relaxes as she senses the sincerity in my words, and Rhett pushes his agreement through me to her. He envelops us both in an embrace, and I relax despite myself.

"I've put safeguards in place. The agreement is that I won't bother him again and he won't bother us, but my cousin Gideon is keeping tabs on him. I'm getting regular updates, so if Seth makes any suspicious moves, we'll know," Lex says.

"And nothing is going to come back to us?" Rhett questions seriously.

Lex nods. "I've been very careful about this. And I do regret not telling you, but I was trying to protect us. Mateo had to know because we needed to break our bonds. But I didn't want you to have to lie for me. And if worse came to the worst, and we got charged, pack mates can be compelled to testify against each other. Bond mates can't."

I frown, and despite my better judgment, I do have to give her credit where it's due. Her actions were extreme, but it's not like we had much choice left. Even if Seth went to prison, that didn't automatically mean their bonds would be dissolved. This way, we're free to move on so long as Seth keeps to the terms of this agreement.

"You're going to tell Lydia when this is over. Not now, but after we're all bonded and she can feel what I'm feeling and understand why you did it," I say at last.

She nods, and the relief coming from her is palpable. I kiss the top of her head and look up to Rhett, and I see my own wariness in his blue orbs. Seth can't be trusted, and we know that while Lex is pragmatic, she tends to hope for the best while preparing for the worst. I want to believe that this peace will last, but we've been burned by that sociopath too many times. Only time will tell who is right, and I can only hope like hell it won't be me.

CHAPTER THIRTY-FIVE

Mateo

WE FELL BACK INTO bed after Lex and Lucas bonded, and it's now several hours later judging by the sunlight coming through the windows when I'm pulled from sleep again, this time by Lucas exiting the bed and throwing on a pair of basketball shorts before leaving the room entirely. Lydia whines, but Rhett is there, touching her and soothing her for the moment. I look over in question to Lex, who is blinking sleep from her eyes.

"He's getting us some food and hydration. He'll be back in a minute," she rasps, voice full of sleepy gravel.

I nod and look back to Lydia and Rhett, and his fingers are buried between her thighs, her hips rocking rhythmically. My cock is already hard from the smell of sex in the air, coating my tongue in sweet honey and spices. Lex rolls until she's curled against my side, and we watch Lydia climax again and fall into a blissed-out doze. Rhett licks his fingers and settles Lydia against his chest and looks back to Lex and me, smirking.

"So when did this happen?" he asks softly, nodding at our position. "After Seth's accident," Lex answers as honestly as she can.

I nod and kiss her cheek, avoiding Rhett's gaze. He chuckles and sighs, and I glance back up at him, relaxing slightly at the amusement on his face.

"How do the bonds feel?" I ask, redirecting the conversation toward a less fraught subject.

Lex hums and Rhett smiles to himself, and I have to admit that while I'm delighted at their happiness, a tiny petty voice in the back of my mind is a little jealous. But I shove that away, not in the mood to deal with my baggage right now.

"It's different than with Seth, but I think that's a good thing, you know? I don't feel as... tangled, if that makes sense?" Lex says, voice lifting in a question.

I nod understandingly, and I hate that the jealousy in my heart grows a little more at that. Rhett clears his throat pointedly, and I have to look away from him. Damn him. I need to get better at controlling my facial expressions.

"Lydia is going to need one of us soon, and I don't think we should put off bonding for much longer. From what Lucas has said, having those bonds will help her come down from her heat faster," Rhett comments.

I nod, doing my best to swallow my protests and disappointment. It should be Rhett or Lex first, the logical part of me reasons. Rhett already has his pseudo-bond with her, and Lex is our prime alpha. There's no world where it makes sense for me to bond with Lydia before either of them does.

"We can go and give you two some privacy if you want it, or we can stay. It's up to you," Lex says, brushing a strand of hair away from my forehead.

I blink dumbly at her, my mind not quite comprehending her at first. But then I snap my gaze to Rhett, and the sparkle in his icy blue eyes makes my heart beat a little faster. They're giving me this choice, the opportunity to decide how I want to do this. And I know they know what this means, judging by their smiles and soft eyes. I nod, too choked up to speak for a long time.

"I'd... I think I'd like to be alone. I'll shout if I need anything, but I think—"

Lex kisses me before I can ramble too far, and I chuckle as she pulls away. She climbs out of bed and slips into her black robe, sauntering gracefully out of the room. I watch the swing of her hips as they disappear through the door before I turn to Rhett and scoot closer, working with him to maneuver Lydia from his embrace to mine. I give him a long look, feeling the need to speak, but not sure what to say. He spares me the mental torment, leaning in and clasping a hand to the back of my neck before brushing his lips against mine.

"I know, Matty. But don't worry about a thing. It won't be like last time; I promise," Rhett whispers against my mouth.

Nodding again, I take a deep breath. Of course, he'd pick up on my nerves. He's far too observant for his own good, truly a menace to society. But he doesn't elaborate, just clapping my shoulder before walking naked from the room, closing the door gently behind him. I sigh and nuzzle into the crease of Lydia's throat, breathing in her scent. She's warm again, and I want to touch her, but I don't want to wake her either. She needs to rest as much as she can, and who knows how long this is going to last.

Thankfully, she moans a moment or two later, turning over to press her face to my chest without even opening her eyes.

"Good morning, baby girl," I mutter, kissing her neck over and over.

"It's morning?" she sighs, words slurring together slightly.

"A glorious one. The sun makes your hair look like melted caramel right now," I gush, not even sure where the words come from.

She chuckles, hands sliding out over the sheets, searching. I pull her back in with a kiss, trying to distract her. While she's in heat, she's not going to take kindly to any of her chosen partners leaving her side, even for short periods of time. I don't want her to get upset, but I'm too late. She rears back and looks around, eyes half-lidded and bleary.

"Where is everyone?" she asks, her tone edging toward panicked.

"They're making food, baby. Don't worry, they'll be back soon," I soothe, sitting up to gather her in my arms again.

She nods, but she's still tense. I run my hands over her stomach and up to her slightly swollen breasts, rubbing them gently and playing with her nipples until she's soft and pliant again. She lets me guide her back down to the bed, and I settle myself over her, kissing her harder this time. Her fingers thread into my hair, holding tight as our tongues dance, her yielding when I push. I shift my knee up to press against her core, and she's already soaked.

"Does my baby girl need something in her pretty pussy?" I coo, nibbling on her throat and collarbones.

"Yes, please," she moans, head tipping back to give me better access.

I chuckle under my breath, basking in her gasping cries as I pinch her nipples hard, only to soothe away the hurt with my mouth. She grinds against my leg, trying to get some relief. But I pull back over and over, teasing her with pressure, only to ease off and leave her whining.

"Daddy, please don't tease me. I need you," Lydia finally whines, pulling my hair hard.

"But I want to tease you. And you want to give Daddy what he wants, don't you, baby girl?" I taunt, sliding a hand down to brush feather light over her throbbing clit.

"I do, but it hurts. It aches and I can't take it, please. Daddy, please—please help me," Lydia sobs, begging desperately.

Moving back to kiss her deeply, I nudge her legs apart as I line my aching cock up with her entrance. I don't know why or how, but hearing that honorific on her lips as she begs me to fuck her does something to me, bringing out the primal caregiver that I didn't even know I had inside of me. I want her to need me, and I need to please her. And as I slide into her tight heat with no resistance, the look of joy and relief that spreads across her face brings me to my metaphorical knees. Seeing her look at me like I'm the center of her universe fills my heart with so much warmth that I can feel it trying to leak from behind my eyes.

"I love you so much, Lydia," I whisper passionately, driving deep into her.

As she gazes up at me, a touch of clarity returns to her expression, the smile on her face not the heat-induced kind from a few moments ago, but more like the woman who holds my heart in her delicate little hands.

"I love you, too, Mateo."

Lydia trails off with a groan as I shift my hips, driving against her inner pleasure point as I rise up, bringing her with me so she's in my lap. We're nearly eye to eye in this position, and she has more leverage to fuck herself deeper onto my cock. Her arms are tight around my shoulders, her nipples hard as they brush my chest each time our hips come together. Words fail us both as we race toward release, and I swallow, nervous again. As if she can already sense my emotions, she cups my cheek with her left palm, the arm we agreed I'd bite to bond with her.

"I'm close, and I can feel it trying to reach out toward you," she whispers breathlessly.

My brow twitches in confusion, but she shudders and arches her back, her pussy clamping down on me out of nowhere. I suck in sharply, slowing to fuck her through it like I normally do. But she whines, nails digging into my skin.

"Faster, please. I need to feel you," she begs.

The primal part of me surges forward at the slight quavering to her plea, desperate to soothe whatever is hurting my omega. I grasp her hips and help her to ride me, eventually turning to put her on her side, lifting one of her legs to my shoulder so I can drive harder and deeper than before. Her hand slips down to my chest, settling over my heart, and our eyes meet. The emerald green irises are nearly swallowed by the blacks of her pupils, the void pulling me down until I'm lost. The world could be burning to the ground around us, and I still wouldn't be able to look away from this miraculous creature.

"Will you mark me, Alpha? Make me yours?" Lydia asks, voice small and thin, like she's on the verge of tears again.

"You're mine, Omega. And I'm yours. Until this stops beating," I declare, pressing a hand over hers on my chest.

She cries out my name, throwing her head back as she crests her peak once more, her muscles sucking me in until my knot slips into place, swelling as I fill her with my seed. My body tingles and something surges in my stomach, more than my orgasm, something deeper and more intrinsic. I lean down and close my teeth over her wrist, biting with enough force to break her skin for the first time since we met. My mind races and slows at the same time as her blood coats my tongue and throat and I take several long pulls of the sweet nectar. She tastes like the first rain after a drought, and my soul fills with light. There's a pull in my chest, and I gasp and release Lydia's wrist as feelings of trust and rightness, and true, unconditional love, fill me. I look down, tears on my cheeks, and I let Lydia's leg fall to the side, groaning at the increase in pressure when I hold her to my chest, our legs tangled together and faces inches apart.

"You're here," she whispers reverently, almost disbelieving.

I nod, lower lip trembling. I can feel our connection growing brighter and stronger, each little touch adding to the tether and bringing us closer. Chest to chest, nose to nose, sharing breaths, we kiss away each other's tears, just feeling and experiencing this moment. I feel lighter than I have in years, like I'd be bobbing along the ceiling if she wasn't holding me to the ground. My impulse to fill the silence with talk fades, because I realize I can tell her how much I love her without words now.

Giving a short, experimental tug on the invisible string between us, I send her pleasure and joy. She giggles brightly, squirming and then going still as the movement triggers another orgasm. I pull her arm up and kiss at the wound I've created, licking the tender flesh. Almost instantly, she relaxes, head flopping back against me. And faintly, a matching tingle spreads through my own wrist. It's not possible for an alpha to retain a bond mark like omegas and betas can, but that doesn't mean we don't experience the effects of the marks we leave on our mates. Everything is super sensitive right now, which is why I can feel it so strongly, but I hope that never fades. That every time she touches my mark, I'll know.

"That feels like the world's best massage, and eating the most delicious dessert all at once," she drawls sleepily.

"Then I'll do it every day, until you're sick of it," I promise, only half teasing.

"Don't threaten me with a good time." She yawns, falling even deeper into relaxation until she's fully asleep. But even after my knot deflates and my cock is soft, I don't move an inch.

The need to be close to her is overwhelming, and I let my head rest on hers as I close my eyes, slipping into a light sleep as well.

CHAPTER THIRTY-SIX

Rhett

THAT EVENING, WE'RE ALL piled in the nest, limbs tangled as we try to catch our breaths from the most recent round. I don't remember much from the disaster of Seth's heat, but I know it wasn't like this. I've never felt more comfortable in my life than I do in this moment, skin on skin with my pack. The air is thick and warm, everything hazy with endorphins. Lucas backs in with a tray of finger foods and bottles of sports drinks, setting them on the edge of the bed before crawling into Lex's waiting arms. Mateo leans over and plucks up a string of grapes, feeding them to a half-conscious Lydia.

The pure love shining between Mateo's and Lydia's faces warms my heart in a way I don't think I could have ever prepared myself for. Maybe it's because the shadows and darkness I've grown accustomed to seeing on my best friend's face for the last few years are finally, truly gone. Maybe it's because I'm watching Lydia receive the care she deserves from someone who understands how special she is. Or maybe it's something else entirely. Regardless of the reason, seeing them together, speaking without words, makes me smile with soul-deep contentment.

I watch them for a while, but my attention shifts as Lex moves in and rests her head on my bicep, with Lucas curled into her other side. She chuckles a little to herself, and I look at her, pushing a little curiosity down the bond through Lucas to her.

"I haven't thought about work or Seth once in the last few days. I can't remember the last time that happened," she whispers, just for me and Lucas.

Wrapping my arm around her, I press a lingering kiss to her temple. "I'm glad. It's time for us to move on from the past," I mutter against her skin.

She sighs, and I feel a strange, bitter flash in my chest before it's gone. Lucas looks up in alarm, feeling it, too.

"We've still got one last string to cut," Lex mutters darkly, eyes fixed on Lydia and Mateo.

I nod, keeping my face blank even as righteous fury fills me for a moment before Lucas is there, soothing it away. He casts me a quick glance, and I smile gratefully. Lydia whimpers, drawing our attention, and Lucas rolls away to assist, giving Mateo a little bit of a break. Not that he moves far, but he can only get it up so fast. I look down at Lex, frowning.

"I gave Jason my access card to the Wickland suite. He should be there by tonight, if not tomorrow morning," I mutter, trying not to let my words carry.

"If I can get away to send a text, I'll have Steph get in contact with him so they can get the documents to a forensic accountant," she replies just as softly.

I shake my head, gathering her close. "We can worry about that later. I want to enjoy being back home, with everyone I love. Let's get through this and through the holidays, then we can teach t'ose abusive fuckers tha lesson t'ey deserve."

Lex chuckles, a low, dangerous sound that only feeds the petty, vengeful part of my soul. I can feel her own desire for revenge, to show the people who hurt our omega the consequences of their actions. But we have to be patient. Our moment will come. I know a thing or two about delayed gratification and how sweet the rewards can be for those who wait.

Lucas tugs on the bond, and I look up to find him buried between Lydia's thighs, thrusting deep and slow, making her writhe and buck as she tries to get him to go faster. She's reclining against Mateo's chest, and he has a finger on her clit, tracing lazy circles. Their teasing has her panting and whimpering, and my heart twists at the noise. Lex kisses my cheek and sits up, gathering up the food before it can spill everywhere while I crawl toward my omega. She sniffs a little, her eyes cracking open as her hands stretch out toward me on instinct.

"Sir, please, I need you," she mutters, tone almost bordering on pained.

I smile kindly, nudging Lucas out of the way. He leans down and kisses Lydia thoroughly, withdrawing to allow me to kneel in his place.

"No, don't leave," Lydia gasps, grabbing Lucas's wrist.

He twists in her grip until he can reciprocate the hold, bringing her hand up to his lips and kissing her knuckles tenderly. "I'm right here, sweetheart. But our sir wants to ask you something, doesn't he?"

Lucas looks at me, and I feel his meaning even as I can read it in his eyes. He's seeing something we aren't, some sign that Lydia needs an alpha, and it's time for me to bond with her. I swallow at the thought, and my cock hardens so fast I go a little lightheaded from the sudden reallocation of blood in my system. I've thought about this moment for so long, dreamed about the day when I'd take this stunning woman as my bond mate. And as she looks up at me, my best friend still toying idly with her dripping pussy and swollen clit, I've never felt more sure of anything in my life.

"Look at me, sweet girl," I purr, pushing an ounce of my alpha bark into the words. Not enough to force her compliance, but enough to get her attention on me.

I can almost feel the effort it takes for her to open her eyes and drag them up to meet mine, how hard she's struggling to obey me. My heart swells with love, and I reach down and cup her jaw, running my thumb along her lower lip. Without missing a beat, she takes the tip inside of her mouth, swirling her tongue as she sucks, emerald eyes never leaving mine. I hum my approval, delighting in the spark of joy the simple sound brings to her eyes.

"I love you, my perfect girl. Will you take me as your bond mate?" I whisper.

She gasps as Mateo dips a finger inside of her slit, but her attention is entirely fixed on me now. The world falls away as I watch her climb toward release, higher and higher, until her chest heaves and she's shaking with the effort to hold back. I wait to see what she'll do, if she'll give in to what her body wants, or if she'll remember her training.

"Yes. Yes, sir… please," she breathes, hardly able to get the words out.

"Such a good girl, my love. Can you hold it just a moment longer for me?" I prompt, leaning in and lining my cock up with her entrance.

She blinks slowly and nods, biting her lip. I press forward, her tight heat quivering around me. Her arms dart out, wrapping around my shoulders and clinging to me as I set a hard and fast pace, groaning low in his chest at the wet slide of her cunt. I whisper praise with each roll of my hips, my hands clutching her waist hard enough to bruise.

"You gonna come all over his cock, baby girl? Or do you want more? Want us to fill you up all the way?"

Mateo's voice startles me, and I'm a little ashamed to admit I'd forgotten he was there. Lydia throws her head back, nodding as she moans her pleasure and frustration. I shift slightly, bearing her weight so Mateo can get himself into position. Lydia hitches her legs over my thighs, and I spread her ass for Mateo, presenting her rear entrance to his cock. She's so wet and open that he's able to slip past that ring of muscle without much resistance, and the feeling of his cock sliding against mine, only separated by a thin muscle, is incredible. Lydia shouts a string of curses, but quickly dissolves into wordless screams as we find our rhythm. One of us withdrawing as the other thrusts forward, chasing our release.

"Alpha, mark me, claim me, please," Lydia begs, nails scratching my back as she holds on for dear life.

It's like a tether snaps inside of my soul, and my vision goes black for a moment as my primal instincts flood my rational mind. My fingers dig into the soft flesh of her ass, and I don't even care if I leave bruises. In fact, the image of Lydia covered in marks, *my* marks, spurs me on harder, and

I pound into her, snarling wordlessly. My knot swells, and I can't stop even if I wanted to. It slides into her heat, locking in place. My spine zings with my release, but something more powerful pushes past those feelings, and I turn my head and lock my jaw around Lydia's right bicep. Mateo shouts at the same moment Lydia's blood fills my mouth, but it's like he's at the other end of a tunnel. I close my eyes, stars bursting behind my lids, and my body floats for a moment before I crash back into myself. But now, the balance of my life has shifted irreparably. My center of gravity, the sun at the center of my solar system, is now the woman in my arms.

A flash of pain along my back draws me back slightly, and then another at my shoulder has me releasing Lydia's arm. I try to turn to look, but I can't because Lydia has latched onto the spot between my shoulder and throat, her little teeth digging into me. I nuzzle her slightly, licking at my mating bond. She sighs, pulling back and doing the same to her own mark.

"Mine," she whispers, over and over, her left hand smearing blood over my chest, over her chest, even onto Mateo's arms, where they wrap around her ribcage.

"Yours," Mateo replies, bringing her fingers to his mouth and licking them clean before kissing his mark.

I act on the overwhelming impulse that rises in my chest, and I take their clasped hands and bring them to my mouth, biting Mateo enough to draw his blood. He growls, but I soothe the small wound with a kiss before dragging a stripe of red across my heart, mixing my blood with his and Lydia's on my skin.

"Mine," Lydia says again, squeezing our interlaced fingers tight.

Mateo and I look at each other, and something blossoms between us, a connection that wasn't there before. He's been my best friend, my occasional lover, my pack mate. But now our threads are woven tighter, more completely. Our family is almost complete, a tapestry of love and support that grows stronger with each connection. And at our center is one omega, the piece we were missing.

"Ours."

Mateo and I speak at the same time, but I'm surprised by the third voice joins us. Lucas is there, stroking Lydia's hair and kissing her temple. I can feel him now as well, the web of bonds growing stronger as we touch and stay close, until Lydia looks up at our beta, feeling the wave of love he sends to her through me, tears in her eyes.

"Yours," she replies at last, voice cracking.

I move to kiss away the tear that slips free, but I'm not fast enough. Because Lex is there, wiping it away. We all look, and she's smiling brightly, but there's something in her eyes, a longing on the edges of her happiness.

"One more, my love," I whisper, kissing my bond mark, savoring the little shiver it sends through her body.

Lydia nods, and Mateo and I move at last, allowing Lydia to crawl into Lex's lap. She falls asleep almost immediately, not that Lex seems to mind. Mateo, Lucas, and I look at each other, then almost simultaneously burst into laughter. We're covered in sweat and blood, and my shoulder aches from where Lydia bit me.

"Let's clean up," Lucas suggests breathlessly.

We look at our omega, and Lex gives us an encouraging nod. So I stumble on weak legs into Lydia's bathroom. But even if the physical evidence washes away, nothing will ever remove this newfound warmth in my soul.

CHAPTER THIRTY-SEVEN

Alexandra

I CAN HEAR THE shower running as Lydia dozes in my arms, and I play with the ends of her toffee-colored hair. Her skin is cooler than it was a few days ago, and the realization makes my stomach sink a little. She must be nearing the end of her heat. Will there still be enough time for her to be satisfied with the state of her bonds with Mateo and Rhett, and to bond with me? We'd taken it for granted that we'd be able to complete all the bonds, but with Lucas co-opting her first two bonding chemical surges, it's possible her body will decide she's done before we're ready. I can't deny the pulse of disappointment that thought brings to my chest, but I push it down and away, hoping Rhett and Lucas don't feel it. I have to keep it together, and she needs to rest after such an intense moment.

"Lex," Lydia whimpers, wriggling slightly.

I slide down to hold her closer, kissing her forehead. "I'm here, sweetness," I coo, stroking up and down her back.

"I love you," she says dreamily, blindly seeking out my neck to nuzzle against.

I smile, my stomach doing a little flip. "I love you, too. Rest now; I've got you."

She shakes her head and pulls back to look at my face. There's a clarity to her eyes that wasn't there a few minutes ago, a fire I haven't seen before.

"I don't want to," she snaps, growling adorably.

I roll my eyes, ready to laugh, but that only makes her growl more. And then suddenly, she's flipping me onto my back, kissing me hard. I'm too stunned by her sudden shift to do anything than kiss her back, tasting the last traces of Rhett's blood still on her lips. The honey and whiskey and ozone flavor of her makes my pussy pulse, and I run my hands down her chest to cup her breasts. They're so perfect, the right size to fill my palms with nipples so responsive and sensitive to each twist and pinch.

"I can feel you, just a little bit," she mutters against my skin as she trails kisses down my jaw and neck.

I gasp at the scrape of her teeth on my collarbone, then the slide of her pussy against my thigh as she moves lower and lower, until she's sucking on my nipples, her perfect tongue swirling around the hardened buds until they ache. The primal part of my mind is roaring for me to stop this, to take control and make her relax like she needs. But then phantom touches soothe that savage part of me, until I'm a puddle on the mattress, completely at Lydia's will.

"You don't think I'd let you out of my nest without claiming your rightful place as my alpha, did you?" Lydia asks lightly, the sultry omega purr under her words tickling my heart.

"I don't want you hurting yourself—"

Lydia bites the swell of my breast hard enough to make me gasp, and I try to push back against the syrupy pool filling my head. Lydia's fingers play at my entrance, swirling in my arousal until she can push one slim digit inside of me, curling it slowly. Her touch is hesitant, unsure, but something about her boldness makes it feel so good. And when she finds that perfect spot inside of me, I groan through gritted teeth, bucking as I ride her finger. She adds a second finger, growing more confident as I respond to her, but her pace stays slow. I look up at her with a growl, and she's smirking. This little brat is *teasing* me.

That's all it takes for me to finally throw off the influence holding me back, and I snap. I flip Lydia over, grabbing her wrist and holding her still as I writhe on her fingers. She has the audacity to laugh, raking the nails on her other hand down my chest hard enough to leave bright red streaks across my pale skin. Marking me, claiming me.

"Come for me, Alpha. Come for your omega," Lydia taunts, twisting to rub her thumb on my clit.

I gasp and tense up, and she takes full advantage, shifting her weight until I'm knocked backward and onto my stomach, the air whooshing out of my lungs. But I don't get a chance to recover as Lydia pounces, driving her hand into my channel, the noises she pulls out of my throat almost embarrassing. The pleasure is worth it, though, and I can only hang on as she pushes me over the edge, refusing to let up even as my muscles try to lock around her fingers. With her soft purr, I'm butter on hot pavement, coming apart again and again in quick succession.

"That's a good girl," Lydia coos, only slowing her hand as I'm coming down from my third orgasm.

Snarling weakly, I'm boneless for the moment. She laughs and pulls out, humming with delight. I turn to look, and she's using the fingers she just fucked me into the mattress with to play with herself. And she's looking at me like the cat who got the cream, a challenge for me to try to stop her.

"Someone seems to have forgotten something," I start, softly but not weakly.

She doesn't respond, putting on a full show as she chases her own release, eyes locked with mine the whole time. I finally get enough strength back in my limbs to get on all fours, and I prowl toward her, teeth bared. She's close; I can smell it in the electrified air between us. I wait, biding my time as she gets closer and closer to the edge. And right as she's poised to fall, I dart forward, one hand around her throat as I tackle her into the bed, the other pinning that traitorous hand right beside her face.

"Your cunt is mine, Omega," I growl, nose only millimeters away from hers as I straddle her chest.

"Then fucking claim it, Alpha," she rasps, barely able to speak around my fingers squeezing her slender neck.

I snarl a wordless admonishment, not liking her tone one bit. "You're going to take what I choose to give you, my greedy little omega. If I want to edge you all night, make you cry and beg until you can't stand it anymore, then that's what I'll do. And you'll thank me for taking the time out of my day to touch you, for deigning to give you anything at all. Isn't that right?"

She swallows and something shifts in her eyes, and there's a whisper of caution along my bond with Lucas, a touch I recognize as Rhett's. I loosen my hold on her throat a touch, and she gulps in a breath, lower lip shaking. Is she shutting down? Did I go too far? I'm about to pull away, to stop this before I really hurt her, but then she speaks, and I'm struck dumb.

"If that's what you wanted, I would do it happily. I'd beg, cry, kill for you. I'd do anything for you, Alexandra."

The bald honesty of her shaky words strikes me to my core, and there's something at the edge of my senses, a caress I don't recognize, and I swallow a growl of frustration. She's reaching out to me, trying to tell me something, but it's muffled by too many intermediaries. Her fingers come up to brush along my cheekbone, her other hand pressing something into my entrance. My toy.

"Please," she says simply, but her eyes speak volumes.

We work together to slide the toy into her folds, and I feel a pang of longing. I might be able to knot her this way, but I wish I could feel how wet she is, or how she squeezes my length. My eyes never leave hers as I rock into her, our hips meeting over and over. We're both so close already that it doesn't take much until we're both panting, holding on to each other as we race toward the cliff's edge.

"I'm yours, and you're mine," Lydia mutters, holding my face with both hands.

I nod, not able to deny her. She pulls me into a kiss, only letting me linger for a moment before she redirects my mouth to her throat. The place everyone left alone, even when they could have marked her over and over. My teeth ache, and I scream as a tsunami of an orgasm crashes down on me, and I press my knot inside of her at the same moment as I bite down.

Light and color explode through me, everything swirling together until I can't tell up from down. Lydia's blood tastes like ambrosia, liquid gold filling me with warmth and love and so many other things. And suddenly, I can feel the depth of her trust, her love for me. She's giving herself to me completely, letting me into her heart to see every flicker of emotion. The fear of rejection, the anticipation for the future, her excitement, her physical pleasure. When I test that connection, she pushes back against me. Not trying to pull away, but so eager for me that she barrels into my heart, pushing out every fear and insecurity. She loves me so much, loves every flaw and quirk. She loves me for who I am, not what I could do for her.

"I'm here, Alpha," she whispers in my ear, holding me close.

My eyes burn, and I release my teeth, licking the blood away tenderly. I'm too full, too overcome with emotion to respond. And it only gets worse as I smell lemons and fresh cut grass, Mateo's smile flashing behind my eyes even though I know he's still in the other room. Then Rhett, his little brush of dark chocolate-scented reassurance, easier to feel than Mateo's, but just as strong. And Lucas, my patient beta, who smells of clean sheets and campfires of my childhood, filling me to the brim with his love.

Eventually, I'm able to pull away from Lydia, but I don't let her go far. The boys return to the nest, and we spend the rest of the night wrapped in each other. I don't bother to hide my tears, and I'm not the only one shedding them. We linger in our freshly formed connections, testing them and comforting each other without words, until we fall asleep in a pile, the sun rising on the first day of our lives as a bonded pack.

CHAPTER THIRTY-EIGHT

Lydia

THE FIRST THING I'M aware of as I open my eyes is the distinct lack of an itch under my skin. I don't know what time it is, or even what day it is, but I know I'm not itchy. Instead, I'm cold and profoundly sticky. I shiver, trying to find a blanket to cover up with, but I can't move. This is due in large part to the two sets of arms wrapped around me, pinning my hands to my chest.

I open my eyes and the room is dim, the overhead light off and the faintest bit of sunlight filtering through the curtains. It could be dawn or dusk, and I can't turn my head to see my wall clock. Sighing, I let my head flop down, resigned to being stuck here for a while.

My eyes slide closed, and I jump at the tentative little nudge in my chest. I can taste s'mores on the back of my tongue, and I turn my head on instinct, finding Lucas's blue-gray eyes open and sparkling. He's not the owner of any of the arms around me, but instead my head is resting on his thigh, and the rest of his limbs are lost in the tangled web of flesh around me.

"Welcome back to reality, sweetheart," he says, chuckling under his breath.

"How long have we been..."

"Banging each other's brains out?" Lucas finishes with a laugh. "Six days, give or take a few hours."

I flush a little, only making him laugh more. He wriggles closer until he can press a kiss to my hairline, and the little pulse of affection in my chest makes me smile like a love-struck fool. I look up, realizing that Rhett and Mateo are the ones stuck to me like Velcro, and I can smell Lex, but I'm surrounded by too much man-chest to see her. Rhett grunts as Lucas elbows him in the head "accidentally," reeling back enough for me to breathe as he's pulled back to consciousness.

"Sorry," Lucas says with a wink in my direction.

"What's wrong?" Lex mutters sleepily.

"Lydia's done, and awake," Lucas answers for me.

"And I really need to pee and take a shower," I add.

"I'll join," Mateo mumbles, and I'm not even sure he's fully awake.

"I love you, but the idea of any of you touching me right now makes me want to vomit," I admit, and a chorus of chuckles meets me.

There are a few moments where no one moves, and I can feel the reluctance bouncing around the room. While I admit that it's nice to be warm and in the arms of two of the people I love, my bladder continues to make a strong objection. But eventually I manage to wriggle free with Lucas's help, and he shoos them out of my room to take care of their own hygiene.

I spend a few blissful minutes alone, scrubbing away the last few days of grime and sweat, and Lord knows what else, until my skin is raw. I try to savor it, but the nagging pull in my chest makes me rush. The edge of panic in my chest, like something's missing, catches me off guard, but my pack is there, dulling the edges before it can ever reach truly concerning levels. I'm surprised to find the top few layers of my bedding gone, but the bulk of my nesting materials are still in place. The air still smells like sex, but there's a heavy layer of my mates' scents on every inch of the space.

My mates.

Smiling to myself, happiness bubbles like champagne in my soul. It's unreal to think that these incredible alphas took me for their bond mate, that we made it to this point, and it finally happened. I feel the familiar surge of self-doubt, but then they're there again, like guardian angels taking away my anxieties and leaving only love behind. I finally understand what Sylvie and Caleb meant when they described being bonded as never feeling lonely again. Even if I'm not focused on them, I can still feel the pack in my heart. Things that I could only guess are suddenly and unshakably true. Rhett loves me more than the air he breathes. Lex will do anything she can to make me smile. Lucas adores me. In Mateo's eyes, I'm the most beautiful woman in the world.

I pause and sit with that knowledge for a moment, trying to wrap my head around it. It's not like I didn't know this was coming; I'd spent the last few weeks planning and prepping for my heat. I knew I'd be attempting to bond with this pack, had talked for hours with my omega mentor about how it would work, for both me and Lucas. But now that it's done, and I have the bond mates I'd always dreamed of, I don't know what to do.

For years, I'd lived with the fear of what being bonded would mean. The commands, the subservience, the cage. Never having a private thought or feeling, never able to escape. But now that I have not one, but three bonds, I can see now that my fears were unfounded. I can feel Rhett, Mateo, and Lex on the edges of my mind, and Lucas even more distantly than that, but their presences aren't suffocating. They aren't pressing into my mind, demanding my attention. They're just... there. Sort of like how you can forget you're wearing a seat belt sometimes, but it's still there, ready to protect you if the worst should happen.

Rhett is the first to notice my tentative poking, opening up to me without hesitation. I can taste his happiness like chocolate on my tongue, and I smile to myself. He's not pressuring me to do anything, or reveal anything, letting me exist in our connection for as long as I like, and not stopping me when I withdraw. There's a warm tingle in my right bicep, like phantom lips kissing his bond mark. I can feel Lex and Mateo's curiosity, but I send them a wave of warmth and peace.

The frantic feeling of missing something creeps back into my mind, so I hustle to my closet. I slip into comfortable clothes, finally feeling the ache in my bones from being thoroughly fucked every way to Sunday. But it's a good ache, an ache I would take a thousand times over if it meant having these bonds wrapped around my heart. When I manage to drag myself up the stairs, Lucas is hard at work making our first meal as a mated pack.

Sliding into step with him, I let him speak and guide me through our bond. I don't know if it's the novelty of it, but there's something infinitely more exciting about communicating like this. I hope I don't ever lose the sense of wonder that comes with every affectionate tug on the string that ties me to him through Rhett and Lex.

As if summoned by my thoughts, the two alphas appear in the doorway, hair still damp from their own quick showers. Rhett steps up behind me as I stir the vegetables in the frying pan, kissing my temple as he puts his hands on my hips. There's nothing sexual about his touch, which is the only reason I'm tolerating it. The idea of anyone putting anything in or near any of my holes makes my stomach roll.

"I reckon it'll only take a few hours for that to go away," Lucas teases, responding to my thoughts.

I stick my tongue out at him, making him laugh. Mateo comes back, wearing low-slung gray sweatpants and no shirt, roughly toweling his hair dry. And despite myself, seeing the V-shaped muscles leading suggestively below his waistband, the trail of fine hair extending from his navel like the road to paradise, still makes my heart flutter, and my pussy twinge. Every head in the room snaps to me, and I flush. So maybe it's not as much fun to have my every desire broadcast to the people I love.

"Don't even think about it. This omega is closed for business," I say firmly, taking the pan off the heat to start plating.

Lucas hums skeptically, and I can feel the teasing, but Rhett still throws a reproachful growl his way.

"You take all the time you need, love," he says reassuringly.

"Besides, I think we can keep each other busy in the mean-time. Right, Matty?" Lucas drawls, throwing a wink in the alpha's direction.

"Oh, for sure. We can have lots of fun now that Rhett's home, can't we?" Matty throws back, words light but some-how incredibly seductive.

"Just so long as you boys clean up after yourselves," Lex chides, the undertone of laughter in her voice undermining her a little.

"You can always supervise, Lex. And you, as well, love. Wouldn't want you missing out on a damn good show," Rhett finishes, giving me a wink that makes me blush.

I smile up at him, and the shock of having him here, phys-ically present, comes back all over again. We'll have time to talk about what happened, but I don't want to ruin this moment with anything so serious as all that.

A vibration on the counter draws our attention, and we look to see Rhett's phone light up with an incoming message. And my shock ripples across the bonds as I see Jason's name flash before the screen goes dark.

"Why is my brother texting you?" I ask, turning to look at the alpha in question.

Rhett looks troubled for a moment, but he can't hide the flash of shame that comes down the bond. At least he feels bad for keeping this from me.

"He left Chauvert. He's probably letting me know he made it to Everton, and is settled in at Wickland House," he replies honestly.

I stare at the device, waiting for it to do something, maybe give me a better answer or more details, but when it stays dark and silent, I look at Lex. I can feel Mateo's surprise, but there's nothing like that coming from her, or Lucas, for that matter.

"How long have you known?" I ask.

She has the decency to let her emotions show on her face, and her feelings match Rhett's. Shame. Anxiety. Contrition. It makes it hard to stay mad when I know how bad they feel about hiding this from me.

"He was staying with Rhett for about a week before the charges were dropped. There's more to the story, but it's not mine to tell," Lex says at last.

I nod, sighing. I just want to spend some drama-free time with my mates, not have the real world intrude on my happiness so soon. The idea of anyone coming near us makes the panic rise in my stomach, but Rhett's arms tighten and pull me close, soothing the feeling away.

"Then we don't have to let it. We can address all that after we settle," Lex suggests.

I look at her again, and then at Rhett, asking without words if that's possible. Because the idea of spending even a few weeks without having to deal with my family, or Seth, or Darren, sounds like absolute bliss. Time to really enjoy being mated, to solidify the tenuous bonds without stress. We could recenter, recharge, recover in peace. It sounds like a fantasy, but nothing in the world seems more necessary after the year we've had.

Rhett looks at me for a long time, and then nods, kissing my forehead again. "Yes, I think we can make that work."

"It's about time we took a vacation. I vote for Fiji," Mateo says excitedly.

I look to Mateo, who's grinning from ear to ear. The expression is infectious, and I can't help but return it, even if the idea of leaving the house fills my stomach with unexpected tension. Lex's eyes flash to me, her concern coming down our bond before she turns a hard look onto Mateo.

"We can't go gallivanting all over the world, Mat. Lydia needs her nest," she says sternly.

As soon as she voices it, I know she's right. Even now, I want to drag everyone back downstairs and pile back into bed. The idea of leaving the house, let alone the city, is out of the question, at least for now.

Mateo, to his credit, is unfazed. "All right, then it's a stay-cation. Movie marathons, cuddling, and my favorite takeout places? Sounds amazing to me," he chirps brightly.

The unspoken tension in the room seems to dissipate, enough for me to feel the distant brush of something passing between Lex and Lucas, though neither of them speaks. A glance between them, and Lucas throws up his hands. I look at her curiously, but she shakes her head.

"Another thing that can wait, sweetness," she says.

I give her a wary look, but let it go. If it were important, she would insist on telling me. I know that as truth, sensing her agreement across our bond. So instead, I let myself get swept up in the affection of my mates, the laughter and banter as we share our first meal as a mated pack and forget about it. We deserve a moment's peace, I remind myself. We earned this, and I won't let my anxiety ruin this.

CHAPTER THIRTY-NINE

Lydia

"HARDER, LOVE. REALLY GIVE it to me," Rhett instructs, bracing himself.

I grunt and throw my whole body into the next strike, feeling the burn up my arm as my fist connects with the punching bag. Rhett's pride pulses down our bond as I manage to shift him ever so slightly, and I grin savagely, shaking a few beads of sweat from my brows as I throw another punch, then another in rapid succession.

It's mid-November, and I've started training with Rhett a few times a week now. It started off as self-defense lessons, basic hold-breaking techniques and that sort of thing, but we've since moved on to more offensive training. I don't have the brute strength to take on an opponent like Rhett, but I can throw a decent punch now without hurting myself in the process. Caleb joined us the other day, when my mates decided that they weren't going to lose their marbles about me spending time alone with another alpha, even a mated one. He'd supplemented Rhett's lessons, and even taught me the very basics of firearm handling. Not that I will ever own a gun, but Caleb wanted to make sure that if there was ever a time when I'd need to use one that I'd at least know how to do it safely.

"Good girl. That's the last of our sets for today," Rhett praises, straightening up from where he'd been holding the bag steady for me.

I smile brightly, bouncing on the balls of my feet. The feel-good work out chemicals mix with the adoration coming from him, making me feel like I'm on Cloud Nine. It doesn't help that he looks absolutely delicious in his gym shorts, his chest bare and glistening. He gives me a look as the flash of desire runs through me, half a challenge, half a warning. I flush and settle down, sending a wordless apology his way.

Ever since my heat, I've been climbing my pack mates like trees any chance I can get. I talked to Sylvie about it a little, and she reckons that it's the mating hormones doing their thing. According to her, I won't have another heat cycle for a while, up to a year in her experience. Something about making sure that the bonds are fully locked in before my body returns to anything resembling a normal cycle. In the meantime, the primal part of my mind will be screaming for me to jump on any of my mates' dicks whenever possible. Sylvie started talking about how it's my body's way of trying its best to take advantage of the increased fertility mating bonds can cause, but I'd stopped her before she got too far along that path. The breeding kink my pack and I like to indulge in is one thing, but I'm not anywhere remotely ready to be a mother.

Rhett helps me unwrap my hands before we head back into the house from the gym above the garage. Mateo's SUV is missing, as is Lex's sedan, and the reminder that they'd had to go to work today stings all over again. I push the irrational feeling aside, though. They'd been more than indulgent of me and my unrelenting demands to have them near me at all times at first, because our bonds were new and being apart for even a few minutes was uncomfortable. But they couldn't put off their work commitments anymore. They aren't leaving me totally alone, though, as an attempt to ease me back into normal life. At first, only one of them would leave at a time, but now, I only need one of my mates at home with me, though everyone has adjusted their schedules to be home for supper these days.

Not that I've been slacking, either. They've thrown me into the deep end with the Magnolia Garden Theater, now that the structural repairs are underway. I've got a little work area set up in the basement lounge area, piled high with papers and folders of things for me to look through. I'm making decisions about floor plans and which event furniture to purchase for The Garden, but it feels like too much fun to really be called work. It's like a dream come true, and even though the feeling has diminished a little more each day, I'm still waiting for the day I have to wake up.

Rhett and I take separate showers and then meet back in the kitchen to get started on cooking for everyone. We've just chosen a recipe—Cajun-style seafood scampi—when Rhett's phone rings, the number for the gate guard flashing.

"That's Jason. He'll be here in a few," Rhett announces, almost tentatively after he hangs up.

I sigh and nod, stomach sinking a little. Jason and I silently agreed to pretend he's been in Everton on an extended visit, enjoying the time we have together to reconnect. It hasn't been easy, but I was determined to not let the real world intrude. My pack was content enough to play along, which was good enough for me at the time. But we can't avoid it anymore. He owes me one hell of an explanation, and I'm going to get what I'm due.

Pulling out a chair at the dining room table, I pull one leg up to my chest while tucking my other foot under my hips as I wait. My mind tries to take off in anxious thought spirals, but my mates are there every time, filling me with their unshaking calm. I hope I never get used to that. I've struggled with anxiety my whole life, and usually I'd have to try to talk myself down from the edge, with varying degrees of success. Now that I have these incredible people in my life and in my heart, I've never felt more grounded and safe. Before, I had to trust that they would protect me and care for me, and that I wasn't a bother or a burden, which was, at times, impossible to accept with the voice of unreason whispering in the back of my mind that I didn't deserve that sort of treatment. Now, I don't have to take it on faith; I can feel the truth of those things in the very center of my being. There's nothing to argue or doubt anymore. Pack St. Clair loves me and wants to care for me in every possible way, and that's a fact as real and irrefutable as the sunrise.

I'm yanked from my happy thoughts by a knock at the door, followed by Rhett welcoming my brother inside. I don't move, watching down the hallway as the two approach the open doorway into the open-plan living space. I'd seen Jason a few times since Christmas, so I'd known he's been on the mend, but he looks good. There isn't the heaviness to his gait or posture anymore, and the bags under his eyes have all but vanished. He comes over to the table and pulls out the chair on my right, turning to face me as he places a messenger bag on the table in front of us.

"So," I start.

"So," Jason echoes with a smirk.

I give him a half-hearted glare, and he smirks back. He'll always be my little brother, driving me crazy until the day they put me in the ground. His cucumber and juniper scent is a cool, refreshing change to the constant sea of familiar aromas, and as he takes a deep breath, he cocks his head a little.

"I can smell them now. I thought it was the proximity and scent marking, but no. That's all you, Lydi," Jason says, almost to himself.

I smile fondly, looking at Rhett, who's busied himself in the kitchen while I talk with my brother. He looks up and winks at me, the tickle of his primal satisfaction in my chest. I roll my eyes. Just like a man to enjoy having his claim recognized by another alpha, even if he's my blood relative.

"Anyway, I guess we should talk about what happened in October." Jason sighs, shifting in his seat.

I give him an ironic chuckle. "Yeah, I guess we should. There's an elephant in this room, dying for attention," I joke, rolling my eyes.

Jason holds up his hands. "I thought y'all were charging him rent, considering how long he's been hanging around," he volleys.

We share another laugh, but fall silent. The hurt I've been feeling, about being lied to and being kept in the dark, resurfaces, but I try to keep my face impassive.

"I am sorry, Lydi. If things hadn't been... what they were, I would have told you right away. But when Lex told me y'all wanted some time to adjust, I just..." Jason trails off, leaning back in his chair and twisting his fingers together nervously.

I stay silent, waiting for him to go on. I don't like that he lied to me, even by omission, and I'm not about to make this easy on him.

"You deserve to be happy, Lydia. And damn it all if I wanted you to have that, even for a little while. But you want the truth now, so I'll give it to you."

He launches into his explanation, describing the fallout after Sam's wedding, our mother, Diane's, fall from grace within our church, and then the insanity of the brawl that took place the night Jason finally left them all behind. I try to hold on to my anger, to stay mad at him for keeping this from me, but the more I think on it, the harder that becomes. With everything that was going on at the time, would it really have made things better if I'd known what Jason was dealing with? I would have stormed back there to try to rescue him without hesitation, even though it would have been stupid and, frankly, suicidal. He did it to keep me safe and out of harm's way, yet again.

Jason finishes his tale, and we lapse into silence, a heavy, charged thing that almost feels like another presence in the room. My brother jumps when I reach out and take his hand, and I'm surprised by how cold it is. He looks at our clasped fingers for a moment before turning his wide-eyed gaze onto me.

"I'm sorry you had to go through all that alone, Jace," I murmur at last, speaking slowly but clearly so he can truly hear the emotion in my words.

He nods and gives my hand a little squeeze. "It's done, in the past. I'm out now," he says, trying to sound unruffled, but there's still a catch in his voice.

"We'll make it right. They've gone on long enough without consequences for the way they've treated us. I don't know how, but I swear to God—"

"I do," Jason interrupts, pulling the messenger bag toward us.

I blink as he lets go of my hand and digs in the bag for a minute, pulling out several manila envelopes of documents and piling them neatly on the table. It's a relatively small stack, only about an inch or two high, but the care with which he's handling them piques my curiosity.

"This is just the tip of the iceberg, Lydi, and you're not going to believe what I've found."

By the time I've looked through the documents Jason put in front of me, my head is swimming with numbers. And I'm not bad at math; I had to take my fair share of business accounting classes as part of my hospitality degree. It's been a few years since I've had to use any of that knowledge, but I can recall enough to see the patterns laid out in black and white.

Embezzlement. Lots of it. Like, hundreds of millions of dollars of embezzlement going back before Jason and I were even born.

From the very beginning, my father was skimming off the top of contracts, double charging for materials that sup- posedly went missing, but then magically reappeared on another job, based on the "in-house supplies" expense lines. It's subtle, but the proof is undeniable, especially as Jason explains the missing pieces that he didn't bring with him, but are in boxes and on hard drives he brought when he left Louisiana in October.

"Do you recognize that account number?" Jason asks at one point, pointing to a line on a spreadsheet.

And with a rush of ice through my veins, I nod. Because I do. That's my mother's personal account. I know those numbers because I had to put them down on every direct deposit form I filled out while I lived under her roof. I was never allowed to keep my paychecks, because I had to contribute to the upkeep of the pack. But these numbers I'm seeing show that she never needed my measly minimum wage pay. She had no reason to take my money, other than to make sure I didn't have it. And when Jason shows me the lavish purchases, the designer clothes she bought to wear once to a business party and then never again; the luxury vacations she said were business trips for Dad and his clients, but then he always had some reason to back out of; the high-end cars that she always claimed belonged to the company and us children could never touch. All of it was a lie.

"They're both implicated in this shit. Because there's no way Dad wasn't aware of how much he was paying her every week," Jason snarls, low and dangerous.

"Not that he wasn't doing his own dirty dealings. Why did he think he could get away with invoicing the company $10,000 a month for 'office supplies?'" I snap.

"Because he never thought I'd leave," Jason says with a heavy finality.

I take his hand again, my heart on fire with rage. They used us, lied to us, treated us like pawns for their own gain. I was nothing more than a bargaining chip, something they could sell off to the highest bidder. And Jason was the unquestioning, dutiful son, never allowed to ask questions but always expected to do as commanded. And when we stepped out of line and couldn't be brought to heel, they cast us out.

"Who else knows?" I ask, my voice cutting through the tense silence.

"About the fraud? Hard to say, but I know Adam is too much of a pussy-ass bitch to—"

"Watch yourself," Rhett snaps, speaking for the first time.

Jason sighs and rubs his eyes. "Adam doesn't work, but he's still getting a six-figure salary. He's a junkie, about as useful as a one-legged man in an ass-kicking contest, and has his head shoved so far up our parents' collective ass that he can taste the back of their tonsils. Pardon me if I wanted to use a shorthand to explain all that."

"We don't use that sort of language in this pack. Get used to it, Jace," Rhett says simply, not even looking up from the vegetables he's prepping.

I smother my amusement for Jason's sake, but I don't miss the sly wink Rhett throws in my direction. I've heard him say far worse than that about my family, but his willingness to force sexist language out of the house is admirable. My brother heaves another sigh, but thankfully lets the matter drop for now.

"Sammy's good, by the way. I had a feeling he didn't know what's been happening, so I asked him straight up before I left. He's furious that he's been busting his hump for Dad, basically doing all the hard work while getting none of the benefits, and even getting robbed in the process," he says, going back to my original question.

"Who knows you have all this hard evidence?" I press, wheels turning in my head.

"Besides y'all? Sammy, and that's it. Trish, the secretary, noticed I was taking a ton of stuff out of the office, but she didn't question it. Honestly, if the business went under, she wouldn't be shedding any tears. I've seen the way the crews treat her," Jason answers, trailing off in a growl.

"So it's just slime from top to bottom, then? There's nothing worth salvaging?" I snap, looking over the documents again.

Silence meets my questions, and I look up after it stretches on for a few minutes. I look between Jason and Rhett, and find them both staring at me like I've suddenly grown fangs and claws like some kind of demon. And to be honest, there's so much righteous fury in my chest that I wouldn't be surprised to find that to be true. I want to tear the people who birthed me to shreds, not even leaving enough for the buzzards to snack on. They've preached on and on about honesty and integrity for my whole life, how we have a duty to those around us to treat them fairly. The number of times I was lectured about not cheating or stealing or double crossing is far too many to count, but I can still remember the scriptures I was forced to memorize and recite.

Proverbs 12:22. *Lying lips are an abomination to the Lord. But they that deal truly are His delight.*

Proverbs 10:2. *Treasures from wickedness profit nothing, but righteousness delivereth from death.*

1 Corinthians 6:10. *Nor thieves, nor the covetous, nor the drunk-ards, nor revilers, nor extortioners shall inherit the Kingdom of God.*

Exodus 20. The Eighth fucking Commandment. *Thou shalt not steal.*

But then one last verse comes to mind. Mark 4:22.

Everything that is hidden will be made clear. Every secret thing will be made known.

A plan solidifies in my mind, as clear and strong as a diamond. They would pay for their hypocrisy and abuse, even if it's the last thing I ever do.

CHAPTER FORTY

Lydia

I THOUGHT THE MOST difficult part of enacting my plan would be getting my parents to agree to meet. Turns out, they've been asking Lex for a meeting since before my heat. They have things they need to discuss with me and my new pack, and it's only been through carefully executed delay tactics from Ted that we've kept them at bay for this long.

In addition to an obscene alpha dowry, they are demanding that I sign an NDA so I don't disclose "sensitive pack secrets" to a "business competitor." Only my parents would delude themselves into thinking their tiny local contracting business is in competition with my pack, but it was easy to see through their flimsy excuse. They wanted to make me sign a gag order so I couldn't go public with the abuse I'd been subjected to my whole life.

I'd wanted to use the information Jason gathered to force them to give up their demands entirely, but Lex made me pump the brakes. We are better than extortion, and even if they deserve the humiliation, we need to do this right. It's not what I'd wanted to hear, or Jason, for that matter, but I could concede to her point. She was a victim of that exact sort of malice, and while she'd never say it, I could always feel her general dismay at the thought of doing the very thing she'd fought so hard to escape. For her sake, I could let go of my own righteous thirst for vengeance.

After a few weeks of going back and forth, the day finally arrives where we're all piled onto the pack's private plane, heading toward New Orleans for what should be the last time. I try not to fidget with my clothes, but I can feel every brush of the material against my mating bites, and it's driving me mad. Lex had helped me choose this blouse, and while it is more expensive than anything I would have ever picked for myself, I can't deny how good I look in it. Sheer sleeves that flow beautifully and cinch at my wrists, stretchy and comfortable, but still structured enough to make my boobs look amazing. We'd paired it with high-waisted trousers to complete the professional image, which is definitely outside of my comfort zone, but the heated stares and pulses of unbridled desire I'd gotten from my mates make me feel a little better.

Jason is next to me at the table, with Rhett and Lex sitting across from us, both of them absorbed in their tablets as they try to get some work done. Mateo and Lucas are on the couches, watching a sports talk show. I didn't think we'd all end up on this trip, but it was hard to tell them no. Lex had to be there as my Prime Alpha, and Rhett wouldn't stand to let me be within arm's reach of my parents without him being there. Mateo insisted he has a promise to keep to my mother, so he had to come with us, and it was hard to deny Lucas when everyone else is going. I didn't fight Lex when she insisted on bringing a small squad of security on the trip, with Caleb in charge. I glance over at where he's reading a newspaper in the seating area closer to the nose of the plane, and I happen to catch his gunmetal gray eyes as he looks around. He gives me a slight incline of his head before turning back to his paper. I'm more than a little relieved to have him on the trip with us. I didn't realize how much I'd missed his solid, unshakable presence at my back until he'd slipped into place behind me at the airport. My shadow returned, his cedar and cookie scent greeting me like an old friend.

After a smooth landing, my heart hammers a little in my chest as I recognize the hangar we're parked in. It's been three months since that day, but I can still feel the last tendrils of guilt in my chest, the little voice in my head starting to whisper how I failed my alpha by leaving him behind. And as we disembark, I freeze when I see a dark stain on the concrete. But Rhett is there, both physically and through our bond, a hand on my lower back, thumb rubbing soothing circles as he purrs gently and pushes calming warmth into my chest.

"I'm safe, my love. I'm here. It's almost over," he whispers into my ear, applying soft pressure to spur me into movement toward the pair of black SUVs waiting for us.

I look up at him, and then around. Lex is beside Lucas, their hands clasped as she leans into him, speaking too softly for me to hear over the ambient airport noise. He blinks and glances up, catching my eye. His anger looms on the edges of my mind, a splash of bitter pine on the back of my tongue before it's gone, replaced by liquor and spices. I allow myself to be led away, and into the back of the first vehicle, curling into Rhett's side as my fingers trace a slight bump on his thigh. He holds me close, and I let myself get lost in the flood of emotion he sends my way. He's safe, and he's happy. He loves me, and doesn't blame me for what happened. None of them do, at least from what I'm feeling through our bonds.

Caleb climbs into the driver's seat of our car, with another guard throwing himself into the front passenger's seat. Mateo slides in on my other side, one of his hands finding mine after his door is closed. Having them with me helps to settle me, and as we leave the hangar behind, my mind slows and goes placid. It's not a long drive, but mid-morning traffic is slowing our convoy. We're in the lazy stop-and-go traffic typical of the Deep South when my phone pings in my purse.

Jason: Sammy wants to meet at the house instead of downtown.
Me: What? Why?
Jason: Ally's been put on bedrest, and he's not willing to leave her. He's promised we'll be alone.

I bite my lip and show the messages to Rhett and Mateo, who look as troubled as I feel. My eldest brother wanted to meet to talk about something, and we'd agreed to meet at an open-air café on the main drag of Chauvert. But having to reroute to my family's home might be a detour we can't manage.

"What does Lex say?" Rhett asks seriously.

I message my brother the question, and his response comes quickly.

Jason: She's hesitant, but I don't think we should blow him off, Lydi. Sammy has been really adamant about this. And can you really blame him for not wanting to leave his pregnant wife?

I hum a little, but he's got me there. I haven't heard much, but I know that Ally's only a few months along in her first pregnancy. And if she's on bed rest this soon...

Me: We'll have to be quick. But if anyone is home, we're not staying. I don't want to jeopardize this deal.
Jason: Heard. I'll let him know.

I relay my decision to Rhett and Mateo, who don't say anything against the idea verbally, but I can feel their worry. We've worked hard to get to this point, and last-minute changes have never worked out in our favor in the past. When I give Caleb the address, he only nods and the secondary guard, a burly alpha with curly brown hair and freckles, makes the change in the GPS.

"Honestly, why do we even bother," Mateo sighs after a minute, a touch of ironic laughter under his words.

"Bother with what?" I ask, confused.

He shakes his head and pushes back some sandy brown locks that fall into his eyes. "Making plans."

Pulling off the beaten-up country road and into the long gravel driveway that leads to my childhood home sends a chill up my spine. The last time I was here, Darren and I were packing up my car for our trip to the cabin that fateful Christmas just over five years ago. His Jeep had been in the shop, and he'd made pointed remarks about how my beat-up old sedan might not even make it to our destination and how we should have gotten a rental. And as we round the last bend, and the house comes into view, my blood runs a little colder.

I remember the white farmhouse feeling like a palace growing up. It'd been bigger than the houses of almost all the other kids in my school, and I'd felt like a princess trapped in her ivory tower, waiting for a prince to slay the dragon and rescue me. But I'd had to learn that sometimes the prince isn't all he's cracked up to be, and the real noble heroes aren't parading around in the shiny armor their daddy bought them. The house itself looks dingy and cold, in need of a new coat of white paint, a couple of the blue shutters hanging crookedly. There's no warmth in my chest, no relief of returning to a safe place to rest. I can't help but compare it to the St. Clair Pack House, with its pale yellow siding and welcoming aura.

"It's a bit much," Rhett mumbles as we pull into a place in the wide gravel circle in front of the house.

I smirk. The architect in him would have a lot of critique here. It doesn't have enough turrets to be declared a McMansion, but Rhett still frowns in disapproval as he exits the car and looks over the exterior with a trained eye. Mateo helps me out on his side, not letting go of my hand as we wait for the other SUV to park and for the rest of our party to exit. Jason jumps out of the back seat like someone hit the release button on an ejector seat, stalking up to the porch steps without pausing to wait for the rest of us. Of course, he'd be eager to be done. The last time he'd been here, he'd been insulted and beaten by our own brother. I scurry after him, dragging Mateo with me, a new sense of urgency in my chest.

Jason doesn't bother knocking, but opens the unlocked door and strides through the foyer and into the great room beyond. My vision blurs slightly as I take in the décor, noticing not a detail has changed since the last time I was here. Signs with platitudes and Bible verses hang on the walls, mixed in among the framed photos of our family. School pictures, graduation candids, professional family portraits, all perfectly posed to present the image of a solid family unit. A lie, of course, but the illusion was enough to fool visitors.

"Sammy! It's Jace!" my brother shouts as the hallway opens up into the informal living room.

"In here!" Sammy calls back.

I follow numbly behind Jason until I'm in the open-plan space, my eyes lingering on the long farmhouse dining table I'd spent so many meals at, sitting silent and obedient while the adults talked. The kitchen where I'd learned the skills my mother ruled had been necessary for me to have to be a good wife and mate to my future Alpha. I drag my eyes away toward the collection of couches positioned around the fireplace and television, heart skipping a beat as I see Ally reclining in an overstuffed armchair, feet up on the ottoman, with a blanket covering her remarkably pregnant belly. Sammy is at her side, his green eyes flicking back and forth between me and his wife, like he can't stand to look away from her for too long or something bad will happen.

"Lydia! You look so good! I'd get up and hug y'all, but they've decided to make my life difficult before they're even born." Ally laughs, rubbing the top of her bump affectionately.

My mind catches her choice of words, and I quirk a confused eyebrow at her. "They?" I repeat.

Ally beams and nods, her bright blue eyes flashing with pride and affection. "It's twins! Can you believe it?" she gushes, laughing freely.

I smile at her, and then look at Sammy, who's looking equal parts nervous and excited. He's about to be a father to not one, but two children, and he already looks ready to burst from the stress. I let go of Mateo's hand and cross to him, wrapping my arms around his chest. He's tall like Jason, so the top of my head only reaches his shoulders, but I can feel the strength he's acquired from years of hard labor. He tenses for a moment before returning the embrace fiercely.

"Congrats, Sammy. You'll make a great dad," I mutter, just loud enough for him to hear.

"I don't know about all that. I couldn't even protect my baby sister," he grumbles.

I pull back and look at him, alarm furrowing my brow. His expression has darkened, and he's looking at Ally again, but not actually seeing. I take his hand and draw his attention back to me. The dark look in his emerald eyes, the mirror to my own in shape and color, makes my heart ache. My mates are there trying to soothe me, even as they linger at the edges of the room, giving me space.

"I don't blame you for what happened, Sammy. You know that, right?" I ask, low and emotional.

"I know, but after talking with Jason, I can't—I didn't know, Lydia. You have to believe me. If I had—"

As I squeeze his hand, his words die in a cough, and a series of rapid blinks as he looks away. Ally groans as she sits up, and Sammy is at her side instantly, trying to get her to move back. She shoos him away, giving him the stern look only teachers can. She manages to get herself into a sitting position on the edge of the chair cushion, her legs wide enough for her belly to rest between her thighs. If I didn't know better, I would have thought she was ready to pop at any moment. I step closer as she reaches for my hand, sitting down on the ottoman in front of her. Sammy kneels on the floor at her side, hand rubbing soothing circles on her back.

"Sammy's been beating himself up for weeks, ever since the wedding. I didn't see what happened, but I'll tell you what, I sure as heck got an earful after the fact. Your Momma and I haven't always gotten along, but I'd never thought her capable of half the horrors Jason's told us about. I'm so glad you got out and found yourself a pack like that one behind you," she says emphatically.

I give her a watery smile, and look at Sammy again, who still looks like he's drowning in a sea of guilt. But I've moved past the point of being angry at him. He was a kid, the golden child. He never had to go through what I did, but he had his own set of pressures and expectations to live up to. The only people worthy of blame are Samuel Sr. and Diane. She was the one who would degrade me, make me feel like I was unworthy of love and respect, and he allowed it. Even if he never participated in my abuse, his lack of intervention makes him just as guilty. I can only hope that one day Adam is able to see how toxic and harmful our upbringing was, but until then, and as long as he continues to side with our parents, I can't begin to forgive him.

But Sammy has seen the light, such as it is, and I can tell by the look on his face, and the sour edge to his normally calm eucalyptus and ginger scent, how hard he's taken this perceived failing.

"I forgive you, Sam. You may not have been there for me when we were growing up, or when I was trapped with Darren, but you're here now. That counts for a lot in my book. I'm done living in the past, and I'd like you to do the same," I say.

My brother looks up at me, eyes glassy with unshed tears. I put a hand on his shoulder and smile. We've got a long way to go to build the sort of relationship Jason and I have, but this is a start. And it's high time we stop letting our parents ruin our relationships with each other. If we're united against them, then it's so much harder to control us and keep us obedient. And that's a very empowering thought, I'd like to think.

I'm about to say as much, but there's a sudden shift in the air, a tension that ripples outward from the guards by the door like a stone tossed into a still pond. Caleb moves first, responding to some sort of signal, but Jason is right behind him.

"What's going on?" Lex demands, taking a step toward the door.

"Vehicle. White SUV. Cadillac," Caleb replies, clipped and efficient.

Jason, Sammy, and I look at each other with similar blood-less expressions of panic. Mom and Dad are pulling up outside.

Chapter Forty-One

Alexandra

LYDIA'S SPIKE OF FEAR runs through my heart like a javelin, and it takes all my willpower not to go to her, gather her in my arms, and take her away from this. But running at this point would be completely counterproductive. So instead, I step forward, putting myself between her and the doorway to the foyer. Rhett moves on silent feet to my right side, fully obscuring Lydia from view. Mateo and Lucas move toward the edges of the room, positioning themselves on either side of the foyer doorway, strategically making themselves less noticeable. Caleb maintains his place closest to the door, and I don't miss the subtle shift of his arms as they cross over his chest, one hand slipping inside his jacket inconspicuously.

I don't see where the rest of the guards, or Sammy and Ally, move to, as my focus shifts to the door when it opens, revealing a man and a woman entering with shoulders back and heads high. The family resemblance is obvious. The man, who I can only assume to be Lydia's father, is average in most respects. His height, weight, attractiveness, all just mediocre at best, but his eyes are the same striking shade of emerald green as my omega's. His hair is a similar shade of blond as Jason's, combed back in a careful swoop that reminds me of World War II army portraits. It ages him beyond his true years, but I can't deny that it has the desired effect of making him appear more severe and respectable than he really is. He's dressed in pressed pants, and a crisp white short-sleeved shirt, exposing muscular arms that have been darkened by his time working outdoors. He scans the room, and I can tell by the way his eyes skate right past me that he hasn't identified me as the alpha in charge yet, which is surprising, but is fine with me. He'll learn soon enough how big of a mistake it is to underestimate Alexandra St. Clair.

"What is all this? Samuel, what's going on here? Who are you—"

"Good to finally meet in person, Diane. We've spoken on the phone a few times. Mateo Hutchenson," Mateo says, stepping out of a shadow to present his hand for her to shake.

Only years of rigorous control keep me from laughing out loud at the frightened expression that crosses Diane Anderson's face. I'd heard about that phone call, when Mateo vowed to ruin her if she continued to harass Lydia, and I'm glad she remembers, too. She ducks behind her husband as they continue forward, and the patriarch shakes Mateo's hand, too much of a Southern gentleman to refuse a handshake, even with a known enemy. Mateo pours on the charm, his smile incandescent as he steps back and motions to the rest of us in the room.

"We were just stoppin' by for a spell, and were about to head your way. Seems like we've crossed paths at the wrong time," Mateo goes on, his words smoothing out as he puts on the mask he so often wears as the face of my organization. The way he can calm anxious clients with just a few short sentences makes him the perfect salesman, and it's why, more often than not, I trust him to be the first person an investor interacts with when dealing with the St. Clair Foundation.

In our strategy for dealing with Lydia's parents, I wanted to have the chance to feel them out before I make my first move, which is why Mateo was supposed to start our introductions. He's adapted the plan, and is taking point now to allow me time to evaluate. The couple is tense, nearly vibrating with discomfort. Samuel Sr. keeps looking around, trying to find something, but only seeing the small army I'd assembled. Could we have gone on this trip with Caleb alone as security and been just fine? Sure, but there's something to be said about bigger posse diplomacy.

"What business do you have in my home?" Diane asks tartly, her aging face twisting like she's sucked on too many lemons.

I don't see much of Lydia when I look at her mother, not compared to her father. They might share the same nose shape, same ears, but beyond that, it's hard to tell. Whatever Diane's natural hair color was, it's now covered with a truly horrendous shade of chestnut brown, one that makes her spray tanned skin lean an unflattering shade of orange. She'd dressed modestly, but the style of her skirt suit is very dated. The coral color is almost hard to look at, not that I want to give her any more attention than is absolutely necessary.

"Sammy asked us to stop by," Jason adds, stepping out from behind Ally's armchair.

Diane's hair whips around her face as her head snaps to look at her youngest son, and she immediately flushes an angry red. She opens her mouth, but Samuel's hand on her shoulder halts whatever she's about to say. Which is for the best, in all honesty. I can feel Rhett through Lydia and Lucas, and he's hovering at the very limits of his temper. If she tried to go after Jason again like she did the last time mother and son were in the same room, I doubt there would be much I could do to stop him. And, if Samuel Sr.'s nervous glances to the alpha by my side are anything to go by, he's thinking the same thing. So he's not entirely oblivious, and avoids conflict whenever possible.

"Where's Adam?" Jason asks, somehow both pointed and casual simultaneously.

"On a job. With Sammy needing to take care of Ally, and this meeting, I had to leave him in charge," Samuel says, almost no inflection to the words. Straight forward, honest, no nonsense.

A strategy emerges, and further solidifies as Diane huffs a sigh, looking at Ally with open contempt in every line of her face. To her credit, Ally doesn't balk, tossing her hair over her shoulder and returning the look with a sweet smile. A woman after my own heart.

"Like I said, we were just on our way out. We didn't mean to interrupt whatever brought you back home, so we can leave and meet y'all at our previously agreed upon location," Mateo offers genially, taking back control of the conversation.

His subtle point catches in my mind, and I narrow my eyes. Why *are* they here? Lydia told us the office is about a half hour away from the house, and we're coming up on our original meeting time quickly. It'd always been my plan to be late, a power play straight out of my father's handbook, but they should have already been at the office, if not on their way. Samuel Sr.'s eyes flick to me, something stirring in them, but I can't identify it before he looks away.

"If it's all the same to y'all, we could get this done and over with here rather than driving all the way out to the office," he says, addressing Mateo now.

Mateo looks at me in question, and I consider. I don't like the idea of staying here. Lydia's discomfort lingers on the edges of my senses, her fingers against my back, her steady, measured breathing as she tries to collect herself. Rhett is there, lending her his strength, but the idea of my omega's distress makes my stomach roil. And even with Samuel Sr. claiming that Adam is out on a job, it's already been proven that people will show up where they're not supposed to be. I'd spoken to Jason a lot about the family dynamics in preparation for this meeting, and we both agreed that if we wanted to keep this as civil as possible, Adam should not be present. Lucas might be a bratty little shit stirrer, but he always knows where the line is. Adam, according to all accounts, finds the line, spits on it, and then marches boldly across it without a backward glance.

But we're here, and it would be better to get this done sooner rather than later. I look to Caleb, and the tension around his eyes tells me all I need to know. We had the floor plan of the office memorized, but we have no idea where anything is, where the exits are, or even if we're alone. I shift to glance at Jason, and he's tense, but not obviously so. He gives me a little shrug, and I purse my lips. Mateo gives me a nod of deference, and Lucas is too busy trying to set the back of Diane's hair on fire with his eyes to notice my questioning glance. Lydia slides her fingers into mine and squeezes twice, silently giving her consent. I turn my attention to Samuel Sr., but before I can respond, Diane is opening her mouth.

"I'll get drinks. I think we've still got some lemonade," Diane says, striding off through the frankly crowded room toward the kitchen on my left.

Mateo, Rhett, Lucas, and I share a look before I turn and look at Lydia, whose face is nearly as pale as the white walls around us. I squeeze her hand, frowning at how cold her fingers are despite the warmth of the room, pulling her eyes from the middle distance. She blinks, and her nerves echo my own. Not giving a single flying fuck about the company around us, I lean in and kiss her hairline, feeling her little spark of joy at the gesture.

"It'll be okay, sweetness. We've got this," I whisper reassuringly.

She gives me a shaky smile, but her eyes flick over my shoulder at the same time I hear heavy footsteps approaching. I turn and lift my chin as Samuel Sr. comes within arm's reach of me, Rhett, and Lydia. We're still standing partially in front of our omega, but he looks past us to his daughter, giving her an assessing stare. There's a long stretch of silence, and I give Lydia the room to decide how she wants to handle the waves of rolling off the older alpha. Our fingers are still entwined, and I can tell the moment he notices by the flare of his nostrils, and the tightening in the corners of his mouth. Rhett straightens, the air filling with leather and burning paper. So he doesn't like that look, either.

"Lydia, help me bring these to the table," Diane calls pointedly, breaking the tense silence before either alpha can start.

Lydia stiffens, biting her lower lip as her eyes move toward her mother and then to me, her conflict sour like artificial sweetener on the roof of my mouth. But before I can tell Lydia not to listen and to sit with me, movement in the corner of my eye catches my attention.

"Let me help, Mrs. Anderson," Lucas says, jumping to attention and scurrying over to the kitchen island and the tray of glasses she's put together.

Diane startles, not having noticed him previously, and then narrows her eyes at my beta, and I feel his amusement and vindication across the room. So he noticed her thinly veiled attempt to order her daughter around, too. One last glance over Samuel Sr.'s shoulder at Mateo, and it only takes a look for him to understand the shift in the room. I've seen enough, and it's time to get down to business. He gives me a nod, settling to lean against the wall near the door. He's stepping back and letting me assume the lead, an eager grin on his face as he settles in for the show.

Taking that as my cue, I walk away from Samuel, and over to the dining room table, pulling Lydia with me. Before anyone can stop me, I sit at the head of the table, my back to the patio doors as I guide Lydia to sit in the chair to my right. It's a bit truculent, but the look on Samuel's face is worth it. He looks at Rhett, confusion and shock pulling his jaw slack, but Rhett just smirks and moves to the seat on my other side, making himself comfortable. Jason sits on Lydia's other side, unbuttoning his blazer as he sighs. When Samuel looks back to me again, his face grows steadily redder with each tick of the hall clock. Lucas appears at my shoulder, the heavy tray balanced expertly on one arm, a tall glass of lemonade extended to me. I take it and sip gently, maintaining eye contact with Samuel, who is still frozen in place where I left him.

"I'm sorry, where are my manners? My name is Alexandra St. Clair, Prime Alpha of Pack St. Clair."

CHAPTER FORTY-TWO

Mateo

LEX'S INTRODUCTION HANGS IN the air like a penny, wheeling and turning until it finally pings to the ground. Her family name and their reputation, as well as her own, have preceded her, it seems. Most of his letters were only addressed to the "Prime Alpha of Pack Saint Clair" so he may not have realized our leader is, in fact, a woman. Ally mutters something about going to have a lie down, and her husband escorts her out hastily, leaving a silence about as pregnant as she is behind. Samuel Sr. clears his throat, shifting his weight, like he can't decide if he should go shake her hand or demand she get out of his chair.

There's nothing like watching my Lex totally emasculate an alpha in fifteen words or less. I may have to take her somewhere quiet on the plane home and show her how much I appreciate her.

"Yes, well, hmm. Ms. St. Clair, I'm—"

"Samuel Anderson Sr., my omega's father and previous Prime Alpha. I'm very aware of who you are, sir," Lex interjects icily.

I press my lips together and try to think of The Loneliest Whale to keep a straight face, and soft cock. It becomes infinitely harder to remain serious as Samuel flushes red and plops down in the chair at the opposite end of the table from Lex. It's a bold move for Lex to take the seat of power away from a man, an alpha, in his own home. But my prime alpha has never been anything but bold. And watching her settle into the wooden chair like it's a golden throne, it strikes me like a bolt out of the blue at how much she's changed since we met. This imperious woman more than earned her nickname from me when we first started working together, but the Ice Queen has melted away in recent months. Seeing her slip back behind the mask is almost disconcerting, only helped by the hand she keeps clasped with Lydia's over the table.

Diane scampers over, sitting at her husband's right hand, not that he acknowledges her. Lucas finishes passing out glasses of lemonade, not spilling a drop despite the questionable integrity of the tray he's balancing. Lydia's eyes track him as he moves, and I can feel the spark of her arousal in my lower belly. Not that I can blame her. Lucas's muscles pull tantalizingly at his black button-down as he moves with practiced ease around the table and back to the kitchen island. And like the menace he is, he hops up to sit on the island counter, perched perfectly in Diane's line of sight. I can't see her face from where I'm standing by the foot of the stairs, but her shoulders tense, rising steadily toward her ears. Good. It's about time someone got under her skin like she's gotten under ours.

"Regarding your demands, I've had a chance to review them with Lydia and we have some questions," Lex starts, pulling my attention back to her.

"They aren't demands," Samuel counters, but he doesn't sound all that convincing.

"Strongly worded requests, then. However you want to split that hair. In any case, I have to ask: how did you arrive at the sum for the dowry?" she continues, leveling a hard stare at him that I've seen rattle lesser men to their core.

"Our lawyer advised that it's fair," Diane snaps.

I can only see the back of Samuel Sr., but there's a distinct tensing of his shoulders as his wife speaks in his place. Even still, he doesn't move to correct her. That tracks with what Jason and Lydia have told us. Samuel Sr. might be an alpha, but Diane Anderson has her mate on a tight leash, using his instinctual need to stand with her and not embarrass her against him in situations exactly like this. To do anything other than give a very short, very tense, nod of agreement would show his omega is going rogue and outside of his control. Which, for a man like that, is a fate worse than death.

It's one-thousand percent horse shit, of course. But that's his grave to dig. Far be it from me to take away his shovel.

"That wasn't my question. Because Lydia has pointed out a strange coincidence, but I'd like to hear your explanation," Lex replies, unruffled.

I have to swallow my growl. Coincidence, my ass. Not when the request they've asked for is the precise ending balance of Lydia's trust on the day the transfer went through, down to the penny.

Samuel shifts backward slightly in his chair, arms crossing over his chest. "It was a complicated equation, taking into account the costs of raising her, her college education, housing, the list goes on. I didn't get too into the weeds with the specifics—"

"Clearly," Lex intones sardonically, the single word enough to silence the alpha opposite her.

"I don't know why it's so difficult for you to understand that you're never going to get any part of my trust fund," Lydia snarls, the words spilling out like she couldn't keep them back any longer.

Her anger is like a red-hot coal settling behind my heart, and I brush a calming mental finger across our bond. My pride still leaks through, despite my attempt to hold it back. She wants to say more, and she's doing so well. I don't know if I could keep my composure if I were in her position. Lydia's eyes flick to me for an instant, and I feel her returning gratitude. I cross my arms over my chest and lean against the banister, nodding once. Her thumb finds my mating mark through the fabric of her sleeve, and I smile at the phantom touch I swear I can feel under the little lightning bolt tattooed on my wrist.

Diane waves a dismissive hand at her daughter. "This isn't about your grandmother's money, Lydia. Our lawyer arrived at that figure based on the hardship we went through getting you into such a prestigious pack—"

Rhett growls low in his throat. "Lydia becoming a member of our pack had nothing to do with you," he snarls, hands clenching into tight fists over the table.

There's a collective wave of annoyance across our web of bonds, but my focus is pulled by the shock coming from

Lydia. I don't know if the others feel it, being so worked up and in their own heads, but I stand up straight and watch Lydia's face closely. She's staring at her parents like she's seeing them for the first time. Disbelief wells up in her, and I take a step closer on instinct, but a sharp look from Lex stops me.

"And as far as you getting what you're 'owed,'" Lex adds, her voice steady, even as it twists skeptically around that last word, "considering how little you've been involved with Lydia's life over the last five years, the figure you are asking for is out of the question."

"That wasn't our choice! Lydia pushed us away, cut off contact, and kept us in the dark about everything. I didn't even know where my own daughter was, didn't know if she was alive or dead until—"

"If you could do us a kindness and stop pretendin' like you gave a shite 'bout your daughter's well-being, things would go much smoother," Rhett growls, his accent coming out with his anger.

"*A false witness will not go unpunished, and he who speaks lies shall perish,*" Jason adds, just loud enough for everyone to hear, even as he picks a piece of invisible lint off his shirt sleeve.

"I'm not sure exactly how much your wife told you about what she's been doing over the last few years, but it doesn't exactly paint a picture of a worried mother," Lex drawls, a challenging look flashing in her hazel eyes.

Samuel doesn't answer right away, and I have to stop myself from moving to look at his face. Lex has backed him into a corner with no way out. He either has to admit that he wasn't in charge, and the wife he's supposed to rule over acted without his knowledge or consent, or he has to admit that he was fully aware of the smear campaign and harassment she orchestrated. Either way, not a good look. Especially as Lydia stares at her father, eyes glassy with unshed tears as she waits for confirmation of things she has only ever been able to speculate about. And the longer he stays silent, the worse it looks for him.

Diane scoffs a sarcastic chuckle. "I'm not sure what you're trying to accuse me of—"

"Oh, how discourteous of me. I would hate for there to be any misunderstandings, so allow me to enlighten you," Lex says, shifting forward to rest on her elbows, looking down the table. "You pretended your daughter was a missing person to stop her from rightfully claiming her trust fund, because you thought you were entitled to it. You tried to convince her to return home for the express purpose of marrying and mating her abuser, again in an effort to get your hands on that money and whatever other kickbacks that sack of rotting horse shit promised you. When that didn't work, you colluded with my pack's ex-omega to stalk, harass and, I believe, ultimately force Lydia into a bond with Mr. McLaughlin against her will. And now, as a last-ditch effort, you've convinced your lawyer and your husband that you're owed over ten million dollars in an alpha dowry for a daughter who was never more than a pawn for you to sell to the highest bidder. Is that clear enough for you, Diane? Or did I miss anything?"

"You forgot about how she knew Darren's plan to rape me on that Christmas Eve, when I refused his proposal, and forced me back to him anyway," Lydia pipes up, not looking at her parents but at her lap.

"My apologies, sweetness. How could I forget a mother not only ignoring her daughter's distress, but adding to it?" Lex says, petting Lydia's hair in comfort while continuing to glare at Samuel and Diane.

"How dare you—"

"Silence," Samuel snaps, and even I can feel the ripple of power as the word cracks through the air like a whip. "As far as I was aware, Lydia wasn't in distress, and was staying with friends of Jason's. There was some sort of work placement she'd received, and would be coming home when her contract expired."

I rock back onto my heels as the wave of realization hits me. Jason isn't looking at his parents, but instead is staring at a spot on the table, eyes a thousand miles away. Lydia swallows hard, lifting her chin as she comes to the same conclusions as the rest of us. Samuel Anderson Sr. might not have been a part of Diane's schemes at all. Instead, she's been lying for over five years to keep him out of the way while she made my omega's life a living hell.

I don't know if there's a place low enough in hell for that woman to rot.

"Partially true. I was staying with Jason's friend, but I was hiding from Darren. I lived in fear of the day you found out where I was, when you would call the police to drag me back to him," Lydia replies bitterly, pulling me out of the beginnings of my rage spiral.

"I thought you were... taking some time apart. That things were..." Samuel trails off, and I can practically hear the wheels turning in his head. I can only fathom how many lies he's been fed over the years, and what's now starting to look a little different with this new information.

"Samuel, you can't possibly believe this. All of this for what, money? They're just spinning tales to get out of paying what we're rightfully owed," Diane says, a noticeable edge of panic to her words.

"Whose idea was it to have Lydia sign an NDA?" Rhett asks harshly. "Was it you, Diane? Too afraid of what Lydia knows, what so-called tales she could tell about you and what you did to her? Or was it someone else's idea?"

Diane sputters and pushes back from the table, and to my surprise, Samuel doesn't stop her. "I don't have to sit here and listen to this in my own home. What do you faithless deviants know about anything? Just whatever my ungrateful children have told you. They can't possibly understand what I've done, what I had to do to keep them walking the correct path."

"You wanted me to bond with a man who beat me regularly, Diane! He raped me over and over, and would have carved my mating mark from my skin in the bathroom at Sammy's wedding if Rhett didn't stop him," Lydia cries, getting to her feet and slamming her hands on the table.

There's a little inhale from over my shoulder, and I realize that Sammy is back from putting his wife to bed, standing out of sight as he listens. Judging by the look on his face, it seems that details of his wedding reception were kept from him. I don't draw attention to him, but it's good that he's hearing this directly from the source. Samuel Sr. is looking between his wife and daughter as they volley back and forth, growing steadily paler by the moment. I don't know if I should go to my omega, to soothe the hurt in her soul, or if I should teach Diane a lesson in manners.

"You've always been an unruly, disobedient child, so it wouldn't surprise me if you need a firm hand to guide you—"

A chorus of growls fills the room from my pack, and I stand up straight, ready to show this woman how firm my hand can be. Caleb is there at Lydia's side as she stares in mute horror at her mother, her shock rippling tangibly through our bond.

"The past isn't why we're here, Ms. St. Clair. We want to put this behind us so we can live our lives, and Lydia can live hers," Samuel says, trying to deescalate the tension in the room.

"And I'm sure a multi-million-dollar payday will make it so much easier to sleep at night. How could you not know what was going on, what was happening to me?" Lydia shouts, words wavering with unshed tears.

"This is how these things are done. I'm not sure what else you wanted me to do." Samuel sighs, and he has the audacity to sound annoyed with Lydia for asking a fair question.

"You can get your fucking harpy of a wife under control, for a start," Lucas says acidly.

Samuel stands and points an angry finger at our beta, who is still lounging on the island, one leg crossed over the other as he leans back on his hands. The picture of nonchalance, but with the way his foot is bouncing, that picture is about as fragile as his patience.

"Mind your tone and show some respect, boy," Samuel snarls, showing anger for the first time.

Rhett is on his feet now, but I'm faster. Three strides and I'm there between the alpha and my beta, spine stiff and hands curled into fists at my sides. Samuel blinks, as if he'd forgotten me in the chaos.

Before I can speak, Lucas just rolls his eyes. "I'll get right on that," Lucas sighs, almost sounding bored.

"We're not paying the dowry. You will never get another dime from me or my pack, so help me God," Lydia declares firmly.

Samuel turns back to his daughter, and my eyes lock on Rhett, muscles coiled to step in and intervene if things get physical, but an almost inhuman shriek draws the eyes of everyone in the room. Diane is visibly shaking with rage, but with her back to me, I can only imagine the look on her face. Whatever it is, Lex stands at last and takes a half step toward Lydia, her perfectly groomed brows pulled down.

"After everything I've done for you, you are going to stand there and pretend like you're better than us?" Diane fumes, pacing toward her daughter.

The air in the room shifts, the already tense atmosphere almost quivering. Rhett turns toward Diane, his fighter's instincts detecting the real threat in the room. I keep my attention on Samuel, watching how his expression changes as his wife descends into furious madness. Lucas sits up and edges toward the floor, and Caleb nods to the other guards in the room. Jason is still seated, deep in thought, and not looking at anyone. No one moves, waiting for whatever is about to happen. Lydia's rage sweeps through her bonds, and I flinch involuntarily, recovering quickly. She walks around Lex until she's only a few yards from her mother, staring her down.

A showdown, one a long time coming.

CHAPTER FORTY-THREE

Rhett

I STARE AT DIANE Anderson, her spray-tanned face nearly purple in her rage. Lydia and her mother are face to face, only a few feet between them, and I'm right there at my omega's elbow. If Diane makes one move to hurt my mate, I'm ready to pull her out of harm's way and show Diane the consequences of her actions.

"After everything you've done for me? You didn't do shit to help me," Lydia snarls.

"Watch your language," Samuel Sr. warns, but I snap a glare at him.

My omega has held her tongue long enough; she can speak her mind however she wishes at this point. Mateo is just over his shoulder, standing between him and Lucas, and edging closer. Putting himself in range if he should try to make a move to escalate the situation.

Diane snarls, mouth twisting into an ugly sneer. "Your life was perfect. You were going to be the perfect omega for the perfect alpha—"

Lydia throws her head back and laughs manically, but there's no humor in the sound. "Perfect? I didn't have any of the skills a real omega needs to survive in a relationship with an alpha. I didn't know how to purr, or actually form bonds. You didn't teach me anything other than how to duck my head and take my abuse without complaint or question."

"You weren't abused, Lydia. It's disrespectful to real victims to say such things," Diane sniffs, crossing her arms over her chest and throwing her nose in the air.

I can't stay still any longer, not with Lydia's heartbreak along our bond. No. We've worked too hard for this. I won't let Lydia go back to that darkness. Never again. I step forward and take my omega in my arms, holding her against my chest. She's stiff and a little cold to the touch, her face pale. Mateo is around the table, behind Diane's back, and I hear Lex come up beside me, one of her hands touching Lydia's shoulder before she steps forward, putting herself in front of me.

"That's completely out of order, Mom. You're going to try to sit there and say that Lydi wasn't abused?" Jason snaps, aghast, finally getting to his feet.

"I never saw anything. Darren has always been the most respectful boy, perfectly courteous to me. If you were so abused, where were the marks? I never once saw you with anything," Diane counters, making my blood boil. She rocks back onto her heel and crosses her arms over her chest like the petulant child she is.

Lydia's tether to my soul shakes like a spider's silk in a storm, hurt and anger radiating from it. Her eyes swim with tears, and I can see the ghosts of her past creeping closer. I kiss her forehead and hold her as close as she'll allow, trying to get her to shift so she doesn't have to look at this complete monster.

"Not all abuse has physical signs, Diane," Lex says in a low, serious monotone.

I growl as that disgusting trash heap masquerading as my omega's mother rolls her eyes. The insults don't seem to be stopping, and I've just about had enough of her and her lies. I look to Samuel Sr., and the older alpha is also staring at his wife. But not in anger, but in shock, like he's never seen her before in his life. And maybe he hasn't; I doubt she shows how ugly her soul is very often.

"Even if you had a few... altercations with Darren, it still doesn't change the facts. We're entitled to compensation for you," Diane says haughtily.

"You're not getting my trust fund. You've taken enough from me," Lydia says, voice weaker than before.

"Nothing I wasn't owed, and it's not like you deserve that money anyway," Diane huffs, jerking her chin in the air.

"Oh, for fuck's sake!"

"Bullshit."

Mateo and Lucas snap at the same time, but Diane jumps as she suddenly realizes how close Mateo has gotten without her noticing. She takes a step back before she remembers that Lex and I are behind her, leaving her paralyzed in the middle.

"You don't get to decide what I do and don't deserve. Not anymore," Lydia says, pulling away a little as she finds her strength again.

I can feel my pack through her, showing their support without words, filling her with love and kindness to counter the hate being thrown at her. I take her hand and lace our fingers together, pushing my pride and belief her way. If this is what she wants, then she can do this, even if it's hard.

"You'll always be my daughter, so I'll always have a say in your life. Not that you ever take anything I say seriously. I warned you what giving in to your... unnatural urges would do. Perhaps God was punishing you for—"

"My urges aren't unnatural, and are frankly none of your business. I had to fight to figure out who I am, and I won't be shamed for loving the people I do. They've shown me more support and love and care in the last twenty minutes than you've shown me in my entire lifetime. And maybe instead of judging me, you should take a long, hard look in the mirror, Diane. Unless you're too afraid of the disgusting bigot who'll be looking back at you," Lydia says, starting as a low snarl and building to nearly a shout.

I don't bother to contain my smug smile as I watch Diane's face turn from red to nearly plum purple with rage, her mouth opening and closing as she struggles to speak.

"You—you jezebel, abomination of a—I can't believe—I am not a—"

Mateo takes a step forward, hands clenching and un-clenching, like he's struggling not to put them around the woman's throat. I growl in my throat, ready to jump to my omega's defense, but Lydia just lifts her chin and sets her shoulders.

"You have done nothing but cause me pain, and I won't stand for it anymore. I have a pack who loves me for me, and I don't need you. You can live the rest of your life in misery, but I won't be in it. We're not paying the dowry, and I'm sure as hell not going to sign that fucking NDA," Lydia finishes.

She looks back to me and Lex as her mother sputters, turning to her husband for support, but the man appears to be too stunned to speak. Lydia starts toward the door, and the rest of us move to follow. Lydia has made herself quite clear, and to say anything else would be to undermine her. Not that any of the words I have for Diane Anderson would be ones fit for polite company.

But as Lydia and I move past Diane, she moves faster than I can react to. One of her hands shoots out and locks around Lydia's upper arm, the other cracks across Lydia's cheek hard enough to send her head whipping around and stumbling into me.

I blink, my vision going red. Absolutely the fuck not.

"Omega, let go," I command, stepping into Diane's space and towering over her as I bring the full force of my alpha bark down on her.

Diane whimpers and complies, cowering back a step. She's shaking again, but then again, so am I. I've never put my hands on a woman who didn't ask for it, but I want to hurt this trash dump of a human in front of me.

"Sam—"

"You don't get to speak, Omega. Get down and beg," Mateo barks, appearing at my side.

Diane crashes to the floor at our feet, head bowed even as she fights against the commands. She's trying to throw me off, but I push back, hard enough to make her drop her chest to her lap as she curls into a ball.

"Matty, Rhett—"

Lydia's whimper from behind me feels distant, secondary to the task at hand. I want to punish this omega at my feet, make her hurt like she made my love hurt. Lex is there, watching us, and very specifically, not stopping us. That's all the permission I need to continue.

"Hands flat on the floor," I order, ice cold.

"Sam, help—"

"I said, quiet!" Mateo shouts, and Diane whimpers.

I catch movement out of the corner of my eye. Sammy's returned, it seems. He's looking at his father in disbelief. "Dad, why—"

"She overstepped. Lydia isn't ours to discipline anymore. Your mother had no right to put her hands on another pack's omega," Samuel Sr. states simply.

I look up at him, finding him glaring at his wife as she kneels on the floor, both of her hands pressed flat, with palms down on either side of her. There's a moment of silent communication between us, and someone solidifies. He'd wanted to believe his wife wasn't capable of the things we claimed, because he loves her, even if I'm skeptical that the toxic cesspit masquerading as a heart in her chest is even capable of the emotion. But he's seen with his own eyes what she's truly capable of.

"Okay. Whatever crock of shit you were trying to peddle didn't work. So, it's my turn. This is what's going to happen," Jason says, stepping around me and Mateo to stand between us and his father.

I blink, careful not to let my surprise shake my hold on Diane and her supplication. I still haven't decided what I'm going to do with her yet, and I don't want her scampering away.

"We're going to walk away from this house, and never come back. You're going to release me from my pack bond, and Lydia from this bullshit dowry demand. We're going to get a written guarantee that you'll never darken our doorway again, and you're going to make Pastor Joe and his fucking son leave Lydia alone. You're never going to contact us again," Jason explains calmly.

"That's one hell of a proposal, son. Why should I agree? What's the benefit for me?" Samuel Sr. responds, sounding intrigued despite himself.

I swallow, throat going dry. We agreed that we weren't going to go down that road. What does Jason think he's doing? Lex tenses at my side as she comes to the same realization a moment later. Her scent shifts, turning bitter, and the hurt coming from her is sour, like unripe fruit.

"You'll stay out of jail, probably," Jason says simply.

Diane squeaks, and Mateo and I growl a reprimand, forcing her forehead to the floor now without even needing to speak. I look to Lex, and the only sign of her distress is the tightness around her mouth and eyes. Otherwise, she looks as cold and calculating as ever. Lydia is tucked into her side, and Lex's fingers are making gentle circles over the bond mark on her throat. But I return my focus to the standoff before me as Samuel Sr. speaks.

"That so? I don't think you know how negotiations work, Jason. See, you need to make proposals that are mutually beneficial for both parties, not make empty threats," he says, the patronizing tone making my teeth grind.

"Oh, you misunderstand me, Dad. This isn't a negotiation, and these aren't empty threats. We're going to walk away. You're going to leave us alone, and we're going to get a legally binding contract to confirm that. Or my new friends at the FTC are going to get a special delivery," Jason replies, not remotely shaken.

I blink. We'd agreed not to extort Samuel and Diane. We're better than that, better than Seth. And looking at Lex, she's as silently furious as I've ever seen her. But she can't undermine Jason, not now that he finally seems to have gotten his father's attention.

"The documents..."

"I promised that you'd regret taking your children and their loyalty for granted," Jason says, picking up when his father trails off.

"And how do I know that you won't blow the whistle, even if I agree to this extortion?" Samuel demands, an edge of panic creeping in now.

Jason sucks his teeth and rubs his lower lip with one thumb. "My word, I suppose. But of the two of us, I'm not the one who's committed fraud, so..."

"Bastard!" Diane shouts, trying to lunge for her son.

"Apologize, Omega," Mateo orders, the force of his command slamming her to the floor on her belly.

Diane shakes her head and fights hard, and I struggle to maintain my hold. She has to be in agony, ignoring a direct order like this, but it doesn't stop her from flopping around like a fish out of water.

Samuel Sr. looks at his youngest son, really considering him for the first time. I can almost smell the smoke coming out of his ears as he tries to find a way to make this come out in his favor. But after spending several long nights with Jason poring over the documents, I know there isn't a happy ending in this for the patriarch. But then his next words catch me entirely off guard.

"What if I gave you the company? Would you sign a contract then? My company and promise to leave you and Lydia and this pack alone until the end of my days, and you'll return the documents and any copies, and promise to never speak a word of this?" Samuel asks, sounding desperate now.

I blink several times. Of all the counterarguments, that wasn't one I expected. But clearly, his son did. Jason hums like he's considering, then looks to Lex. But she doesn't have a sympathetic line in her expression anymore. He's on his own with this deal.

"You'll sign it over to Sammy, make a show of retiring early. And you'll get the McLaughlins under control. No lawsuits, gag orders—"

"I can't speak for Pastor Joe, son," Samuel hedges.

Jason shrugs. "I wonder if Thom is in the office on Saturdays," he wonders idly, pulling out his phone.

Samuel Sr. growls, and I can't help but feel a little bit of affection for Lydia's brother. If he weren't blackmailing his own father, I'd almost have to admire his negotiation skills.

"I'll do what I can. But you'll have to talk to them on your own to get something better," Samuel spits after a minute.

"I'm sure Pastor Joe and I can come to some sort of agreement. I'm sure he'll find my spreadsheets and balance statements just as fascinating as Thom did," Jason returns with a chuckle.

"Wait, what? I thought—"

"I had to show them something, Dad. But don't worry, you'll be able to afford the fine if you sell a few of the cars and boats," Jason replies.

He turns on his heel and starts toward the door, hands in his pockets as he whistles cheerfully. The room is silent for several minutes after the front door slams shut, with none of us sure what to do.

"You'll be hearing from our lawyer, Mr. Anderson. I'll have the agreement to you by end of business this week," Lex says smoothly, her heels clicking decisively on the floor as she heads toward the door herself.

"Is your city-slicker conman used to drawing up blackmail deals?" Samuel snarls.

Lex chuckles ironically. "My personal attorney? No. But I'll be recommending a family friend to handle this personally. He's much more familiar with this sort of thing," she says.

I blink, curiosity blooming. I wonder who she's going to ask to draw up a vaguely legal contract like this? But as the question floats across my mind, I already know the answer. However, my thoughts are interrupted as Diane howls on the floor. I look down just in time to see Lex pulling her foot back, and I see the bloody red puncture wound on the back of Diane's hand, the same one she used to strike Lydia. It isn't lost on me that the hole is about the same size as her stiletto heel.

"Oops. Didn't see you there. You should really be more careful where you put your hands. You never know what can happen," Lex says mildly.

Lex walks away with Lydia at her side, their hands still intertwined. My omega doesn't spare a glance backwards as she holds her head high, and I couldn't be any prouder of her. Lucas moves next, the bodyguards following right after, leaving me, Mateo, and Caleb alone with the two Sams, and Diane. Father and son lock eyes and the air crackles.

"Were you part of this?" Samuel Sr. asks in a low rasp.

Sammy shakes his head and looks to Mateo and me. I look between them, the resemblance even more pronounced with proximity. Diane is still frozen between all of us, her hand bleeding rather profusely now. I'm not exerting much willpower to keep her pinned, so it must be Mateo that's preventing her from staunching the flow of blood.

"Your daughter deserves better than what you've given to her," Mateo says, low and dangerous.

Samuel Sr. swallows, and I'm glad he looks uncomfortable. I shift, drawing his attention. I look him up and down once more, not bothering to disguise the disgust and disrespect in my expression.

"She's been through the absolute worst life can throw at a person, and is still the most beautiful soul I've ever known, not because of your rearing, but in spite of it. Your son has more restraint than I ever will. But I promise you this: come near Lydia again, try to contact her again, and everything you love will be ash. Am I clear?" I ask, speaking slowly so there can be no misunderstandings.

Diane whimpers, but before Mateo or I can react, her mate snarls, silencing her last protest.

"Crystal," Samuel responds promptly.

I nod and look to Mateo, jerking my chin toward the door. I'm ready to put this place in the past once and for all. He nods, but then moves to crouch down in front of Diane. He surprises me by tilting her chin up to look at his eyes, touch gentle and almost tender. Her face is ugly, makeup smeared from her tears and snot.

"I made you a promise, Diane, and I've kept it. And I mean this with the utmost disrespect, but I hope you have the life you deserve, and that it's a long one," he says softly.

Her jaw hangs open as she watches him stand and brush his hands together, removing any trace of her from his skin.

He looks to me, and without needing to speak, we walk away and out of the front door.

CHAPTER FORTY-FOUR

Lydia

LEX'S ANGER PULSES ACROSS our bond as we exit the farmhouse, and it takes a lot of my concentration not to flinch away from her, to try to flee, even if I know it's not directed at me. Some old habits are harder to break than others. She gives me a kiss on the forehead, depositing me in one SUV before moving off, pulling out her phone, and texting furiously.

I'm still in shock as I sit in the backseat of Caleb's rental SUV, turned sideways to look out over the front lawn through the open car door. I can hear Lex's voice as she tears Jason a new asshole, and him fighting back. But their words lose meaning as my face continues to throb from where my mother struck me.

I touch my cheek gingerly, the heat and swelling making it tender, but it's not even close to the worst facial injury I've ever had. It hurts, but it's more of an emotional ache than a physical one. My mother spanked me growing up, but that stopped around my pre-teen years, when I got too big for her to overpower. A psychiatrist would probably have a field day knowing how much I enjoy it when my lovers spank me now, but I've never even remotely enjoyed being slapped in the face. And having my own mother, the woman who gave birth to me, strike me in such a demeaning and disrespectful way cuts deeper. Not to mention the things she said.

You weren't abused.

Maybe God is punishing you.

She doesn't deserve it.

Old, ugly thoughts I thought I'd buried resurface as my mother's words replay over and over again. I don't deserve this pack, or the happiness they've brought me. I only cause trouble, because God is upset at me for some reason. Why would these wonderful, perfect people want someone like me? Damaged, unworthy, insignificant.

"Lydi-bug."

Lucas's voice draws my gaze up from the ground, and I can barely look at him. His blue-gray eyes are bright with concern, and the cyclone of doubt in my chest immediately rebuffs it. I look away, even as he steps closer and brushes my hair back from my face. For the first time in weeks, I struggle to feel his cotton-soft touch through my alpha bonds, all of them so consumed with their anger that it blocks out everything he's trying to send my way. We aren't connected in any way that matters, and he could walk away now that he has what he wants. What use am I to him now that he has his bonds?

"Let me in, sweetheart. I can't feel you," he begs, and I whimper.

"I can't feel you, either," I mutter, voice cracking as tears slip from my eyes.

Lucas gathers me in his arms, and while it's not a true fix, I let myself give in to the physical sensation of his arms around me, one hand in my hair, the other rubbing up and down my back. I spread my knees a little to allow him closer, breathing in his smoke and sugar scent until everything else fades away.

"You were so strong and so brave in there. I'm so proud of you," he whispers in my ear, rocking me slightly side to side.

I don't feel brave or strong, not when I've allowed a few simple words to throw me so far off balance and undo all the work I've done to feel good about myself. Sinking further into my own misery, I stay quiet.

"Let's get out of here before you have to bail me out again," Rhett's voice grumbles.

There's some soft conversation, but I don't hear anything over the buzzing of my anxiety spiral. The world is drifting away, like a balloon in the vast blue sky. I don't even bother to try to reach for the string. My face and chest hurt, throbbing in time with my heartbeat. It's easy to slip into the void again, like riding a bike. You never forget how to let your worst fears consume you.

But then there's a burst of color and light in the dark, a wave of pine smoke and leather and dark chocolate. I can almost sense it in my navel region, a tether yanking me upward, a strong line wrapped in a softer thread. Rhett and Lucas are there as I open my eyes, blocking out the sun as they squeeze to fit in the open car door.

"You have done nothing wrong, Lydia. We're here, and we aren't going anywhere," Rhett says, voice soft but not lacking in emotion.

"We love you so much, Lydi-bug. You're our everything, and we wouldn't change a thing about you, or your past. We fell in love with your kindness, your heart, your passion, and nothing anyone can say changes those things. Least of all those monsters in that house," Lucas adds, the hand still in my hair clenching tight for a moment in emphasis.

Their words are accompanied by an equally intense surge of love down our bond, and the truth of their declarations is impossible to ignore or dismiss. They love me, every part of me, even the most damaged parts of my soul that I haven't been able to fully heal yet. They don't want me to change, or for things to have been different in my past, because that would mean I wouldn't be the person I am today. These thoughts and more fill my head, replacing the nasty ones the last hour triggered. They don't stop even as we slide into the backseat and the door closes. Mateo joins their effort from the front passenger seat while Caleb drives us away from the house that's haunted me.

The hour-long ride back to the airport is quiet, but I don't mind. Rhett, Lucas, and Mateo use the time to continue to reassure me and help me through the last traces of my anxiety attack. I'm feeling drowsy and ready for a good nap by the time we're pulling into the airport, curled on my side with my head resting on Lucas's chest and my feet in Rhett's lap, one of my hands twined with Mateo's. When we stop, I don't miss how he casually tries to roll his shoulder to work out the kinks, not that he once complained about the awkward position he'd held for the last half hour of the drive.

The second SUV pulls up behind us, and Jason leaps out of the back seat before it's even fully parked. His face is twisted in annoyance, hair rumpled like he's been running his hands through it nearly constantly.

"I'm not going to apologize for what I did," he shouts over his shoulder as he heads for the door to the private lounge.

"If you want me to pay for Gideon's help, you sure as hell will," Lex snarls, storming after him.

I'd been so overwhelmed with the boys' soothing that I'd lost track of Lex's simmering rage. Now it's back, settling in my chest like heartburn. We all follow the two of them up the stairs to the plush sitting room, the panoramic windows filling the space with afternoon light. I sit between Rhett and Lucas, both of them still reluctant to let go of my hands. Mateo leans against the wall closest to the couch we're on, the security guards milling around. Caleb is close to where Jason and Lex are standing in the middle of the room, with Lex's weight having shifted onto her back foot as she crosses her arms over her chest, Jason's back ramrod straight.

"I don't want your help if it means having to compromise my integrity," Jason snaps, lifting his chin.

Lex scoffs harshly. "And extortion doesn't compromise it enough already?"

"Like you're so fond of saying, I did what I had to do. I let you try it your way, and it didn't work. Like I fucking told you it wouldn't," Jason retorts, not even flinching at her accusation.

I exchange a glance with Rhett and Lucas, both of whom have similarly tight expressions. Jason is hitting a little below the belt, but I don't know if it's right to stop him.

"We're better than this, Jason," Lex says simply.

"Give me a fucking break with that shit. You can climb down off your high horse anytime now and join the rest of us down here in reality," Jason groans angrily.

"I'm sorry if I don't want to become the type of monster I spent so long trying to escape. Forgive me for not wanting to inflict my trauma on someone else," Lex says sarcastically.

"You're acting like my parents are these innocent little lambs, and they just aren't, Lex. Even if we'd agreed to their terms as written, they would never agree to let us leave. Now we are rid of them, once and for all."

"But at what cost, Jason? What did we give up to obtain that?" Lex shouts, raising her voice for the first time.

Lex's words hang in the air, as a frown pulls at my lips. Jason has a point. With this deal, we're finally going to be free of our parents. With Seth dead and them handled, I can finally move on and have a future with my pack. But Lex isn't entirely wrong either. Are we any better than them, using blackmail and extortion to get what we want? I look to Mateo, and his fawn-colored eyes are shadowed, the bond between us tense and dry, like grass under the summer sun. He doesn't like this either, but he's not speaking up to defend Lex.

"You didn't give up anything. I specifically didn't tell you what I did, so you wouldn't have to live with the consequences. This is on me," Jason says, volume rising as well.

"And what are you going to do now? Run this company you just stole from your father?" Lex throws back, more venomous than ever.

"If you'd paid attention, I specifically wanted Dad to give the company to Sammy. I don't want anything to do with them, and this will give Sammy the freedom to get our parents off his back now. I just wanted out, no matter what it took," Jason says, hackles up.

Lex growls, and I sit up, trying to reach her down our bond to calm her. But she's blocking me, and I can't deny the little pulse of hurt in my chest as I realize it. I look at Rhett, who's looking back and forth between Jason and Lex, as if trying to decide whose side he's going to take. But when I look to Lucas, he's wearing an almost exasperated frown.

"I don't know why you're so mad about this, Lex. You've done some shady things, too, all in the name of 'ends jus-tifying the means.'" Lucas adds, tone much darker than I'd expected.

Lex throws him a look, and I'm caught off guard by the sudden flash of panic in her. Whatever he's referencing scares the daylights out of my prime alpha, but it can't be the business with Wickland House again. We've already cleared the air on that matter, and she knows we accept her mistake. This is fresh fear, something new.

"What's he talking about?" I ask softly.

Lex gives me a long look, and the dread creeping across our bond shakes me to my core. I'm wide awake now, shifting to the edge of my seat. The longer she hesitates, the harder my heart thumps in my chest. And then the rest of my mates flinch back, bracing themselves. What do they know that I don't?

I look at Mateo, trying to figure out the tension in the air. But my blood turns to ice as I realize he's blocking me. I can't feel him at all, and he won't look at me. Panic and worry bubble up like bile in my throat, and I whip my head around to Rhett and Lucas. Rhett is focused on me, and I can feel his attempts to soothe me, but it's distant. Lucas is still looking at Lex, not that she's noticed.

"I'll get my own lawyer, and you can keep your fixer out of this," Jason says, voice ice cold.

I furrow my brow, even more confused. Who is Gideon, and why is Jason calling him a fixer? What does that even mean? Lex is still looking at me, not even acknowledging Jason's comment, or the way he brushes past her toward a table of refreshments.

"What's going on, Lex? What aren't you telling me?" I demand, palms getting sweaty.

She hesitates again, and I'm about to insist on an answer, when an employee comes in and informs us that our plane is ready for us to board. The air between us is tense, ready to snap at a moment's notice as we head out into the hangar and onto the plane. No one speaks through pre-flight checks, or take-off, though I keep my eyes locked on Lex's face, waiting for her to explain. There's a warring swirl of emotions on her end of the bond, though she's careful to keep them to herself now. It bothers me that she's trying to block me out, not that it's successful. But even the attempt hurts. Finally, once we reach cruising altitude, she sighs and looks me in the eye.

"I'm sorry, sweetness. But I've been keeping something from you. I was waiting for a better time to talk, but I guess I don't have a choice now," she starts.

I nod, hurt and anger flaring in my heart. We'd promised each other no more secrets, no more plots, no more lies. To find out that she's gone back on her word after so much work breaks my heart a little. Whatever it is, must have been eating her up inside, judging by what she's allowing through the bond. I can only hope it's nothing earth-shattering.

"Seth is still alive."

Chapter Forty-Five

Lydia

LEX'S WORDS FALL LIKE an anvil off a cliff, each syllable hammering against the inside of my skull. My whole body locks up, my heart beating erratically against my ribs as I struggle to breathe. It can't be true. I refuse to believe it. But the longer the silence stretches and no one contradicts her, I know it is. Seth is still alive.

I think back to all the times I'd been essentially alone since Seth's "accident." How I thought I was safe enough to be at home by myself, to not be as worried about locking the doors and windows and trust that no one was watching me anymore. He could have been there the whole time, waiting and biding his time. He could be anywhere, waiting to hurt me again.

I stand up, trying to move away, to be anywhere other than this room, but Rhett and Lucas refuse to let go of my hands. I try to pull away, fighting them, but they won't release me.

"Lydia, stop. We need to talk—"

Whipping my head around to look at Lex, my eyes burn with hot betrayal. "You lied to me. Again. After you promised not to," I snap, still struggling to get Rhett and Lucas to let me go.

"I know, sweetness. And I'm so so—"

"You're sorry?!" I shout, shaking now. "Sorry doesn't cover this, Alexandra. You promised!"

I shriek in frustration, spinning around to Rhett, who's now on his feet, looking down at me with concern. He's trying to calm me through our bond, but I slam down a wall between us. He doesn't have the right to manipulate me like that. Mateo's refusal to look at me speaks volumes, along with the guilt spilling through the wall he's maintaining between us. Even Lucas, who I can only feel faintly, doesn't seem surprised or betrayed by this. And that only hurts more.

"You knew. You all knew and didn't tell me," I snarl, looking around at my pack.

Mateo ducks his head, the shame rolling off him heavy and sour on my tongue. Lucas shifts in his seat, letting go of my hand at last, not looking at me. Even Jason doesn't look surprised by this news. Rhett keeps pushing to get through the barrier I've set, but there's no hint that he's been caught off guard like I have. The ONLY person who seems surprised is Caleb, but his expression is more confused than angry, which I get. He wasn't promised truth and transparency, only to have the people he trusted go back on their word.

"Please let me explain. It's not as simple as it seems, and you deserve to know the whole truth," Lex begs.

I huff out a few sighs, trying to move away from Rhett. But his grip is too tight, one hand around my wrist, the other holding my upper arm. His ice-blue stare is too intense, too full of things I don't want to see right now. I want to be angry with him, with all of them. But the longer I stand here, unable to escape the flood of feelings coming down my bonds, the harder it becomes to maintain that fury. Feeling their contrition, their guilt, the longing for me, all the while struggling with my own feelings of hurt and betrayal, is confusing and unhelpful.

I stop fighting and focus my energy on sorting through the tangle in my chest, pushing out anything I don't recognize as mine. Rhett loosens his grip just enough for me to pull away, and I move to sit in one of the armchairs, glaring at Rhett as he tries to follow. Pulling my knees to my chest, I look at Lex expectantly. Rhett moves to come to me, but I growl low in my throat.

"You just... don't. Don't move," I snap through gritted teeth, clutching my knees a little harder.

I catch Mateo shifting uncomfortably out of the corner of my eye, and Rhett sinks back into his seat, frowning. But I can't let myself give in to their touch right now. I have to figure out how I'm feeling, and hearing her out while I try to do so wouldn't hurt. It's not like I could go far, anyway. She relaxes slightly, sitting in a chair by the dining area. Mateo stays on the sofa he'd thrown himself into, and Rhett returns to sit next to Lucas on the adjacent one. Caleb shifts toward me, coming to rest in the seat across the aisle from me. There's a long moment of silence, but I refuse to be the first to break it.

"I tried to think of other ways to get rid of Seth, but everything would have taken time we didn't have," Lex starts, picking her words with care.

I narrow my eyes skeptically, and she flinches as she feels that, even through the wall I've constructed between us. Good.

"It wasn't long after you came back from the wedding when your father—or probably more likely your mother—started to hound us for proof of your pack status. They were calling the bluff. And we didn't know if we'd be able to get a new court date before the deadline they forced on us. Our options were limited, and it seemed like a mating bond would be the fastest way to secure your safety. But with Rhett on house arrest..."

Lex trails off, shrinking back into herself, expression darkening. I can feel her swirling doubt, guilt, the resurfacing of her fear. I try to finish her thought, but nothing makes sense. With Rhett on house arrest, I wouldn't be able to go to him and bond?

"We made a pact, Lex, Lucas, and I, long before we ever met you. I vowed that I wouldn't take a bond mate until my pack mates were free to do the same. You didn't want me to be forced to choose between protecting Lydia, and breaking my promise to Lucas," Rhett says, speaking first to me and then to Lex.

"I thought about it. I thought long and hard about asking you to choose. But I couldn't do that. And before any of you say that it would have been an easy choice, even if everyone agreed, it would have meant forcing Lydia to go into heat, and to only have Rhett there to break it. I think we can all agree that none of us would have been happy with that outcome," Lex says, raising her voice for a moment as Lucas and Rhett both open their mouths to object.

I frown as I consider. Setting aside the swoop of instinctual fear at the mention of forcing my body into heat, would I have been able to go through my heat without all of my pack mates there? Maybe, but it wouldn't have been easy on me or Rhett. I remember flashes of my heat, remember the absolute, all-consuming agony that would come whenever one of them was out of my line of sight, even for a few moments. It was only because I had every one of them there with me that I was able to make it through that week. And then to add the guilt of knowing Rhett had broken a promise for me...

"When Lydia came to us and said she was taking her supplements, I made a choice. Seth had to go, one way or another. She was ready for us, and it was time to stop pussyfooting around. So yes, I made arrangements with my father to fake Seth's death," Lex finishes, words firmer now.

"She brought me in only once she had a plan in place," Mateo adds in a low monotone. "But once I heard it, I couldn't say no. I didn't like the idea of not telling y'all, but I still agreed not to."

We all feel their embarrassment, but she doesn't deny it. "He did object, but I wanted to make sure you all had plaus—"

"Plausible deniability," Rhett, Mateo, and Lucas finish in annoyed unison.

I roll my eyes at that. That seems to be her favorite two-word phrase. At least she has the decency to blush.

"So, The Valencia. That's what he wanted?" Lucas asks, the question bursting forward like he'd been dying to ask since the conversation started.

Lex barks out a single ironic chuckle. "Oh, no. The heartless gargoyle *wanted* Bright Hills. I told him to pound sand and he could have The Valencia," she spits.

I furrow my eyebrows for a moment before it dawns on me. Bright Hills Estate is the first property Lex ever acquired, the one she had to break away from her father's company and form her own to complete. Because Leopold St. Clair didn't think it was worth the cost it would take to restore it. Asking her to give up her metaphorical first-born child is low, even for his standards.

"He didn't like it, but eventually agreed, so long as he could get it for a price insultingly below market value. It's only been six months, and I know for a fact he's already made his money back twice over," Lex continues with an annoyed huff.

"I thought your father was an upstanding businessman. How could he possibly help you commit a crime like this?" Jason interjects, and it sounds more like an accusation than a question.

Lex throws him a patronizing smile. "Of course, he is. And his friends in high and low places help him stay that way. My cousin, Gideon, acts as a consulting lawyer for St. Clair Holdings, but his real job is to be the middleman to the Argentieri Crime Family."

"Wait... Delano is the mob guy? I would have thought it was Hunter, for sure," Mateo splutters, perking up a little.

"You've met them?" I ask sternly.

Mateo looks at me and ducks his chin, shame and guilt coming back after that brief moment of curiosity.

"They didn't give me much to go on, but I did my own research. Delano is the son of Alonzo Argentieri, the current head of the family. He and Gideon were school friends, along with Hunter Navarro. Hunter now runs a funeral home and crematory in Baltimore," Lex explains.

"They were there when we took the bond breakers," Mateo adds, not looking at me. "That weekend we went to Savannah. We made sure we were seen looking at property on that first day, made purchases with our credit cards, laid a paper trail so wide you could see it from space. But then that night, we went to my beach house to hunker down as the drugs worked."

The scale of this operation just keeps expanding, and I feel almost ashamed of myself for not putting the pieces together sooner. In hindsight, it all makes sense. Being out of town is an excellent alibi, and by not telling Lucas or me about it, we didn't have to lie to the police.

"Why didn't you tell me about any of this sooner?" I ask slowly, trying not to put any inflection on the words.

Lex sighs and rubs her face, smudging her eyeliner slightly. It almost annoys me to see it because Lex should never look anything less than perfect. And seeing her weary expression, the shadows in her eyes, along with that streak of black, is almost too human for my goddess. Subconsciously, I send a whisper of calm in her direction, and the way her shoulders sag tugs at my heart. She's been so strong for us, done all this in the name of protecting us.

"I could never decide if I wanted to take this to my grave or tell you at the first possible opportunity," Lex says, not really an answer, but the uncertainty and fear across our bond clarifies.

"She didn't want to tell me because she didn't want to do it," Mateo says, picking up where Lex trails off. "If there had been another way to keep you safe, and get rid of Seth, then she... *we* would have done it in a heartbeat. But we made the choice, and we knew how much it would hurt everyone when you found out."

Lex doesn't deny any of it, and my heart pulses with empathy. She only ever wanted to do right by us, and did what she thought she had to. She goes on to explain the details of the deal, how Seth got paid and has had to start over outside of the US, how she's been having him monitored through intermediaries, so she's not technically breaking her side of the no-contact agreement but she's still able to keep an eye on him. As of her last check-in, he's currently in Brazil, which is all well and good, but it's a bit of a cold comfort.

All it would take is for him to send out one status, one picture, one little tweet, and his ravenous fans would go back to harassing me, or worse. He's proven that he doesn't need to be physically present to make my life a living hell, and that he's perfectly content with letting people commit atrocities in his name. My best friend and my adoptive grandmother lost their business and home because of Seth's fans, and the only reason things died down was because Seth had to go into hiding to avoid arrest. I can only imagine the devastation that would come down on us if that pack of jackals ever found out that Pack Saint Clair forced their false idol into exile.

Over time, I'm sure he'd find someone new to victimize, but I'm going to have to live with the fear of his return for the rest of my life. Maybe there would be days, months, even years where I could forget about him, but I'd never be able to shake that feeling of knowing someone out there hates me and wishes harm on me. I'd have to look over my shoulder every time I leave the house, just to make sure I'm not being stalked again. How am I supposed to live like this?

"Lydia, I know what I did is wrong. I broke my word to you, and that's not okay, regardless of the reason, and I'm so, so sorry for keeping this from you for so long. But now you know. All of you know everything. If you want to be included in the updates I get on Seth's location and activity, I'm more than happy to include you. This is the last time I will ever hide anything from you," Lex finishes emphatically.

I sit with her words for a long time, not responding. The initial flood of anger is gone, and I can tell how awful my mates feel about this, their pain a dull throbbing in my chest. Lex's passionate words are backed up by her conviction and true remorse. All of them feel like that, and it's hard for me to ignore that and stay mad. I'm hurt, and they know it. Lex truly believed she didn't have any other options, and did this horrible thing because she loves me and wants to protect me. And realistically, is there anything I wouldn't do to protect my pack? Any lie I wouldn't tell, any crime I wouldn't commit if it meant keeping the people I love safe? So how can I stay angry at them for trying to do right by me.

"I've been burned too many times after giving second and third chances to people who broke their promises to me," I start, speaking to a spot on the carpet near the center of the space.

Everyone tenses and seems to hold their collective breath as they wait for me to go on. I can feel Lex and Rhett already panicking, and Mateo's despair, as he braces for the worst.

"Don't burn me again," I finish.

There's a scramble of bodies toward me, a babble of over-lapping voices as everyone thanks me for my kindness, promises to do better, declares their love for me, saying all the right things. And even if the damaged part of my heart is screaming at me not to believe them, that words are empty promises and that they're going to hurt me again, I let myself believe them. Their words mean something, but the bonds and what they bring to me mean more. There's no duplicity or malintent, just relief and love and gratitude.

"We don't deserve you," Rhett mutters under his breath.

I flush a little, hiding my face as a pulse of deep, all-consuming love hits me from his bond. The others echo the feeling, agreeing without speaking. God, I don't know if I'll ever get used to that.

Suddenly, Lucas gasps, pulling me from my thoughts. "Oh, my God, guys. This is our first fight as mates, and first make-up session," he coos overdramatically.

A small chorus of laughter fills the air, and the last bits of lingering tension fade away. We still don't move, physical touches and emotions bouncing from person to person, bond to bond. Somewhere in the tangle, I smell mulled wine and smoke, then the brush of lips caressing my hairline.

"Thank you, Lydia," Lex whispers in my ear.

My heart warms, feeling what she's not saying. So many people have run out on her, and her gratitude for my forgiveness runs deep, almost as deep as her love for me. That feeling is enough to help me settle into their arms for the rest of the flight.

CHAPTER FORTY-SIX

Lydia

FOR A FEW DAYS after we get home from Louisiana, every shadow, loud noise, and errant leaf in the breeze makes me jump out of my skin like I've been shot. I don't leave my room for a while, but after a good round of self-castigation, I manage to suck it up and try to return to my life. Lex offers me security again, and it's tempting, but I decline. I need to figure out a way to live with this knowledge, and not let fear rule my life. Hiding is tantamount to admitting defeat, and I can't let that sick bastard win. Not again.

So, I try to find a routine, going to the Magnolia Garden in the mornings to check on progress, and then to the new shop to hang out with Gabby, or to visit Sylvie and the baby, Olena Marie, in the afternoons. I'm borrowing Rhett's car for the time being, not quite comfortable with the idea of spending my trust fund yet. I could buy a dozen cars if I wanted to, but if I spend the money, then that makes it real, and I'd much rather pretend like it doesn't exist. Or even better, let Lex use it to pay for the Garden's restoration. But she won't agree to that plan, so in the bank it'll sit.

Lex keeps her word over the next week or so, giving me updates about Seth's movements as she receives them from her cousin. I've yet to speak to the man, but I've been assured that it's for the best. Mateo described Gideon as what Lex would be like if her heart pulled a reverse-Grinch and shrunk three sizes, and the woman herself didn't disagree. The updates aren't especially interesting, just that Seth is partying and living large in Brazil. It irks me that he gets to live the high life on my pack's money, but as long as he stays far away from us, then I suppose I can live with it. And having the confirmation that no one has made the connection between this new party animal in the Brazilian club scene and Seth's former influencer career helps me feel more comfortable when I'm outside of the pack house. The attention from the gossip magazines and his fans has all but disappeared now that there's no juicy drama to follow. Instead, they have to focus on things I'm doing, like the restoration.

Progress at the Garden is steady, and I've been told that a summer completion date isn't unrealistic, barring any complications. I've started working with Lex to hire staff, and she keeps pushing me to book my first events, but I put my foot down. Until I have a confirmed date, I won't commit to even hosting a child's birthday party, let alone something as big as a wedding. A lot of the things I'd learned years ago have come back the more I work on this project, and some of the most important lessons were about managing clients' expectations. If you're going to promise something, you better be able to provide. Maybe my tune will change once the painting is done, but right now, the entire inside of the building is a maze of scaffolding and plastic sheeting. I did have to give a tour to some local journalists, for the Everton Review, and the TV News station, but I can't say I enjoyed the experience. Still, the press coverage is positive and good for business, so I'll just have to grin and bear it. Though I did secretly ask about hiring a public relations manager, so I can focus on the things that I'm actually qualified to do.

Spring comes with its usual bouts of spontaneous thunderstorms and muggy weather, but it's all worth it to see the trees lining State Street in full bloom. I pull up outside the new Grandmother Wila's Flower Shoppe, smiling to myself. Gabby and Wila have been busting their asses to get this place up and running in time for wedding season, and their hard work finally paid off. It was weird waking up on a Saturday in March, knowing full well there's a wedding on the calendar and not heading into the shop to load up the truck before sunrise. But from what I'd heard, my former employer wasn't without help. Jason refused Lex's job offer, not wanting a handout, but instead agreed to work with Wila to help balance her books and prepare the inventory for the opening. He'd only managed a day of number crunching before Wila, in her usual fashion, strong-armed him into working the floor while she and Gabby handled a delivery. Then, before he knew it, Jason had a sky-blue apron of his own, and was out at Bright Hills, distributing centerpieces and pinning boutonnieres on groomsmen. Now, I can see my brother through the front window, filling up the pre-made bouquet display.

After cutting the engine, I dash inside, making sure to lock the car behind me. Once inside, the fragrant scent of dozens of flowers fills my lungs like a hug from an old friend. Jason looks up from his task and gives me a warm grin and a nod, which I return. Gabby comes out from the back room, smiling brightly as she hops the counter and bounds over to meet me halfway. She scoops me up in a tight hug, and I can't help but melt into her a little before we pull apart and settle onto stools around the register.

"I saw that article, babe. And Gran called up everyone and their brother to make sure they saw your segment on Channel 5," Gabby starts, dark eyes sparkling.

I flush, but roll my eyes. "I was so awkward. I didn't know what to do with my hands half the time," I complain, trying for levity.

Gabby cackles at my misery. "To anyone who doesn't know you, the interview looked perfectly professional. But you looked about ready to pass out."

"Yeah, no kidding. If I have to do another one of those anytime in the next century, it'll be too soon," I scoff, and Gabby laughs more.

Jason goes back to his task, but I catch the proud little smile he's wearing. He's too much of a "man's man" to ever admit it out loud, but I know he's over the moon about what I'm doing with my pack. He was the one I'd always cast as my assistant when I planned teddy bear weddings growing up, after all. His own situation might not be as rosy as mine at the moment, but I know he's happy I'm finally able to achieve my dream.

Gabby's phone goes off, and she lets out an annoyed huff as she reads the message, typing out a furious reply before chucking the device onto the glass-topped counter. I give her a questioning look, and she rolls her eyes.

"It's just Wes. You'd think that boy'd get the hint after a while, but he's been blowing up my DMs for weeks. Some guys are so dense," she says, with only a slight hint of dramatic flare.

"I thought he was seeing what's-her-face? Deanna?" I reply, confused.

"Daniella, and yeah. They're still together, but he keeps talking about how he "misses the good times we had" and "he knows he fucked up" but "thinks we could really be something." Like, come on, dude," Gabby says, aggressively finger quoting his bullshit lines.

I'm about to respond when Jason storms by, wheeling the cart through the door to the workroom with an unusual amount of force. And I swear I hear him growling low in his chest. I look at Gabby with raised eyebrows, but she rolls her eyes.

"I have half a nerve to send his girl screenshots of all the thirsty messages this prick keeps sending me," Gabby goes on, completely ignoring my silent question.

We chat a little bit more about Gabby's love life, and I keep waiting for Jason to come back out and join the conversation. But as the minutes stretch, and as he bangs around in the workroom, my curiosity grows until the point where I can't keep it contained any longer. I wait until the backdoor opens before leaning close toward Gabby.

"What the hell is up with Jason?" I whisper frantically.

Gabby blinks at me, all innocent confusion, but I'm not buying it. I give her a hard look, and she sighs.

"I don't know, Lyds. He's staying in my fucking guest room, for crying out loud. But even before that, we talked all the time. But every time I bring up one of my exes, he gets his panties in a twist and acts like a fucking caveman. I don't need that kind of energy in my life," Gabby says, glancing over her shoulder toward the door.

I sigh and hold back the urge to roll my eyes. I want to point out that he's an alpha, and "caveman" is basically their second nature, but she doesn't need a lesson in designation mechanics right now. And I don't think it would be helpful for me to point out that this is pretty much exactly how Jason acted whenever I mentioned I had a crush growing up. He'd start stomping around, listing all the horrible things about the objects of my infatuation and, more than once, he even scared a few off before I could even have a chance. Gabby has always been the more romantically inclined one in our friendship, and if my instincts are correct, she'll see that this isn't just friendly protectiveness soon enough.

"But enough about me. How's your harem?" Gabby redirects, propping her chin up on her fist, elbow on her knee.

I shove her a little in jest, and we share a laugh, and conversation flows. It hits me again how this used to be my life before I met Pack Saint Clair. My best friend and I would chat away for hours, about anything and everything, before I'd go home alone to my empty studio apartment, pretending I was just fine with the way my life was going. It's been a year, almost to the day, since Rhett walked into my life and changed it forever, but I wouldn't have it any other way.

Almost as if summoned by my thoughts, my phone buzzes in my pocket, a message from the man himself on my screen.

Rhett: I'm done for the day, love. When you're ready, meet me at Wickland House?

Me: Yes, sir.

Rhett: Good girl. See you soon xo

I don't stay much longer, as it's almost closing time and I have a date. Jason reemerges long enough to say goodbye, but he ducks out again, mumbling something about invoices to avoid having to answer my pointed looks.

As I make the short drive over to Wickland House, my stomach twists and untwists itself over and over in eager anticipation. Rhett and I haven't really had a night alone together in a few months, not that either of us has really complained about the quality time our pack has been spending together. Still, it'll be the first time in a while that we're going to play alone. By the time I pull into one of the reserved parking spaces, my mind is whirring. I grin as I see Lucas's car, the one Rhett is borrowing for the time being, already parked outside. I manage to contain myself as I stride through the lobby, making a conscious effort not to pace or bounce as I wait for the elevator doors to open and close, whisking me upward toward what I have planned for this evening.

CHAPTER FORTY-SEVEN

Rhett

I'D FORGOTTEN HOW MUCH I love spending one-on-one time with Lydia. Lucas and I have had time to reconnect after my house arrest, but I've had to share Lydia more often than not with the rest of my pack. Not that I mind, because I know how happy it makes her to have all of us close. But nights like this, when we curl up on the couch together and talk and relax without worrying about anyone or anything diverting our attention away, are rare, which only makes me treasure this moment more.

Lydia is curled into my side, slipping in and out of a food coma as I play with her caramel-colored hair. Her scent is everywhere, the florals drifting throughout the room with her contentment. The sun set a while ago, and the lights of the city shine through the glass sliding doors, the only light in the living room of the Wickland House suite. We'd watched the sun set together, and have settled into a blissful silence.

"Happy anniversary, my love," I whisper, pressing a kiss to her hair as I gather her a little tighter in my arms.

Lydia hums happily, returning the sentiment before turning her face up to meet me in a brief but sweet kiss. One of her hands comes up to cup my jaw, nails scraping pleasantly in my beard. She shifts to face me more fully, kissing me again, deeper this time. There's a spark of heat and desire between us, bouncing back and forth along our bond, growing hotter with each round. I moan at the first taste of her, my hands moving to her hips to help her straddle me. I could lose myself in her kiss, the sensation of her lips on mine, the way she rolls her hips to grind her core against my rapidly hardening cock.

"Do you... can we play a game, sir?" Lydia asks, pulling away enough to pant out the question.

I hum an amused chuckle, nuzzling the tip of my nose against hers. "What did you have in mind, little one?"

She hesitates, but I wait, giving her space without judgment to ask for what she wants. She's been getting better, bolder with her requests, and it's been a joy to see her grow into the confident, sexy omega I knew she could be. When she pulls away slightly to look into my eyes, the flash of mischief in her emerald gaze intrigues me.

"I want... can I be in charge? For a little while?" she says, framing the request like a question.

I hum like I'm considering it, but quite frankly, I don't know if there's anything I wouldn't do for this woman. I've given up control a few times, mostly to Lex when we play with Lucas, letting her use me as her living fuck doll to torture our poor beta, but it's been a long time since I've gone full submissive. And the few times I have taken on that role have just reinforced my desire to be the dominant partner. For Lydia, though, I'm at least willing to try.

"How long is a little while, sweet girl?" I ask, tucking a loose strand of hair behind her ear.

She bites her lower lip and gives me the most adorably devious smile, making my cock twitch.

"Until you can't stand it anymore. Then I can be the submissive again, if you're able to take control back, that is," she replies, all innocence.

I chuckle under my breath, smiling even as I shake my head. I have a feeling I know who might have suggested this particular scene to her, but damn it if it doesn't sound like fun. So I look back up into her eyes and kiss her, one of my hands wrapped around the back of her neck. When I pull away, I'm still smiling, excitement bubbling inside me.

"Shall I call you Mistress, then? Or goddess? Or my queen?" I ask huskily, my lips brushing hers as I speak.

She giggles and bats at my shoulder. "Don't make fun of me, Rhett," she says with a playful whine.

"But you are my goddess, and I'd love to worship you like you deserve, queen of my heart," I reply, only partially joking.

She still scoffs, but I kiss her again. I store away the idea for another day to have her submit to my compliments and praise without complaint or back talk, but for now, I will follow where she leads.

"Shall we go to the bedroom?" I suggest.

"To the playroom, actually," she says, spine straightening.

I contain my eager grin as I let her up and follow her obediently into the play space I helped design. Closing the door behind me, I stride over to where she's stopped in the middle of the room, hands on her hips. I want to laugh, to praise her for her imperious look, but I would hate to undermine her confidence.

"Clothes off, then, please," she says, tacking on the nicety almost like an afterthought.

"Yes, my goddess," I reply, following her command without hesitation.

Peeling off my clothes hastily, I throw them in a corner to be dealt with later. Once I'm down to my skin, Lydia's eyes rake up and down my body, her desire like an open flame licking at our bond, warming me from the inside. My cock is standing nearly straight up, leaking fluid steadily. Lydia's tongue darts out to wet her lips absently as she watches a pearly bead form on the tip, stepping forward to catch it on a single digit before it can drip onto the floor. She purrs as she sucks her finger clean, eyes rolling back into her head with pleasure at the taste. I bring one hand up to pump more out for her, but she slaps my wrist away before I can get close.

"Onto the bed, hands above your head," she orders, remembering herself at last.

I give her a little smirk before following her instructions, lying on my back with my hands stretched above me toward the headboard. We'd ordered this bed specifically so someone of my stature could assume such a position without my feet hanging off the end, but it's close. Lydia has to climb onto the mattress beside my shoulder in order to reach across and secure my wrists together with ice-blue rope. She fusses for a while, and once she's finished, I test the binding. There's no emergency escape pull for me to use, but after so many years, I know how to break out of pretty much any tie, and this is no exception. I let her carry on thinking I'm secure, but I'm only as trapped as I allow myself to be.

"We'll use the regular safe words, if that's okay?" Lydia says, framing it like a question.

"Red to stop, yellow to slow down. Understood, my goddess," I say with a nod.

She gives me a stern look, and then out of nowhere, she grabs my cock firmly, gripping the base as my knot begins to swell. I shout a curse involuntarily, not prepared for the sudden stimulation. But she doesn't let up, squeezing hard as my knot pulses with my heartbeat, the pressure incredible and unlike anything I've experienced. My knot can't inflate fully with the way she's holding me, and the ache builds until I almost feel the beginnings of an orgasm at the base of my spine. But it's not enough for me to come yet, and the look on her face tells me she knows it, too.

I pant, closing my eyes as I try to thrust up into her hand, to get any kind of friction, but she only moves with me. I'm on the verge of asking for more, but then she lets go and slides off the bed, leaving me with a twitching cock and aching balls. And to make matters worse, she saunters to the end of the bed and slowly, ever so slowly, peels away her clothes.

"You're so beautiful," I whisper reverently, salivating as she reaches behind her back and deftly pops the hooks of her bra.

She just smiles, shrugging out of the straps, holding the cups in place until the last moment. My cock twitches as I watch her breasts bounce with the movement, and I groan, licking my lips. Her nipples are already hard, a dark dusty rose against her pale skin. I try to sit up, forgetting for a moment about my bindings, only to be pulled back down. She giggles, flipping her hair over her shoulder.

"Someone's an eager beaver," she teases, playing up her twang for effect.

"I'm always aching for you, love," I murmur, words raw with honesty.

She flushes under my praise, and I fight the urge to do more. That light pink spreading across her cheeks and chest as she turns away and goes to my dresser might be my favorite color in the entire world.

As she pulls out a bottle of lube from a drawer, she makes sure to bend over enough for me to catch a glimpse of her glistening pussy and—oh God, I don't know how or when, but she's nestled a plug between the cheeks of her perfect ass, the glittering green gem catching the light from the bedside table. I try to figure out when she would have had time to do that, but my train of thought goes off the rails completely as she crawls over the footboard between my legs, nudging them apart until she can settle on her knees, poised directly above my pulsing, leaking dick.

The first drop of lube along the shaft makes me hiss from the chill, and I arch up as several more hit me seconds later. The contrast in temperature shocks my system, the orgasm that seemed so close a moment ago drifting away. Lydia doesn't waste time, spreading the gel over every inch of me, until I'm bucking up into her hands again. But then my jaw falls open as she spreads the excess between the valley of her breasts, playing with her nipples and massaging them. The entire time, she holds eye contact, watching my every reaction, and I can feel her satisfaction with what she's seeing. Because I'm truly hypnotized by the way her tits move and fall, the heft of them overflowing her lithe fingers. And when she leans down and positions them around my cock, squeezing until I'm completely surrounded, sliding her breasts up and down, I'm a goner.

I try to match her movements, to make her go faster, harder, anything other than the slow, teasing pace she's set. The softness of her supple flesh combined with the slick lube almost feels like I'm inside her, and I need more. I groan and pant with abandon, chasing my orgasm as she works hard to fuck me with her perfect tits. I've dreamed of this moment, but it's better than I could have ever imagined.

"Lydia, please. God, you feel so good," I moan between heaving breaths.

"Tell me what you want," she prompts, girlish and full of teasing laughter.

I growl and clench my fists. I could break loose and take what I want right now, and she'd be nearly powerless to stop me. But the joy and pleasure she's getting from this power exchange tastes like honey candy on my tongue. I can hold out a little longer for her. So I grit my teeth and swallow, trying to regain some semblance of control.

"Please, can I have your perfect pussy, my goddess? I need you, need to feel you," I plead.

Lydia chuckles, and I realize my mistake a moment too late. She sits up and wipes away some of the lube from her skin and mine with a cloth she'd had laid out before crawling up my chest and settling with her dripping core above my face.

"Since you asked so nicely," she practically purrs, leaning forward to drape herself across my chest and stomach, and putting her cunt in perfect feasting position.

I dive in without another moment of thought, not even caring about the obscene slurping sounds I make as I drink deep. Licking and sucking on her clit, thrusting my tongue as far as I can inside of her, doing everything I possibly can to please my omega. She whines as I flick the tip of my tongue rapidly over her clit, grinding down against my mouth. I can feel the end of the plug against my nose, and I use that to my advantage, moving my head so I can press against it, fucking her as best as I can. She moans, her legs starting to shake as she approaches the edge. I want to tease, to pull back and delay her release, but then the warm heat of her mouth surrounds the head of my cock, and all reason abandons me.

Bending my knees until my feet are against the mattress, I jostle Lydia farther down onto my face, even as I thrust up into her mouth. The vibrations of her moans around my cock feel like heaven, and I return the favor by sucking her clit between my lips and humming, making her whole body twitch from the intensity of the pleasure. It's a race now, to see who can make the other come first, and damn her if she isn't testing the limits of my control. The sloppy sounds of her mouth as she sucks more and more of me down her throat, combined with her shameless moans, make my spine tingle. But I'm giving as good as I'm getting, using every trick I've learned in the last year to push her closer and closer to the edge of oblivion.

"Fuck, yes! Rhett, don't stop. I'm going to come!" Lydia screams, releasing my cock with an obscene pop.

She loses herself in the pleasure, reaching back and grabbing a fistful of my hair to keep me pressed against her core. I wouldn't be able to stop if God himself came down and commanded it. Her whole body vibrates until, at last, she throws her head back and screams my name, riding my tongue through the waves of her climax. I do my best to clean her juices from between her quivering folds, but I can still feel it soaking into my facial hair. She finally releases me and collapses forward onto my chest, breathing hard. The position unfortunately shifts her pussy out of my reach, but I've had enough of this game. She's had her fun, and now I need to fuck her in the worst way.

She doesn't seem to notice as I shift, twisting my wrists around until the rope loosens just enough for me to slip free. I keep my hands above my head, sighing.

"Have you enjoyed yourself so far, my love?" I ask mildly.

She hums, nodding against my abs. I chuckle, cracking my neck slightly.

"Good. Because it's my turn," I say, my voice dropping a full octave.

Before she can respond, I bring my hands down hard onto the cheeks of her peachy ass, the crack filling the room. She jumps, trying to twist to face me, but I'm too quick. I buck my hips at the same time as I grip her around the waist, moving her until she's poised over the tip of my cock. Lydia makes a noise of protest, but I still feel her reach down and align the tip of my cock with her entrance in the moment before I slam her down, filling her completely with one stroke. Her hands scramble for balance as I set a brutal pace, my teeth gritting as I watch her ass bounce on my lower stomach. Her pussy is still soaked and pulsing from the aftershocks of her orgasm, and it squeezes me tight as she hurtles toward another. She's sensitive, and she screams every time the head of my cock brushes against her G-spot.

"Sir, please, I'm sorry. I didn't mean to tease you," Lydia moans, and the playful little tug on our bond makes me smirk. So this is how she wants to play? Fine with me.

I growl, planting my feet before flipping us over, pressing her face down to the bed without ever withdrawing. Her palms slide on the soft sheets as she struggles to lift herself up, but I catch her wrists and drag them up toward the headboard, securing them with the same rope she'd used on me. She whimpers, pulling at the bonds, but I sit back and admire the view before me. The love of my life, my perfect omega, speared on my cock, a plug in her ass, and her hands bound above her head. Beautiful.

"You're going to have to earn my forgiveness, little one. So be a good girl, and fuck yourself on my cock," I say, lacing my words with false disappointment.

Lydia nods and does her best to get her knees and elbows under her before she sets to following my instructions with vigor. She doesn't hold back, fucking herself deep and hard as I stay still, admiring her from behind. My hands drift to rub at the globes of her ass, and she gasps, her rhythm faltering for a moment before she finds it again.

"You've been naughty, haven't you, sweet girl?" I coo, still rubbing gentle circles on her cheeks.

She nods, not pausing her rocking motion. I chuckle and bring my left hand down hard onto her ass, soothing away the sting. She gasps, and her pussy clenches around my cock, our bond sparking like a live wire. I take over the thrusting as I spank her again, this time on the right, and her head drops as she just lets go and slides into sub space. I spank her twice more, marveling as I feel her bliss, her peace as she gives in to her base instincts and submits to me. Her skin turns red and warm under my hands, and she whimpers as I grip the soft mounds and really pound into her.

"You're so tight, so full with this deep in your perfect ass," I growl, using my thumb to press against her plug.

Her muscles spasm, and her moans grow higher and higher, but right as I know she's about to peak, I slow down, waiting. She turns her head, looking over one shoulder at me. Her eyes are glassy with need, face flushed and lips parted. She arches her back, trying to get me to move, but another swat on the ass makes her go still.

"Please..." she whimpers, voice breaking.

"Please, what, little one?" I prompt, rolling my hips and pressing harder on her plug, enjoying the sensation of it against my cock even as Lydia shakes beneath me.

"Please let me come on your cock, sir," she begs, making my heart soar.

I purr, fucking into her hard and fast. But my good girl holds back, waiting for my permission. So, I lean in until my lips are brushing the shell of her ear.

"Come. Now."

She shatters with a scream, her cunt squeezing me over and over, sucking my cock in and almost refusing to let go. I don't slow my pace, and she peaks again and again in quick succession. I want to keep going, to give her more pleasure than she's ever dreamed possible, but soon, it's all too much. My balls pull up into my pelvis, and my whole body tingles with the oncoming force of my release.

The world explodes with light and fire as I shout her name and slam home, my knot locking into place. Even still, my cock pulses over and over, filling her tight channel with enough cum that it leaks out around the sides. I'm a little lightheaded as I lean forward, catching myself on my hands not to crush Lydia beneath me. She makes the cutest little whimpering sounds as I release her wrists and gather her in my arms, rolling us onto our sides, my body curled protectively around hers.

I center myself as I massage her wrists, checking for any redness or tender spots. Heat radiates off her ass from my spanking, and I make a mental note to find some soothing cream before we settle in for the night, or maybe sooner. I can feel her coming up out of sub space, and her desire is flaring again as she shifts her hips against mine.

"How did you get free?" Lydia rasps, clearing her throat a little.

I chuckle. "Wouldn't you like to know," I tease, squeezing her a little tighter.

I can almost hear her rolling her eyes, and I smile. With the way we're positioned, I can nuzzle my nose against our mating mark, and she hums with delight, a bubbly lightness filling both of our chests from the touch.

"As a matter of fact, I would like to know how you did it. Could come in handy the next time you've got me all trussed up," she snarks.

My laugh is darker this time, and while my knot has deflated, my cock is hard again. I nip at our mark, and thrust up into her, taking her breath away.

"Then allow me to teach you a lesson, my sweet omega. We'll see how well you can focus once I replace that plug of yours with something altogether more satisfying."

CHAPTER FORTY-EIGHT

Alexandra

THE SUNSET THROUGH THE picture window of the kitchen has to be one of my favorite views in the entire world. It's even better with a glass of wine in my hand, watching my beta do his thing at the stove. Even Mateo's hand on my lower back is pleasant, something I'd never thought possible a year ago. It's the weekend, and I have these two all to myself for the night while Rhett and Lydia have some alone time at Wickland House.

I'd made the call to give myself the weekends off a while ago, and I'm honestly regretting not having done it sooner. Having the time to unplug and relax with my pack has done wonders for my overall productivity during the week, and I love how happy it makes them.

My phone pings on the counter beside me, and I sigh as I see Gideon's name appear with the incoming call notification. I consider letting it go to voicemail, but this could be the update on the Anderson situation I've been waiting for. I do let him stew for a while as I excuse myself to my office, letting it ring until the last possible moment before swiping to answer.

"This is Alexandra," I state professionally.

"Weird. I dialed the number for the brothel. Picking up a side hustle, Lexi?" Gideon snipes, making my blood boil.

"What do you want, Gideon? I don't have time for your inane dribble," I retort, rubbing the bridge of my nose.

"I just got done with the paperwork for your latest scheme. Everything is signed and sealed, as promised," he says with a self-satisfied sigh.

I roll my eyes. "Not my scheme, but I'm glad to hear it's done. I'll wire you the rest of your payment on Monday."

"You're going to want to send me extra," Gideon replies.

I blink. "And why would I possibly *want* to send you more money than we agreed on?"

"Because your problem child has gone missing, and if you want my help tracking him down, I need the resources."

My fingers spasm and my heart stops, my whole body going cold as panic surges. Almost immediately, my bond mates are there, sending their concern and comfort to fill me, but I can't stop the rising tide of panic filling all the empty spaces. My focus narrows to the conversation, everything else ceasing to matter. I find my office chair on instinct and sink into it to stop myself from collapsing onto the floor.

"What do you mean, missing?" I rasp.

"I don't know if he finally got wise to the tail I had on him, but he's given my people the slip. We're trying to find him again, but in a city like Buenos Aires, that's a little easier said than done," Gideon says, a little too casual for my nerves right now.

"I thought you said your people are the best," I growl, trying to keep my tone even.

"They're the best your payment could buy. I could get better ones, but that'd mean more investment from you," Gideon says flippantly, and I've never wanted to strangle another human being more in my life.

"Where was the last place you had eyes on him?"

"He went home with a bartender. You don't pay enough to have them watch two dudes going at it, so as far as they knew, he stayed the night there. But he never came out in the morning."

"And when was this?"

Gideon sucks his teeth and hums, like he has to try to remember this. I know it's an act, a negotiation tactic to make nervous marks think they have to do more, provide more in order to get more information. With the right type of person—or wrong type, depending on your point of view—these seconds of silence would lead to offers of more money in exchange for whatever you're holding back. But I know this play because my father taught it to me first. So I stay quiet, my patience far exceeding my cousin's. Eventually, he huffs out an annoyed sigh.

"Two nights ago. We've been trying to pick up his trail, but it's not going great," Gideon says eventually.

I curse colorfully under my breath. Seth Douglas has been left unaccounted and unsupervised for forty-eight hours. There's no telling where he could have gotten to. I'd like to think this is just like a few weeks back when we thought we lost him when he was out partying, but he'd passed out in the bathroom of a club. Maybe he's gone into heat and is bunked down with that bartender? It'd be naïve of me to assume the best when it comes to Seth, so until we know for sure, I can't take chances. Rhett and Lydia are safe at Wickland House for tonight, but I'll let them know to come home first thing tomorrow morning. Then we can figure out what our next move is.

"You need to fucking find him," I press, my brain restarting and going straight into emergency planning mode.

"I don't work for free, you know. I've got bills to pay, a lifestyle to uphold," Gideon says, sounding for all the world like he doesn't want to extort my pack's safety to make a quick buck.

"Leopold, is that you? God, it's almost uncanny how much you sound like him," I toss back in a light, overly sarcastic tone.

"You say that like it's a bad thing, Lexi. Maybe if you were more like your father, you wouldn't be in this mess in the first place."

I growl low in my throat. "And what exactly is that supposed to mean?"

"Remember when he took us to the homeless camp under the bridge? We were, what? Twelve?" Gideon asks randomly.

I have to swallow a bitter laugh. "Ten," I correct.

I'll never forget that day for as long as I live. My father took Gideon and me to one of the many tent cities in Baltimore, pulling up in our Rolls Royce to stare at people who had nothing except the clothes on their backs. He'd talked about how much of a problem those "leeches" were on the city and the hardworking taxpayer, but all I could see were people in need of help. And my father told us how he was working with the city council to turn this spot into something useful to society, not the ugly eyesore. He was right about it being ugly, but that was because it was a reflection of the ugliness inside of people like my father. People who were too busy chasing a dollar to stop and think about their fellow human beings.

"He saw a problem and solved it. He didn't spend years going back and forth, trying to appease people who didn't deserve it. Decisive, firm action," Gideon says, pulling me out of my memories.

"Is that what you took away from that day?" I ask in a dry monotone.

"All I'm saying is that maybe if you'd had a bit more of that, then we wouldn't be out here trying to chase down your loose end," he replies.

"I don't tell you how to live your life, so I'd thank you not to tell me how to live mine," I say, words cold and clipped.

"You've always thought you were better than us, but you're still a St. Clair," he says, and now I know he's just trying to get a rise out of me.

"You're wasting time. Find Seth, or—"

"Or what? Listen, we both know you're out of options. So pay me, and we'll do our jobs. And if you send me enough, we can make sure this doesn't happen again, if you catch my drift," he cuts in, dropping to a murmur toward the end.

Unfortunately, I do catch the smoke he's blowing in my face. And for a split second, I'm tempted. But an inquisitive little tug on my bond with Lucas stops that thought in its tracks, along with a series of hard knocks on my office door. No, I'm better than murder. Seth is still a person, and unlike what my father thinks of himself and our family, having money and power doesn't mean we get to play God.

"I'll send you what I can tonight, but it's after hours, so you'll have to wait until banks open on Monday for the rest," I reply, trying not to give away how much it pains me to do this.

"Then I guess we'll do what we can. I hope whatever you send will cover it. Who knows what can happen in a few days?" he says in mock concern.

He's officially hit the end of my patience, and a little voice in the back of my mind unhelpfully reminds me that this is exactly why I had to get away from my family in the first place. This is what unfettered arrogance and affluence will do to a person. But I've had enough with the games. My pack's safety isn't up for debate, and I won't let this megalomaniac in training get away with thinking he can play with our lives for kicks.

"Fuck you, you greedy little fuck knuckle. That sociopath you lost wants my omega dead, and you're over here demanding money. My father must be so proud to have an heir just as heartless as he is!" I whisper-shout, increasingly aware of Mateo and Lucas outside of my door.

"You don't have to resort to name calling, Lex. I only need a couple thousand, enough to cover some bribes, equipment, et cetera," Gideon replies, seemingly unruffled.

I pull the phone away to let out a closed-lipped scream before going back. "I hope someday that you find someone who can worm their way into your black heart, make you love them, and then I hope something happens to her, so you'll know what it's like to—"

"If you want my help with anything ever again, you're going to shut your fucking mouth, Alexandra."

Gideon's alpha bark catches me off guard, and I can only sit in stunned silence for a moment. Not because the bark actually works on me, but because of the sudden shift in his demeanor. The snide, cocky ball-busting of a moment ago is gone, replaced by an angry, bitter alpha lashing out. I don't know how or why, but it seems I may have it a little too close to home.

"I'm going to send you a request for what I need. Pay it, and we'll find the omega," Gideon continues, words clipped and cold as ice.

"And if I don't?" I ask, unable to stop the question from escaping.

"Do you want to find out?" Gideon spits harshly.

I want to tell him where he can shove his sanctimonious bullshit. I want to tell him to fuck off in a hundred different ways. But I can't. And judging by his silence, he knows it, too.

"Find him. Or you'll learn how dirty I'm willing to get my hands to protect my pack," I snap.

I don't even bother waiting for an answer. Pulling the phone away from my ear, I hang up before tossing it carelessly onto my desk. My heart aches with worry, but I do my best to stop those feelings from leaking down my bonds. I send out a reassuring pulse to Lucas, and I can hear their muffled voices on the other side of my door before they eventually leave me be. My first impulse is to take care of my business and not involve them, but those days are over. I'll explain everything in a few minutes, but I still sit motionless for another long moment. I need to get it together, and do what I have to do to protect my pack. But first, I need to call the bank to get this fucking money sent. I wish I could send it in pennies.

CHAPTER FORTY-NINE

Lydia

A LITTLE WHILE LATER, I'm drifting in and out of awareness as Rhett and I snuggle together in his bed. I've been bathed and massaged until my muscles feel like cooked spaghetti, all the soreness from our play gone. Rain patters against the glass of the sliding door to the balcony, growing more intense with each passing minute.

"Is everything okay, love?" Rhett murmurs into my hair, half asleep himself.

I hum noncommittally. Something is bothering me, an unease I can't quite place, strong enough to keep me awake, but not strong enough for me to be able to find the source. My bonds with Mateo and Lex are muted, but I'm not surprised. Considering the time, they're probably asleep and the connections are always weaker then. Also, we've had to practice blocking the bonds temporarily when we're having intimate moments, so we don't make everyone else suddenly horny at potentially problematic times. But I can't find a reason for my fight-or-flight response to be kicking in right now. I'm safe in Rhett's arms, and I know the rest of the pack is at home. Maybe my instincts are picking up on something else?

"I want to text Gabby and Jason, see if they're okay," I say at last.

Rhett nods and lets me slide out of his embrace without fighting me. I look back at him, sprawled out on the bed, the sheets covering him from the waist down. The faint light coming through the sheer curtains gives his normally golden hair a silvery sheen, shadows stark against his pale skin. The ink of his pack motto tattoo almost seems to swallow light, rising gently as his breathing evens out. I smile a little to myself. Once I find my phone, I'll have to try to get a picture of him like this. Though I'm not sure I could ever adequately capture the breathtaking beauty of my alpha in a single image.

Throwing on Rhett's t-shirt and a pair of sleep shorts, I pad out into the hallway on bare feet. I stop in the playroom to rummage through my clothes, but my phone isn't in the pockets of my jeans. I search around, but no luck. Huffing a sigh, I head out into the living room, trying to find my purse, but that's not here either. Where did I leave it? I'm about to give up and wait until morning, but another pulse of worry fills my chest. I know better than to ignore my instincts, and if they're giving me warnings this strong, then I need to listen. What if something happened to Wila? She's not a spring chicken anymore, and the stress of opening the new location might have finally taken its toll. Or maybe Jason has run into a problem with our parents and that agreement he's forcing them to sign.

I'm in the middle of pulling apart the couch cushions when the first clap of thunder rolls through the night outside of the glass. The storm is getting worse, and I suddenly wonder if I left the sunroof open in Rhett's car. Then it hits me. I must have forgotten my bag in the car in my rush to get up here this afternoon. The rain comes down in sheets, hammering the sliding glass doors. Can this not wait until morning? I bite my lip before sighing, resigning myself to braving the weather for a few minutes if it means being able to put my anxiety to rest and get some sleep. Besides, if I get too cold and wet, Rhett will no doubt take care of warming me back up. I giggle at the thought, grabbing the keys off the kitchen island, heading toward the elevator and slipping into my flats, while I wait for the car to arrive. Even though I'm expecting it, the ring of the bell still makes me jump as it cracks through the silence, louder than even the growing thunder outside.

The ride down is slow, and I hum along to the generic jazz music playing softly through the hidden speakers. I fiddle with the car remote as I watch the floors count down, not that this elevator can stop at any of them. About halfway down, the lights flicker, following a massive thunder crash that I can hear even from here. There's a brief pause and I send a quick prayer to whoever might be listening that the power doesn't go out and leave me trapped in here. Small spaces don't bother me, but spending time with nothing but my thoughts sounds like literal torture. I don't even have my phone to keep me entertained. Thankfully, my prayer is answered as the car finally arrives at the bottom floor, the doors opening smoothly.

The lobby is graciously empty, not even an attendant at the front desk. I consider trying to find them, or a security guard, and ask where the stairs are, just so I don't have to risk riding the elevator again during this storm. I even wander around the lobby for a minute, trying to find an employee of any kind, but it's completely deserted. I eventually decide that I can manage. If I do get stuck on the way back up, at least I'll have my phone with me to let someone know.

The rain hammers on the black stone overhang, thunder rolling almost constantly now, blinding flashes of lightning going off at random intervals. The torrent is almost biblical, and I pause one last time at the edge of the covered sidewalk closest to the reserved parking spots. It's only a few hundred feet, but I'd still end up drenched. Sucking it up, I grit my teeth and take off at a jog toward the car. The doors unlock with a soft beep that's barely audible over the pounding rain. My clothes are soaked within seconds, my hair growing heavy as it gets saturated, too. I pull open the driver's side door and let out a triumphant little laugh as I spot my bag on the floor of the passenger's side. Leaning in, I stretch until I manage to close my fingers around the strap.

As I shift back, the hairs on the back of my neck stand on end, and I'm suddenly filled with the certainty that I'm not alone. I freeze, panic filling me so completely that I can't even breathe. It could be nothing, maybe a security officer coming to check on who's climbing into one of the owner's cars, but my primal fear instincts are in overdrive. My heart hammers in my chest, the rain on my back and hips not even registering as I strain for any sound or movement on the edges of my senses. I force myself to take a deep breath, adjusting my grip on my bag so I can swing it at anyone who gets too close. I used to have a self-defense key chain on my old keyring, but I haven't carried those since the accident. I could try to put Rhett's keys between my fingers, but would that take too much time? I've already wasted precious seconds. I need to move, get to safety, and I need to do it fast.

Steeling myself, I swallow against the sudden lump in my throat. Then, moving faster than I've ever done before, I pull my top half out of the car and whip around, looking frantically for anyone nearby. But the parking lot is dark, the lampposts in power-saving mode at this time of night. The only light is coming from the lobby, and it barely illuminates where I'm standing, let alone a few feet behind me. My eyes aren't adjusted to the dark anymore, and I can only blink uselessly, unable to see anything through the rain splashing onto my face.

I glance behind me toward the doors, plotting my route. I just have to run, and not look back. If anyone is following me, I'll be able to see them once I'm inside the lobby. One last glance into the parking lot, and then I'm off. I slip a little in my soaked shoes, but I don't stop. As my foot comes down on a sharp rock, my ankle rolling painfully, I stop for a moment as not to lose my shoe.

But in that moment, my heart jumps into my throat as a thick-fingered hand closes around my bicep. My lips part to scream, but another hand comes up to cover my mouth, pulling me back into a broad chest. The training I'd done kicks in, pushing out the panic enough for me to remember what Rhett and Caleb taught me. I throw my elbows into my attacker's ribs, trying to get them to loosen their grip enough for me to break free, to try to stomp on their instep as they drag me backwards away from the door. I scream as loud as I can, even with the hand pressed hard over my mouth and nose, hoping like hell someone might hear the struggle. I'm pulled back into him, an arm coming around my chest and ribs, pinning my arms down so I can't fight, and I'm lifted off my feet for a moment as I try to dead weight, making me yelp in surprise.

"Just knock her out already," a voice grumbles.

It's getting harder and harder to breathe, and my vision blurs, but that sound shakes something in my core. I know that voice, that gravelly smoker's rasp. But before I can think much more than that, there's a sharp prick of pain on the side of my neck, a needle. I try to fight more, but it's too late. All too soon, my movements slow as whatever drug they've injected into me drags me under into unconsciousness.

CHAPTER FIFTY

Mateo

SETH HAS GONE MISSING.

Lex describes her phone call with her cousin, but I can't take in anything she's saying. My mind is stuck on those four words. I could almost kick myself for letting myself relax. I should have known this would happen. We should have known better than to trust Seth to keep his word. And now we have to sit on our asses, waiting for him to be found, and hope like hell that happens before anyone gets hurt.

I don't trust Gideon St. Clair as far as I can throw him, and having to listen to his blatant profiteering off our misery, even secondhand, only makes me dislike him more. And once Lex is done speaking, we sit in the quiet for a long time, not sure what to say.

"We should call Rhett and Lydia," Lucas rasps, barely above a whisper.

Lex shakes her head, running her fingers through her hair in agitation. I can't feel her, but the shame on her face is obvious even without the bond. She doesn't want to admit to failure, even if this isn't her fault. I move from my station at the kitchen island to the sectional, gathering Lex in my arms and pulling her tight to my chest.

"They're safe at Wickland for the night," I say to Lucas, purring for Lex.

She doesn't respond like an omega, but she at least melts into me, which I take as a good sign. Lucas gives me a disapproving frown, but lets it go for the moment. I don't like keeping them in the dark either, but right now, we have nothing to tell them except Seth is in the wind. For all we know, he's still in Brazil, and we could be raising the alarm over nothing. Lydia doesn't need any unnecessary anxiety. So better to wait for more concrete information and plan from there.

Silence is where fear grows, and the longer no one speaks, the harder it is to push away my creeping doubts. Lucas eventually tosses the dinner we didn't eat before coming to sit on the sectional with Lex and me, close enough for all of us to touch. Seth could be anywhere, doing anything. Increasingly unlikely scenarios play out in my mind despite my best efforts to push them aside. Rhett and Lydia are safe in the Wickland House suite, I remind myself over and over. The elevator is the only way in, and the emergency stairs out of the suite only go down two floors, and the door to them is only able to be opened from the inside. We have security around the entire perimeter of Bristol Point, and no one comes in or out without going through the guard.

Lex's phone chimes with an incoming message, making us all jump. She fishes it out and opens the new message from Gideon, Lucas and I looking over her shoulder. My stomach drops as she opens the photo. The image is of a chaotic airport, but centered on a man wearing a baseball cap and huge sunglasses under a hoodie, which might have disguised him in an airport like Chicago, but the ensemble only makes him stand out in tropical Brazil. My brain is telling me that the silhouette is off somehow, but it's still unmistakably Seth. Same huge shoulders, same oddly shaped legs sticking out from his cargo shorts.

Lex closes the image and pulls up Gideon's message, which only serves to confirm my sinking suspicions.

Gideon: We pulled this off airport security. He left Brazil a day and a half ago.

"Mother *fucker*. Everything's in Portuguese. I couldn't tell where he was going," Lucas curses darkly.

"Even if you could, who knows if he had any connecting flights," I add morosely.

"Let me ask if Gideon has any more info," Lex says with clipped efficiency.

She types out her message and we wait, each second ticking by feeling like a year as we all watch the three little dots appear and disappear, only to appear again seconds later. And then, at last, the news we all dreaded comes through.

Lex: Do you know what his final destination was?
Gideon: Atlanta.

Fuck.

I sit frozen even as Lex springs into motion, dialing Rhett. Seth is here, in the state. There's not a single doubt in my mind that he's back in the city, too. But why? What could have possibly driven him to do this? What are we going to do now?

"Rhett! Oh, thank God!" Lex shouts, making me jump. "Why didn't—you know what, never mind. You and Lydia need to get home. Right now."

I watch her get up and pace away, and Lucas looks up from his phone. I can't quite hear Rhett's response, but from the sound of his voice, it definitely seems like we woke him up.

"I got a call from Gideon, and Seth's—well, Seth's back. In Georgia... No, I don't have time to explain—" Lex presses her lips together, and even I can hear the string of curse words he's shouting loud and clear. "It's a long story, and I'll tell you once you and Lydia get home."

There's a pause as he responds, but Lex's next words die in a gasp. At the same moment, my chest floods with ice cold panic, my entire body freezing and burning with a terror so profound that tears spring from my eyes and fall down my cheeks. I lean forward, trying to get my lungs to cooperate, but I can't get them to inflate around the raw fear exploding in my soul. But then, just as suddenly as it came, it's gone. Like a candle snuffed out, leaving only the bitter aftertaste of burning sugar in my throat.

"Rhett... where is Lydia," Lex rasps, her voice hoarse.

I don't have to hear the answer to know the truth in my bones.

Seth has Lydia.

I can't sit still, but Lex won't let me out of her sight now. So instead of taking to the streets to try to find her, I pace around the open space between the sitting room and the kitchen. The illusion of movement is better than doing nothing. Lucas is next to Lex, trying to calm her as best he can, but I'm afraid she's gone over the edge at last. Caleb is on his way to meet Rhett at Wickland House, something about security footage to figure out where to go from here.

I stop at the picture window and stare out into the stormy blackness beyond. Lightning paints the trees and rolling hills behind the house, coating everything in mercury for a moment before the world is plunged back into inky black. The thunder comes a moment later, a clash of atoms in the sky loud enough to pierce through the panic.

I have to do something to find Lydia. I can't stand not trying.

Closing my eyes as I lean forward, I let my head rest on the cool glass. The bond I share with Lydia is muted, like it is when she's asleep, but somehow even more distant. I pull on it, but there's no response, no little flicker of vanilla-flavored delight I've grown used to feeling when I reach out to her like this. I try again and again, each attempt more frantic. The fact that the bond is still there is a small comfort. If it wasn't...

I don't dare let myself finish that thought. We'll find her in time. We have to.

I'm about to give up when I feel the slightest pulse along our bond, like a violinist plucking at the string. My nose fills with burnt sugar, and I try my best to control the shaking in my limbs as her fear fills my chest.

We're coming, baby girl. Just hold on.

I push the comfort and reassurance down the tether between us, picturing the golden thread in my mind's eye. I'm about to do it again when a strange, disconnected feeling of levity and arousal fills my chest. Excitement, anticipation, determination. She's purposefully sending those emotions across all her bonds, flipping from one to the other faster and faster. Then there's arousal again, followed by anticipation, and then nostalgia? What is she trying to tell us?

"Do you feel that?" Lucas asks, pulling me out of my head.

"I don't understand," I mutter, clenching my eyes shut tighter as I fight to maintain focus.

She's trying to tell us something, I know it. I send back confusion and desperation. I need more. I don't understand how she's feeling aroused right now. I can feel how terrified she is, but maybe it has to do with where she is?

I need to get my head out of my ass and figure this out. She's counting on us. I know Seth, and I know how he would operate. Another flood of anticipation, determination, excitement, arousal, and then there's nostalgia again. A longing for the past, but excitement for the future, maybe? There's a blip of confidence, maybe a moment of safety, and the more I focus, the more I'm sure of the fact that she knows where she is. That's what the safety means. She's somewhere she knows, and knows well. But that could be a dozen different places.

But Seth would want to create a spectacle, to make a statement with his actions. He wouldn't choose somewhere random. It would mean something to her and to us. Maybe it's one of the restaurants? I try to send back feelings of warmth and satisfaction, the kind you would get after a meal. But I'm met with a strong hit of rejection. So that's a no. And besides, if someone broke into one of the restaurants, we'd have heard about it.

"Have we contacted the security companies? Any flags on the systems?" I ask aloud, just to make sure.

"Caleb says no. Wherever they are, it isn't someplace on the network," Lucas returns, speaking for Lex as she continues arguing with someone on the phone.

So it's somewhere connected to us, but not on our security network. Somewhere that makes her feel safe, and aroused? I try to send back another questioning tug, but as I search for the bond, something's wrong. Instead of the pristine golden thread, there's only jagged edges, and the connection is blurry, like an old television not quite tuned correctly. I can feel blips of fear and pain, but they're so faint as to almost be non-existent.

"Oh, God. I can't feel—what happened? Where is she?"

My eyes fly open as I whip around, my concerns abandoned at the agony in Lucas's voice. He's on his feet, looking around wildly, hands clutching at his thin t-shirt like he's about to rip it from his chest. Lex has finally stopped and is looking up at her beta with wide, horrified eyes. She looks to me, the silent question on her face. I reach deep in my chest, and my bond with Lydia is still there, but it's only a tiny ember compared to the inferno of only moments ago. What has he done?

"The bonds..." Lex whispers, the wheels turning in her eyes.

Things start to fall into place. I don't know how, but Seth is attacking our bonds. He's been silent for months, and the first thing he does is attack our omega and the bonds we've formed with her. What's changed? What set him off and made him pick this moment to strike? I look around, searching desperately for answers, even as I'm half focused on trying to solve the riddle of Lydia's messages, all the while clinging to the disintegrating fragments of our bond. Then my eyes spy the most recent copy of The Everton Review, the issue with the feature about Lydia and The Magnolia Garden.

Jesus H. Christ on a pogo stick.

I scramble to pull out my phone, dialing Rhett. I know where he's taken her.

CHAPTER FIFTY-ONE

Lydia

MY HEAD POUNDS AS I slowly come back into my body. For a moment, all I can hear is my blood pounding through my ears as the world spins. I feel like I've been hit by a parade of buses, and then run over by a freight train. I try to stretch my limbs, but I freeze as I realize with a jolt that I can't. A surge of adrenaline brings the world into sharp focus, and I can finally take stock of my situation.

My hands are tied behind my back with rough hemp rope, and my ankles secured to the front two legs of the hard wooden chair I'm in. My torso isn't tied back, or my thighs, but a short tug of my arms reveals that they're connected to a cross brace. I've kept my eyes closed until now, trying to feign unconsciousness for as long as I can get away with, but I dare to open them a sliver to get my bearings.

Even through my lashes, I recognize the room I'm in immediately as the ballroom of The Magnolia Garden Theater. I was here this morning, watching as the work crew erected the scaffolding. Now everything is covered with plastic drop cloths, creating a clearing-like space in the center of an industrial forest. I can still hear the rain on the roof, but there's a strange heat against my left side that's growing hotter with each moment. A quick glance out of the corner of my eye reveals a bright work light, pointing up from the floor toward me like a spotlight.

"You can stop pretending, little omega. I know you're awake," a gravelly voice drones from out of sight.

I take a deep breath before lifting my chin up from my chest, eyes wide as I finally come face to face with Seth Douglas. Though, if I didn't know better, I would never know it was him. His face is nothing like I remember, his nose thinner, brows more pronounced, lips positively enormous, almost grotesquely so. He hasn't been wasting time spending his bribe money, it seems.

"Seth! Oh, my–you're alive!" I gasp, trying my best to make my surprise sound convincing.

Fear and adrenaline snap things into sharp focus, and my mind whirs into planning mode. I need to buy time, time for my pack to realize I'm gone and find me. If I can get Seth talking, it might just work. But even if Rhett realizes something is up once I don't come back up to the suite, how will they know where I am?

"Did Alex not tell you? Well, I can't say I'm surprised. The St. Clairs love their dirty little secrets," Seth says, sounding bored and annoyed in equal measure.

"What are you talking about? There was a crash. It was all over the news," I counter, letting the very real fear in my chest leak through as disbelief in my words.

My bonds quiver in my chest as each of my alphas tries to reach out with varying degrees of success. Rhett's thread is hot with fury, while Lex's is freezing cold with guilt and fear.

Mateo's link is soft, and I latch onto it for calm. It's slippery, and it takes me several tries to focus enough to push away my other emotions and try to send something useful.

"Oh, honey, that wasn't me in that accident. I hate to break it to you, but your pack paid me off and faked my death. They thought they'd toss me aside when the new model came out," Seth replies, not sounding sorry at all.

I gasp, trying to keep up the act while my mind searches for clues to send. I focus on my excitement for the restoration project, my hopes and dreams for what this place will be one day, anything relevant that could help them find me. Hell, I even remember the intimate moment I shared with Mateo on the day he first brought me here.

"That's what Pack Saint Clair does to omegas like us. They use us, make us think we're special, but then toss us aside when we're not needed," he continues, pacing forward with his hands behind his back.

"I'm nothing like you," I snap, my mouth working before my brain.

Seth throws his head back and laughs like I've told the world's funniest joke. He even wipes away a fake tear from his eye. My facade slips for a moment as my irritation with his theatrics surges, not that he notices. I manage to slip back into the role of frightened victim before he looks back at me, shaking his head.

"It's so cute how naive you are, little omega. You think those alphas give a shit about you? That's a laugh and a half. But you'll find out how right I am soon enough," Seth says, taking another couple of steps toward me.

There's a strange, wavering pulse of satisfaction from Mateo, like he's just eaten a meal and wants to collapse into a food coma. *He's trying to guess.* I send back a hard denial. I'm not at a restaurant, and he needs to figure that out. But something's off with the connection, almost like interference.

"Something wrong?" Seth questions with mock innocence.

He's within arm's reach of me now, and in the harsh beam of the work light, the work he's had done is even more obvious, and it is not pretty. Before, he'd been muscular and overly tanned, but I could see the appeal in him. He wasn't my type by any stretch of the imagination, but he had been undeniably attractive in a conventional sort of way. But now, with his too-big lips and almost beak-like nose, all of that appeal is lost. His clothes are tight in strange places, and his scent is all wrong. Harsh, sour limes and the sickly-sweet rot of fruit surround us, blocking out everything else. And when he leans down, bracing one arm against the back of the chair so our faces are level, I have to swallow back a cough.

"Your bonds feel strange, don't they, little omega? Like you can't quite hold on to them?" Seth asks, eyes boring into mine.

I swallow, but don't answer. Real fear pulls at me now. What has he done to me? I try to find my bond with Mateo again, but it keeps sliding through my mental grasp. Seth chuckles, a low, dangerous noise that makes the hair on the back of my neck stand on end.

"That's how it was for me. First this, then the pain starts. Days of soul-shredding agony, alone except for those fuckers Alex hired to make sure the drugs worked," Seth goes on, the lightness and mocking energy gone and replaced with pure hatred and malice.

My stomach sinks as his words register. The drugs. The bond breakers. I squirm in my seat, as if I can outrun whatever chemicals he's pumped into my body. Seth only laughs again, and then his hand is around my throat, squeezing until I can hardly breathe.

"While I'd love to watch you go through that minute by minute, I'm afraid we don't have that sort of time at our disposal. So, let's pick up the pace, shall we?" he gloats.

I want to fight, but between his hand on my throat and my bindings, I can only wiggle a few inches. Not enough to escape him. I can't even beg or plead, not with my air cut off like this. I watch in horror as he pulls out a syringe of clear liquid from behind his back, pushing the plunger until a little comes out of the sharp tip.

"Getting one dose of this shit felt like getting dragged behind a horse through the pits of hell. Three doses... well, I almost feel bad for you. Almost," he comments all too casually.

In the movies, the moments before something dramatic happens to the hero always occur in slow motion. We get to see the knife sailing through the air, or the bullet racing toward its target. But in reality, there's no special effects department granting me extra time to shout or beg or cry. One moment, I'm staring at the silver flash of the needle above me. The next, a stab of pain in my arm. Seth shouts triumphantly as he pulls the syringe away, stepping back to admire me like a painting he's just completed.

I'm frozen, my heart pounding even as I will it to slow, to not spread the drugs through my system, but nothing can stop biology. The bond breaker hits me like a wave crashing on the shore, inexorable and crushing. I scream, my chest exploding with fire. I can see the bonds above me, like strands in a spider's web. Gold and blue and crimson and even a faint violet, stretching off into the darkness around me. I sob, full body cries as, one by one, the threads snap and break. First violet, fading away as the others connecting him to me fray further and further. Then gold, my sweet summer light winking out. Then crimson, my lifeblood and passion, then lastly blue, the one who helped me love again after I'd lost all hope. They're gone, and I'm left hollow, my heart bleeding.

"You can cry all you want, little omega, but it won't change a thing. By the time any of your precious alphas find you, it'll be too late. Your bonds will be broken, and with any luck, you'll never be able to bond again. Then you'll see. You'll see how Pack Saint Clair treats people who've outlived their usefulness," Seth crows, voice rising to nearly a shout.

I shake my head, dropping my chin to my chest as I struggle again. I need to run, need to get out of here. But my head is a mess, full and empty, and my eyes struggle to focus on anything. My hair whips around my face as I look around frantically, but all I can see are shadows moving just beyond the circle of light.

"Please, help me!" I scream, desperate and frantic.

"There's no one here but us, at least for now. Though, I'm sure we'll have company soon enough. I have some souvenirs to deliver to some mutual friends. Why don't you hang tight, and I'll go wait for them out front?" Seth drawls.

The shadows, dozens of them now, dance around behind the sheets of plastic, disappearing as thunder booms overhead. There's a rustle of plastic, and then I'm alone. I look down at my ankle and yelp as the floor falls out from under me, and I'm hurtling down. I screw my eyes closed and brace myself, but I take a deep breath, and a hint of dark chocolate comes to my nose. Rhett.

No. This isn't real. I'm not falling. I'm on the ground. Tied to a chair.

When I open my eyes, the world is right again, and a quick glance confirms that I am alone. Seth left me alone. Now's my chance!

I take another steadying breath and try to calm my racing heart. One step at a time. I can do this. First, get free of the rope. I twist my wrists around as much as I can, pushing away the errant thought that the fibers suddenly feel like snake scales. No, it's just rope. I've been tied up before, not even that long ago. Rhett taught me how to escape ties like this. I slide my arms up and down against each other, working the loops of rope as far down my hands as I can until I can get my thumb under one and yes! I can get it over my knuckles, and the whole tangle suddenly comes loose enough for me to break free.

A few quick tugs later, and I have my ankles untied and I'm up out of the chair, looking around. I need to find an exit, and fast. But the world rocks under my feet and I fall to one knee, trying not to vomit. I have to close my eyes, but suddenly my head is full of whispers. Voices familiar and foreign overlap, no words able to be heard above the cacophony. Laughter, they're laughing at me because I can't even get to my feet. I have to try. I can't stay here. Move!

I grunt a yell as I push myself up, staggering forward until I run into a support pole, and then I cling to it like a lifeline. I look around, and I gasp as I see my brother, Jason, standing on the other side of the cleared area from me.

"What the hell! How long have you been there?!" I shout, pushing off and charging at him.

He doesn't speak, just turns and walks away, pushing through a gap in the plastic. I jog the last couple of steps to catch up, but as I pull back the sheet I saw him walk through, I'm met with empty darkness. No sign of him.

"Jason! Where are you?" I shout, taking a step forward but thinking better of it. I don't need to chase him, I need to get out of here.

I turn back around, trying to sort through the pudding in my brain to remember which way the doors are, only to see Lex sitting in the chair I escaped from. She's perched imperiously, like the queen she is, staring straight ahead. I stumble in my haste to go to her, my knees cracking hard on the concrete, and I crawl the last few feet. But as I reach out, her eyes slide to mine, and she disappears in a cloud of smoke.

I'm hyperventilating now, and I can only collapse to my hands and knees, trying to get my mind under control. What is happening to me? My throat is too tight for me to cry out, to try to call for help again, and I watch as my tears splash onto the plastic under me. A footstep makes me freeze, and out of the corner of my eye, I see a shape getting closer. What visions has my mind brought out to haunt me this time?

But then there's a gentle hand on the middle of my back, and the smell of tobacco hits my nose moments before a voice rings out, low and smooth.

"It's okay, petal. It'll all be over soon."

CHAPTER FIFTY-TWO

Rhett

MUD FLIES OUT FROM under Caleb's tires as we pull into the makeshift parking lot outside of The Garden. I've been buzzing with barely contained rage ever since we left Wickland House, and I don't even wait for the vehicle to come to a complete stop before I'm throwing the door open and jumping out. My shoes sink into the soft ground, and I have to blink through the soaking rain pelting me as I stalk toward the front doors, which sit slightly ajar. I'm about to charge straight inside when Caleb grabs my arm and pulls me behind him. I growl, but he pulls out his gun and nudges the door open, checking the corners before motioning me forward.

We move on silent feet, water dripping from our clothes and onto the plastic under us as we enter the foyer. The sound of the rain echoes strangely around the high ceilings and empty space, and I can't hear anything beyond our breathing and footsteps. The plastic is doing an incredible job of hiding any sounds of voices or movement.

"Two floors," Caleb mutters.

I grunt an affirmative reply. "She could be anywhere," I reply, just as softly.

"Split up. We'll cover more ground," Caleb instructs, his accent more pronounced with his seriousness.

"You go up," I say, nodding in agreement.

Caleb doesn't respond, heading around the perimeter of the room toward the grand staircase directly across from the main doors. I look around, my eyes adjusted to the semi-darkness better now. The central part of the room is mostly clear, with scaffolding towering high above to allow workers to reach the rafters. I know one side of the room has a bank of doors that lead into the ballroom, while the other has doors leading to lounge spaces and storage rooms. Clearing the ballroom is going to be a task, so I'll check off the smaller rooms first. Edging through the shadows to the right, I keep my eyes and ears open for any sign of movement, though it's nearly impossible to hear anything over the rain.

The first room I find is an office, stacked high with boxes of furniture in need of assembly. There's hardly room to swing a cat in here, let alone hide, so I close the door and move on. The next room is empty save for an industrial work light, powered off at the moment. My heart beats a wild tempo in my throat as I move from room to room, each as still and silent as the last. Maybe Mateo is wrong, and she's not here. If so, we're wasting time.

I pause at the corner of a hallway that leads down toward the row of suites set aside as spaces for bridal parties to prepare in, checking for any signs of life. I dare not call out for Lydia; I'd might as well shout for Seth to come and find me. It's better if I ambush him, not the other way around.

The space is only lit by the watery light that's able to make it in through the rain from the street, casting deep shadows behind stacks of boxes and covered furniture. I drop to a crouch, moving from cover to cover as I make my way toward the first door, my entire body alive with adrenaline. The building creaks as the wind picks up, and I use the sound to mask my movements into the first room. The light is even weaker in here, and I nearly pull out my cell phone to use as a flashlight before I think better of it. Light would just as surely announce my presence as shouting.

A scuff of a shoe on plastic makes me freeze, and I duck behind a pile of boxes, hoping I've hidden myself fast enough. I wait, trying not to breathe too loudly, but no other sound comes. I give it another few seconds before I move again, pulling back a sheet to look under a table. But then, there's running footsteps right behind me. The space is crowded, and I don't move fast enough. A massive weight jumps on my back, one arm banding around my throat to wrench me upright. Sour limes and rotting fruit fill my nose even as I struggle to breathe and throw off my attacker. Then there's a sharp stab of pain in my left shoulder, only there for a moment before I manage to connect with someone's ribs with my elbow, making them cough and pull back.

I whip around, reaching for whatever stabbed me. My heart sinks as I pull out a syringe, the plunger down. Looking up, I find Seth grinning like a madman.

"One down, two to go. I hope your friends join us soon. I've missed them so much," Seth drawls, half laughing.

Oh, no. What the fuck did he give me? I take a step toward him, but my head spins, and I stumble like I've run into an invisible wall. It's like there's something in my chest, its tiny claws shredding my organs apart like paper as it tries to escape. I gasp as my bonds start to wither, but I mentally grab hold of them and refuse to let go.

Seth, taking advantage of my momentary distraction, charges forward, dropping his shoulder. I manage to spin partially out of the way, but it still knocks the wind out of me, even with a glancing blow. With more grace than I would have thought possible, he stops and pivots, and I can't move fast enough to escape his arms as they lock around my waist. The already dizzying effect of the drug is only intensified as Seth lifts me off the ground, and up over his shoulder, slamming me into a table. I land on my tailbone, and my limbs go numb for a minute as the pain ricochets up my spine.

I look up in time to see Seth get back on his feet and turn, winding up with a soccer kick aimed straight at my face. My instincts take over and I barely manage to catch his foot in midair, using his own momentum to hurl him backward. Fortunately, there isn't any furniture behind him to break his fall. There's a sickening crack as his head smacks against the concrete floor, and I give it two long heartbeats while I get to my feet to see if he'll get up again. When he doesn't, I stumble toward the door but stop short as his words finally sink in.

One down, two to go. Shit! He's got more of this drug.

As I hustle back over to where Seth is sprawled out on his back, I can't deny the disappointment as I realize he's still breathing. I get my first good look at him, and I'm frankly repulsed by what I see. He's spent his bribe money on more cosmetic procedures than I can identify with my quick glance, leaving hardly any of his original features untouched. The overall picture is that of a hulking brute of a man, almost a caricature of masculinity. Is this truly what he believes to be his ideal appearance?

I let out a triumphant gasp as I feel two more syringes and a vial in an inner pocket of his jacket, pulling them out and clutching them tight in a fist as I head for the door. I'm both hot and cold at the same time, and my drying clothes don't help the feverish trembling in my limbs. Managing to get out into the hall and back to the foyer, I lean heavily against a set of scaffolding, trying to figure out what to do next. I know where Seth is, so I could shout for Caleb, find out where he is, and we could search together. Or we could secure Seth to make sure he can't get free before we find Lydia.

I'm in the middle of debating when, out of nowhere, a fist connects with the back of my skull, sending me flying forward, and I only just get my arm out in time to prevent my face from breaking my fall. I try to get up, but a heavy kick to my back sends me down again. And this time, I lose my grip on the drugs, sending them skittering off toward the doors.

"Should have done this years ago. It's about time someone brought you down a fucking peg," Seth snarls, jumping on my back as I try to make my way toward the last place I saw the vial.

His words strike something in my core, igniting a fire that, until now, has been smoldering in the background. If it's a fight Seth wants, then it's a fight he's going to get. I roll onto my back, arms up to guard my face as he rains down blow after blow, but I have patience. And when the time is right, I pull my fist back and catch Seth's jaw, stunning him long enough to push him off me and get up into a crouch.

"Couldn't have said it better myself," I spit before launching myself at him with a savage snarl.

CHAPTER FIFTY-THREE

Lydia

MY MIND REJECTS THE words, the voice above me. No. This isn't real. I'm hallucinating again. But as I scramble away, turning around to look back, the figure standing there is as real as I thought Jason and Lex were only moments ago. Darren's copper hair burns like fire in the harsh light of the work light, his lanky figure rising impossibly tall as he unfolds from his crouched position. I shake my head, trying to clear this vision so I can focus on escaping. But no matter how hard I try, he's still there.

"You just had to misbehave, didn't you? If you'd done as your daddy told you, then we wouldn't be here, and I wouldn't have to do this," Darren drawls, disappointment dripping like acid from every word.

I whimper and tremble, clambering backward, away from him as he stalks forward, slow and methodical. The whispers are back, the ghostly laughter ringing around me. This can't be real, can't be happening. My back hits a scaffolding cross brace, and I'm trapped as he gets within arm's reach of me.

I try to breathe through my panic, but my nose only smells tobacco and clay, the scent of my nightmares.

"I had a lot of time to think in the hospital, petal. I'd decided you were too much fucking trouble, and that if you wanted to be someone else's problem, then so be it," Darren goes on.

I can only look up into his face, and I realize with a cold bolt of shock that it's not the same one I remember. An ugly scar mars his sharp jawline, giving him a distinctly lopsided look. His nose is crooked, and as he sneers at me, I see that he's missing part of a tooth. There's almost nothing left of the strikingly handsome alpha who swept me off my feet all those years ago. Only his eyes, muddy pools of hatred, are unchanged.

But before I can inspect him any further, he cocks his leg back and kicks me hard in my exposed stomach, the blow knocking the wind out of me and making me double over in agony. Hallucinations can't hurt you, right? So why do I feel like I'm going to be sick from the pain?

"All you had to do was sign one little form, a protection for both of us. We could have put this behind us, but no," Darren snarls, kicking me again.

I cry out, trying to roll out of his reach, but I've effectively cornered myself. My vision swims with tears, and I can't even speak as I try to regain my breath. I hold up a hand, a feeble attempt to shield myself, but he only smacks it aside before kicking me again and again, and I swear I hear something crack. Then suddenly, Darren has a fist in my hair, dragging me away from the edge of the clearing and back toward the chair. I kick and squirm, clawing at his wrist until blood flows onto my fingers. He growls and throws me onto the ground, but I've regained a bit of my senses. This time when he goes to kick me, he's aiming for my face. But I manage to grab him by the ankle just in time, and something feral breaks loose in my mind. I lean in and bite, hard enough for blood to fill my mouth. He screams and tumbles backward, hitting the ground with a solid thump. I spit out the foul-tasting liquid, moving to a low, defensive crouch. I still don't know the way out, so that eliminates the flight part of my fight-or-flight response.

Darren recovers faster than I would have thought, rolling and pouncing onto me in one smooth motion. He knocks me onto my back, straddling my chest as he tries to strike down at my face. But I get my arms up, blocking like Caleb and Rhett taught me. My bare feet struggle for purchase on the plastic under us, preventing me from getting enough leverage to throw him off.

"Just lie down and take it, you omega bitch!" Darren shouts, but there's no bark to his words.

I shout a wordless refusal, trying to throw punches of my own now, but it leaves me exposed for a moment. Darren seizes the opportunity, catching me on the side of the head and stunning me. My head spins, and I turn my face, feeling the vomit trying to rise in the back of my throat. In the shadows of the mezzanine, I swear I see movement, but I can't trust my own senses anymore. I have to focus on what's real, and right now that's Darren, grabbing me by the hair and yanking my head back hard. There's a flash of silver in the light, a knife. I get my arms up as he tries to bring the blade down, and the bite of pain brings a strange clarity. I finally manage to get my foot under me, and I tip my hips, getting Darren off balance enough for me to wriggle a few inches, but he recovers too fast. This time, I'm on my stomach, with no way to protect myself.

"There's no knight in shining armor to save you this time, my petal. You're alone, worthless, friendless, packless. Just what an omega like you deserves," Darren spits, hand fisting in my shirt.

Bucking and fighting, I try to escape with everything I have left in me, but I can't stop him as he slices through the cloth like hot butter. The only thing my squirming accomplishes is making his hand slip, the knife slicing into the skin along my spine. The cuts sting as I throw my arms back, trying to hit him, anything to prevent him from finishing what he'd started months ago.

The first cut of his knife into the flesh on the back of my shoulder makes me scream, pain like I've never experienced before, blocking out all other sensations. I arch and try to twist, but he pushes me down with an elbow to the back of my neck. He's laughing, taking his sweet time to torture me one last time. Black dots swim in my vision, and I sob, but I'm losing energy fast. I can't fight him, not anymore.

But as a second wave of nausea comes over me, there's a roar, and then suddenly, Darren's weight is gone from my back. I cough, my shoulder throbbing as I roll onto my side, trying to figure out what happened. My sob this time is one of pure relief as I see my friend and protector, Caleb Novak, wrestling the knife out of Darren's grip and throwing it away into the darkness. They trade blows back and forth, Darren eventually knocking Caleb off of him, and then the two are on their feet, scrambling over something else now. I sit up, holding the front of my shirt in place as the back gapes open, and I realize with a start that the object they're fighting over is Caleb's gun.

I gasp, distracting Caleb for a moment, but it's too late. Darren punches Caleb hard in the side of the head, sending the larger man staggering backward, but it also sends the gun flying through the air. I watch it until it clatters to a stop just feet from me, and Darren takes a step in my direction, so I act without thinking. I pick up the gun and point it up into Darren's face.

No one moves for a long moment, all of us breathing hard as the world stops. Darren's eyes are brown pits of fury, but he doesn't move any closer now that I've got a weapon trained on him. Caleb is just behind Darren, but he doesn't move either. I don't dare move my attention away from Darren, even as I struggle to my feet, slipping slightly on the blood now splattering the floor.

"So, what now, petal?" Darren snarks, far too confident for someone in point-blank range of a gun.

"Did you know what Seth planned? Where did he get those bond breakers?" I ask shakily.

Darren snorts. "Like I give a shit. You got what you fucking deserved, as far as I'm concerned."

I grip the gun tighter, thumbing the safety for a moment as I consider what to do. "Did you come alone?" I ask, directing my question toward Caleb.

"Rhett's with me, *voyin*," he responds simply.

Darren snarls and turns back to lunge at him, but I step forward, raising my other hand to stabilize my grip. But the shift in Darren's stance reveals another flash of silver, the knife coated with blood. My blood. Darren looks back at me, a mocking smirk pulling at his uneven lips.

"You're a coward, my petal. Always have been," he tosses at me, completely unafraid.

"Stop calling me that!" I screech, pulling the hammer back on the gun.

"What are you going to do? Shoot me?" Darren nearly shouts, letting out a bark of a laugh even as he turns toward Caleb again.

Something about the taunt and his dismissal snaps what little control I have left, sending my fear scattering like fog under the sunlight. Protective rage fills my chest and I step forward again, taking careful aim before bracing myself and pulling the trigger. The crack of the shot feels distant as I watch Darren fall to his knees, clutching at the gushing wound between his legs. He howls and looks up at me, honest to God, tears streaming down his face. And for the first time, there's true fear in his eyes as he finally recognizes me as a threat. I want to pity him, to see him as a human being in pain, but all I can see is the face of a man who beat me for years, just because he could. I can't hear his cries for mercy, only the abuse he's thrown at me echoing back through time. And that knife, still clutched in his hand. The one he was going to use on me, on Caleb, maybe even on the rest of my pack.

No. It ends here.

Another crack, louder than thunder. A splatter. Smoke. Silence.

CHAPTER FIFTY-FOUR

Alexandra

LUCAS IS A MESS in the passenger seat beside me as we race through the winding, rainy streets of Everton. Only moments ago, I'd felt my tangential connection to Rhett go dark, but I haven't allowed myself to think or dwell on what that could mean. Mateo is a statue in the backseat of my car, and hasn't said a word since we ran out of the pack house. Only years of practice with compartmentalizing my emotions has kept me from breaking down.

Caleb's SUV is parked haphazardly outside of the front doors to the Garden, the passenger door wide open and the seat soaked from the driving rain. I pull alongside, Lucas jumping out of the door the moment I put it in park, Mateo not far behind. As we're climbing the steps leading up into the building, there's a sharp crack, and I look around, confused. That was too short to be thunder, and I didn't see any lightning. Another pop, and my gut drops to my knees. That's not thunder.

"Lydia!" Mateo roars, charging inside.

The foyer is a mess of plastic sheets and scaffolding, but in the middle of it all are Seth and Rhett, fighting like their lives depend on it. We all stop dead and watch as Seth throws wild haymakers, Rhett dodging, but only barely. His movements are sluggish, and I can tell even from this distance how badly he's shaking. What did Seth do to him?

Mateo surges forward, but Rhett snarls out a savage growl; not territorial, but a warning I feel in my bones. Even without the bond, the message is clear. Stay back. Leave. Run.

"He's got drugs! Bond breakers! Find them!" he shouts, breaking Seth's guard and pummeling his stomach with a short series of blows.

"Where?" Mateo asks, looking around.

"Dropped them. Get them," Rhett snaps, hardly able to finish his sentence before he grunts with pain, Seth landing a body shot to his ribs.

Lucas moves first, pulling out his phone and turning on the flashlight as he starts scanning the area. There's a new focus in his red-rimmed eyes, and his relief is palpable through my bond. I don't allow myself that sort of comfort yet, not until we find Lydia.

I'm crawling on the floor, looking under tables and in between boxes and bins, trying to find any trace of these drugs, my mind racing. But a shout of triumph pulls my attention away, Mateo holding a vial up in the light. It's similar to the one Hunter had in Savannah, and my heart slows a fraction. But then Seth breaks away from his fight with Rhett, charging toward Mateo like a bull toward a red flag. I don't have time to shout a warning before they collide, Mateo collapsing sideways as the vial flies out of his hand in a graceful arc. I scramble to my feet, but Lucas beats me to it, and I see he's got an empty syringe in one hand, along with the half full vial.

"Here!" I shout, motioning for Lucas as Seth gets to his feet, leaving a stunned Mateo in a heap.

Lucas hesitates, and I almost shout again, but then I see his plan. Seth is nearly foaming at the mouth, more feral animal than man, as he races in my beta's direction. And Lucas, my smart, brave Lucas, makes sure Seth has fully committed to the maneuver before he lobs the vial toward me, taking the full impact of Seth's tackle.

As the glass lands in my hands, I raise it above my head, ready to smash it into pieces, but then I pause. What if we need this? Could this be laced with something and the hospital will need it to run tests for an antidote? But my momentary hesitation costs me. Seth is back on his feet, and I can only stand there as he sprints toward me, murder in his eyes. But before he can reach me, Rhett and Mateo are there, tackling Seth from behind, all of them sprawling onto the ground. Rhett is breathing heavily, clutching his chest, and he can barely get to his hands and knees. Mateo is fighting with Seth again, but there's something in the omega that I've never seen before. A strength that defies logic.

"Omega, stop!" I shout, putting the full force of my bark behind the command.

Seth freezes for a moment, giving Mateo enough time to gather himself and wipe the blood away from a corner of his mouth. Seth turns ever so slowly to look at me, and as our eyes connect, thunder booms overhead, echoing through the building. And then he rolls his neck, cracking it, and the tether I'd cast to hold him down snaps. I stagger sideways, and Seth grins at me, advancing a step. But then Lucas is there, a fierce war cry spilling from his throat as he tries to jump onto Seth's back.

In one smooth motion, Seth grabs Lucas by the shirt and lifts him like he weighs nothing, holding him above the floor. Lucas kicks and writhes, trying to break free. I can only watch in horror as Seth winds up, throwing Luc ten feet away, into a pile of plastic paint buckets. I want to run to him, but I'm frozen in place by the inhuman stare coming from my former omega.

"Omega, no! Stop!" Mateo barks, and even I can feel the ripple of dominance in the air.

But Seth keeps staring at me, completely ignoring Mateo's command. Rhett is back on his feet, if just barely, and tries to lunge at Seth. Faster than I thought humanly possible, Seth turns and punches Rhett square in the jaw, making the alpha drop, out cold.

"Alex," Seth coos, the sing-song lilt to my name all the more sinister in his gravelly voice.

"No!" Mateo screams, rushing forward, fists raised.

Stepping back a few paces, I tuck the vial into my bra while Seth is distracted, for lack of a safer place to keep it right now. I move away, heading farther into the building where I can hear shouting. A voice, female, hysterical. Lydia.

"Look out!" Mateo screams.

I whip back around in time to see Seth releasing a pipe, launching it in Mateo's direction, and mine. Mateo leaps out of the way, and for a heartbeat, I can only watch the metal bar wheeling through the air directly toward my face. Then instinct takes over, and I drop to the floor, knees protesting at the sudden landing. There's a rush of wind as the pipe sails over my head, missing me by mere inches. I look up and let out a wordless cry as Mateo crumples to the floor, Seth standing over him with bloody fists.

My blood runs cold as Seth turns to me, his manic grin bloody. He spits a glob onto the floor, splattering Rhett and Lucas with the spray before stepping over them and advancing on me.

"What have you done?" I ask, getting to my feet again, mind whirring at the speed of sound. I need time. Need to find Lydia and Caleb.

"You're gonna have to be more specific, sweetie. I've been a busy little bee," Seth snarks, slowly advancing on me, flexing his fingers.

"Clearly. Did you at least get the name of the quack who botched your plastic surgery?" I taunt, glad my voice is steady for the moment.

"Don't like it? I thought it made me look manly. No more soft edges," he replies.

I dart around a pile of boxes, putting as many barriers between us as he tracks me around the room. The boys are still out for the count, and I don't hear voices in the ballroom anymore. As Seth takes another step forward, something crunches under his foot, and I use the moment he looks down to rush farther into the lobby, closing in on the bottom of the stairs. I know I'm faster than him, so if it comes down to a chase, I can head upstairs. It's a maze up there, and if I'm lucky, I might be able to lose him.

But my blood runs cold as Seth looks back up, his grin a vicious snarl.

"Where's the vial, Alex?" Seth asks, too calm.

"Gone. Smashed," I bluff, thankful my voice isn't as shaky as my hands.

"Smart, I suppose. I wouldn't want to go through that again, either," Seth drawls, shrugging one shoulder.

I lift my chin. He's still stalking forward, but my back is to the stairs. I need him to get closer, to think he's got me. If he thinks he's won, then he might get sloppy. I can't match him physically, but I can sure as hell out-think this asshole.

"It wasn't so bad. A few days holed up, getting fucked by a real man over and over again—"

"You bitch," Seth snarls, lunging for me with an open palm.

I dodge, using my speed to outmaneuver his bulk. I have to keep him from grabbing me. Stall, dodge, weave. Under the scaffolding, over the table. He's slow through the obstacles, and I get my space back.

"I've been called far worse by far better people than the likes of you, Omega," I taunt, carefully backing away and keeping myself out of arm's reach.

Seth tries his best to mimic an alpha growl, but it's such a pathetic attempt that I can't help but laugh. Though a moment later, I yelp as I dance out of his way once more, moving toward the stairs again. I'm about to dash up the steps when he strikes, and as I move back, my foot catches on a wrinkle in the plastic, and I swing my arms wildly, trying to get my balance. But that's all the opportunity Seth needs.

My back hits the edge of a step with a painful crack, and I gasp, trying to move, but Seth jumps on top of me, straddling my chest as his hands come down around my throat. I can only stare up as he squeezes tighter and tighter, the manic glint in his eyes all I can see.

"I was going to let you live, Alex. You would have had to live with the scraps of your pack and never be able to fix it. That seemed fitting enough punishment for you. But you had to go and ruin my plans, didn't you? You could never give me what I needed, so I'm just going to have to take it," Seth hisses, and I'm not even sure he's speaking to me anymore.

My head pounds as I try to breathe, but no air comes. I claw at his arms and fingers, trying to get him to let go, but he won't let up. Reality drops on me like a lead weight. I'm going to die, and then Seth is going to kill my pack, or worse, tear their bonds apart. I couldn't save them. I couldn't protect them when they needed me the most. And I didn't even get to tell them that I loved them one last time.

My vision tunnels, going black around the edges, and I close my eyes, resigned. Tears leak from my eyes, and I wait for the darkness to envelop me. But then, a crack like thunder breaks through the haze of oncoming oblivion. And then another. No, not thunder. Gunshots.

The fingers around my throat go slack and I take in gasping, coughing, burning breaths, trying to regain my bearings. A groan from beside me draws my attention, and I turn to see Seth collapsed on his stomach, two dark spots in his shirt growing larger. He rolls over and coughs, red-tinged spittle coming up.

"Mine," a familiar female voice snarls.

Chapter Fifty-Five

Lydia

THE BODY OF MY abuser hits the floor with an unceremonious thump, a growing pool of red spreading out from under him into the plastic. I can only stare into his wide, unseeing eyes, his expression of surprise frozen in place for eternity.

Darren McLaughlin is dead. And I killed him.

I want to feel horror, or guilt, or *something*, but all I can feel inside of me is all-consuming relief. He's gone, and he can never hurt me again. I did that. I'm a murderer, but I'm light enough to float to the ceiling and never come down. I can breathe deep, even with the slight twinge of pain in my ribs, and I smile. He's gone. He's dead. I killed him. And, I realize with no small amount of shock, I'd do it again.

"Lydia, *voyin*, you're hurt," Caleb says, coming up to my side.

He tries to turn my face away from the dead man at my feet, but I refuse to be moved. I lower the gun to my side, carefully keeping my finger off the trigger, even as I reengage the safety. I can't believe I can remember those simple safety steps under the weight of what I've done, but my training seems to have stuck better than he'd intended. Giving up on turning my face, I jump as Caleb takes my shoulders in his hands and forces me into a quarter turn, stepping close enough to block out everything else. His snickerdoodle and cedar scent pushes past the lingering tobacco in the air, and I take a deep inhale of it. Or at least I try to, because anything deeper than my normal breathing makes my ribs scream in agony. I wince and clutch at them with my free hand, and Caleb makes a sympathetic noise.

"Your shoulder, let me see that," he urges, fingers gentle as he guides me.

I wince again as he touches the tender stripe of skin Darren managed to cut open, but my body is a tangle of confusing signals, and the pain gets lost among them. My heart is slowing bit by bit, but I don't trust the calm. Seth is out there somewhere.

The lightness and relief disappears, as that thought crosses my mind. My body hums with newfound energy, my mind spinning back up. My heart races and I look around wildly, as if Seth is going to leap out of the shadows and attack. But no. He went out front. I need to find him before he finds my pack and… oh God, the bond breakers!

"Where's Rhett?" I ask, suddenly, pulling away from Caleb to take a step toward the doors.

He's about to answer when raised voices echo through the space, and I take off. I don't know where my shoes got to, but I don't even care. I know those voices. My pack. They're here. Seth's promise flashes through my mind again, and I grit my teeth as I shoulder open one of the doors leading from the ballroom to the foyer.

But my feet freeze in place as I take in the scene in front of me. Rhett is out cold in the middle of the floor, his face bloody from a wound I can't identify. Mateo is in a heap a few yards from me, partially on his side, limbs splayed out. And Lucas is trying to get to his feet, but can't manage it, falling onto the floor, even as he tries to crawl toward the grand staircase.

And on the stairs is Seth. His back is to me, blocking the upper body of the woman he has under him. But I don't need to see her face to know it's Lex, her feeble coughs and cries fading as Seth laughs.

My blood boils as I step forward. No. He won't hurt her. Not while I have breath in my body. The instinct to protect my pack at all costs overpowers common sense, and I raise the gun to shoulder height, taking careful aim as I reach the bottom of the stairs.

"Mine," I snarl under my breath, pulling the trigger twice.

The bullets strike his back, one after the other, and Seth's arms jerk with the shock of each impact. I climb the stairs, keeping the gun trained on him as he slips to the side, giving Lex enough room to roll away, coughing and sputtering.

"Mine," I repeat, louder and fiercer.

Seth rolls over onto his back, looking up at me with wide, terrified eyes. He coughs, red spittle covering his lips as he struggles to speak. But my next gunshot drowns out whatever pathetic plea he might have tried to utter. This pathetic excuse of a man has hurt my pack for the last time. He's proved he can't be trusted to do the right thing and leave us alone. So he can't be allowed the chance to run and hide. No more.

No more fear. No more looking over our shoulders. This pack, my pack, has suffered long enough, and it ends here. We have worked too hard for too long for this worm to haunt us. I won't allow it. My pack deserves better than this, better than him. And I won't let them hurt anymore. I will protect them, even if it means destroying my soul. There isn't anything I wouldn't do for them.

I pull the trigger again and again, sealing his fate. I can't stop, not until the threat is gone. Seth Douglas needs to be destroyed, once and for all. The bullets stop, and I'm crying, sobbing at the empty *click, click, click* of the magazine.

"Lydia, enough, *voyin*. It's done," a deep voice calls from behind me.

I know the voice, but my mind is lost in the blood frenzy. I snarl and keep pulling the trigger, but nothing else comes out. I need more. There aren't enough bullets in the world to make Seth suffer like he's made me and my pack suffer, but I won't let something as trivial as that stop me from trying.

"Enough, my sweet omega. It's done."

Lex's voice cuts through the haze of murder, the subaudible hum of her not-quite-bark bringing me back down. Her fingers smooth over mine, gently prying them apart until another set of hands pulls the gun from my grip at last. I tense, ready to turn and protect my pack from the new threat, but then I smell cedar, snickerdoodles, and I relax again. Caleb. I don't look up as Lex gathers me to her chest, staring at the mess that is Seth's unmoving body. Blood is trickling down the steps, warm for now as it pools around my toes, but growing colder with every moment. There's something pulling at the back of my mind, and I whimper, pain I'd all but forgotten resurfacing. My bonds, so frail and close to snapping.

"Thank you, my love. You saved me," Lex whispers into my hair.

I don't respond, lost in my head as I try to find the scraps of the tethers to my mates. I can't feel Lucas at all, and Mateo and Rhett are just blips on the edges of my consciousness.

"He gave me bond breakers. Three doses. I couldn't—"

"Shhh, it's okay. We'll fix this. I promise," Lex says, low and calm.

Sobs bubble up as the ache of the loss returns. I don't know how we could possibly fix this. Even in death, he's won. I want to spit and scream and cry and crawl into my nest, never to come out again. This is grief on a scale I never thought possible.

A groan pulls my attention, and Lex and I turn to see Rhett struggling to his feet. I try to run down to him, but my feet are slick with blood, and I nearly fall over. But Rhett is there, moving faster than I'd expected him to, catching me and gathering me close.

"I thought I'd lost you," he whispers, voice cracking as he buries his face into my hair.

"I'm sorry. I'm so—I shouldn't have gone outside, I should—"

"No, Lydia. Don't apologize. You're safe, and that's all that matters," Rhett chides, and I can feel his tears against my skin.

"I have the vial, Rhett. I don't know what—should we go get checked out? I..." Lex trails off as Rhett and I turn to look at her. Her lower lip is trembling as she holds up a half-full vial of clear liquid, the bond breaker. I want to smash it into a million pieces, but that would mean leaving Rhett's embrace, and I don't know if I could do that for all the money in the world.

"Call Delano, or Gideon, Lex. They deal with this stuff all the time, right? Maybe they'll know what to do," Mateo says, staggering to my side.

Gasping, I lean far enough out of Rhett's arms to drag Mateo close, clinging to him.

"I got your message, baby girl. I'm sorry we didn't get here sooner," he murmurs, stroking the back of my head.

I shake my head, heart too full for words. I can still feel him, his relief like sugar on my tongue. He was my first bond, and he's always been the easiest to reach, and right now, I'm just glad that I can get anything. But I don't trust it to last, not with how much of the drug Seth pumped into me. I look up at him, tears in my eyes, and I can hear Lex out of reach, talking rapidly into her phone. Mateo gives me a sad smile, like he knows what I want to say. I don't want to lose him, or any of them. Not after we fought so hard to get to this point.

"I love you so much. Both of you. I'll tell you every day for the rest of my life, so you'll always know it's true, even without the bond," I manage to get out through my tears.

"Don't talk like that, love. There might be a way," Rhett says, cupping the side of my face with one of his warm, rough hands.

I lean into the touch, enjoying what little I can feel of our bond. It's the weakest, hanging on by a thread. Even still, he's fighting like hell to hold on.

"I'm not giving up on you yet, Lydia. Don't you give up on me," Mateo whispers emphatically into my hair.

I swallow, marveling at the depths of his determination and strength. When I look up at him again, his lips brush mine in a soft but intense kiss. Words fail me, and I blink back more tears.

"Never," I promise, burying my face in his chest for a moment.

A shuffle of footsteps pulls my head up, and I turn to see Caleb helping Lucas limp over to us, and I suck in a sharp breath. Lex is still on the phone, but she's looking him over, brushing back his hair and checking for bleeding. He's got a split lip, and he winces every time he breathes, but it's the pain in his eyes that strikes me the deepest. I extract myself fully from Rhett's arms before gathering Lucas to me. He leans heavily on me, and his undisguised sobs break my heart all over again.

"I thought I lost you, Lydi-bug. I can't feel you, I can't—"

"I know, Luc. I'm sorry," I hush, my ribs protesting as he squeezes me tight, like he's afraid I'm going to float away.

"I hate this, hate not being enough—"

"No, don't say that. I love you just the way you are, Lucas," I protest, shaking my head.

"I love you so much, Lydia. I need you, but I can't—I can't be what you need," Lucas goes on, like he can't or won't listen to me.

"You are enough, Lucas. You hear me? Look at me," I say, much firmer, pulling away to take his face in my hands. "I don't need another alpha, I need you. I need my beta, who knows me better than I know myself, who can always make me feel better, even before we had the bonds. I don't need a bond with you to know you love me. You show me every day, and that's enough. I love you, Lucas Klausen."

"But if—"

I cut him off with a kiss, the metallic tang of his blood only enhancing his smoke and sugar flavor. It's not a long kiss, but it does the job, and Lucas's shoulders slump. I don't delude myself into thinking this is over, but only time is going to reassure him if the bonds can't be fixed.

"Thanks, Gid. Oh, fuck you, you little shit... Yeah, yeah. Just text me when it's done," Lex says, hanging up her call with an angry press of her thumb.

We all turn to her, and she sighs, running a hand through her hair. I frown as I see the bruises forming around her throat, the distinct finger-shaped splotches making my temper flare all over again.

"Well? What did they say?" Rhett asks urgently.

She doesn't speak for a moment, then turns to Caleb. "Do you think you'll be able to wait here for a bit? My cousin is calling in some friends to... take care of this," she says, swallowing with some difficulty.

Caleb nods, eyes bright with emotion. "I'll use the time to think of what I'm going to put on my expense report when I have to replace my weapon," he says dryly.

I want to laugh, but Lex's face gives me pause. At last, she turns to us. "There might be a way, but I'm not sure if you'll like it," she says.

Chapter Fifty-Six

Mateo

I'm squeezed into the backseat of Lex's car as we race back to the pack house. Rhett is just as cramped as I am, but with Lydia in the middle seat, I don't mind as much. I can't stop touching her, trying to maintain the tenuous connection between us. We grabbed the first aid kit out of Caleb's SUV, and we've more or less patched ourselves up. My face is sore, but thankfully, it seems like nothing's broken. Rhett has a black eye forming, but he's holding a disposable ice pack over it to keep the swelling down. Lydia's shoulder is the worst of the physical wounds, but between the two of us, Rhett and I managed to get it bandaged. We'll have to see if it holds up, or if we need more advanced medical care later. Right now, we have more pressing concerns.

The silence is charged as we wait for Lex to speak. She refused to give details of whatever her cousin and his friends told her could help us until we were in private, and each moment she doesn't talk makes me want to scream with frustration. We're almost halfway home, and she's still staring out the window like she's waiting for a miracle to jump out of the tree line and into our path. Lucas clears his throat, and it seems to break whatever spell she's under.

"The bond breaker Seth got from Brazil isn't as strong as the medical grade stuff we were given, so Rhett, you shouldn't lose your bond with Lucas if we're fast. Lydia getting three doses is a concern, but mostly because it's impossible to know if that shit was laced with anything without lab testing," Lex starts, speaking to the windshield as she concentrates on the road.

My heart drops, and my grip tightens slightly on Lydia. She's shivering, from nerves or the cold, I'm not sure, but I rub her skin to warm her up, regardless.

"What do you mean, if we're fast?" Rhett asks, words more of a growl.

"That's the part you're not going to like. We need to reestablish the bonds, and we need to do it tonight. And to do that..."

"I need to go into heat," Lydia mutters, saying what Lex won't or can't.

Lex trails off, audibly swallowing and nodding. My tired mind is slow to work, and I feel like I'm missing something. Instinctually, there's an unease building in my chest, and I can't put words to the source of the feeling. But I don't get to puzzle it out as Rhett's growl rattles the silence.

"No, we find another way," Rhett interjects firmly.

"What happens if we don't?" Lucas questions.

Lex sighs, rolling through a stop sign without hesitation. "The bonds would break for good. We'd all have to take another dose and start over. And even then, there's a significant chance that the next time we try to bond, it won't work."

I swallow hard and look down at Lydia. Even in the darkness of the car, with only the occasional streetlight to see by, I can see the fear on her face. A little bubble of hope forms in my chest as I feel the flickering of our bond, and I try to soothe her gently. Though I can't tell if it works, because her expression doesn't change. The wheels are starting to turn, and I furrow my brow in concentration.

"I won't go into heat again naturally for a while. Months, at least," Lydia rasps, barely above a whisper.

"I know, sweetness. That's... that's the part I don't like, but I can't see another way," Lex says, voice cracking with unshed tears.

Then it hits me. If Lydia won't go into heat naturally, then it would have to be forced. And the only way to force an omega into heat is with an alpha bark.

"We couldn't try without Lydia going into heat?" Lucas asks, sounding almost frantic.

"An omega only produces the hormones that bonds need to form when they're in heat," Lydia says flatly.

I gather her close, kissing the top of her head as my heart twists painfully in my chest. Of all the things that I thought we'd need to do, forcing Lydia into heat never once crossed my mind. And after everything she's been through, both tonight and in her life up to this point, this wound shouldn't need to be torn open. Rhett has his arms around both of us, trying to shield us from reality with his body, but it's no use. Lydia feels so small and fragile like this, shaking and scared in the dark with no one but us to protect her. But what if helping only hurts her more?

Lucas makes a noise of frustration from the front seat, and I look up to find him ruffling his hair.

"We can't go to the hospital? Maybe a doctor—"

"How would we explain everything that happened, Lucas? She just tripped and fell onto three doses of illegal bond breakers?" Lex says, nearly shouting.

"I'm trying to think of ways to fix this that don't involve Lydia having to relive her trauma, Lex!" Lucas returns, getting heated himself now.

I look down at Lydia, and find her staring off into space, lost in her thoughts or memories, I can't tell which. I stroke her cheekbone with my thumb, and she jumps a little, coming back to the present and looking up at me.

"If you don't want to do it, I'll take the risk," I say softly.

"But what if we can't bond ever again?" Lydia asks, a low, terrified squeak.

I swallow and close my eyes, the idea of losing the thing I'd worked so long to gain spiking through my chest like a spear. But no, it doesn't matter.

"Then I'll have to spend the rest of my life telling you how much I love you in other ways. I'm yours, bond or no bond," I declare, softly but not weakly.

"You are our omega, Lydia. We're in this together, and we don't need bonds or pieces of paper or a judge's signature to prove anything," Rhett adds, leaning in to rest his forehead against Lydia's uninjured shoulder.

"But... I..." Lydia says, trailing off and swallowing a sob.

"We'll keep looking for other ways. This can't be the first time someone got a wrong dosage," Lucas says, sounding more relaxed now.

"But what if I want you to do it?" Lydia exclaims, words tumbling out fast, like she's afraid she won't get them out in time.

We're all silent for several heartbeats, long enough for us to get through the Bristol Point security gate. I stare in awe, waiting for her to take it back. We've made it clear that this doesn't have to happen, that we can try to find another way. This has been her hard limit for as long as I've known her, and if forcing her heat is going to do more harm than good to her mental health, then I want no part of it.

"We don't have to," Lex says, sounding almost defeated.

"I know. And I can't tell you how much it means to me that you, all of you, are trying to find another way. But... I trust you. I love you. And I don't want to lose these bonds, not after everything. I want to try," Lydia says, the conviction in her voice making the backs of my eyes burn.

"We should sleep on it, not make any hasty decisions—"

"But Lex said we don't have time, Rhett!" Lydia snaps, speaking over my best friend's reasonable suggestion.

"It's not worth it," Rhett grumbles.

"What isn't worth it? Saving our bonds?" Lydia demands, hackles rising.

Lex pulls into the garage, but none of us move to exit the car. Not while Lydia's question hangs in the air like a penny. He's put down the ice pack, and I can see that a bruise is forming on Rhett's cheek, and the cut above his eyebrow has scabbed over, but it only makes the bright blue of his irises that much more intense. And the look he's leveling at our omega speaks volumes to his fear and worry.

"I won't be like *him*, Lydia. It wouldn't be right, and I can't—I won't do that to you, not when there's another choice," Rhett says.

Lydia shifts to face Rhett more fully, putting a hand to his cheek. The cuts on her forearms make my stomach flip, but

I push the lingering rage to the side. Rhett's eyes soften, and I can see the tears forming at the edges of his lashes.

"You will never be him, Rhett Cooper. If I could do this myself, I would, but I need you, need all of you. Being your bond mate has made me the happiest person in the world, and I don't want to lose that tonight. You've done so much to help me heal from what he did to me; help me with this last thing. Please," Lydia begs, speaking first to Rhett, and then to the rest of us.

Lucas doesn't look at her, but then she reaches out over the center console and takes his hand, drawing his attention. There's a darkness in his blue-gray eyes I don't like, but without my connection through Lydia, I can't tell where it's coming from. I reach over the back of the seat and grip his shoulder, looking around. Slowly, Lex reaches out and clasps her hand around Lydia's and Lucas's entwined fingers.

"I want this, and want all of you," Lydia presses, looking at Lucas.

I swallow and nod, squeezing Lucas's shoulder in reassurance. "If this is what you want, baby, then I'm in," I say into the silence.

Rhett sighs, and then he turns to kiss Lydia's palm. "Okay," he says simply.

I don't need a bond to tell me how much it's paining him to agree to this. Even with her permission, forcing a woman, especially one he cares so deeply about, to do anything, goes against his very nature. I reach out with my other hand and take his, lacing our fingers together. He looks up at me, and I give him a soft, understanding smile and a little dip of my chin. I won't let him beat himself up over this, not when there's so much on the line.

"We won't let your trust go misplaced, sweetness," Lex says with a short nod.

Lydia looks to Lucas, but his expression is distant. Reaching out, Lex puts a hand on his shoulder, making him jump. I see the shadows under his steel-blue eyes as he looks back through the rearview mirror. He's not looking at me, but at Lydia, and something shifts between them. Some sort of silent exchange. But thankfully, it's enough.

"We're going to have to be careful with this," he sighs at last.

Rhett nods, and I look down at Lydia. Our bond is little more than a few hairs stretching across an endless void, but her trepidation is written across her green irises. I give her the most reassuring smile I'm capable of, but I'm not sure she buys it.

But we're pulled out of our bubble as Lex opens her door, flooding the car with light. Lydia sets her shoulders, and my chest fills with pride. And as we pile out of the car, I follow her example. She's facing her greatest fear for us, and it's our job as her pack to see her through this.

Chapter Fifty-Seven

Lydia

My stomach twists over itself into ever tightening knots as my pack waits at the door to my room, watching me. I'm standing at the edge of my nest, looking down at the carefully arranged blankets and pillows lining the edges of the mattress, leaving enough room in the middle for all of us to fit. Sudden nerves hit me, and I swallow. I'd been so sure of this in the car, but now that the moment is here, old fear is resurfacing.

A hand on my lower back makes me jump and I turn to face Lucas, who's looking down at me with concern pulling his brow low. I lean into his touch, his presence a comfort, even without any bonds. He doesn't hesitate to hold me close, rubbing in slow, up-and-down motions on my back.

"You're in your head, aren't you?" he asks, soft enough for only me to hear.

I nod, flushing with embarrassment. I thought I was ready, but I can't shake the fear my past has instilled in me at the mere thought of an alpha barking at me until I go into heat.

But I don't want to lose the bonds I have with my wonderful, extraordinary pack.

"Look at me, sweetheart," Lucas says firmly.

I obey, locking onto his intense blue-gray eyes. I couldn't look away now, even if I wanted to. His hands slide down to the hem of my borrowed shirt, slipping below the fabric and pushing it up and up until it's over my head and then on the floor. I shiver as the cool air glides over my overly warm skin, and Lucas hums his approval.

"You are so beautiful, Lydia. God, I can't get over how fucking perfect you are," Lucas whispers, almost speaking to himself.

I suck in a sharp breath as his hands come up to cup my breasts, massaging them with just the right amount of pressure to melt the knots in my stomach and turn my core molten. His thumbs roll over my nipples until they're hard and aching for more. I cling to his biceps, nails digging into his skin and making him moan. He guides me backwards until my knees hit the edge of the bed and I ease onto my back, bringing him with me. He slips a leg between my thighs, his knee pressing against the apex. I grind against him, my thin sleep shorts and his jeans the only thing separating us, and that suddenly feels like too much. I try to pull my shorts down, but Lucas growls at me, and I freeze from the ferocity of it.

"Don't move, not until I say so," he says, low and husky.

I nod and whimper, going completely still. I don't get to see the dominant side of Lucas very often, but I wish he would show it more. And in this moment, when it would be so easy for me to slip over the edge of anxiety, having his strong, steady guidance is a Godsend. The intensity of his gaze stokes the fire in my belly higher and higher, but he won't do more than touch my breasts and grind his thigh into my soaking pussy. I don't even dare roll my hips anymore, hoping my obedience will be rewarded.

"Such a good girl for me," he purrs, dipping his head to nuzzle against my breasts before he finally takes one of my nipples between his lips.

I gasp and arch into his mouth, my hands going to his hair and pulling just like I know he loves. He groans and shifts, slipping my shorts off before nudging my legs apart so he can press the hard bulge at the front of his jeans against me. Despite everything I've been through tonight, my body still reacts to his touch, his scent, his everything. I want more, need to feel him completely. I try to wrap my legs around his hips, but I'm met with a sharp, chastising bite to the swell of my breast, making me whine.

"If you want to play games, we can play games, but I'm not sure you'll like consequences for your naughty behavior," Lucas says, a strong warning tone coating his otherwise playful words.

I blink, swallowing. His gaze is so stern that I almost forget that this is just a game, part of the plan to get me into the right headspace. My heart flips and I want to apologize, but then I remember myself. So, I let my lips pull up into what I hope is a sly, seductive smile.

"Maybe I deserve a bit of punishment," I croon, trying to pull his face to mine, but he refuses to budge.

The fire flares hot in Lucas's eyes, and his dark chuckle makes me shiver. "If that's what you want, then I know some alphas who would be more than happy to oblige you. What do you say if you want to stop?" Lucas prompts, finally looking me in the face.

"Red. And yellow if I need a breather," I reply automatically.

Lucas nods and leans down to kiss me tenderly. "Remember, Lydi-bug, I'm right here, and I'm not going anywhere. I'm going to hold your hands the whole time. If you can't speak, I'll squeeze your hand to check in. If you're okay, squeeze twice, and if you want out, just squeeze my hands three times in a row and I'll call it, okay? You're safe with us. Never forget that," Lucas whispers against my lips.

I nod, heart swelling a little with affection. Lucas is my lifeline, always has been, and I'm grateful beyond words to have him here with me. His kiss is soft and sweet, but not lacking in heat. The taste of him, marshmallow and pine smoke, is like coming home, and my eyes burn from the sudden surge of emotions inside me. When we pull away, he rests his forehead against mine.

"I love you, Lydi-bug," he whispers.

"I love you, too, Lucas. So much," I reply.

"If you're having second thoughts, it's okay. We don't—"

"But we do. I want this. And I know you'll be with me, and you'll keep me safe," I say, stroking the tips of my fingers along his sharp cheekbones.

He nods and the corners of his mouth lift in a small smile. When he sits back on his heels, I can only stare in awe at how beautiful he is. The dark, tousled hair falling into his bright eyes, the slope of his muscular shoulders, the toned forearms. Everything about him oozes sex appeal, and I lick my suddenly dry lips.

"Naughty girl, looking at me like that," he teases, raising his voice a little.

"But you look good enough to eat," I say with a fake pout.

He laughs, a dark sound that makes my pussy clench on air. "You need to be taught some patience, don't you?" he asks.

I nod, tucking my chin demurely. Lucas shakes his head and laughs again, this one sounding more like his normal chuckle, and I smile, batting my eyelashes.

"I think our omega needs her alphas to teach her a lesson," Lucas calls over his shoulder.

Glancing at the door, I suck in a sharp breath as Rhett and Mateo stride into the room, shirtless. Rhett has several bundles of rope in his hands, and Mateo is holding a vibrating wand in one hand, and a paddle in the other. Lex follows behind them, now wearing her black silk robe.

Rhett and Mateo pause at the edge of the mattress, and I sit up as Lucas moves to my left side, his fingers slipping perfectly into the spaces between mine. The remnants of my bonds hum feebly, a silent question from both of the men before me. Permission to enter my nest. I nod mutely, and their shoulders relax a fraction before they climb up beside me. Lex moves my vanity stool to the edge of the bed and perches herself on it, directly in front of me. She elegantly crosses one leg over the other, and I glimpse her bare sex for a moment before she settles back and gives me a hard stare.

Mateo's hand goes to my throat as he positions himself on my right side. He's not squeezing, but the weight of his hand is familiar and almost comforting. He tilts my chin up so I can't look anywhere but at his face. His tawny eyes search mine, and I have to struggle not to look away. There's no softness left in his expression, just stern, unshaking dominance.

It's so potent, making my primal instincts perk up and take notice.

"You're going to take your punishment like the good girl I know you are, aren't you?" he asks, speaking slowly.

"Yes, Daddy. Please," I beg mindlessly.

There's a purr from behind me, Rhett's hands massaging my back, loosening the muscles and making me melt. He's careful of my shoulder, brushing his lips against the bandages, making me shiver. Mateo's fingers flex, making me jump and whimper.

"Let go, Omega. Let go and obey," he says, and I gasp at the same sub-audible rumble I'm used to hearing only from Lex in his voice. Not quite a bark, but tuned directly to the primal part of my mind.

I can only nod, mouth open on a pant as my heart suddenly kicks into high gear. There's a gentle double-squeeze on my left hand. I squeeze twice in return.

"On your knees, thighs spread, lovely," Lex orders, a cold snap through the warm haze of Mateo's stare.

My movements are sluggish, but they don't rush me. Eventually Rhett's hands are on me, sure and steady, as he ties his knots. The web of rope across my chest and back holds me like an embrace, allowing me to slip a little further out of my body. I'm tethered into position, lines running to anchor points in the walls and ceiling until I barely need to support my own weight and I can relax into the ropes. Once he's finished, I know I can't move an inch. Somehow, that knowledge allows me to slip even further down.

I'm secure, safe, surrounded by the people I trust the most in the world. Lucas is behind me now, as my hands are tied behind my back and secured at my waist. Rhett gave me my usual emergency release pull, which I hold tight in my right fist, while my left hand is still entwined with Lucas's. While Rhett works, Mateo traces feather-light teasing touches over my skin until I'm covered with goosebumps. I want to squirm, to whine and plead for more, but with how serious his expression is, I know better than to try my luck.

"How many?" Lex asks, drawing my attention.

"Domina?" I question, the word a little slurred in my hazy mental state.

"How many times did you disobey?" she asks, purposefully leaving the question open-ended.

I struggle to think, but I don't know if it's worth traveling down that road. This isn't about wrongdoings, I realize. This is a question as to how much I can take right now. I have a feeling as to what they have planned, based on the toys they brought, and I know my limits.

"Ten," I gasp as Mateo flicks at my nipple.

She only nods, and I scream as Mateo presses the vibrator to my exposed clit, turning the speed up to the max. I can't flinch away, can't escape the sudden surge of pleasure and the orgasm barreling toward me. My moans rise higher and higher, but just as I'm reaching my peak, he pulls the toy away, leaving me dripping and aching.

"Count for me, sweet girl," Rhett purrs, rubbing a hand along my ass.

"Yes, sir," I reply automatically.

The first strike of the paddle comes softer than I know he's capable of, but still hard enough for the ache to linger. I count each of the five strikes, my mind starting to detach from my body as pleasure and pain blur together.

"You want to surrender to us, don't you, my love? To give us whatever we want?" Lex purrs as Mateo starts up again with the vibrator.

I nod frantically, the primal part of my mind screaming in enthusiastic agreement. I'm pulled back from the edge again, and Rhett's strikes are harder this time, but my brain can't separate the ache in my ass from the ache in my core. Empty, so empty.

"Please, Domina, please," I practically sob as the pleasure starts again.

"Your body isn't ready for us, baby girl," Mateo chides, his stern disappointment like an ice spike through my heart.

This time, instead of the paddle, Rhett's fingers slide into my aching pussy, thrusting up hard and fast, but he withdraws before I can orgasm, and I feel the tears leaking from my eyes and sliding down my face.

Two squeezes on my left hand. I return the gesture, even as my body shakes and my head falls back. I can feel my bonds stretching out into the darkness, warmth filling me as the overwhelming demand for my body's submission crashes down. They don't have to speak their wish, but there's a small part of my mind still fighting.

"More," I gasp, my half-lidded eyes staring at the ceiling.

The paddle again, then the vibrator. Over and over, the pleasure curling tighter, with no release in sight. But I can hardly feel it. I'm starting to float, and I try to let myself go, to sink into that place where I'm only a vessel for sensation, but something is keeping me tethered to the ground.

"Omega, let go. Give in and give us what we need," Rhett rasps in my ear, his true alpha bark shaking me to my bones.

Heat flares in my belly, but I whimper, flinching back from it. Primal fear overwhelms my senses, but I do my best to push past it, focusing on the scents of my alphas. The love I can feel surrounding me, even without the bonds.

"You can do it, baby girl. Just let go."

Mateo's bark isn't as strong without the use of my designation, but the fire under my skin grows hotter all the same. The vibrator returns, and I can feel myself dripping onto the mattress, my pussy clenching on nothing. The familiar ache builds, and I try to reach for it, but it remains just out of reach. I sob, shaking and panting.

"Obey, my sweet omega. Be our good girl, and let go," Lex orders, the power of her true alpha bark pushing everything else aside except for my primal drives and urges.

Sweat covers my skin, the pressure of the ropes digging in, adding that extra layer of pain and pleasure wrapped in one. Fingers fill my pussy, even pressing against my rear entrance, stretching me out. The command is there, so close I can taste it like ambrosia from the gods. I'm on the edge of the cliff, a sea of fire below me. But my mind won't let me fall. I can't do this.

"I'm here, sweetheart. It's okay," Lucas whispers in my ear.

Cool, crisp, sweet. A breath of fresh air. A breeze at my back. My safety. My lifeline.

I close my eyes, seeing the waves of flame and sparks in my mind's eye. I squeeze my left hand twice and then I tumble forward, arms spread wide.

Chapter Fifty-Eight

Lucas

THE MOMENT LYDIA FALLS into her heat, the air around us becomes saturated with lilacs and honey, sweet and floral and delicious. My mouth waters and I move in as close as I can, kissing the skin between the intricate weave of emerald green rope Rhett twisted around her upper body. She whines, leaning into me, her hand still clutching mine, almost painfully hard. But I don't let go, not for a moment. Lex stands from her stool, shedding her robe to leave her in nothing but her skin before climbing into Lydia's nest and prowling toward us.

"Fuck, yes," Mateo sighs, words rumbling with a purr and a growl all in one.

Rhett has emergency shears in his hands, cutting away ropes until Lydia is free, limp and utterly pliant to Mateo's touch. He pulls Lydia toward him, his lips capturing hers with a hunger I'd felt building over the last several minutes. I want to go with them, but Rhett takes my chin in his hand, pulling my attention back to him.

"I need you, pet. Please," Rhett begs, eyes hooded and cheeks flushed.

I nod, swallowing hard. There's a little tug in my chest, but I can't tell who it's coming from with emotions running so high. I toss my shirt aside, and shuck my jeans with a little twinge of protest from my ribs. I'll probably be feeling the full effects of the ass-kicking I got tomorrow, but for now, the pain only makes my throbbing cock twitch. Rhett undresses with haste, and then he's on me, arms around my chest and waist, mouth on mine. God, he tastes amazing, the burn of whiskey on my tongue, a perfect counterpoint to the sweetness in the air. His cock is leaking as he ruts against me, and I reach down to grip both of our cocks together, spreading our pre-cum as we grind against one another. I moan as slick fingers probe at my tight entrance, smelling Lex moments later as she curls against my back.

"You did so good for us, such a good boy. That's it, work yourself open for your sir. You've earned it," Lex praises, nibbling on my ear as she works.

I can feel her relief and love through our bond, like a warm fire chasing away the chill of doubt that lingered all the way from The Garden. The hard part is over, and by the sounds of it, Lydia is getting the relief she needs as she bounces on Mateo's cock. I glance over for a moment, but then get lost in the beauty of the two of them together.

Mateo is on his back, Lydia riding him hard and fast. He has a fistful of her hair, pulling hard enough to make her arch nearly in half backwards as he thrusts up, slamming into her over and over. Her breasts bounce heavily, her nipples peaked and jutting out, just begging to be sucked. And her face is the picture of bliss, eyes unfocused as she stares up, too lost in her pleasure to mask. The wet sounds of their bodies coming together, her cries of ecstasy as she shatters from the pleasure, gushing all over Mateo's stomach might be the most erotic thing I've ever seen.

I let out a curse as my hand is knocked aside and lips close around my cock at the same time as another slides with ease into my ass. I look down and see Rhett sucking my dick like his life depends on it, looking up at me with enough reverence in his icy eyes to knock the wind out of me. That is, to knock whatever wind is left as Lex thrusts up hard into me, perfectly angled to hit my sweet spot with each roll of her perfect hips.

"I love you," Lex moans as she pulls my hair, angling my chest for better leverage.

"Oh, fuck! I love you, too. Jesus Christ, that's—" I choke out a moan as Rhett takes my cock all the way down his throat, swallowing around me.

The warm slide of his tongue as he pulls back before diving down again makes my eyes roll back into my head and my toes curl. Lex's nails dig into my chest, clinging to me as she fucks me deep. I don't know what to do with my hands, or any other part of me. I try to find some sort of rhythm, but it's too much, too fast. Rhett looks up at me as he takes me all the way again, his blue eyes ablaze with lust and unshaking love. My heart jumps around my ribcage, but then drops to my belly as Lex bites my neck, over her mating mark. I can't hold back, and I don't get a chance to warn them as my spine tingles and I shoot my cum down Rhett's eager throat. But he doesn't balk or complain, only moans as he swallows every last drop.

Lex pulls out with a light chuckle, and as Rhett licks me clean and sits up on his knees, I twist to look at her. She's grinning like the cat that got the canary, the sparkle in her hazel eyes making my stomach flip with a strange mix of excitement and trepidation. But I don't get to question her, as Rhett grabs my hips and manhandles me onto all fours, pushing his entire cock into me in one smooth motion. I'm still sensitive, and the pleasure of his deep, slow thrusts is almost too good, making me see stars with each brush of the head over my prostate.

"Take my knot, baby girl. Just like that, fuck yes!" Mateo shouts.

I look up and find that I'm perfectly positioned to watch as his knot slips inside of Lydia's waiting channel, making her cry out again. Mateo grabs hold of her left wrist, bringing it to his mouth and biting down hard. She gasps, eyes flying open to stare at the ceiling, face breaking out into a wild, almost manic smile. Mateo licks at his bite, her blood smeared around his mouth like war paint, moaning and sighing.

"Yes, oh, God, Matty—you're—I can—" Lydia squeaks, a tear sliding down her cheek.

"I know, baby girl. I feel it, too. I'm here," Mateo soothes.

I sigh in relief, even as Rhett's purr rumbles through me like thunder. It's working. Lex moves behind Lydia and tips her forward, lining her strap-on up with Lydia's peachy ass. Our omega is limp and come-drunk, resting her head on Mateo's chest as Lex fucks her deep. Rhett matches her pace, and I grunt with each hard thrust. Lydia's emerald eyes meet mine, and she smiles, reaching out with her other hand toward me. I try to reach for her, but Rhett has me too far. I stretch, but Rhett growls.

"Sir, she needs me," I pant, grunting against the pain of his fingers digging into my hips.

Rhett's rhythm falters for a moment, and he sucks in a sharp breath. Moments later, he releases me, and I crawl over to Lydia's side, threading our fingers together while using my other hand to push some of her hair from her face. I'm partially prone, and Mateo's hand brushes idly against my bicep, so light, I'm not even sure he knows he's doing it. But my attention is fixed on our omega, and the vulnerable smile pulling at her lips.

"What's the matter, sweetheart? You okay?" I push, concern filling me.

She shakes her head, squeezing my hand twice. "Just want you close, too," she whispers.

My heart skips a beat, and my face heats with an honest-to-God blush at the raw emotion in her eyes. Rhett moves behind me again, leaning over me to kiss Lydia's forehead. She preens and hums her delight at his attention, and I can't help but smile. He tilts her chin and claims her mouth with his, even as one of his hands glides over my back and around my stomach. He purrs as he reaches his destination, stroking my half-hard cock. I hiss, still a little sensitive from my earlier climax.

"Such a good girl, taking your Domina's cock in your pretty little ass," Mateo purrs.

"Thank you, Daddy. You both feel so good," Lydia replies, closing her eyes and arching as Lex adjusts her angle slightly.

"Does my greedy girl want more?" Mateo prompts, his hand drifting away from my arm until he finds Rhett's rock-hard length.

"Yes, Daddy. Can I come, Domina, please?" Lydia says, breaking off with a moan.

"Hold it just a minute for me, my love. Stay right there," Lex grunts, pushing deep and grinding.

Mateo and Lydia both moan, and he thrusts up again, as well. His knot hasn't deflated, so he's barely able to circle his hips. Lydia's eyes pop open before sliding closed again, and I can see her shaking.

"Be good and take care of our beta, sweet girl. Then you can come," Rhett prompts, resting his chin on my shoulder.

Lydia looks up at him, then at me, and she squeezes my hand twice in question. I don't know how, but I'm suddenly aching again at the idea of Lydia's mouth on me. I return her question with confirmation, and she sits up slightly. Rhett guides my cock to her waiting mouth, and I sigh, resting my head on Rhett's shoulder as she works up and down my shaft. Her tongue dances along every vein, swirling around my head and even dipping into my slit to taste me. Her moans and whimpers send goosebumps over my body, and I do my best to not thrust down her throat before she's ready.

"Yes, fuck, yes, I'm going to come," Lex pants, pushing as deep as she can without knotting and grinding her hips in rapid circles.

"Can you take it, baby? Can you take two knots?" Mateo asks, kissing Lydia's breasts as they swing above his face.

Lydia moans and nods, thrusting back onto Lex and Mateo as she chases her pleasure. Rhett groans, grinding against my ass, his pre-cum sticky against my skin. I tilt my hips, and he gets the silent message, sliding back inside of me with a soft sigh. I've never felt more connected with my pack, all of us touching, panting, sweating, and on the edge of bliss. One of Mateo's hands is between my legs, alternating between playing with my balls and Rhett's. Lex's nails find my arm and scratch long lines down my skin. Rhett pounds hard, careful not to force my cock down Lydia's throat, not that it matters. She swallows me all the way down, and the vibrations of her muffled screams are almost more than I can handle.

Lex's release sets off a chain reaction. She pushes her knot into Lydia's ass, making them both scream, which sends me barreling over the edge, and I drag Rhett with me. Lex's teeth clamp down on the side of Lydia's throat at the same moment Rhett's teeth find our bond mark, and with a flash of pain, his knot slips past the clenching ring of muscle stretched around his thick length. The world tilts as a flood of emotions fills my chest, and I nearly sob as I taste dark chocolate and wine together again. Rhett releases me a moment later, and reaches down to Lydia, shifting us both forward so I can support her chest as he bites her bicep, directly over his original mating mark.

And then, to my shock, Lydia lifts our intertwined hands, and bites the webbing between my thumb and pointer finger. I know it won't do anything, but the gesture, the symbolism of her claiming bite, fills my heart with joy until it leaks from my eyes. She lets go and cleans her bite with little kitten licks before looking up at me.

"Mine," she says deliberately.

"Yours," Mateo sighs, head thumping back to the mattress.

"Yours," Rhett and Lex echo in unison.

I swallow, continuing to hold eye contact with Lydia. There's a fire in her gaze, and her love comes across the reforming bonds like an inferno. She loves me, and needs me just as much as she needs the rest of our pack. She couldn't have done this without me. These thoughts and more are suddenly irrefutable truths in my soul. I nod and give her a wide, genuine smile as I lean my forehead against hers.

"Yours," I say, meaning it with my whole heart.

CHAPTER FIFTY-NINE

Lydia

A HAND AROUND MY throat. Sharp pain in my arm. Laughter, taunting. Shadowy hands push and shove me until I'm on my hands and knees, tears splashing onto the plastic below me.

Lie down and take it, you omega bitch.

The weight of the gun in my steady hands, unflinching as I fire over and over, the shock ricocheting up my arms. The acrid burn of gunpowder in the air. Muddy brown eyes staring up at me but never seeing again. Red hair. Blood. So much blood.

This is what you deserve.

There's no one here to save you.

Alone. Friendless. Packless.

Pain as my bonds shred, disappearing before my eyes.

Dead eyes. So many dead eyes.

"Come back, love. We're here," Rhett mutters in my ear, pulling me from my nightmare.

A warm touch, not on my skin but in my soul, brushes away the lingering fear, and I swallow, trying to rehydrate my desiccated mouth. I open my eyes and I find him immediately, his icy-blue gaze full of worry even as our repaired bond hums with soothing calm. I roll over and snuggle close, letting him wrap his arms around me as I bury my nose in his bare chest. His scent of leather and old books and dark chocolate helps to slow my frantic heartbeat, and the traces of pine smoke and even honey work like a tonic on my nerves. I wouldn't be smelling those unless the bonds were repaired.

Everything is normal for the first time in days, but it's not like last time. I feel like I'm covered in a thin exoskeleton of sweat and various other bodily fluids, but there's no driving need in my chest to get clean. In fact, anything that would take me out of physical contact with my pack sounds like the worst possible thing right now. I lift my head up as a bolt of worry shoots through me, but it passes just as quickly as I see Lucas and Mateo cuddling nearby, Lex barely visible between them. Before I can even voice the need, Rhett rolls us until my back is touching Lucas's back, settling the little restless tickle in my chest at last.

"Are you hurting at all?" Rhett asks, nuzzling against my neck.

Shaking my head, I close my eyes for a moment. I'm sore, but it's not unbearable. My shoulder hurts the worst, but I'm sure a few painkillers will take care of that. As I take stock of my body, I realize how many bite marks I have on my arms, chest, stomach, thighs, and other places I can feel but can't see. I look at one of the random bruises, the teeth marks still visible even though they didn't break the skin, and then back up to Rhett pointedly.

"We wanted to make sure the bonds stuck." Rhett chuckles, his cheeks a little flushed.

I giggle and tentatively search in my heart for the places I was used to feeling my bonds. Bone-deep relief floods my system as I feel four bonds, three bright and strong, the fourth less bright, but still rock solid. It worked.

"Are you okay? With... what happened?" Rhett questions, drawing my attention back to his face.

I bring my fingers up and brush them over the worry line between his brows, not stopping until his face is smooth. Only then do I smile and stretch my neck up to kiss him. When I pull away, I stroke my fingers through his beard absently, making him purr into my palm as I try to sort through my feelings.

Before I met Pack Saint Clair, the idea of bonding with anyone terrified me to my core. But they proved themselves worthy of my trust and my love over and over again. Every time they stopped to really listen to me, and hear what I said, or when they took my refusals at face value, and didn't pressure me into changing my mind. Those bonds were worth facing my fears to save. While I don't remember much of the aftermath, I was aware enough during the process to know how much care my alphas took to make sure I had ways to communicate if I needed to stop or if I reached my limit. And I know in the deepest part of my soul that if their efforts to force my heat instead forced me into a panic attack, they would have stopped and would have never blamed me for it not working.

"I know it wasn't easy, for me or for anyone. But it wasn't like before. I never felt unsafe or unloved. I knew you would take care of me and... I think I needed that. Now I can put my past well and truly behind me, and we can move on together, as a family," I say, picking my words with care.

Rhett hums his agreement, burying his face in my hair, kissing my temple every now and then as we sit in silence for a few long heartbeats. I can almost hear his brain working, but I leave him be. Forcing me into heat goes against everything Rhett stands for, even if he was acting with my permission.

"I almost couldn't do it. You mean so much to me, and I never want to put you in a position where you feel you can't say no," Rhett stammers, words tumbling out.

I brush my fingers along his cheekbone, careful of the tender bruise forming there. His black eye is fading to yellows and greens, but the colors only make the blue of his irises more intense. I stare into them for a long while, getting lost in the depths, swallowed whole by the love pouring out of them. But as I pull back, I smile softly.

"And it's because you feel that way that I knew I was safe. Even though we didn't have time to plan or prep, we still had so many safeguards in place. My mind and my heart knew what had to be done. We just needed to convince my body to get with the program," I say, ending with a little laugh.

Rhett chuckles at my joke before falling silent. His lips brush my hairline, forehead, cheeks, and then finally, he presses a tender kiss to my lips. I close my eyes and bask in the taste and warmth of him, the way he guides me through the motions, the feeling of his tongue on my bottom lip, always asking permission. And I open for him gladly, like I know I always will.

When we pull away, Rhett leans in and rests his forehead against mine. "Thank you for trusting me, trusting us with that," Rhett mutters.

"Thank you for trusting me, too," I reply, closing my eyes and smiling.

We settle back into silence, and the steady thump of Rhett's heartbeat nearly drags me back under, but then Lucas turns over, gathering me up in his arms. I laugh a little as he smiles against my skin, nipping at it gently.

"You're not hot," he mutters, gravelly with sleep.

I let out a sarcastic scoff, rolling my eyes and making Rhett laugh. "Gee, thanks. I know I've had a rough few days, but—"

Lucas bites a little harder, making me yelp, but he soothes away the hurt with his tongue. But at the sound of my momentary distress, Lex and Mateo both bolt upright, looking down at me in alarm. Seeing me laughing relaxes them, and I manage to untangle one of my hands and extend it in their direction. Lex doesn't hesitate, interlacing her fingers with mine as she shifts up toward my head. Mateo follows her, spooning her from behind and draping one arm over her waist to play with my hair.

"How are you feeling, sweetness?" Lex asks tenderly, bringing my hand up to her lips and kissing the back of it.

"Good," I sigh, relaxing into my pillows.

And I smile to myself as I realize it's true. I'm sore, and sort of a mess, but I feel… good. Unburdened. Light. Free.

"I'm glad. You did a very brave thing, letting us force your heat like that," Lex replies, tone turning serious.

I look up and find her staring at me, searching for something in my face. Our bond hums with low-level anxiety, like she's waiting for me to come to my senses or something. But I send her reassuring waves, watching her relax into Mateo as she realizes I'm not about to have a breakdown.

"I couldn't have done it without you, without all of you," I say, shifting my gaze to each member of my pack in turn. The sun peeking through the windows warms the air around us, and I drift away, watching the dust motes dance in the beams. We're all quiet, but it's a peaceful silence. There's no pressure to fill the air. We're content to be here, together as a pack. But of course, it can't last forever. A phone going off makes me jump, and Lucas sits up, still half asleep, but fists raised all the same.

"Come say that to my face, you pencil-dick twat waffle," Lucas grumbles, swaying slightly.

I chuckle and reach up, putting a hand on one of his fists. "Stand down, soldier. It's just a phone," I say through my giggles.

"I'll phone you," Lucas says, yawning and flopping on top of me, already asleep again.

The device beeps again, and Lex sighs. "I think it's mine," she says, stretching and groaning.

She starts to get up, but Mateo growls, wrapping his arms around her to pin her to his chest. She lets out a huff of protest, but he doesn't relent, even as she starts to squirm.

"Leave it," Mateo says, voice muffled slightly.

"It could be Gideon," she returns irritably.

"Even more of a reason not to answer. That trumped-up asshole can learn some fucking patience."

"Or it could be Caleb—"

"He would know better than to call until we've given him the all-clear."

"Or the police—"

"Why? No one called them."

"Mateo, seriously—"

"Shut the fuck up and stop moving. I'm trying to sleep," Mateo growls.

Rhett and I chuckle, and I can hear them bicker and struggle, though I'm pinned down by Lucas's snoring form. A moment later, Mateo curses and Lex cackles in triumph before she manages to extract herself from his embrace. She goes to leave my nest, and my heart jumps into my throat with sudden anxiety. Too far, she's too far.

"Lydia?" she asks, whipping back around to look at me.

"Please don't go," I say, extricating one of my hands to reach for her.

She pauses, looking out toward the door for a moment, and I pull ever so gently on our bond, too afraid of snapping it again. I prepare myself for the rejection, but she sighs and turns back with a smile.

"It can wait," she says at last.

My smile could power the whole city as she settles back down on Lucas's other side, lacing her fingers through mine over his hip. Rhett smiles against my head, and the mattress shifts as Mateo scoots over to spoon Lex from behind.

"Oh, I see how it is. I ask you not to get up, and I get an elbow to the diaphragm. But Lydia asks, and it's all smiles and cuddles. You're not supposed to play favorites, you know,"

Mateo grumbles, and even without seeing his face, I know he's smiling.

"She said please," Lex says simply.

They bicker back and forth some more, but I don't mind. Especially not when Mateo's hand wraps around my wrist, thumb gently stroking his mating mark, and Lucas shifts to be less on top of me and more holding me with one leg hitched up over mine. Rhett's arm drapes over me, his fingers resting on Lucas's thigh.

My heart slows, peace filling every corner of my body. I breathe deep, filling my lungs with whiskey, mulled wine, graham crackers, and lemonade. My pack is here. And nothing will tear us apart again.

CHAPTER SIXTY

Alexandra

RAIN PATTERS AGAINST MY umbrella as I stand beside the ornamental duck pond of Everton Park. I roll my eyes again over Gideon's choice of a meeting location. If we wanted to be less conspicuous, we could have met at my office. But no, we have to be a cliché. He's definitely inherited my father's flair for the dramatic.

I pull my phone out of my coat pocket and check the time. He's cutting it too close. I don't have all day to wait. The wind picks up a little, the remnants of last week's storm bringing an unseasonable chill to the air. Gideon's been on my ass for the last few days about finishing this mess, but today's the first time Lydia's felt okay enough to let any of us leave the house. But even still, I can feel her longing for me in my chest like heartburn. I want to rub at the phantom ache under my sternum, but that would mean exposing my skin to the biting wind.

"We said eleven," a familiar voice drawls behind me.

I turn to see the Trio of Trouble approaching. Hunter stays back toward where the path around the duck pond breaks off from the main walking trail, back to us as he keeps watch. Delano and Gideon come right up to me, our umbrellas bumping. Delano strolls casually, moving to my other side, but still within conversation range.

"It is eleven, exactly," I snap, already irritated.

Gideon flicks his arm to lift his sleeve, revealing a Rolex on his wrist. He hums and frowns a little in surprise. "Huh, so it is. My mistake," he says simply.

I roll my eyes. That's as close to an apology as I'm ever likely to get from him, so I don't bother responding.

"For your collection," Delano says from behind me.

As I face him, he's extending a manila envelope toward me. I take it, startled when he steps up and slides my umbrella from my grip, holding it for me so I can have both hands free. As I blink up at him, he nods at the envelope expectantly. I break the seal and open it to find half a dozen photos, polaroids by the look of them. My stomach turns as I flick through them, but I force my face to take on a mask of unruffled calm.

Darren McLaughlin and Seth Douglas piled together like crash test dummies. Darren and Seth in a vat of greenish liquid. The same vat, now reddish brown with chunks floating in it. The chunks in a bucket, now with bones included. The bucket at a pig farm, a pair of arms tipping it into a feeding trough. A fire, plastic sheets visible in the blaze.

"Where's the gun?" I ask, shoving the photos back into the envelope so I don't have to think about them anymore.

"About a mile out in Baltimore Harbor. It fell overboard when we went deep sea fishing last weekend," Gideon says with a sigh, like he's annoyed I even asked.

I nod and go to stick the envelope in my pocket. But before I can, Delano snatches it away, handing me back my umbrella. I can only watch in shock as he pulls out a lighter and, in one smooth, practiced motion, flicks it open, ignites it, and sets the envelope ablaze.

"What—"

"No evidence, Lexi. No witnesses," he says simply.

A wave of ice sends shivers down my spine, and I watch the ashes drop from his leather-clad fingers and into the water below. I don't dare ask what happened to the men who did the clean-up. Plausible deniability.

"Though it seems like this mess has sorted itself out, I take responsibility for it happening in the first place. I made you a promise that he wouldn't ever darken your doorway again, and I failed. So we've done a full debrief and dealt with the men who lost sight of Mr. Douglas accordingly," Gideon says suddenly.

I blink at him, too stunned to speak. That's... more than I ever expected from him. Admitting you've made a mistake is most assuredly not part of the St. Clair playbook. There's something flickering in the depths of his hazel eyes, a sadness I recognize. Guilt. If I were a different sort of person, I'd take my well-deserved victory lap, but instead, I just nod graciously.

He clears his throat and adjusts his stance before nodding at me. "Your turn," Gideon prompts.

I swallow and pull the half-full vial of bond breaker from my pocket, passing it to him. He holds it up to the sky, not that there's much light to see by. But whatever he detects, it makes his frown deepen. Especially after he shakes the liquid a little and then lets it settle.

"Same shit?" Delano asks, an edge to his voice that cuts through the tense silence.

"Yep," Gideon grunts in response before slipping the vial into an inner pocket of his wool coat.

"What's going on?" I ask, concern and curiosity rising.

"Nothing you need to worry about, Alexandra. Just a supply chain issue," Gideon says, a little too casually.

I give him a long, searching look, considering my options. If there's something he's not telling me, and it could affect my pack, then I do have something to worry about. I hold eye contact, lifting my chin slightly as I adjust my weight into a more imperious posture, like I'd been taught. Gideon sighs and rolls his eyes after only a few seconds.

"Someone's trying to move in on our market, okay? And it looks like your problem child and the thorn in our side might have been using the same supplier," he says.

"Anything dangerous in there I should know about? Fentanyl? Meth?" I demand.

Gideon is about to answer, when a bark of laughter takes us both by surprise moments before an arm drapes across my shoulders. I look up to see Delano grinning at me like I've just told the most amusing joke he's ever heard.

"No one would waste perfectly valuable pharma to cut bond breakers. Not to mention the reactions between the two would render both inert," he says, like it's obvious.

"Pardon me, Doctor Covalent Bonds. Chemistry of street drugs isn't exactly one of my fields of expertise," I drone sarcastically.

"Lucky for you, it's one of mine. But you don't have to worry your pretty little head. We haven't found anything toxic in the samples we've collected and tested. But if something shows up, you'll be the first to know," he says with an infuriatingly patronizing ruffle of my hair.

I swat his hand away, sniffing with indignation. My brow twitches in confusion as my nose detects something new, something I've never smelt on any of them before. There's Delano's usual phosphorus and smoke, but there's something distinctly sweet under that. Like peaches and brown sugar and cinnamon, a cobbler resting out to cool.

"Who's the omega?" I ask out loud, looking up with a little smile.

Delano's humor vanishes immediately, and he takes two quick steps back, turning to walk toward Hunter. I look to Gideon, and take a long inhale through my nose. It's on him, too. He gives me a dark glare and lifts his chin.

"A pleasure doing business with you, as always," he says sharply, running a hand down the front of his coat to smooth out the non-existent wrinkles.

Before I can respond, he's turning on his heel and marching away. Delano and Hunter move aside to let him take point, neither looking back as they fade into the misty afternoon. I shake my head with a bemused smile still pulling at my lips. Lord help that woman if she's caught the attention of that posse.

I walk around the pond in the opposite direction, my steps lighter than they've been in months. The world is brighter somehow, the future wide open now that we've dealt with this last hanging loose end. There aren't any more secrets to keep quiet, no need to stick to the shadows. We're free.

Epilogue

RHETT

SIX MONTHS LATER...

The summer air buzzes with excitement, voices bouncing off the walls of The Magnolia Garden Theater. The restoration is complete, and I think it's our best work yet. Hardwood floors gleam in the light of the chandeliers hanging above. Delicious smells waft out from the state-of-the-art kitchen we'd installed, skillfully hidden from view but still easily accessible for the staff. Every detail has been considered, and seeing the results of our hard work makes my chest swell with pride. And in a few short minutes, the public will be allowed in to see it. Or at least, the public who paid for a ticket to the opening gala. We're hoping to woo more investors for future projects, and to show off the venue's potential to planners, bloggers, and anyone else who might want to book with us in the future.

But as I stand at the edge of the foyer, looking out over the flurry of activity, my eyes catch on the staircase and my blood runs a little colder. It'd taken months before any of us could step foot in here again, and I doubt I'll be able to completely forget the events of that night. Not that there's any evidence left. All that remains are the memories that haunt us, but those fade with each passing day. And tonight, we're going to replace those with new, much happier ones.

I catch a trace of lilacs in the air, and I find my omega in the crowd immediately. She's absolutely stunning, wearing a vintage black silk dress that hugs her curves in all the right ways. She's instructing a few of the staff on the correct placement of the display items we'd put together to show the history of the building around us. Many of the photos I'd found in my research are in frames, along with treasures we'd discovered buried in the basement storage. Watching Lydia work always brings a smile to my face, but seeing her in her element like this is a special sort of joy.

I scent Mateo before I see him, his happy, bubbly lemonade aura pulling the corners of my mouth up just a little bit higher. Like me, he's dressed in a well-tailored tuxedo, but his sandy brown hair is in his usual ruffled, just rolled out of bed "style." Grinning from ear to ear, his tawny eyes sparkle as he also watches Lydia work. He sighs heavily once Lydia rounds a corner toward the kitchen, pulling my attention to his face.

"What's up, Matty?" I ask conversationally.

He shrugs and looks around, smile falling slightly. "Still doesn't feel real. Like, I keep waiting to wake up, back before..."

I put a hand to his lower back, nodding as he trails off. He doesn't need to finish the sentence for me to know what he means. But as my heart sinks a little, vanilla-scented comfort fills my chest. She's there, soothing away my fears, and judging by the look on Mateo's face, he's feeling something similar. It never ceases to amaze me how in tune with our emotions she's become, caring for us even when she's busy. I truly don't know what I ever did to deserve a woman like her.

"Let's get something to drink," I suggest, nodding toward the open doors to the ballroom.

Mateo and I make our way from the foyer, and I can't help but smile again as we cross the threshold. Circular tables are arranged across most of the floor, leaving space in the front of the room near the stage for a dancefloor. The place settings gleam and glitter, reflecting the candlelight from the centerpieces. I'm not surprised to see the small gathering of people near the bar, but my heart still lifts at the sight of them.

Lydia's eldest brother, Sammy, has one arm around Ally, his other hand holding out his phone to show Wila Fitzgerald what I assume to be the same slideshow of baby photos he'd presented to me not that long ago. Zeke and Zoey just turned five months old, and I've never seen prouder parents. Ally indulges her husband, laughing at the same jokes over and over as he tells everyone who will listen—and several people who probably don't—every little detail of his children's lives.

Wila nods along, *oooh-ing* and *ahh-ing* at the appropriate places as Sammy follows her from table to table. We'd told her specifically she's not working tonight, but I see our instructions are being ignored. She's adjusting centerpieces and shifting flowers in their arrangements, not even trying to hide it. I roll my eyes and continue on toward the bar. The day Wilhelmina Fitzgerald listens to anyone will be the day hell freezes over.

Her granddaughter, on the other hand, is taking full advantage of her night off and is leaning heavily on a cocktail table, listening intensely as a waiter talks animatedly about something. Though, judging by the glassed-over look in her eyes, her attention is mostly for show. Not that I blame her. The object of her attention is an undeniably attractive man, his shoulders and arms filling out his uniform nicely. But just out of her line of sight, Jason is glaring daggers at the pair over the rim of his glass. Lydia has speculated about their relationship, but I've cautioned her to stay out of it. If it's going to happen, it'll happen. Though I do hope for his sake, he doesn't wait too long. Gabby is a catch, and any man of any designation would be lucky to be with her.

Mateo and I order our drinks, and I glance around again as I take my first sip. Finally, I spy Lex, entering the ballroom with Caleb, with Sylvie on his arm. The pair look good in their cocktail attire, even if they make an odd picture. Him with his clean-shaven face and ramrod straight posture, and her with her bubblegum pink hair and animated hand gestures as she talks Lex's ear off. My prime alpha looks good enough to eat tonight, with her sleek waves and signature red lips, the same shade as the bottom of her stiletto heels. She gracefully extracts herself from the conversation with the Novaks, eyes scanning the room once before she spots Mateo and me and makes a beeline in our direction. She doesn't hesitate before lifting the drink from Mateo's hand

and taking a pull before handing it back. He rolls his eyes, but his smile is still fond.

"Have you seen Lucas?" she asks lightly, eyes sparkling.

I shake my head, taking a moment to feel for him. He's close, and the bond between us vibrates with nervous energy. I send him a pulse of reassurance, which is met with a returning touch of gratitude. I smile to myself, taking another sip of my drink.

"It's almost time," Mateo mutters, looking at his watch.

"Don't rush them," Lex chastises.

Thankfully, before they can start bickering in earnest, there's a clatter of chains and pullies, and everyone in the room turns to see the red velvet curtain parting on the stage. In the middle stand Lucas and Lydia, the latter's mouth parted on a little gasp. She's lost her clipboard and radio at some point, but Lucas has her hands in his, preventing her from running.

"Lydia," Lucas says, pulling her attention back to him.

Lydia's gasp echoes through the now silent space as Lucas drops smoothly to one knee, still holding both of her hands in his.

"When you came into my life, I didn't know what to think. You were so different from anything I ever expected, and earning the privilege of your trust and your love has been the most incredible gift you could have ever given me and our pack," Lucas starts, speaking loud enough for everyone to hear him.

Lex's hand slips into mine, and I squeeze it gently. Her joy is a bright citrus note on the back of my tongue, strong enough to detect even through Lucas's nerves and Lydia's shock and overwhelming joy. I send out my happiness across the web of bonds, reassuring both of them at the same time. Mateo moves in close, his arm brushing across my back as he reaches for Lex, too. The physical connection between us grounds me, keeping me in the moment. My eyes burn, but I don't do anything to stop the happy tears that are forming at the edges of my vision.

"You've never asked any of us to be anything other than who we are. Your love for us is unconditional, and I hope you know that I feel the same. I thought I knew what it was to live a complete life, but time and again, you've brought joy and wonder into my world. But I realized not too long ago that there is something missing, and I don't want to go another day without it," Lucas continues, voice cracking.

He reaches down into his coat and pulls out a little black box, opening it and holding it up to the light. I don't need to be close to see the ring, as we'd all been there to help him pick it out. A pristine oval diamond set between two smaller ones on a platinum band embossed with delicate filigree. Simple from a distance, but remarkably stunning up close, exactly the perfect style for our omega. Lydia's hands go to her mouth, and I can see the tears on her cheeks as she stares with wide eyes.

"I told you once that I didn't think I could ever get married because it would mean having to choose one of our alphas over the others. And I'm not asking you to choose me over them. I'm asking you to marry me to complete our family. So will you do me the honor of agreeing to be my wife?"

There's a moment's pause where Lydia looks out into the crowd, her eyes finding me and my pack mates right away. I give her a little nod, sending her love and support across our bond. Out of the corners of my eyes, I see Lex and Mateo giving her similar nods. We'd talked about this for a while, and I couldn't be happier for my beta. His love for Lydia fills me with joy, and if they want to take this step together, then I will support them every step of the way.

Lydia looks back down to Lucas and lowers her shaky hands, reaching for him. She nods frantically, lips pressed together in a thin, watery smile. Lucas's face lights up with a wide, easy smile, and he takes her left hand in his as he gets to his feet. The room erupts into cheers as he slides the ring onto her finger and then gathers her into his arms, kissing her deeply.

When the pair comes down off the stage, they're immediately swarmed by our guests. The next several minutes are a cacophony of excited congratulations, but my pack hangs back. It's only after the assistant event coordinator rushes into the room that we realize we're late. Lex moves off to handle the opening of the doors to the gala attendees, but Mateo and I follow Lydia and Lucas out of the ballroom and back to one of the private suites.

Once the doors are closed, Lydia doesn't hesitate before throwing herself into my arms, kissing my cheeks over and over, sobbing with wordless joy. I can only laugh, especially after she attacks Mateo, nearly knocking him over with her enthusiasm. I step to Lucas's side and gather him in a one-armed embrace, kissing the top of his head.

"You did amazing," I whisper.

Lucas lets out a puff of air and shakes his head. Lydia and Mateo turn to us a moment before the door opens, Lex slipping inside. She rushes over to Lydia, gathering her up in an embrace, both women smiling brightly. Then I move over to the side of the room and lift the bottle of champagne

I'd prepared earlier from its ice bucket. We gather close after I pop the cork and pour, lifting our flutes in unison.

"To Lydia and Lucas, and the wedding she's not allowed to plan herself," Mateo jokes, nudging her playfully with an elbow.

"To Pack Saint Clair," Lucas says over our chuckles.

"To our future, together," I say, voice soft with emotion.

"To us, and everything it took to get here," Lex continues, voice cracking with her joy.

"To bonds stronger than blood," Lydia finishes, smiling brightly.

With those toasts, we drink deeply as one family, one pack. Complete at last.

THE END

Acknowledgments

I don't quite know where to start. So many people have helped me bring Pack Saint Clair to life over the last year and a half, so I'll start where I can.

The list of shoutouts has to start with my invaluable PA, Halla. You've been with me through the good and the bad as this book came into being, keeping me on task, talking me off the imposter-syndrome ledge more times that I'd like to admit. You're not just my PA, but my friend, and I can't wait to drag you all over Hell's half acre.

Next, I have to thank my writing group and support system. My dear readers, you may know them as M.F. Moody, Micca Michaels, and Shannon French Scott, but I know them as my fellow members of the Council of Potatoes. These ladies have been my rocks throughout this writing process, and more than a few of my favorite moments in this book may have been inspired by them, or they may have given me an idea, or just let me talk through my writer's block. No matter which way you slice it, this book wouldn't have been written without them.

Merri Bright, my book wife, you are an angel among men. From early drafts to last minute panics, you have helped me more than you know. I only dream of one day being able to fully return the favor. Until then, I am your grateful servant/beta reader.

No book is complete without its cover. And this series has been blessed by the talents of Sandra Maldo Designs. Thank you for everything you do, babe.

NiceGirlNaughtyEdits has once again helped me shape the lumpy meh-burger of a first draft into the stunning masterpiece you've just consumed. You're a bad influence, in the best way. One day, I'll write that football Sunday scene, just for you.

My penultimate thanks goes to my husband. Mr. Theodore Woods is a gentleman of the highest quality, and his influence can be felt on every page. Not only as my brainstorming partner and violence consultant, but in countless other ways. Rhett's eyes. Lucas's humor. Lex's take-no-prisoners work ethic. Mateo's laugh. The list of ways you've made me a better writer and a better person could fill three more novels. Thank you for holding my hand as we took this leap of faith together, and for being my eternal hype man and support.

And lastly, dear reader, if you've gotten this far and you can still see the page through the tears, I want to take one last moment to thank you. I wouldn't have had the courage to chase my dreams without each and every one of you. Whether you're following me on social media, liking and commenting on my posts, or you've left a review on Amazon or Goodreads, or even you just read my books and enjoyed them, you matter to me. I think about you every day, grateful for your time and your attention. It means the world to me that, of all the things you could be doing at any given moment, you choose to spend these precious few minutes with me and the characters I've created. Pressing "Publish" on Lilacs and Leather was the scariest thing I've ever done, but you, my dear, beloved reader, made all of that fear and work worth it. So again, thank you. Thank you for your time. Thank you for your love. And thank you for being here. I'm glad we found each other, and I hope to see you again soon.

XOXO
Thora Woods

Want more?

Pack Saint Clair: The Complete Series

The books you love, together at last. With exclusive, never-before-seen short stories, a brand new extended epilogue, and other exciting surprises!
Coming to Amazon and KU...

February 9, 2023

Join the Conversation!

LIKED WHAT YOU JUST read? Want to let everyone know? Leave a review!

Amazon

Goodreads

Bookbub

If you review on social media, please tag Thora.

Instagram: @thora_woods_author

Twitter: @_thora_woods

TikTok: @thora_wood_sauthor

Want to hear the latest news? See what Thora's working on next? Or just want to hang out with other people who love omegaverse? Click the link below to learn more!

Thora Woods, Author

About the Author

Thora Woods is a lifelong writer, reader, and creator. Born in New Orleans, LA, she began her writing journey in her pre-teens, growing her skills at SUNY Fredonia in their Creative Writing program. Thora lives in Western New York with her two dogs, Fritter and Pepper, two cats, Impala and Hoagie, and her husband.

Made in the USA
Middletown, DE
02 September 2024

60237113R00326